A BUSINESS PROPOSITION

Money. Leonie needed it. And quickly. Or else she would see the restaurant upon which she had banked all her dreams, the restaurant she had slaved to make succeed, be taken from her.

There was only one person she could get it from. Jimmy Newland. The bright young lawyer who had wanted her ever since they first met—even after she told him she was in love with another man and already carrying that man's child within her.

Now she could feel the pulse throbbing in her throat as she told him, "I have four more months before the child will be born. But," she said meaningfully, "if you can bear it . . ."

"A business arrangement?" he said somewhat coldly.

"I will be faithful to you," she said softly, "and available whenever you like . . ."

And Leonie knew from the look in Jimmy Newland's eyes that she had won . . . and at the same time, lost. . . .

TIMES OF TRIUMPH

Big Bestsellers from SIGNET

- ☑ **MOMENTS OF MEANING** by Charlotte Vale Allen. (#J8817—$1.95)*
- ☑ **ACTS OF KINDNESS** by Charlotte Vale Allen. (#J8690—$1.95)
- ☑ **GIFTS OF LOVE** by Charlotte Vale Allen. (#J8388—$1.95)
- ☐ **THIS IS THE HOUSE** by Deborah Hill. (#E8877—$2.50)
- ☐ **THE CRAZY LOVERS** by Joyce Elbert. (#E8917—$2.75)*
- ☐ **THE CRAZY LADIES** by Joyce Elbert. (#E8923—$2.75)
- ☐ **THE HOUSE ON TWYFORD STREET** by Constance Gluyas. (#E8924—$2.25)*
- ☐ **FLAME OF THE SOUTH** by Constance Gluyas. (#E8648—$2.50)
- ☐ **ROGUE'S MISTRESS** by Constance Gluyas. (#E8339—$2.25)
- ☐ **SAVAGE EDEN** by Constance Gluyas. (#E8338—$2.25)
- ☐ **WOMAN OF FURY** by Constance Gluyas. (#E8075—$2.25)*
- ☐ **BELOVED CAPTIVE** by Catherine Dillon. (#E8921—$2.25)*
- ☐ **THE RAGING WINDS OF HEAVEN** by June Lund Shiplett. (#E8981—$2.25)
- ☐ **REAP THE BITTER WINDS** by June Lund Shiplett. (#E8884—$2.25)*
- ☐ **ALADALE** by Shaun Herron. (#E8882—$2.50)*

*Price slightly higher in Canada

Buy them at your local bookstore or use this convenient coupon for ordering.

THE NEW AMERICAN LIBRARY, INC.,
P.O. Box 999, Bergenfield, New Jersey 07621

Please send me the SIGNET BOOKS I have checked above. I am enclosing $_____ (please add 50¢ to this order to cover postage and handling). Send check or money order—no cash or C.O.D.'s. Prices and numbers are subject to change without notice.

Name _____

Address _____

City_____ State_____ Zip Code_____

Allow 4-6 weeks for delivery.
This offer is subject to withdrawal without notice.

Times of Triumph

Charlotte Vale Allen

A SIGNET BOOK
NEW AMERICAN LIBRARY
TIMES MIRROR

PUBLISHED BY
THE NEW AMERICAN LIBRARY
OF CANADA LIMITED

NAL BOOKS ARE ALSO AVAILABLE AT DISCOUNTS IN BULK
QUANTITY FOR INDUSTRIAL OR SALES-PROMOTIONAL USE.
FOR DETAILS, WRITE TO PREMIUM MARKETING DIVISION,
NEW AMERICAN LIBRARY, INC., 1301 AVENUE OF THE
AMERICAS, NEW YORK, NEW YORK 10019.

Copyright © 1979 by Charlotte Vale Allen

All rights reserved

First Printing, December, 1979

1 2 3 4 5 6 7 8 9

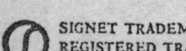 SIGNET TRADEMARK REG. U.S. PAT. OFF. AND FOREIGN COUNTRIES
REGISTERED TRADEMARK - MARCA REGISTRADA
HECHO EN WINNIPEG, CANADA

SIGNET, SIGNET CLASSICS, MENTOR, PLUME, MERIDIAN
and NAL BOOKS are published in Canada by The New American
Library of Canada, Limited, Scarborough, Ontario

PRINTED IN CANADA

COVER PRINTED IN U.S.A.

For Stephanie and Gail

Part ONE
1913-1914

1

Hayes, the manager, hired Leonie firstly because what he thought was her English accent would lend the distinctive touch to the place that O'Hara's liked to maintain. And secondly because she was so unusually tall and strikingly good-looking the male customers were bound to be pleased dealing with her. Thirdly because she was young enough and seemed to lack the preening vanity that might offend the female clientele. And finally because he was convinced it would be a fairly easy matter to charm and seduce her, thereby keeping her firmly in her place as well as sufficiently on edge to be readily at his disposal. After all, she *was* young, and newly arrived—just three weeks off the boat, she'd told him, and admitted to being uncertain of the ways of city life.

His initial impression, however, underwent a quick reevaluation when, within an hour of starting work, she'd managed to make sense of the system and was properly directing customers to their tables, making certain that no one section of the restaurant was overloaded; seeing to it people were evenly distributed so that each station had its fair share of people to see to. She took it upon herself to approach the tables of those already well into their meals, to smile and ask if everything was to their liking. And, obviously charmed, the customers responded to her warmly. Which irked Hayes, because he liked gliding among the tables, chatting with the customers, and this too-tall girl with her airs and graces was usurping him. He'd have to see about that, he thought, rushing out to the kitchen to supervise the slow-moving waitresses.

For her part, after the first day, it seemed less of a job and more of an obstacle course: avoiding the oily overtures of Mr. Hayes, dealing with people who arbitrarily decided they didn't like the table to which she'd shown them and turned asking, "Why can't we have that table?" so that she had, smoothly and without pause, to fabricate some flattering lie that would convince them their original table was infinitely more desirable. "That one's so close to the kitchen," she'd say in a confidential undertone. "This one's much quieter."

She coped with boldly whispered invitations a number of men ventured to make. Outrageous sexual invitations she was forced to smile and laugh off gracefully, without offense. It wouldn't do to alienate the customers.

One or two of the waitresses quite often—too often, perhaps?—bumped into her, several times resulting in stains to her clothing. The girls challenged her with their eyes, waiting to see how she'd respond. Feeling sympathetic—their job being considerably less pleasant than hers—she'd say, "Just an accident," or, "My fault," and the collisions ceased. They accepted her. Although their eyes were still puzzled when connecting with hers. They couldn't make sense of her. Leonie didn't mind.

Frequently, things were dropped or spilled in the restaurant. And then Hayes materialized to apologize to the diners, hissing at the waitress or busboy in question to clean up the mess at once and then see him in his office off the kitchen.

In the kitchen, Leonie knew—having seen it happen almost immediately upon starting work at O'Hara's—Hayes, slit-eyed and furious, shouted at the girls, taking careful note of breakages, advising the damage would be subtracted from their week's wages. The girls, almost every time, began to cry, trying to explain. Hayes didn't hear, hadn't time. Unless the girl happened to be willing to meet him in the slack time, between three and six, in his office. And even then, the girl in question couldn't be certain that her wages at week's end mightn't still come into her hands less the cost of the broken dishes. When this happened, there was usually a scene—most often ugly—that resulted in the girl's quitting. Hayes was unperturbed. The turnover in staff was tremendous, Leonie saw by her third day. The waitresses seemed to be the arena where Hayes proved his potency and superior strength. After each slack-hours encounter, he emerged from his office positively glowing with satisfaction. He beamed at Leonie as if the two of them shared some malevolent secret. When she failed to return his smiles, he stopped giving them, and began regarding her with some of the same slit-eyed malice with which he followed the comings and goings of the waitresses.

She didn't like him, but failed to share the waitresses' fear of him. She simply wanted him to leave her alone, to let her get on with her job, collect her wages at the end of the week, and go home. But her every instinct warned her from the first that it wasn't going to be quite that simple. Hayes, she thought, lacked the intelligence to deal well with people, and preferred perfecting his role of martinet to attempting to keep both staff and customers happy. It was easier to charm the clients and keep the staff on their toes by use of threats, sexual abuse if necessary, and the exercise of power.

From the beginning, everything about the place was alarming. And rather than becoming accustomed to any of it, she found it all more nightmarish with each day's passing.

The kitchen, hot, steamy, reeked of the clashing smells of too many different types of food all being prepared simultaneously. The sharp odor of broiling fish did battle with the fatty smell of roasting meat. Harried-looking boys frantically scurried around with trays of dirty dishes, slipping on the greasy floor while another boy of not more than ten tried never-endingly to mop up the spills, twice being in the wrong spot at the wrong time so that incoming waitresses pushing through the door crashed into him. Once toppling him backwards into his bucket and sending a flood of gray sudsy water cascading over the already slippery floor. The bottom of the waitress's uniform got drenched with dirty water, bits of food clung to her shoes. The girl, erupting angrily, kicked the child hard in the shin before flying over to the dishwashing area to grab up a wet cloth, trying desperately to repair some of the damage.

The second time, the boy was swabbing the floor by the sinks where the spillage was greatest. Flies hovered over the garbage barrels, the sinks. One of the busboys hurrying in with a fully loaded tray skidded on the soapy floor and the tray crashed with a long roar of shattering crockery and glass that was heard throughout the restaurant, so that everyone outside looked up, listening. A pause of several seconds before laughter began here and there and people returned to their meals, commenting about how startled they'd been. Leonie looked toward the kitchen doors, knowing someone would pay dearly for that resounding crash.

Hayes fired both the boys on the spot. In the back alley

outside the restaurant, the busboy—a sturdy lad of about fourteen—beat the other, smaller boy so severely the child was left dazed and bleeding behind the trash bins, where Leonie, coming out for a much-needed breath of air, found him.

She held the child upright and got him back inside to a relatively quiet corner of the kitchen, where she sat him on a chair and began cleaning him up, when Mr. Hayes arrived demanding to know, "Just what do you think you're doing, Miss Benedict?"

"The other lad beat him," she explained, gently examining around the boy's already purpling eye. "He's just a child," she said, touched by the thin vulnerability of the boy's neck, by his tears.

"It's none of your concern," he said evenly. "Your *job* is *out there!*"

"I'll only be a moment." She turned to smile, hoping to deflect him.

The clatter and din of the kitchen continued on as always. Waitresses demanded meals they'd ordered that weren't yet ready. The chef, a huge, truly alarming fat man brandished a carving knife, hurling obscene expletives the waitresses simply ignored; while the salad boys, and the pastry chef, and the dishwashers, and the cashier all continued at their jobs, everyone moving within the steaming cloud of colliding doors. Pats of butter slid from their saucers to the floor. Soup splattered, sloshing over the rims of bowls. A blancmange slithered off its plate to lie whitely quivering near the OUT door while the waitress, near tears, turned with her tray and went back for another dessert.

"Get him out of here!" Hayes said dismissingly. "And get back to your post at once! You're not here as a nurse."

"At once, sir," Leonie said, wishing he'd go away so she might talk to the boy. He didn't look well enough to get home on his own.

"Be quick about it!" he snapped, studying her as she bent over the boy, feeling hot inside his clothes as he looked at her long hands gingerly dabbing at the child's nose, cleaning away the blood. Noting the slender, tapering lines of her back, the swell of her breasts. He wanted to strip her down, tear her apart. He moved away, saying, "See me in my office at three. I think it's time you and I had a little talk."

She nodded, not really hearing, hurriedly attending to the boy. Concerned. "Are you going to be able to get home on your own?" she asked, raising his chin in order to look into deep brown eyes, framed by thick dark lashes.

"Aw, I'm okay," he sniffed. "Wasn't my fault, though."

"I know," she murmured, bathing his face with a wet cloth. "How old are you?"

"Said I was ten." He near-smiled conspiratorially. "But I'm not. Won't be till next April."

"You should be in school," she said, rinsing the cloth.

He laughed, then winced. "School! Lemme go now," he said, suddenly impatient. "I gotta see about finding someplace else, maybe get another job before closing time."

He wouldn't stay, wouldn't allow his injuries to be seen to. He had to go, he said; had to get another job or his ma would be mad. He scooted out, darting through the kitchen, pushing his way out to the back alley. Cautiously he looked out just in case the older boy might still be waiting, then ran off. The alley door slowly swung to.

She returned the cloth and bowl to the dishwasher, then collected her stack of menus and went out once more to the front of the restaurant, where Mr. Hayes turned her job back over to her, smiling for the benefit of the four waiting to be seated at table six, saying so pleasantly, "Don't forget, now, Miss Benedict. My office at three." You'd better be there, his thin mouth told her.

What was he on about? she wondered. Nothing here really made overmuch sense to her, she thought, showing the four to table six, giving out the menus once they'd seated themselves. Saying, "Have a pleasant meal," before heading back to her post near the front door, shivering in the surge of cold air every time the door opened and more customers came in. She couldn't get warm. The only relief came in those minutes she could snatch in the kitchen when she claimed her employee's meal, which wasn't anything like the food served to the clientele. Strange, sauce-disguised plates of leftovers, the scraps given to the staff; smelling foul, tasting worse. She couldn't imagine serving food of such deplorable quality to anyone. But all the staff, except the chefs, ate it. Quickly. Mopping up the sauce with crusts the chef saved in a large bowl, cut from the croutons for the French onion soup. Everyone ate fast in their ten-minute breaks, gulping the food down before hurrying back to the restaurant. She gave up on the sick-making meals and nibbled the crusts of bread, drank cups of tea, feeding herself a proper meal once she got home at night after her twelve-hour day at the restaurant.

The tea-and-coffee lady was a dear old soul to whom Leonie took an instant liking. And Mrs. Blainey provided Leonie with those cups of good strong tea, urging her in a whisper to drink them quickly, ". . . . before that Hayes one comes in, sees." Going off into a corner of the kitchen to drink down the bracing tea, she tried to make sense of this chaotic place, of why she was here. She had to do something, couldn't sit idle in her apartment waiting for a letter or for Gray to come find her. And the only thing she knew about was food, having prepared all the bread, the meals for her father and herself at the mission; working her way through the old cookery book of her mother's. She'd gone right the way through "Salads" and almost all the way through "Soups and Stews," making substitutions when the recipes called for items she'd never heard of. Things she'd supposed the English must eat. During her time in England she'd discovered that the English with whom she came into contact seemed to eat mainly gammon rashers and runny eggs, roasts of beef with soggy Yorkshire puddings and overdone roasted potatoes. No salads, to speak of. And Cousin Augusta had informed her she disliked stews intensely, considered them fit only for the help belowstairs. In any event, Augusta refused to allow Leonie anywhere near the kitchen.

Now, here she was in this mad, dirty, noisy city; working in this mad, dirty, noisy restaurant, and Mr. Hayes was storming across the kitchen toward her, red in the face, coming up to her to hiss, "I've been waiting *fifteen* minutes! When I tell someone to be in my office, I expect that someone to *be* in my office!"

"I'm sorry, Mr. Hayes," she said, setting down her cup. "I'll come straightaway. Is something the matter?" she asked his departing back, her eyes moving to take in three of the waitresses standing by the small counter built to accommodate staff meals—to be eaten standing, and as quickly as possible—pushing food in, wiping at their mouths with agitated fingers as more food went in. Everything so fast. The chef screamed something at the pastry chef, who grabbed up a long-bladed knife and screamed back at the huge fat man whose face glistened with running sweat; his sweat dripping into the food he was preparing. Leonie's stomach rose, imagining some customer hungrily dipping into a plate of something containing that fat man's exudings.

Mr. Hayes was small, dapper; hair meticulously center-parted, combed down to the sides, kept flat with some sort of lavender-scented pomade. Pin-striped suit, white spats, highly polished black shoes, a white carnation pinned to his lapel. His shirt collar looked lethally sharp. She entered his office, her nose assaulted by his various smells. The pomade as well as some sort of cologne. And underlying these was the faintly rank odor of not especially clean male flesh. What am I doing in this place? she wondered, seeing this man as a banty little rooster. Chest outthrust, face arranged into an indulgent smile.

"Come sit down, Miss Benedict." He turned his smile on her full-force. "We'll have a little chat."

"I'd prefer to stand, thank you, sir." She smiled back, finding him odious, knowing at once he was offended by her refusal to accept his generous hospitality. The smile lost much of its self-indulgent pleasure, hardened at the edges, like the blancmange congealing on the kitchen floor. She wanted to be somewhere clean and silent, somewhere green and warm; wanted not to feel as close to vomiting as she did.

"You're taking a little too much time to yourself," he said. "I understand that you're new, that you don't know how things are done here, so I'm prepared to be a bit more lenient with you. But you're going to have to pay closer attention. We don't pay you good wages so you can waste time involving yourself in the petty squabbles of the kitchen staff. You're to be out there at the door, ready to seat the customers as they come in. Not in the kitchen."

"I understand."

"And all this talking with Mrs. Blainey. You're holding the woman back from doing her job—"

"But—"

"And you're being a little overly familiar with the customers. That's *my* job, not yours. Furthermore, it's none of your business if one of the waitresses cuts herself."

"But it was a nasty cut—"

"It's *none of* your *business!*" he repeated, coming around from behind his desk to stand near her. Too near. He was slightly shorter than she, so that she had the distinct feeling she was looking down at him. He seemed aware of her advantage in height, and as if to emphasize his control of the situation, perched on the edge of his desk, crossing his arms comfortably across his chest, smiling again; saying nothing, simply gazing at her, smiling.

"Will that be all, then?" she asked, his many smells too strong now at this range; battling down a tremendous desire to move well away from him, but knowing he'd take immediate offense. She noticed his small hands. Exceptionally small, like a child's, except for the black hairs escaping from beneath his shirt cuffs, like dozens of miniature snakes crawling over the back of his too-white, tiny hands.

"You've got a lot to learn," he said, as if doing her a great service in imparting this bit of information.

"I expect I do," she agreed, closely watching his hands; bothered by them.

She was too clean, too properly put together. He'd have liked, right at that moment, to see her take a spill on the kitchen floor; to stand in the doorway of his office and see her go down, come up soiled. Putting on airs and graces. He knew the type. Airs and graces. Having to work, nonetheless, for her four dollars a week. Niggled, though, by her qualities. Because in spite of himself, he recognized that her air and her grace were not manufactured, but infuriatingly genuine. Effortlessly, naturally, she possessed the dignity and elegance he'd never have. It made him all the more anxious to see her debased, soiled in some critical fashion.

"Will there be anything else, Mr. Hayes?" she asked again, her stomach going tighter and tighter, the floor of her mouth filling unpleasantly with fluid.

His hands itched to fasten themselves to her breasts, to pull at her clothing.

"Just make sure you stay where you're supposed to be," he said. "This isn't a social club."

"It's frightfully cold by the front door."

"Cold? It's not cold."

"Where I come from—"

"Wear a shawl," he said, becoming annoyed. "Unless, of course, you're not interested in the job . . . ?" He left the question dangling.

"Yes," she said, risking taking a step away. "I will. I hadn't thought of that." She escaped.

It was like entering hell every morning. Leaving the relative quiet and comfort of her apartment on Tenth Street, she made her way to the restaurant, where the waitresses and busboys were frenziedly setting up the tables for breakfast. Latecomers were shouted at by the ever-present Mr. Hayes, while in the kitchen the chef screeched and raged over his steaming pots and brandished his carving knife, and Mrs. Blainey with a bandage wrapped around her scalded hand filled the huge urns, standing on a chair to do it. A new little boy pushed the wet mop back and forth across the already fouled floor. The noise echoed as Leonie hung away her coat in the staff room—a tiny cubicle designed to hold all the outer garments of the staff as well as supposedly being of a size to accommodate those of the staff taking their ten-minute breaks. There wasn't anywhere to sit. And Mr. Hayes kept the room locked, to protect, he said, the staff's valuables.

On her fifth day, someone rifled her handbag which she'd left in the supposed safety of the staff room, taking eleven dollars and change, a lace handkerchief that had belonged to her mother, and, puzzlingly, her smelling salts. It was as if whoever had perpetrated the theft knew how dependent she was upon those whiffs of salts to enable her to tolerate both the stink of the kitchen and of the staff, who, for the most part, reeked of body odor from their frenzied rushing about.

She doubted seriously any of the waitresses or busboys was responsible, because she'd managed to gain their trust, even a kind of fleeting friendship with the majority of them. Mr. Hayes, she suspected, was walking about with her money, her handkerchief, and the small bottle of smelling salts. But why?

On her eighth day, he cornered her in the staff room, his eyes screwed down to slits, silently advancing upon her with a terrifying twist to his mouth; muttering something about her place—why wasn't she in her place instead of forever sneaking off either to disrupt the staff or hide herself in here—allowing her no room for response, allowing her no room, forcing her into a corner.

"I've only just arrived," she tried to explain.

He said nothing, his hand moving out as if he was going to touch her. Something inside her head seemed to click, and she put out both her hands, shoving him away from her, exclaiming, "Get back from me!" She stood breathing hard, prepared to kill him; wanting to. For his cruel ways with the waitresses and busboys, the kitchen staff; for his forays among the girls, his invitations into his office to the more innocent of them; for his lack of stature, his meanness, his complete failure to possess any redeeming qualities whatsoever. She pushed him, and his hand shot out, catching her hard across the side of her face.

"You don't *push me!*" he said in a voice soprano with barely controlled rage. Visibly trembling, he again advanced on her. But not before closing the staff-room door. Meaningfully.

No one had ever hit her. No one. Not ever. Her vision seemed to be clouded, as if the blow had caused her eyes to fill with blood. And she struck back with all her strength, sending the little man crashing against the wall. She wanted to scream, feeling all the anger, the injustice. She leaped at him, hitting him again; losing control of herself temporarily. She hit him, in dreadful silence, while he cowered, defending himself; regarding her with horrified eyes as if a wild animal had suddenly been released in his presence and his life was imperiled, telling her to, "Get away from me! Crazy! Damned crazy . . . !"

"I want my money," she said from deep in her throat, where the outrage pulsed hurtfully. "Eleven dollars and seventeen cents. And my handkerchief, my smelling salts." Her chest heaving, she stood before him with clenched fists, wanting desperately to annihilate him. Her face hurt from his blow and that film of blood was still in her eyes, the stink of him in her nostrils.

"What the hell're you *talking* about?" His eyes gave him away as he drew himself upright, pretending indignation while his eyes carefully tracked her slightest move.

"Four dollars for my week's work, as well as two dollars for this week. Eleven dollars and seventeen cents. All together, that makes seventeen dollars and seventeen cents. Give it to me!"

"You'll get *nothing!* You're crazy!" His eyes were on the door now, as if he'd summon help—the fat chef, perhaps, with his carving knife. "Collect your things and get out before I call the police!"

"You'll *give* me *my money*, Mr. Hayes," she said firmly.

"I'll give you nothing!" he insisted. "Crazy damned foreigner!" He knew at once he shouldn't have said that, because her eyes seemed to ignite.

"I'm an *African*," she said in that deep voice. "And I have powers you've never dreamed of, Mr. Hayes. Are you willing to risk my powers?" It was a bluff. And she could hear her own laughter inside her head. But she'd succeeded in terrifying him. "A bit of your hair," she said quietly, "one of your buttons. That's all I'd need."

In the end, he threw three bills on the floor at her feet, then tore open the door and literally ran out, yelling back at her, "Be out of here in five minutes or I'll have the police come and *take* you out!" He ran straight into the audience of staff gathered by the door. Screaming, "*Get back to work!*" he shoved through them, slamming into his office.

The fat chef bellowed with laughter, clapping the pastry chef on the back, exclaiming, "First time anyone made that son of a bitch wet his pants." He made up a thick roast-beef sandwich for Leonie to take home, pushed it over the counter toward her with a surprisingly shy smile.

And Mrs. Blainey said, "You take care of yourself, dear. Nice girl like you, you don't belong here, in a place like this."

Back at the apartment, she looked at the notes she'd picked up from the floor. Two tens and a five. She laughed, thinking of her threat. A hollow feeling in her chest as she went to stand by the window looking out at the rain, thinking about the madness of the entire episode. No sense, no reason, no logic. All those people running, sweating, colliding. Glasses and dishes smashing, food dropping to the floor. Small children hired to clean up the messes. Big boys beating little boys. Mrs. Blainey scalding herself trying to fill those big urns. It wasn't the way life was supposed to be. I wouldn't treat people that way if it were my restaurant, she thought. Feeling tears easing her eyes, she stood looking out at the rain, wondering if she was supposed to subdue herself, suppress her feelings, abase herself in order to have a job and survive. Surely there was something else, some other way to earn money, have a life.

I'm afraid, she thought, watching the rain make random patterns on the glass. Is that what life is in America? The restaurant. People calmly eating. Well-dressed, affluent people sitting down to expensive meals, while behind the swing doors there was filth and panic and violence. One view for those with money, another for those without. I don't want to be here, she thought, looking past the rain at the nearby buildings.

The nausea caught up with her finally and she was sick. After, with a cup of tea, she went to sit down on her bed, holding her hands around the cup for warmth, deciding she'd get a newspaper first thing in the morning and begin looking for another job. But what, she wondered, if the next job were just like this last one? I couldn't bear that, she thought, more frightened. There had to be something else she could do. Perhaps Gray's answer to her letter would come soon, save her having to offer herself up to another inexplicable, degrading experience. It was only a month since she'd stepped off the ship. It seemed years. Only November, and it was colder than she'd have believed possible.

She sipped the tea, idly wondering if the little boy had managed to find himself another job. Nine years old. Wrong. A little boy with a thin neck, too thin-looking altogether to sustain the weight of his head. And an old woman with bandaged hands grappling with heavy pots of water, struggling up onto a chair to tip the water into the urns. Frantic young girls coping with the demands of the customers, the lunacy of the chefs, the deductions for breakage from their wages, the unwanted attentions of the manager upon whom their jobs depended.

I won't allow myself to be defeated, she vowed. There had to be something else, somewhere else, something.

She unwrapped the sandwich, thought of the fat, red-faced chef who'd displayed such unexpected kindness; thought of his sweat dripping over the blood-oozing beef and put down her cup to go into the bathroom, sick again.

2

The first of her letters to Grayson was returned to her on the morning of her nineteenth birthday. She carried the letter upstairs to her apartment and sat at the kitchen table staring at the word "RETURN" printed across the face of the envelope, feeling shattered and ill. Someone—surely not Grayson—had returned the letter unopened. And it had been forwarded on to her from the hotel where she'd stayed her first two weeks in New York.

Perhaps, she thought, he'd receive her second letter—had, in fact, already received it. Or perhaps Cousin Augusta had made some arrangement that would prevent Grayson from receiving her letters.

She couldn't think clearly and got up to put on her coat. A walk would help clear her head and even possibly ease her fear. Although she doubted that.

The weather was gray and cold. The noise of the city never ceased. Night and day a steady hum lay under what might have been silence had she not experienced the complete and embracing stillness of the mission, where only the sudden laughing cry of a hyena broke the night air. The smell of gasoline fumes from the numberless automobiles and buses sickened her, as did the midday crush of people who materialized on the streets to perform their errands and eat hasty luncheons before returning to their jobs.

Occasionally she saw black people and felt herself lifting in anticipation of a greeting. But their faces were sealed, their eyes nonrevealing. They didn't smile. And this disappointment added to her growing store. Everything seemed so bleak, so cold. Every day she read in the newspapers of yet

15

another building that had been burned, of another missing girl who was thought to have been spirited away by white slavers. Page after page of horrors. What *was* this place? she wondered.

There was, according to the newspapers, a great deal to fear in being abroad alone on the streets of New York. Yet, perversely, she felt no fear whatsoever. She felt only the depression that was settling ever more thickly, more permanently around her. And now that her first letter to Gray had been returned, she couldn't help wondering if Augusta had acted entirely upon her own in sending her away. Could Gray have had a hand in it? Was that possible? Could he have lied so skillfully? She refused to believe that what had passed between them had been nothing more than self-indulgence on his part and a delusion on hers. He'd been sincere, she told herself. He hadn't been dishonest. But why, then, had the letter been returned?

It was all a series of shocks. She was astonished to find herself alone in this enormous city, knowing no one, when just weeks before everything had been lush and green and so optimistic. Gray was to tell Augusta he planned to leave her, that he and Leonie would, in time, marry. He'd been so insistent, saying, "I won't have you as a mistress! I won't! You're to be my wife!"

She'd known from the first time their eyes met that it was wrong of her to fall in love with her cousin's husband. But it had been love, and so real. He did love me, she thought now. He does. But why had the letter come back?

It was terrifying to find herself so utterly alone, living in two rooms on the third floor of a converted house on Tenth Street; rooms she'd managed to find and secure through an advertisement in the New York *Times*. Rooms she felt she was paying far too much for. But the neighborhood, the bank manager had told her, was a good one, a safe one. And he was the only person in the entire city with whom she could talk—even in the most desultory fashion.

She lived in two rooms on the third floor of a house on Tenth Street in a city that felt too large, too cold, too noisy, too dirty—too everything she was ill-equipped to cope with. Pregnant, she was now certain. Augusta had presented her with a sum of money along with the various rail and ship tickets. Money, tickets, bags packed, gone. So quickly. All of it accomplished neatly and effectively while Grayson was in France on an assignment.

She was going to have to find some sort of work, something to provide an income, because the money Augusta had given her wouldn't last indefinitely. Augusta had been surprisingly generous. The letter of credit had translated into almost four thousand dollars. But sitting idle day after day waiting for a letter, for word from Gray, was an impossible, intolerable existence. Idleness, in any case, was completely beyond her capabilities. The problem, though, was her not having had any specific training.

Curving her shoulders inward against the cold, she continued along the street, her eye caught by a man in the act of slapping a coating of whitewash over the interior of a plate-glass window of a shop on the west side of University Place; and, puzzled, she stopped to watch, wondering what he was doing and why.

Crossing the road, she peered in through the window past the man with his brush, seeing chairs piled atop tables, a light on in the rear. On impulse—with no idea what she was doing, or why—she tried the door. It was open, and she stepped inside, asking, "What's become of the restaurant that was here?"

"Closed!" he said around the stub of a cigar clamped between his teeth.

"Oh! Is there to be another restaurant here?"

"Wouldn't know about that, lady. All's I know is, I've gotta finish whitewashing this here window."

"Why?"

He finally turned to look at her. "Why?" he repeated.

"Yes, why?"

"Damned if I know." He laughed.

"Do you know if someone has leased the premises, if there are plans for another restaurant?"

"Don't know a thing, lady."

"Well, who *would* know?"

"Landlord." He paused to dip his brush into the bucket of whitewash.

"And who might the landlord be?"

"Fella name of Rosen."

"Where might I find this Mr. Rosen?"

"Sure do ask a lot of questions, don'tcha?"

She managed, finally, to drag the address out of him, and hurried uptown, coming to an abrupt halt outside the building, wondering just what she was doing. A restaurant? Well, why not a restaurant? She felt a sudden rush of excitement.

She could open it at her convenience—say, for breakfast and lunch—then close when all the other restaurants were serving dinner. That way, she'd have time to herself and the baby, time to prepare the bread and food for the next day. She liked the idea. Yes, very much. Of course, everything would depend upon this Mr. Rosen—if she was or was not about to become the proprietor of a restaurant.

The rather haggard-looking secretary asked her name, said, "Wait," and slipped through an inside door, to return a few moments later saying, "You can come in."

Mr. Rosen was a singularly unattractive man. Not so much in feature but rather in the aura he exuded of disinterest, greed, and suspicion.

"I should like to inquire into the possibility of renting your property on University Place near Twelfth Street," she told him.

"What for?" he asked bluntly, boldly eyeing her.

"To open a restaurant," she replied coolly. "Is the property available or is it not?"

"Could be. You fronting for somebody?"

"I beg your pardon?"

"Never mind. You, yourself, you're going to open a restaurant?"

"Yes, that's right." The more difficult he was, the more determined she became that she would do this. Not only do it, but succeed splendidly.

"And what're you going to use for money, sweetheart?"

"My name is Benedict, not 'sweetheart.' And the money is *my* concern, isn't it? Is the property available?"

"Might be. It depends."

"On what?"

"On whatever," he said, his eyes traveling over her inch by inch, dwelling for long moments on her breasts. "Rent's twelve hundred a year," he said unexpectedly.

"That's too high!"

"Really?" He raised his eyebrows.

"I know for a fact," she lied, "the previous tenants paid nowhere near that amount."

"You do, huh?"

"That's correct, I do. I'll pay you six hundred a year."

"In advance," he said quickly.

"Rubbish!" she snapped. "I shall pay you two months' rental in advance. You will provide me with a properly drawn five-year lease with an option for renewal. And my bank will handle the arrangements. May I have a piece of paper, please, and something with which to write?"

Taken aback, he produced paper and a pencil and watched as she wrote down her name and the address of her branch of the Bank of New York.

"If you will be kind enough to notify Mr. Freeman, my banker, when the lease is ready to be signed, he will duly advise me and I will present you with a draft for one hundred dollars, and you, in turn, will present me with a witnessed copy of a properly executed lease. Is that satisfactory?"

"What's your name again?" he asked, drawing the paper back across the desk.

"Leonie Benedict."

"Some tough cookie, huh." He grinned at her, revealing stained teeth. "Okay, you got yourself a restaurant. Just make sure you pay on time or you'll find your highfalutin bottom out on the street."

"I'd also like to arrange purchase of whatever equipment and furnishings are presently in the restaurant."

"I'll get back to your banker."

"May I go now and inspect the premises?"

"Sure." He opened one of the drawers of his desk and brought out a key. "Might as well take this sooner as later."

"Thank you." She accepted the key and turned to go.

"You've got someone you're fronting for?" he asked again.

She stared at him blankly.

"Never mind." He slammed shut the drawer. "You'll be hearing from me, *Miss Benedict*." He was snorting to himself with amusement as she went out.

She opted to walk back downtown, needing the time to think.

What was she doing? A restaurant. Well, she wouldn't have to pay for a cook. She'd do all of it herself. But she'd need someone to wait tables, someone to do the washing up. Two additional people. If she opened early for breakfast, closed midmorning, then opened again for lunch, she could close for the day by, say, two-thirty and have the rest of the afternoon and evening free. She also wouldn't be competing with other restaurants in the vicinity that only served dinner. The few places she'd seen open for breakfast were small, dreary-looking ones, or dining rooms in the hotels. There didn't seem anyplace pleasant where one might enjoy a good-quality breakfast in cheery surroundings.

She found her excitement building as she hurried back toward the restaurant, whose plate-glass window had, by now, been completely whitewashed. Letting herself in with the key, she found that the man with the cigar had gone.

She moved into the dim body of the restaurant, her excitement evolving into something closer to panic at the sight of the dirt, the shabby quality of the tables and chairs, the grimy wallcovering and flyspecked ceiling. The kitchen was of a good size, and the stove, she ascertained, was more than functional. But everything was filthy beyond belief, encrusted with layers of grease and grime. Blackened pots sat on the table beside the sink. Moving on, she discovered a storeroom, a foul lavatory, and a second fairly large room that had evidently been used as some sort of office. There was a back door off the kitchen leading out to an alleyway where stood rows of trash barrels belonging to other establishments also backing onto the alley. Returning inside, making sure the rear door was securely bolted, she went back to the office to investigate, discovering that what she'd assumed was a closet was, in fact, a door opening onto a narrow stairway that led to a room above, of precisely the same dimensions as the office below. About twelve by fourteen, with a window fronting on University Place and one overlooking the roof of the kitchen below, and beyond, the alleyway. The windows were thick with dirt and the room itself piled high with newspapers and debris.

Downstairs again in the restaurant, she stood looking around, thinking the place would have to be scrubbed down, cleaned thoroughly, disinfected, and painted. No one would want to start the day with a meal in such a dismal, dirty place. But with fresh white paint on the walls and ceiling, and with a white curtain over the lower half of the front window, some plants, and clean tablecloths, it would be a bright, welcoming place.

She got out her notebook, righted one of the chairs, and sat down to make a list of things she'd need to begin with. Buckets and scouring brushes, cleansers, paint, some new pots and pans. Dishes? Were there dishes? Leaving her things on the table, she went to the kitchen to find, with a sigh of relief, a sizable collection of thick white plates, cups, saucers. Good enough to get on with. And, in an ill-fitting drawer in the storeroom, cutlery. She returned to her list.

Sitting tapping the tip of the pencil against her teeth, she wondered if this wasn't some bizzarre dream. Was she mad to attempt a venture about which she knew very little? An ability to cook didn't qualify her to be an employer, a person offering a public service. But Father had said, "Be bold in your endeavors, Leonie." And she would now have to respond, "This is so bold as to be dangerous." But she wanted to try. If she failed, at least she'd have made her best effort.

She'd managed to forget entirely about the letter. But upon arriving home, she went into the kitchen thinking to prepare a meal, and there it was on the table where she'd left it. The sight of it brought her earlier depression back full force as she slumped into a chair, the word "RETURN" leaping up at her as she wondered—again, again—if it were possible for Gray himself to have returned the letter. No, no.

She could write to Bessie, the cook, and enclose a letter for him. But all the post went first through Augusta's hands, and since Augusta knew full well that Bessie knew no one in New York except Leonie, it was all too probable that Bessie would never receive the letter.

With a sigh she opened her notebook and went again over her figures, determining that it would cost her for salaries, rental, and foodstuffs, approximately three thousand dollars to keep the restaurant running for one year. That would include painting and decorating as well as odds and ends she was bound to discover she needed as she went along. And Mr. Rosen hadn't yet informed her of his asking price for the existing equipment. But he would. And his price would be too high, because he was greedy.

If the restaurant failed, at the end of a year's time she'd be in desperate circumstances. It wouldn't fail.

Suddenly exhausted, she got up and went to get ready for bed. Placing her hands on her still-flat belly, she wondered how long it would be before she began to swell. By her estimate, she was in the third month, which meant the child would come in May. Six months from now. And six months was quite a long time, really.

She lay in bed gazing at the ceiling, her hands loosely clasped under her breasts, trying—as she'd done every night for the past two months—to understand where she was, and why; willing Grayson to come to her.

Grayson took a taxi home from the station, urging the driver to hurry, excited and eager to see Leonie, elated at the prospect of the start of their life together. He made his entrance into the Kensington house to be greeted, not, as he'd hoped, by Leonie, but by a strangely effusive and affectionate Augusta, who atypically offered her pouty mouth for a kiss.

"Well," he said, discomfited, freeing himself from her embrace, "this is quite a surprise, Gus."

Beaming, she watched him remove his topcoat, saying, "I have so many plans. I simply can't wait to tell you about them. We've already had masses of invitations and I'm planning a small dinner for forty or so early next month, and—"

"Where is Leonie?" he asked casually, strolling into the sitting room. Sensing something amiss, he turned to look back at Gus.

"Has she taken herself off to the park?" he asked lightly, knowing how Leonie loathed being confined indoors, how she loved to run through the grass.

"She's gone," Augusta answered flatly. "Last month, actually."

"*Gone?* Where?"

"To America."

"What have you done, Gus?" he asked too quietly.

"I haven't done anything." She noticed his temple was throbbing. And the air was suddenly filled with ice.

"What have you done?" he repeated.

"She spoke so often of getting off on her own, leaving. She was so . . . uncomfortable here with us. I simply . . . helped."

"Helped how?"

"Gave her some money, purchased a ticket. Made arrangements."

"Where have you *sent* her?"

"Well, I truly couldn't begin to guess where she might go. The ship was sailing to New York. I . . ." She couldn't continue, intimidated by the throbbing in his temple, the tightening of his lips. He seemed to be losing his color, the flesh somehow melting from his face so that the bones beneath had sudden prominence. "It really was for the best," she said weakly, "for her good."

"For *your* good," he corrected her, struggling with sudden ungovernable rage.

She stood staring at him, wetting her lips, not daring to imagine what he might do should he learn she'd gone to visit his assistant at his office and airily advised that all personal mail for Mr. Marlowe be redirected to her. At Mr. Marlowe's request, she'd added significantly. And she had, that very morning, penned "RETURN" across a letter that had come for Grayson from New York City. He'd strike me down, she thought now, confronting his blazing eyes, perhaps murder me if he knew what I've done.

"Do you know where she is, Augusta?" he asked again.

"I do not," she lied.

He couldn't have stopped himself, hadn't any desire to, and struck her across the face with all his might. She staggered back, blood gushing from her nose.

"Be grateful I'm stopping with one blow," he said in a hiss. "Because the temptation to kill you is overwhelming. You'd better advise your attorney that you'll be commencing divorce proceedings. I'll provide you with whatever evidence is required. It is my intention never to have to set eyes upon you again. I've always known you weren't the world's most intelligent woman, Gus. And I suppose it must have been fairly obvious that something was going on. For that, I am sorry. We were indiscreet. Don't interrupt me. I never, though, suspected you of being capable of such cruelty. Whatever your feelings or guesswork, to send a young girl on such a voyage; knowing perfectly well how terrified she was when she arrived here from Africa. And you laughed, because her terror seemed so amusing to you. But you've never had to be afraid of anything ever, Gus. And it's turned you callous and stupid and monstrously cruel. I hope God will forgive you, because I can promise you that I *never* will!"

He glared at her as she cowered against the doorframe, holding the back of her hand against her streaming nose.

"But I didn't . . ." she tried to explain herself.

"What 'didn't' you?" he demanded.

"I didn't *know*. It was simply that she was so patently out of place and . . . and . . ." She gave up, defeated.

He moved that night to his club, and the next day made arrangements with an international inquiry agency to try to trace Leonie. He did consider sailing to America on the next available ship. But where would he go? She might be anywhere, mightn't have stopped in New York but gone on to somewhere else.

He stood at the window of his room staring sightlessly out at the city, gripped by fear at the prospect of having lost her for good; fearful, guilty. Everything that had happened was his responsibility entirely, because he'd ignored the warnings of his common sense and fallen hopelessly in love with a young girl he'd promised to protect, not seduce.

Dr. Benedict, he thought, I am sorry, so sorry. Gus and I gave our word to care for her. I am guilty of caring too deeply, and Gus of being incapable of caring.

3

She purchased several gallons of white paint, a scrub brush and bucket, two paintbrushes, some turpentine, and a number of other items. The boy from the hardware store delivered everything, then looked around asking a lot of questions before going off whistling, tossing the nickel tip she'd given him into the air. He thought she was a pretty girl, and liked the funny way she talked. But she sure was going to have some swell time of it trying to fix that place up! It'd be interesting, though, taking on a challenge like that, working with someone like her.

With a knife, she scraped clean a small area of the front window, then taped up a "HELP WANTED" sign. That done, she donned an apron, tied a scarf over her hair, rolled up her sleeves, and started in to work on the kitchen; scrubbing down the stove and tabletops, the sink, slowly, painstakingly removing what seemed to be a lot of years' accumulation of grease and dirt. She felt a tremendous sense of satisfaction finally at seeing the stove gleaming and ready for use.

Then the small lavatory. Throwing open the window to air it out, liberally splashing disinfectant into the bowl, holding her breath and half-closing her eyes, she went at this exceedingly unpleasant task. But with the toilet clean and the small window washed, she thought that with fresh paint and a new piece of linoleum on the floor, the room would certainly be usable.

Pausing before moving into the body of the restaurant, she stared into the room, feeling overwhelmed. How on earth would she ever cope single-handedly with all the dirt? The scarred, rickety tables and chairs seemed to challenge and defy her. There wasn't a thing she could think of to do about the tables except, in time, make certain they were hidden beneath fresh cloths. The chairs, though, could be painted. More work. But it would all have to be done.

Pushing the furniture off to one side, she reached for the broom and began methodically sweeping the dirt out from the corners; wondering how people could possibly have taken their meals in a place like this. They couldn't have, she realized, and that was very likely why the place had closed.

Rose saw the sign in the window from the opposite side of the street and stopped, trying to imagine what sort of help they might be wanting. She hated her present job, but it was security, and she needed the money. But just suppose, by some miracle, that whoever had placed that sign in the window was willing to pay a good salary for someone hardworking and loyal? Suppose she, Rose, were exactly the sort of person for whom they'd been looking? She knew she was wasting valuable minutes, yet she continued to stand on the far side of the street looking at the sign, trying to get herself to cross the road and ask. It wouldn't cost her anything.

While standing debating, the door opened and a very tall blond girl wearing an apron and carrying a broom emerged and stood in the doorway looking up at the sky. She was young and lovely-looking, and Rose, on impulse, decided it wouldn't do any harm to ask her what sort of job was going. Surely, if this girl worked there, it couldn't be a too-bad place. She walked across the road and stopped on the sidewalk, saying, "Hello."

Leonie smiled and said, "Hello."

"I saw the sign," Rose said. "I was curious to know what kind of help they're wanting."

Leonie felt lifted, looking at the girl standing in front of her. Very plain except for glossy black hair and large, luminous black eyes, there was something solid and sensible about her, yet something fragile and frightened, too.

"Would you like to come inside?" Leonie offered.

"I really can't. I've only got a few minutes left before I have to get back. Could you tell me about the job?"

"I need someone to help run the restaurant, do a number of different jobs at first, until we're really started. Waiting on tables, taking money. Quite a few things, really."

"You?" Rose asked. "This is your place?"

Leonie's smile widened. "That's right. At least it will be if

I'm ever able to get it clean enough to paint it. May I ask your name?"

"Rose," she answered, looking past Leonie into the restaurant. "Rose Manero."

"Rose. My name is Leonie Benedict."

"What would you be paying?" Rose asked, all too aware of her time slipping away.

"How much salary do you receive now, Rose?"

"Five dollars a week."

"Do you know anything at all about restaurants?"

"I know how to eat," Rose said. "And I know how to cook. I can count, and a little dirt doesn't scare me. I live with my mother and my kid brother and I need every cent of my wages."

I like you, Leonie decided. "I'll pay you six dollars a week," she offered. "But I'll work you to death for it."

Rose's eyes met hers, and she smiled for the first time. A smile that made her black eyes gleam, transformed her from someone plain into a beautiful woman.

"I don't mind working hard," she said.

"May I ask how old you are, Rose?"

"Twenty-two. How old're you?"

Leonie laughed. "Nineteen. When could you start?"

"Monday? Would that be all right? I've got to let them know I'll be leaving."

"Monday will be fine."

"What kind of hours, by the way?"

"Seven A.M. until three."

Rose's mouth opened, her eyes widened. "That's *all*?"

"That's all."

My God! Rose thought. I could be home to help Mama by three-thirty. I could sleep an extra hour or so at night. She looked again at Leonie, wondering if the girl wasn't maybe crazy. She didn't look crazy, but she was a foreigner, and maybe she didn't know how things worked. Still, a dollar more a week.

"You want me to come tomorrow and help with the cleaning?" she offered.

"But what about your other job?"

"I don't owe them anything. I'll be here at seven." On impulse, she extended her hand—something she'd never done with another woman. Leonie took it, reassured by the strength of Rose's grip.

"Where do you live?" she asked as Rose turned to go.

"Brooklyn. But don't worry. I'll be here seven on the dot."

Leonie leaned on her broom and watched Rose walk quickly off up the street. A small, somehow compact woman with an aura of destination.

"It's a dollar more a week," she said, quickly making the bed. "And less hours. I'll be able to spend more time with you." She straightened and looked over at her mother, who sat leaning on her arms on the windowsill, looking out; not listening, not hearing. "I'll make dinner now," she said to her mother's broad back, her unmoving figure. "You must be hungry."

She moved to the stove, hidden behind the cloth curtain, and began getting out pots and pans, then carried a bowl of vegetables over to the table, all the while continuing to describe her brief meeting with Leonie.

"She's about the tallest woman I ever saw," she said, expertly dicing onions. "But really pretty. Sounds English or something. Even if the job doesn't last forever, I figure with what I can save up out of that extra dollar a week, things'll work out just fine. And I'll have more time . . ." She stopped, put down the knife, got up, and walked over to the window, bending to see her mother's face.

Dull, staring eyes moved back and forth, following the movements on the street below.

"Mama?" She put her hand on her mother's shoulder, and the head slowly turned, the eyes fixing on Rose's face. "I'm home, Ma. Getting supper ready now. Angelo's coming up the stairs. I can hear him."

Like a dog, Rose thought. Like a dumb dog. Watching her mother's head turn back, the eyes slowly drift away to follow the traffic on the street. What're we doing, she asked herself for perhaps the thousandth time, talking to you like you hear us? Like you see us?

"What d'you see, Ma?" she asked quietly. "You see anything down there?"

Silence.

"I've got this new job, Ma. It's gonna be good. Ma?"

I'll never be you it'll never happen to me I'll die before it's me at the window.

Several people came knocking at the restaurant door to ask about the jobs. But Leonie didn't get the right feeling about any of them. Until Clark, the boy from the hardware store, came in to ask.

"I'll do anything," he said. "Sweep up, wash up. I'm a hard worker. And real reliable."

"I'm sure you are." She smiled. He was tall and thin, with orange-red hair, paper-white skin and a multitude of freckles, ingenuous brown eyes, and a gap-toothed grin. "How much are you paid now?" she asked, having quickly established that the best way to determine the right wage to pay was by finding out the wage presently received, then offering slightly more.

"Three dollars."

"Do you think you could manage three different jobs?"

"Four, if I had to. What're the jobs?"

"I was thinking if I could find someone to sweep, wash up, and help clear the tables, I might be willing to pay four dollars a week. That would also include stoking the boiler in the basement."

"You got yourself a boy!" he declared. "When do I start?"

"As soon as possible. I could certainly use your help with the painting."

"Oh, I'm a first-class painter." He smiled. "Learned from my dad. And a pretty fair carpenter, too. Know all kinds of things about all kinds of things. What hours?"

"Seven to four." She'd need him an extra hour for the washing and putting away.

"I'll be at the door seven o'clock the day after tomorrow," he promised, and went off, pausing to remove the "HELP WANTED" sign from the window on his way out.

Leonie smiled as she returned inside to the kitchen, where Rose, in a voluminous coverall, was scrubbing away at the pots.

"We've got a kitchen boy," Leonie told her. "And a first-class painter and pretty fair carpenter to boot."

"Isn't it just amazing how dirty some people are?" Rose said from between her teeth, trying to rid the bottom of a large soup kettle of a black layer of burnt-on fat. "I wouldn't eat *anything* that came out of this."

"Nor would I," Leonie agreed, cleaning the kitchen window that gave onto the alleyway. "Tell me about yourself, Rose."

"Not a whole lot to tell," she said, reaching for the scouring powder. "My mama and papa came over from Naples when Mama was carrying me. Papa worked in the fish market. He got run over by a bus a couple of years ago, and Mama went crazy. I mean really crazy." She looked over at Leonie, then once more bent her head to the task at hand. "Me and Angelo, my kid brother, we've been taking care of her ever since. She's not out of her head or anything like that. Just quietly crazy. Sits looking out the window all day, watching the street. She doesn't know a word of English because she always refused to learn. She understands well enough, because me and Angelo never learned much Italian. So we talk to her in English, and she answers—when she's talking, which isn't too often anymore—in Italian. Angelo works downtown at the Exchange. He's a runner. I was working for this publishing company, in the factory. Until I saw your sign. I was there eight years."

"Eight years? From the time you were fourteen?"

"Oh, sure. Angelo's been at the Exchange since he was about ten. He lied, said he was twelve. Nobody cared much."

"What did you do at the publishing company?"

"Put glue on bindings. Stupid job. But it paid all right. I'm going to like this a lot better, though."

"I hope so."

"I will," Rose said confidently. "I can tell."

"Have you a beau, Rose?"

"No," she answered slowly, scared the way she always was when she saw the face of some man who looked good to her and that feeling started happening inside her that she had to fight down, get rid of. "I've got about all I can handle with Mama and trying to pay the rent and getting to work on time. You got somebody?"

"No," Leonie lied, thinking it easier than trying to explain when she herself wasn't in the least sure of the explanation.

"Where d'you come from, anyway?" Rose asked.

"I was born in Africa, the Transvaal, and grew up in Swaziland."

"*Swaziland?* I've never even *heard* of it. Are you some kind of light-colored Negro or like that?"

"My parents were English, Rose. Medical missionaries. I don't remember my mother at all. She died when I was two. My father died almost eighteen months ago. I lived with a married cousin in London for close to a year before I came here. I arrived in New York in September."

"No insult intended. I mean, for all I know, there could be blonde Negroes."

"None taken."

"What's it like, Africa?"

"Beautiful," she said softly, reverently. "Silent and green."

"I guess you must miss it, huh?"

"Yes," Leonie said distractedly, staring into space. *How did I come to be here? What am I attempting to do? Did you ever love me? Or did you simply wish to make your marriage with my body?*

Rose returned her attention to the pots, and Leonie started painting the kitchen walls, stopped suddenly by a wave of nausea that made her put down her brush, open the back door, and step out into the chill air, taking deep breaths.

"What's wrong?" Rose asked, coming over to the doorway.

"I think it's just the smell of the paint."

"It is pretty strong," Rose agreed. "You know, I haven't seen you eat anything today. Maybe you're just hungry."

"I completely forgot about food."

"Come share my lunch. Mama gets carried away, always packs too much. It's the only thing she does anymore, packing our lunchbags, so it'd be kind of mean if we made her stop. Anyway, there's plenty here for both of us."

They sat down at the table, and Rose unpacked a bag of sandwiches, setting one in front of Leonie, who picked up one thick half, suddenly aware of her enormous hunger. "You're right," she said. "I am hungry." She bit into the sandwich, chewed, swallowed, then asked, "What is this, Rose?"

"Genoa salami, cooked peppers, and onions. You don't like it?"

"Oh, I do. I'm just afraid . . ." She couldn't finish. Her stomach was overturning. Jumping up from the table, she ran into the small lavatory and vomited into the toilet. Then she leaned against the wall, blotting her eyes and nose with her handkerchief, waiting to see if there'd be more; thinking about Gray. How tall and powerful he'd seemed from the first, with an air about him of barely suppressed anger; sudden kindnesses and confidences. So truthful, so gentle, with large hands possessed of a great capacity for tenderness, holding her as if she were smaller, more fragile, more valuable than anyone or anything else on earth could ever be to him; placing this child within her. He'd talked so happily of the children they'd one day have. "One day" is here, Gray. And I'm so afraid, moving in alien areas surrounded by strangers.

Returning finally to the kitchen, she ran the cold water, drank some, then apologized. "I'm sorry, Rose. I don't think

I'm going to be able to eat it. It's very good, though, and you're generous to offer to share your lunch with me."

"You're sure you're not sick?" Rose asked, studying her with slightly narrowed eyes.

Leonie sat down slowly, meeting Rose's deep black eyes, feeling all at once she couldn't go on another moment without someone to talk to, confide in, a friend who wouldn't judge or condemn.

"It isn't unusual, Rose," she said, "for someone in my condition."

Rose put down her sandwich. "What condition?" she asked, the last bite lumping in her throat like a clot of knowledge she forced herself to swallow.

"I am going to have a baby."

The words hung in the air between them for several long moments.

"But I thought you didn't *have* anybody," Rose said, not sure how to react. The woman at the window of her mind's eye was all at once possessed of long golden hair, a youthful, narrow back. And she sat in silence, this lovely blonde, while her child asked, "Ma?"

"I thought I did, you see. It's so difficult to explain. I've written to him twice. My first letter was returned over a week ago. And I'm very afraid he hasn't received my second one. I know if he had, he'd have replied. I know it!"

"What're you going to do?"

"What I'm doing. I don't know what else to do. And I suppose it must be obvious I haven't any real idea what I'm doing with . . . all this." She looked around the kitchen apprehensively, as if strangers might be watching and listening. "I'm so frightened," she said, reaching across the table to take hold of Rose's hand. "Are you appalled, Rose?"

"I don't know what I am," she said truthfully, thinking she'd been stupid to count on that extra dollar. In a few weeks she'd most likely be back at the factory asking for her old job. She felt a little sick herself, the disappointment causing her stomach to contract. Mindful of Leonie's hand enclosing hers, her brain rushed here and there, trying to think. "I suppose you don't know about the markets or even where they are."

"Sorry?"

"You were planning to buy from the local shops, weren't you?"

"I suppose . . ."

Rose freed her hand, an urgency overtaking her; a need not to have all this turn out an embarrassing mistake.

"I'm going to have to show you, teach you. The markets. Everything."

"I'm not following you, Rose," Leonie said, unsure where Rose was going.

"I gave up a good steady job to come here," Rose said angrily. "And I'm not going to go back with my tail between my legs, begging to have it back. You know how to cook," she said. "I know where to shop. I know the men in the market. Most of them were friends of my papa's. They'll give me good prices. *Nineteen*," she said, drawing her brows together. "Are you one of these stupid girls who believes everything a man tells her?"

"Gray loves me," she said quietly. "I am not so stupid that I fail to know the difference between lust and caring. I'll understand if you'd prefer to leave."

"Don't be *stupid!*" Rose said impatiently. "I'm trying to tell you I want this thing to work! Because . . . because I gave up a good, steady job. Because . . . My God! I don't even know why! How," she demanded, "are you going to run this place and look after a baby at the same time? Did you think of that?"

"Of course I thought of it. I'd planned to keep the baby in the room next door during working hours. Where I'd hear it, be able to look after it."

"What if it's busy out there"—she pointed to the restaurant—"and the baby starts to cry? What're you going to do?"

"Look after it."

"I don't know," Rose said wearily. "I guess we'll be able to work something out. What're you gonna do if this place doesn't work?"

"It *will* work!"

"Not just because you want it to, Leonie. You're dreaming if you think that's all it takes. You need customers, people with money. Why should they come here and not across the street or up the road? God! It gets worse by the minute. And what about when you're too big to move around?"

Leonie lowered her head to the table and began to cry.

"*That's* not going to get you anywhere!" Rose said, feeling guilty now. "You're in this thing, so we're going to have to *make* it work. Just how long were you thinking of taking getting this place ready?"

"A few weeks," Leonie answered.

"Okay," Rose said more softly, instinctively stroking Leonie's hair. "We'll get it done sooner, get this place open and working. I hope to God you're not really stupid and that I'm not even stupider, giving up a good job."

Wiping her eyes, Leonie sat up, asking, "Why are you so angry, Rose?"

"Men," Rose said bitterly, her mouth thinning. "Love. Look where it gets you! Even without a baby, this wouldn't be easy. But a baby, too . . ." She shook her head. "You're sure you can cook?"

"Quite sure."

"All right. I'm sorry I yelled. But my God! Two stupid women with a restaurant. I guess, if nothing else, we won't go hungry."

4

Rose took her around the market, introduced her to the butcher, the greengrocer, the fishmonger. All old friends of the family who, at Rose's badgering insistence, agreed to supply the restaurant at fair prices.

"You set up standing orders," Rose explained on their way back to the restaurant, "and Clark can come down every morning early to pick everything up."

With Clark, they spent ten days getting the place cleaned up and painted, all three of them working from early morning until late at night. A sign painter was hired to paint the name in gold lettering on the front window. Fliers were printed up, announcing the opening of Lion's, the name being an anglicized version of Leonie, and the three of them set out in different directions to distribute them throughout the neighborhood.

On the Sunday before the restaurant was to open, Leonie worked in the kitchen preparing the bread while Clark and Rose put the finishing touches to the place. Kneading the dough, she flung the heavy mixture down on the pastry board until her arms ached. Setting the loaves to rise under a damp cloth, she finally sat down at the kitchen table with a cup of coffee to go over the week's menus.

> Monday Breakfast. Baked eggs, toast, and fresh sausage; or a bowl of fresh fruit, bread and butter; tea or coffee.
> Monday Luncheon. Beef stew, or thick pea soup with ham, both served with bread and butter, a small green salad, tea or coffee.
> Tuesday Breakfast. Poached eggs, toast, and bacon; or oatmeal with heavy cream; tea or coffee.

Tuesday Luncheon. Chicken stew, or vegetable soup, both with fresh bread and butter, green salad, tea or coffee.

Wednesday Breakfast. Eggs Benedict, or a cup of fresh orange and grapefruit sections, bread and butter, tea or coffee.

Wednesday Luncheon. Ham stew, or chicken soup; bread and butter; green salad; tea or coffee.

Thursday Breakfast. Eggs florentine, or kippers; toast; tea or coffee.

Thursday Luncheon. Lentil soup, or beef stew; bread and butter; small green salad; tea or coffee.

Friday Breakfast. Scrambled eggs with toast and bacon, or rice cereal with heavy cream; tea or coffee.

Friday Luncheon. Fish chowder, or chicken stew; bread and butter; green salad; tea or coffee.

Saturday Breakfast. Cheese omelet with fresh sliced tomatoes; or apple-apricot compote; toast; tea or coffee.

Saturday Luncheon. Ham stew, or chicken soup; bread and butter; green salad; tea or coffee.

By making use of the large icebox, she'd be able to refrigerate and store leftovers to use again. The iceman daily delivered huge blocks of ice.

"Everything's done that's going to get done," Rose said, she and Clark coming in to join Leonie at the table. "All we need now are customers and a lot of help from God."

"C'mon, Rose," Clark said good-naturedly. "It's all gonna work out fine."

"Sure," she said.

"Let's have a last-minute look at everything, shall we?" Leonie said. "Go over it all once more."

They went into the restaurant, where all the tables were set, ready for the next morning. The tables had been stripped down to the bare wood. Clark's idea. Salt and pepper shakers stood on each. Near the kitchen door was a sideboard for the water jugs. In the kitchen, on the serving counter, a stack of wicker trays waited, ready to receive the hot meals. Knives and forks and napkins wrapped and stacked. Spoons. Cups and saucers had been set near the two urns—the one for coffee, the other for hot water. Two huge soup kettles sat on the stove.

"You're gonna stay and do the cooking now?" Rose asked.

"I'm just going over the menus a final time."

"I don't know," Rose said doubtfully. "It all *looks* fine. I just hope it works the way we've planned it. I come in and first thing write up the breakfasts on the blackboard. Then I write down the orders on one of the slips, come out here, give you the order, you fill it, put the food on the trays, I take it back out, deliver the meal and collect for it, then go on to the next table."

"I've been to the bank," Leonie said. "I'll bring the change in in the morning. At the end of the day, I'll tot up the receipts, prepare the slip, and Clark will take the cash to the bank. Have we forgotten anything?"

"I'll stoke the boiler first thing," Clark said, "then come up and fill the urns, sweep the front, then get ready to dish up the salads, wash up."

"That's it then," Leonie said.

God help us, Rose intoned silently.

Clark got on his hat and coat, said, "See you in the morning," and went off. Rose lingered for a few minutes in the kitchen, watching Leonie drain the peas she'd had soaking overnight.

"I was thinking," Leonie said, tipping the peas into one of the soup pots. "If we could somehow prepare sandwiches, sell them to take away, it might bring in some extra money."

"Who'd sell them? How? Where?"

"Just prepare them ahead of time, put a small sign in the window saying they're available."

Rose thought about it, then said, "This isn't that kind of restaurant. I think you'll just be making extra work for yourself. Why don't we wait, see how this goes first?"

"You're probably right," Leonie said, adding water to the pot, then going to the icebox for the bowl of ham she'd chopped earlier. "It's just that I'm anxious to cover all the possibilities."

"You still feel sick all the time?" Rose asked.

"It seems to be passing."

I shouldn't like you, Rose thought. I shouldn't even be here, taking your money every week, just helping to use up your money. A baby. A few more months and you'll hardly be able to move from the stove to the serving counter.

"You'll probably have to hire another girl pretty soon, all things being equal," she said.

Leonie added the ham to the pot, then turned, wiping her hands down her apron. "I'm terrified, Rose," she said softly. "It's not easy to explain. Father always told me to be bold. Perhaps I've managed to mix boldness and madness, get them confused in my own mind. I have a few thousand dollars and a need to do this. Be my friend, Rose. I'm all too well aware of the likelihood that I'm throwing away all the money I have in the world. But if I'm doomed to fail, I'll fail on a grand scale. I refuse to hide, cowering shamefully, waiting for . . . I don't know . . . a miracle, perhaps. I'll do what I have to do, one step at a time."

"Maybe Clark could take a basket of sandwiches round to the factories nearby," Rose said, thinking it through. "And do the washing up after. You might be right about that." She smiled and impulsively put her arms around Leonie, giving her a brief hug. "Be careful going home. I'll see you in the morning."

While the soup was simmering, she uncovered the bread, kneaded it again, then set it to rise a second time; leaving it in the icebox ready to go into the oven first thing in the morning. That done, she got to work on the stew, sitting at the table chopping the vegetables. Letting her mind float while her hands performed, remembering so vividly that afternoon in the country. The house in Surrey. The stream. Lying on the grass, her clothes opened to the sun. How he'd later described his feelings.

Grayson had come along the bank of the stream, halting abruptly some two hundred yards upstream. A ringing in his ears, a giddiness overtaking him at the sight of her, supine on the grass. Her skirt drawn up over her thighs, chemise unfastened, breasts bared to the sun. For a moment he'd been able to do nothing but stare at her, his hands twitching with a desperate need to touch those expanses of exposed flesh, to feel beneath his fingers her softness.

"Cover yourself and go back to the house!" His voice had emerged far louder than intended, startling both of them in the green silence.

She'd jerked upright, her eyes flying open, clutching her chemise closed with one hand while frantically attempting to lower her skirt with the other. Her heart gone mad, pounding painfully. He'd terrified her with his sudden booming command.

"I'm sorry," she'd said, terribly agitated, reaching for her shirtwaist, trying with trembling fingers to fasten the chemise. "I didn't think . . . I came . . . I'm sorry."

"I've frightened you," he'd said then, hating both himself and the situation. "I didn't intend that. I was simply . . . startled . . . at coming upon you here . . . this way."

"But I didn't think anyone would come here," she'd explained, shoving her arms into her shirtwaist with such haste that the chemise had come open again. Completely distraught then, she'd wrapped her arms around herself, dropped her head, and begun to cry. Unhappier than she'd ever been, she'd wished she understood why he was so furious with her. She hadn't intentionally bared herself in anticipation of an audience. It was just that the sun had felt so wonderfully warm and she'd been in need of comforting.

"Please," he'd said helplessly. "Don't. I have no desire to upset you." He'd taken several steps toward her, then stopped, undone by her heartbroken sobbing, feeling too cruel for having so brutally intruded upon her privacy instead of simply leaving her undisturbed and continuing on in a different direction. "It is I who should be apologizing," he'd said, going forward until he was standing over her. "Forgive me. Please?"

Keeping her head bowed, eyes lowered, she'd begun fastening her shirtwaist, wanting nothing more than to get away from him, from this place as quickly as possible, all the confusion of this English way of life climaxing in this moment of piercing shame.

"It's too late," he'd said, bewildered by his own words and actions as he'd dropped down in front of her, gently shifting her hands from the buttons. "Too late."

She'd lifted her head to look at him, still frightened.

"Forgive me," he'd said. "From the moment you stepped from the train . . . Those evenings at the London house . . . All the questions you asked, the interest you've shown in all the things Gus has always found so unutterably boring . . . How golden you are." He'd opened her clothing, unable to stop himself, capitulating to that overwhelming need to touch her. His hands closing over her breasts, he'd sucked in his breath with pleasure as his thumbs pressed into the softness of her nipples. "Forgive me?" he'd whispered, his hand moving up the back of her neck, his mouth against hers. He'd been convinced he was behaving monstrously in forcing himself on her. Until he'd felt her hands on his face and her mouth opened beneath his. Responding. This, in itself, positively extraordinary after more than four years of Gus's cold unresponsive bulk suffering his periodic spasms of need. After those years of Gus's closed lips and lifeless, flinching body, to have Leonie responding, offering him caresses as his mouth moved down her throat, across her shoulder, to her breast was astonishing. To hear the small pleased sounds she'd made as he'd lowered her to the grass, her thighs quivering, parting as his hand sought to touch her. Unbelievable. It had thrown his senses into chaos.

"I love you," he'd whispered. "I haven't the right to say it, or do ... Please, trust me, trust that I won't hurt you."

"Yes," she'd whispered back, knowing. So wonderful to be held, to have his hands—large, sensitive hands—moving tenderly over her, touching her in the most exquisite fashion; his fingers stroking between her thighs creating a heated violence within her, something that demanded to be satisfied, so that she'd kissed him feverishly, exploring the sweet interior of his mouth, lifting closer to him, to the pleasure; longing to have him show himself to her, bring himself into her, make the marriage complete.

Her trembling acceptance of his caresses had alarmed him. What was he doing? What had he embarked upon here, soiling this young girl, this innocent girl with his need? But she was whispering, encouraging him, her hands working at his clothing, and he'd helped free himself of the suddenly hateful garments, thinking it was right, had to be right; it was a caring so profound it left no room for thought.

She'd loved the look and feel of him. Running her hands over his broad, smooth chest, down across his belly, down; closing her hand around him, feeling delirious with wanting this, wanting him deep inside her body; contracting expectantly as she stroked him, learning him. Unprepared for this soft hardness, this warmth, this compelling need to open in anticipation of his entrance into her.

"I will never love anyone but you," she'd told him. "Never. And you must know that."

"You will be my wife if I have to move heaven and earth to do it. And *you* must know that!"

I will have a child, she'd thought. And this child of ours will have your fine gray-green eyes and sensitive hands, your anger and tenderness. And I will have you.

All the things you said, she thought now, chopping the last of the vegetables, then going over to the icebox for the beef, sitting again at the table, methodically cutting the beef into cubes. Marrying Augusta for money. I understood, thought no less of you for that, because I do understand ambition. It is something Father made me come to terms with in my own nature long ago. And you were completely truthful with me about your motives, the reasons why you entered into the marriage; the reasons why you would now extricate yourself.

Perhaps you weakened when faced with Augusta's opposition. Or perhaps I was simply too willing to believe.

She blotted her eyes on her sleeve.

It is still not too late to prepare the herbs, remove this child from me. I might. But I will not. I may never have anything more of you. And even if none of it was truth to you, it was to me.

She got up to lower the flame under the soup pot. Then stood, staring into space, for a moment threatened by depression. She shook herself, rejecting it, and returned to the table to flour the meat cubes while the oil was heating in the second pot. Do what must be done. Then do the next thing and the next.

He was asked to do a piece on the Russian foreign secretary, Sazonov. An interview, to be backed up with a description of general conditions in St. Petersburg. He prepared for the trip and embarked on the fifty-hour train ride preoccupied with thoughts of Leonie, fears for her. And had to force himself to be observant, to take notes of details when doing this was usually effortless and automatic.

It was a brief trip, one that left him with very little free time to himself. Sazonov was courteous, intelligent, subtle; anxious to discuss Russia's difficulties with Austria-Hungary, the Balkan situation.

"A chess game," he said consideringly. "Austria championing Albania in order to prevent Serbia from reaching the sea. Italy is motivated by a desire to control Albania. France, now that we are allied, is uncertain about attempting to effect a conciliation with Germany. Yet they are stepping up their armaments and, as you probably know, have extended their national defense service from two years to three."

"How," Gray asked him, referring to his notes, "do you feel the Tsar will react to a German declaration of war?"

"I see now how you have earned your reputation in journalism, Mr. Marlowe," Sazonov smiled. "An ability to project beyond the immediately obvious, and a somewhat blunt directness."

"I apologize if I have offended you."

"On the contrary. If we had more generals with your skepticism and vision . . . But . . ." He raised his hands in a gesture indicating the impossibility of the situation. "Not for publication," he cautioned.

"I understand." Gray put down his pen.

"She will destroy the Russian empire, this fool of a woman and her hemophiliac child. All of Russian history shall be altered irremediably by the Tsar's love for this hysterical German and her fanatic attachment to this mad priest, Rasputin. I am merely a diplomat who *suggests*," he said with a trace of bitterness. "I do not advocate a war. But it's inevitable. Blunders will be made. Everywhere. And the Tsar . . ." He made a decisive gesture of finality with his hands. "It is my personal sadness and fear that I may have to live to see it all collapse." He smiled suddenly. "You have a gift, Mr. Marlowe, for drawing confidences. You might, under certain circumstances, be a dangerous man."

"No," Gray said soberly. "I have no taste for intrigue. Mine, as you observed, is an analytical brain, not a political one in the sense of achieving personal acclaim. And only to myself," he said carefully, "am I truly dangerous."

"How, may I ask, have you managed to arrive at such a perceptive personal truth?"

"Something I mistook for indiscretion."

"Ah, yes," Sazonov nodded sagely. "Love."

"Will the Tsar sign an order for general mobilization should Germany declare war?"

"In the present circumstances, very possibly. Let me now ask you a question. What will England do?"

"I expect Asquith will attempt to maintain neutrality until the last possible moment. But we will undoubtedly find ourselves at war within the year."

"I fear so," Sazonov said softly, sadly.

With only a few hours' free time, Grayson went out into the streets, struck strongly by the fact that almost every man was in uniform. Not only army officers, but civilians of all professions. The color and variety of the uniforms lent an unreal, almost theatrical atmosphere to the streets.

Horse Guards in tunics and brass helmets, Cossacks in flowing robes and furry busbies, policemen dressed in black, with orange or green facings, and astrakhan caps. Students in green or gray, with peaked caps, concierges in long blue overcoats with gold lace. *Dvorniks*, whose job it was to sweep the front steps and clear the paths, clad in scarlet blouses and caps with brass plates that gave the address of the house to which they were attached. Even wet nurses wore blue uniforms for boys, pink for girls. Dark-haired Caucasians in long-skirted caftans of white or brown, with double rows of cartridge belts across the breast, silver daggers in their belts.

The door porter of the Astoria Hotel where Grayson stayed was spectacular in a long black blouse and twisted pink sash, a row of peacock feathers gracing his black astrakhan cap.

Storing his observations, he made his way to the house of Fabèrgé, thinking he would buy some memento of this trip to present to Leonie when they were reunited, but found, to his considerable disappointment, even the smallest gift there completely beyond his capabilities. And went instead to the Ural Stone Shop, where he selected a small, exquisitely detailed carving of a lion in chalcedony. Then he hurried back to the Astoria to collect his bags.

Watching the countryside from the train window, his notes spread across his knees and on the seat beside him, he studied his reflection in the glass, finding it strange to see the rushing countryside passing across the empty interior of his backlit silhouette, as if he were empty. He felt empty all at once, and filled with outrage at having, so late, come to love, only to have lost it. Damn Augusta! His fists clenched. The train hurtled on.

For her part, Augusta was in a state of shock. She'd had no idea matters had progressed as far as they so evidently had. But Grayson's reaction to Leonie's departure proved beyond any possible doubt that they'd been lovers. And she now regretted her haste, wishing she'd allowed Leonie to stay on. With her to serve as Gray's mistress, all the sexual pressures would have been removed and Augusta would have been free to enjoy being Mrs. Marlowe, reaping the benefits of Gray's presence at his side in society without having to tolerate the sickening thrust of his body within hers. Naturally, it would have been out of the question for her to sit back condoning the presence of her husband's mistress in the same house. But he might have removed the girl to a suitable flat.

What was the use of going over it all again and again, though? Leonie was gone. It had been a mistake. But Gray was determined to have the divorce. What will become of me? Augusta wondered, examining her face in the mirror. If I remarry, I'll simply have to contend with another man's weight upon me, squeezing the air out of my lungs, pushing his hateful way into me. But without a husband, I am nothing. I will have no place in society. Slowly but surely my name will be dropped from one guest list after another, until I have no life left at all.

There were no options. She could see that all too clearly. Just as she'd provided Leonie with no alternatives, those same actions now saw her similarly lost. She'd have to grant Gray the divorce. And she'd have to remarry as quickly as possible in order not to lose her standing socially.

Damn that girl! she thought miserably, feeling the beginning of a headache. Damn the day I ever heard of her! I wish I'd never responded to her father's letter, never set eyes upon her!

"The place looks really nice, Ma," Rose said, taking her mother's arm, urging her to get up from the chair beside the window. "You wouldn't believe the difference now. It's going to work." She led her mother over to the table, pressed on her shoulder to get her to sit, placed the knife and fork in her hands. "Eat, Ma. Before it gets cold."

Angelo, his head bent low over his plate, was shoveling food quickly into his mouth.

"Eat slower, Ange," Rose said, taking her seat. "What's the race?"

"Gotta go out tonight," he said around a mouthful of food. "There's a ball game. We're going."

"Eat, Ma," Rose said, patting her mother on the arm. "Eat."

She sat a moment looking down at her own plate of food, thinking about Leonie alone at the restaurant, preparing all that food. What if nobody came? They're gonna come! she told herself. And they're gonna like it! 'Cause I'm not going back to that stinking factory. She automatically reached out to wipe her mother's mouth with her own napkin.

I'll never be you, Ma. Look at you. Can't even eat because somewhere in your head you think maybe you're missing something on the street. What for? Nobody's coming.

She put the lids on the pots, turned off the stove, washed and dried the bowls and knives, then went for her coat. So tired she felt the ache in her arms as she fitted them into the sleeves. She took a final look around before letting herself out, making sure the door was locked. Walking back toward Tenth Street, the wind fierce, cutting right through her, blowing up her skirt, her sleeves, making her eyes water and her lungs hurt.

As she was going up the stairs, she nearly collided with a young man coming down. He removed his hat with a flourish, smiled, and said, "Good evening," as he moved aside to allow her to pass.

She automatically said, "Good evening," then stopped, asking, "Are you the tenant from the second floor?"

"That's right. We haven't had the pleasure of meeting. James Newland." He bowed theatrically.

"I am Leonie Benedict," she began.

"Oh, yes." He smiled more widely. "The lady of the restaurant. I found one of your fliers in my letter box."

"Perhaps you'll come have breakfast or lunch," she said, staring at him, strongly reminded of Gray. They were of an age, of similar build, although Mr. Newland seemed of a far less serious, less intense nature. Yet there was something about the eyes and chin. And his hands, she noticed, were large and graceful.

"I intend to breakfast first thing in the morning," he said. "A pleasure meeting you, Miss Benedict."

He made his way jauntily down the stairs, and she continued on up to the third floor, thinking he was attractive. And hadn't Jenny Barnes, the landlady, mentioned something about his being an attorney? She might one day have need of an attorney.

She went directly into the bathroom to bathe, and then to bed, to lie unable to sleep, her mind moving restlessly here and there. No word from Gray. Perhaps there never would be. And what would happen, she wondered, when she began to grow bigger and people took notice of her condition? How would she explain herself?

Oh, Lord! She turned her face into the pillow. How will I explain to others what I cannot explain to myself? Please don't let me fail! I have nowhere else left to go.

5

Clark was at the market by five-thirty Monday morning to pick up Lion's provisions. By seven-thirty he'd stoked the boiler, swept the place, and filled both urns, carefully measuring the coffee into the grinder before setting to work grinding.

Leonie had the loaves of bread cooling and the first batch of eggs in the oven, the sausages draining in a pan beside the stove. She was so nervous she could scarcely function, and kept lifting the lids on the two pots—now on the rear burners—to check the soup and stew.

Rose, having tied on her white apron and donned her white cap, was carefully chalking the breakfast selections on the blackboard. Thinking: What if no one comes? Here we all are, and what'll we do if no one comes?

Five people came in to have breakfast that morning. One was James Newland, who, after his meal, came out to the kitchen to say, "Don't be disheartened. I promise you I'll do my best to encourage my friends to come by. The place is charming and the food first-rate. I congratulate you." He tipped his hat, smiled, and on his way out left a ten-cent tip for Rose.

"He's kind of a dandy," Rose said somewhat suspiciously. "But he's a big tipper, that's for sure."

Leonie opened the oven to look at the three eggs still in there, then closed the door, straightened and turned to Rose. "I suppose we might just as well begin clearing for lunch. I don't think anyone else is going to be coming." Her letdown was so total she felt ill.

"It was a good beginning," Rose said. "And once people hear, more will start coming."

"Sure," Clark chimed in. "And didn't that friend of yours say he'd tell his friends? You just wait and see."

"I'd better go change the blackboard," Rose said, wishing she had some magic words to take that awful apprehensive look off Leonie's face.

Between 11:30 and 2:30 that afternoon, they served meals to seven people. Rose took the orders, wrote them down, placed the slips on the serving counter beside Leonie, who then took bowls and filled them either with soup or stew, while Clark put salad on plates, ladled on dressing, and placed them on the trays beside the bowls, along with small plates of bread and pots of butter. None of the customers seemed especially bothered at dining in a near-empty restaurant, and two asked questions, promising to come again. Rose made another ten cents in tips and carefully counted out the money she'd collected into the cash box. Clark silently moved in and out, clearing the tables, carrying the tray of dirty dishes back to the sink, where he quickly washed and dried them. Then the three of them stood in the kitchen looking at each other, waiting to see if anyone else would come.

Finally Clark went to put the "CLOSED" sign on the front door, and Leonie tallied the day's takings. The amount just covered her expenditures for provisions. She sat looking at the one note and scattered change on the table in front of her, fighting down her nausea and a childish-feeling desire to lock herself away somewhere and weep.

"Say," Clark said quietly, "would it be okay if I bought a bowl of that stew?"

She looked up at him blankly for a moment before saying, "I've forgotten all about us. We'll sit down together right now and have a meal. Clark, you bring over the salad. Rose, if you wouldn't mind bringing the bowls." She got up and went to the stove, lifting the lids off the pots. She felt Rose's hand fall lightly on her arm and whispered, "Pray for us, Rose. We've got to do better."

Lion's first week of business saw Leonie with a net loss of twenty-seven dollars. Ten of those dollars went to a doubtful exterminator who came to spread around some kind of chemical he promised would get rid of the cockroaches that seemed to have materialized overnight. Another five got used up for ice and coal. The restaurant itself lost twelve dollars.

Breakfast had averaged half a dozen people daily—James Newland a regular—and luncheon had averaged nine. Nowhere near the number needed to cover all the costs.

On Sunday, in very low spirits, Leonie rode the Fifth Avenue bus uptown to take a long walk through Central Park. The day was bitingly cold but sunny, and she walked along trying to think of some way to get more people to patronize the restaurant, wondering if sending Clark out with the sandwiches, starting Monday afternoon, would see any improvement in revenue.

If she was obliged to carry Lion's at a loss—something that hadn't entered into her considerations when planning the restaurant—most of her capital would be used up in very short order. Her forehead creased with thought, her body stiff with resistance against the cold, she was completely unaware of being addressed until the second time she heard her name spoken, and stopped to see James Newland on the path in front of her, smiling, leaning with both hands on his silver-topped ebony walking stick. She was no longer inclined to smile at the stick, having realized that the majority of his gestures and props were purely for effect and signified little.

"If I had a propensity for concentration such as yours," he observed, "I'd most likely, by now, be an eminently successful attorney."

"You're not successful?" she asked, surprised to find his face had grown familiar after seeing him daily sitting at breakfast with a copy of the *Times* folded beside his tray.

"Not nearly as much as I'd like to be. May I walk along with you?"

"Please."

He fell in beside her, and they continued along the path.

"How is Lion's faring?" he asked politely, well aware it wasn't doing too well.

"What would you do, Mr. Newland, to bring in more people if the restaurant were yours?"

"Now, there's an interesting challenge."

"Have you some ideas?"

"Have you taken out ads in any of the newspapers?"

"I haven't. I wasn't sure an advertisement of the size I could afford would be noticed."

"Do it," he said. "At the very least, an ad will bring in enough new business to pay for itself."

"What more?" she asked.

"I'm honestly not sure." He redirected her to a nearby

bench. "By the way, would you be interested in going to the flickers with me one evening?"

"What are they?"

"Moving pictures. Don't tell me you haven't been yet?"

"I haven't, actually."

"Then I insist you allow me to take you. Friday evening?"

"Yes, all right. Thank you very much."

"I'm wild about them," he admitted with a self-deprecating little shrug. "Now, about this advertisement." He became quite serious. "It's always good to leave a bit of mystery, something to intrigue people." He pulled out his pocket watch. "Have you plans for the remainder of the afternoon?"

"I haven't, no."

"Let's have tea somewhere," he suggested. "I understand the English begin to wither without their afternoon tea."

"I'm not English, Mr. Newland."

"No? My apologies. But what are you, then?"

"African."

"Fascinating! Let's talk about it over tea."

"Why?"

"Because you interest me," he said candidly. "You obviously haven't been taken in or put off by any of my gimmicks, and that's to your credit. You're also totally unlike any other woman I've met."

"You wish to indulge your curiosity."

"Haven't *you* any?"

She wanted to say no, but thought better of it and said nothing at all.

"It isn't a seduction," he coaxed. "It's simply tea and, if you like, some petits fours. I have a terrible sweet tooth. Small iced cakes are almost as good as moving pictures."

You are sweet, she thought, disarmed. "Would you offer me some legal counsel in exchange?" she bargained.

He stood up, offering her his arm, saying, "May I call you Leonie?"

When it came to matters of the law, he showed himself to be completely serious as well as strongly interested. He explained at some length how she might go about naturalization proceedings and offered to assist. "Without charge," he said. "It would be a privilege to be allowed to help." He also offered to scout around to see if he couldn't find someone to do the restaurant's books on a part-time basis.

"May I ask you a personal question?" he asked finally.

"I can't promise to answer."

"Fair enough. A short time ago, you asked me *why* when I invited you to tea. I gave you a truthful answer. I'd like to ask you why it is you've come to New York and taken on so many sizable problems for yourself."

She sighed and shook her head. "Some other time, perhaps, I'll attempt to answer that. I think if I had one wish it would be never again to have to offer explanations for who I am or what I'm doing or why. If it were you who were attempting to make a go of Lion's, no one would question you."

"That's right."

"But it isn't 'right,' Mr. Newland. One does as necessity dictates, and that is precisely what I'm on about."

"That's not strictly accurate," he disagreed. "Most women, especially one as beautiful as you, would seek a husband with all due haste and allow the husband to cope with the problems of necessity and its dictates."

"But I'm not seeking a husband. And my 'beauty' so-called hasn't anything to do with this."

"Which brings us back to my question. I'm sorry if it irritates you. But you're young and evidently quite alone, trying almost single-handedly to succeed at a venture that would defeat any number of men. So naturally my curiosity is aroused. However, in deference to your sensitivity on the matter, I'll stop asking why and hope sometime you'll choose, of your own volition, to tell me. And please"—he smiled—"don't now ask me why you should choose to tell me anything."

"I like you," she said, taking him completely off guard. "I find you very kind. You've made this a pleasant afternoon, and I thank you for it."

"No," he said quietly. "I thank *you*. I've enjoyed being with you immensely, and I'm very much looking forward to Friday evening."

James Newland went ahead and made arrangements with a judge he knew, then advised Leonie several mornings later that she could, the following week, meet with the judge and effect naturalization. She thanked him distractedly and he watched her return to the kitchen, wishing there were more he could do. He'd spread the word among his friends and noted there was a slight increase in the number of people at breakfast. But nowhere near the number the place obviously needed to survive.

Friday morning he sent a note out to her via Rose reminding her of their engagement that evening and promptly at seven presented himself at her door. He complimented her on her dress, then helped her into her coat, both of which he thought were far too lightweight for the time of year.

"What are winters like in England?" he asked as they were heading uptown in a taxi.

"I was only there for one winter. But by comparison, I'd have to say it was fairly mild. Nowhere near as cold as this."

"It will get a lot colder," he said tactfully.

"I expect"—she looked down at her lap—"I'll have to buy some warm clothes. How cold does it actually get?"

"Zero and below."

"I see." She turned to look out the window, thinking: More money to be spent. Always more.

He took her to see the new Sennett flick, *In the Clutches of a Gang*, with Al St. John and Roscoe "Fatty" Arbuckle and reveled in her laughter. Over dinner after, at Delmonico's, she said, "I can quite easily see now why you're so keen. That was wonderfully funny."

"I'm delighted you enjoyed it. Perhaps you'll come again with me."

"I'd like that," she said, her eyes moving over his face feature by feature, drawn to him.

He found himself imagining how she might look without her clothes, at once overheated at the idea, filled with a growing desire to make love to her. It came over him so suddenly, so completely, he felt unable to breathe for several seconds as he stared at the rise of her breasts above the neckline of her pink silk dress.

At her door, she thanked him. "I'm sorry we had to leave so early. But I have to be up at five in the morning."

"I understand."

He made no move to go, and she was tempted to pretend for a few moments that he was Gray and accept the kiss he so plainly wanted to give her, asking herself if it really mattered now whether or not she gave herself to another man. She was a little alarmed to find herself thinking in this manner. But this man could offer her support, assistance, protection, even pleasure.

"Thank you for a lovely time." She gave him her hand. "Tomorrow, you must have breakfast courtesy of Lions."

"Luncheon?"

"Fine."

She opened the door and went inside, then stood listening to his footsteps descending the stairs. Thinking: I must leave an alternative doorway open. I may find myself in need of it.

By Christmas, Lion's was showing a loss of nearly nine hundred dollars. Determined to create some sort of feeling of festivity, Leonie shopped for small gifts for Rose and Clark, and when the last of the customers departed on the twenty-fourth and Clark had placed the "CLOSED" sign on the front door, she made a small ceremony of presenting each of them with their gifts and pay envelopes. They, in turn, offered her gifts.

"Don't open this now," Rose whispered, presenting hers to Leonie with an embarrassed hug.

Clark, his face afire, thrust a small package into her hands, saying, "Hope you like this," then hurried away.

The week had been Lion's best, the income actually meeting the expenditures. She went to stand by the front window, looking out at the thickly falling snow, thinking if they could just keep going for another five or six months, the restaurant would become an established fixture in the neighborhood. Breakfasts were averaging ten or twelve, luncheons up to eighteen or twenty. It was building. But so slowly.

She gazed at the snow, comforted somewhat by the sight of it. Loving the look and feel of it, the way it masked the grime and ugliness of the city, the way it muffled the ceaseless noise. She continued to stand for some time watching, then drew closed the curtains over the lower half of the window. With her packages in a string bag, warmly clad in her new winter coat and overshoes—items she'd managed to find in a nearly-new shop on Eighth Avenue—she walked home through the snow. James would be coming at seven to take her out to dinner.

With three hours to herself, she lit the gas fire in the bed-sitting room, then went to take a long bath and wash her hair, afterward examining her hands, the cuts and redness from her hours in the restaurant kitchen. She smoothed on some cream and stood absently working it into her hands, looking down at the slight swell of her belly. She could feel small movements within and was both elated and fearful. Awed at the reality of the child's existence within her, deeply afraid of the possible repercussions. No, the *probable* ones. The only one whose reactions she was sure of was Rose. And that was now. Once the child arrived, Rose might feel quite differently. She was not easy to predict.

Clad only in her wrapper, she collected her knitting and went to sit before the fire to dry her hair, deciding to open her gifts.

Clark's package contained a pair of fine tortoiseshell combs that had to have cost him the better part of a week's wages. She examined them, perilously close to tears as she reached for Rose's gift and opened it to find Rose had knitted a baby jacket and cap with matching booties in soft yellow wool.

On impulse, Jenny Barnes decided to go up and invite Leonie down for a glass of sherry. She'd seen little of her since the opening of the restaurant and felt she'd perhaps been remiss in not making more of an effort to befriend the girl. After all, Jenny reasoned, Leonie was alone in the city. And it was Christmas.

Leonie got up and went to open the door, smiling at the sight of Jenny, inviting her in, saying, "How nice of you to come visit! Do come in!"

Jenny's eyes went at once to Leonie's belly, lifted to her breasts, went again to her belly. She felt something like a spark igniting in her head and told herself not to be silly as she followed Leonie into the sitting room, saying, "I thought you might like to come down, have a glass of sherry, some fruitcake. It . . ." She stopped, her eyes fixing on the knitting, the baby clothes, turning to look again at Leonie's middle.

"What is it?" Leonie asked, realizing the moment she spoke that Jenny had put it all together.

"No!" she said in a strangely strangled voice. "I won't *have* it!"

"Sorry?"

"You'll have to go! At once! This is a respectable place, a decent . . . I won't have you . . . Not into my home! How *dare* you?" She was vibrating with anger and indignation.

"What are you saying?" Leonie's voice was soft in contrast.

"You'll leave at once! I won't have you here!"

"I have a lease on this apartment," Leonie said even more quietly.

"No one would expect me to condone your actions by allowing you to continue living here! You're to go!" Her voice was so high now it was painful to hear.

"It's Christmas. I can't possibly leave now. Where would I

find another place? I'll leave, of course, if you insist. But at least allow me a few weeks' grace to find another apartment."

"*A week!*" she shrieked, moving to the door. "One week!" She slammed the door so hard that everything inside Leonie's apartment trembled. As she ran down the stairs, she collided with James as he was rounding the second-floor landing.

"What's happened?" he asked. "Is something wrong?"

She shook her head, white-lipped, and raced on down the stairs to her apartment. Again slamming the door hard, so that two small china dogs she'd always treasured fell to the floor and smashed. She knelt down to pick up the pieces, crying, "*See* what you made me *do*!"

Staring after her, hearing the gunfire report of her door slamming, he looked up the stairs and, on a hunch, went up to knock at Leonie's door.

"What's happened?" he asked when she came to the door.

Thrown headlong into a state of panic, she couldn't speak, but erupted instead into convulsive sobs.

"Oh, now . . ." He stepped inside and closed the door. "It can't be all that bad." He placed his arm around her shoulders, acutely aware of her state of undress and still-damp hair as he directed her back into the sitting room to the settee, where he again asked, "Can you tell me what's happened?"

She struggled to stop crying, thinking he, too, would most likely reject her. After all, she'd seen him on several occasions in the company of women, going in or out of his apartment. She'd heard their laughter echoing up the stairwell. He had any number of women. Why should he care or involve himself in her problems?

Distressed by her weeping, he drew her against his chest, holding her.

"She's said I'm to leave here at once," she sobbed against his shoulder. "I begged her to give me a little more time, but she wouldn't listen. What am I to do? It's Christmas. How will I possibly find another apartment now? Has she the legal right to do this, Jimmy? I have a signed lease. Surely she can't do this, can she?"

"You're going to have to explain to me exactly what she's doing." He lifted the wet hair back from her face as he offered her his handkerchief. "I'm sorry, but you have me at quite a disadvantage." Mindlessly, he was stroking her arm, aware of her flesh, warm through the silk, her breasts graphically defined by the fabric.

She moved away from him, feeling chilled, and went to sit

on her knees before the fire. "I'm having a baby," she said coldly, her fingers lifting the sleeve of the baby jacket. "That's what's happening."

"I see," he said in a low voice. "I see."

"I'll understand perfectly if you get up and leave now," she said tonelessly. Saying, as if to herself, "I must think what to do. I must *think*."

"Would you like to tell me about it?" he asked. "May I smoke?"

"I'll fetch an ashtray." She got up, went to the kitchen, and returned with a saucer that she placed on the settee beside him before resuming her seat on the floor by the fire. "There's very little to tell," she said, her fingertips touching the hem of the baby jacket. "I fell in love with my cousin's husband. I haven't any idea whether or not she knew or suspected, but she was most unhappy, in any case, having me there. So when Gray left for an assignment on the Continent—he's a journalist, you see, and abroad quite often—she arranged for me to come to America. I had hoped to hear from him by now."

"I suppose we'll have to put you in a hotel until you find another apartment," he said, trying to think all this through logically. "As you've pointed out, it is Christmas, and not the best time in the world to go looking for rentals. Legally, I'm sorry to say, Jenny does have the right to evict you. I think a hotel's the wisest choice."

"I can't afford it," she said, sitting motionless, waiting for him to pass judgment on her.

"Then I'll simply afford it for you," he said.

"I couldn't accept it."

"Of course you could. Consider it a loan, if you like."

"No. I couldn't."

"Look," he said. "I'm sorry Jenny behaved as she did. She's a very ordinary woman and I can't say I'm surprised one bit by her reaction. It's unfortunate she's giving you so little time, but it *is* her building and she *does* have the right to evict you."

"Aren't you going to add your condemnation to hers, Jimmy?"

"It's hardly my place. I'm scarcely a moralist. You've been admirably discreet in refraining from commenting on the several women you've seen me with, although I make no secret of my affairs. But why should I add to your present troubles by contributing my judgments? I have to admit I'm a little shocked. I am. But not, perhaps, for the reasons you might think."

"Why, then?"

"That afternoon we met in the park. I lied when I said I was inviting you to tea and not a seduction. Because that's been foremost in my mind since the first time we met on the stairs."

"I do care about you, Jimmy," she said carefully. "You've been wonderfully kind."

"It isn't the same thing, and we both know it. What we've got to do right now is decide where you're to go."

"There are the rooms at the restaurant," she said, realizing there was somewhere for her to go. "I'll move there."

"You can't *live* there, can you?"

"I pay the rental. I might just as well. I'll get Clark to help me paint the rooms, move there by the end of the week."

"Why won't you let me help you?" he asked.

"I can't, Jimmy. And I can't tell you why. I simply can't."

"This other man," he said.

"I don't know," she said. "I'm no longer sure of anything. Please don't take offense at my refusing. I'm so . . . that you'd offer . . . want to help."

"Well," he said, clearing his throat. "There's still dinner. Are you up to it?"

She smiled a small smile. "If you still want to."

"I'll come back, then, as arranged, at seven."

I love you, the voice in his head told her. I've never in my life loved anyone the way I love you. And isn't it a pity? You love someone else.

He let himself out, and she sat on by the fire, her fingers blindly stroking the baby jacket; wishing she could turn herself over to Jimmy, allow him to do for her, provide for her; despairing over the substance within her that refused to let her capitulate.

6

Jimmy, displaying unexpected protectiveness, helped her get moved in. But kept saying, "You can do better, Leonie. I don't care for this at all. Won't you let me help you?"

"It's convenient," she said. "And practical. No one's going to rent me an apartment as a single woman who's about to have a baby. Later on, perhaps, once the baby's born, I'll try again. But for now, this will do nicely."

"You'd have no trouble at all if you say you're a widow," he reasoned.

"I hate lying, Jimmy. I simply can't do it."

"You may have to, sooner or later."

"I won't!" she said stubbornly.

"You're young," he said. "And I think you're going to learn soon enough that it's pretty hard to survive in this world going on truth alone. What are you going to tell this child, Leonie?"

"The truth. That I loved her father, that I'm not ashamed of anything I've done, that it was my choice to have her."

"And what will you do when she hates you for all the truth you've told her?"

"Please don't do this," she said. "It doesn't help."

"You defeat me. You know I want to help, that I . . ." He gave up. He'd never encountered a woman as stubbornly determined. It frustrated and angered him. "This . . . shadow," he said. "This man you love. Where is *he*? If the two of you are involved in such a grand passion, why isn't he here helping you?"

"I don't *know* why!" she snapped. "What do you *want* of me, Jimmy?"

He didn't answer, his eyes holding hers. After a moment, sounding very wearied, she said, "I suppose you're right. Partially."

"Marry me," he said, surprising both of them. "Let me give your child a name."

"It has a name," she said, staring at him.

"That's not what I mean."

"I know what you mean."

"I don't *think* you do. Maybe in England—or Africa, wherever—the bastard son of the duke or the earl is rather a romantic figure. But the illegitimate child of a woman who runs a restaurant is hardly going to be welcomed into society with open arms. Why is it so difficult for you to accept help? Not just mine, anyone's. Why?"

"You want to make love to me," she said bluntly. "You don't have to offer help or marriage."

"What in hell does that mean?" he asked hotly, annoyed at being so transparent.

"It means"—she placed her hand on his arm—"that I care for you. And you needn't offer anything but yourself."

"You think I'm a fool," he accused.

"I think you're anything but a fool. I'm not making sport of your feelings. Don't you understand?"

"Frankly, no."

"Jimmy, you're very attractive. I like the way you look, the way you dress. You have wonderful taste, you're generous and very kind. I enjoy talking to you. Even"—she smiled—"arguing with you. But right now I cannot be what you'd like. Leave me to get settled in now. Please? It's been a terribly long day and I'm tired. I've got several girls coming in in the morning to be interviewed. I've got the bread to prepare, and tomorrow's meals. I'd like to thrash it all out with you, but not now."

"Will you come out to dinner tomorrow evening?"

"Yes. Thank you. I'd like that."

He picked up his hat and walking stick and turned to go.

"Jimmy?"

He turned back hopefully.

She put her hand on his face, looking into his eyes for a moment before touching her mouth to his. "Thank you."

"I care so much for you," he said huskily.

She nodded, knowing. He stood a moment longer, then let himself out.

Bathing was an enormous problem, and if she wished to use the toilet in the night, it meant getting up, going downstairs through the office, out through the kitchen, and around into the small lavatory. With the increasing internal pressure of the child, she found herself rising three or four times a night to make the trip downstairs. Then, finally back in bed, she was unable to get back to sleep. At last, feeling horribly obvious, she purchased a chamber pot in a secondhand store and kept it under the bed.

In the morning, she had to make her way to the kitchen to bathe—feeling all the while she was being watched—seeing the cockroaches scurrying to their various hiding places. It made her skin crawl.

The advertisement she'd placed in the New York *Times* had helped improve business, and slowly, steadily, more people were coming in for breakfast and lunch. Working Thursday afternoons with Bill, the bookkeeper Jimmy had found for her, she could see Lion's was breaking even most days, showing a slight profit on others. And now that she was no longer paying the rental for the apartment, that extra money was helping defray the deficits.

"I figure three or four more months building steadily," Bill told her, "and you'll start coming into the black. 'Course, taking on that additional girl's set you back a little. Still, you've got to have the help."

She went to the icebox one morning to get out the meat she'd ordered the day before, and stood staring into the box, wondering if she was becoming absentminded. She'd purchased a small roasting chicken, planning to invite Jimmy round to dinner. Now the chicken seemed to have disappeared. She searched the shelves of the icebox, trying to remember where she'd put the small bird, positive it had been right at the front. It was gone.

Rose said, "You know I never go into the icebox. Why?"

And Clark said, "It was in there last night when I put away the pot of ham stew. Isn't it there now?"

Hazel, the new waitress, looked round-eyed and said, "Did I put something in the wrong place, do something wrong?"

A mystery. Leonie decided that somehow the chicken had mistakenly gone into the trash.

Two days later, in the middle of the luncheon period, Rose came into the kitchen with several order slips, moved to get the bowls, and stopped dead. "We've run out of bowls," she said.

Leonie, at the stove, turned, saying, "That's impossible!"

"Look for yourself!" Rose indicated the serving table.

Clark said, "I'll just dry these and you can use them."

Rose, hand on her hip, looked askance at the bare place on the serving table, saying, "Something's going on around here."

Hazel hurried in with two orders, put the slips down beside Leonie, and hurried out again.

Rose watched her, chewing thoughtfully on the end of her pencil.

"Here you go, Rose!" Leonie dished up two bowls of soup, one of stew. Rose snapped back into action, setting the bowls into the tray while Clark got the salads, the bread and butter.

The following week, half a dozen salt and pepper shakers vanished. In the middle of preparing the day's salad, Clark suddenly had no more lettuce. And Rose, watching from the kitchen, saw Hazel deftly pocket a five-cent tip that had been left on one of Rose's tables.

"That girl's a thief," Rose told her mother and Angelo over dinner that night. "Eat up, Ma."

"What're you gonna do about it?" Angelo asked, forking pasta into his mouth so that his cheeks bulged.

"Eat slower!" Rose said angrily. "The way you eat's disgusting, Ange."

"Mind your own business. I don't tell you howta eat, you don't tell me. Jesus! Look at her!"

"Oh, Ma!" Rose wailed. "Look what you've done. Got sauce all down yourself."

After Angelo had gone out that night, and with her mother finally in bed, Rose sat in her mother's chair by the window, unconsciously falling into her mother's favorite position, with her elbows on the sill, chin on her clasped hands, trying to decide what to do about Hazel. She knew she wasn't wrong. But proving it wasn't going to be easy. And the first thing she was going to have to do was talk to Leonie about it. She gazed out the window, seething, thinking about that round-eyed innocent look of Hazel's, while the girl lied through her stinking teeth.

Leonie listened, then said, "But, Rose, we see her leave every day, and she's not carrying a thing."

"Somebody's in it with her," Rose insisted. "I'm telling you! How else can you explain the missing food and the bowls, even the damned salt shakers?"

"You don't suppose Clark could be helping her, do you?" Leonie asked doubtfully.

"Clark?" Rose looked at her incredulously. "Clark, if he found a penny on the street, would ask everybody in the neighborhood if they'd lost it."

"I really hadn't any doubts about him," Leonie admitted. "I simply wanted to know if you did."

"The one I've got all kinds of doubts about is dear little Hazel. We've gotta trap her! Figure out some way to catch her in the act."

"You have an idea, Rose?"

"I sure do. In fact, I just now figured out how she's doing it."

The next day, Rose put her plan into action. Clark and Leonie were on guard, distractedly serving up the meals, waiting. At twelve-thirty, the restaurant's busiest time, Hazel came out to the kitchen and slipped into the lavatory, as she'd done any number of times before. Clark threw down his dishrag and ran over to lean against the lavatory door, while Leonie hurried to open the rear kitchen door in time to see the policeman Rose had summoned slip his hand down the collar of a young boy standing outside the lavatory window waiting to receive the piece of meat Hazel was passing out.

Upon seeing the policeman, Hazel dropped the meat, climbed down from the seat of the lavatory, and tried to get out, only to find herself barricaded inside. She began to wail and pound on the door, while in the restaurant, the customers looked up, wondering what was going on. Leonie went through to say, "We're awfully sorry, there's a slight disturbance. It'll be cleared up in just a moment. Please, do go on with your meals."

Rose, in the kitchen, was filling her own orders, flying around with the trays while the policeman ushered the young boy into the kitchen and Clark let Hazel out of the lavatory.

"You've got them true to rights," the patrolman told Leonie. "You want to make a formal complaint?"

"Why did you do this?" Leonie asked Hazel quietly. "Who is he?"

Starting to cry, Hazel said, "My brother."

"Why?" Leonie asked again, feeling sorry for the girl in spite of her anger.

Hazel refused to answer, but stood her ground, sniveling. The boy simply glared at everyone, hanging suspended from the policeman's grip on his collar.

"Get her pocketbook from my sitting room, Clark," Leonie said, looking at Hazel.

"What're you doing?" Hazel cried.

"I'm going to have a look through your pocketbook."

"You can't do that!"

"Of course I can. What else have you taken from here?" she asked. "Aside from the food and crockery?"

"Didn't take anything," she lied sullenly.

"You're making me angry, Hazel," Leonie warned. "In the three weeks you've worked here, all sorts of things have turned up missing. I want an explanation."

"Get fucked!" The boy sneered.

The policeman cuffed him on the ear. Leonie's hand flashed out and caught him across the other side of the face.

"Have them arrested!" Clark urged, moving back to the sink to wash the dishes Rose had just brought in on the tray.

"Absolutely!" Rose concurred. "*Thieves!*" she spat out, filling another order hurriedly.

In the girl's pocketbook Leonie found a small roll of bills.

"You leave that alone!" Hazel cried, darting forward, attempting to grab the money away from Leonie.

Lazily, Leonie lifted her arm and effortlessly flung the girl back against the wall as she continued to count the money. Thirty-three dollars. She pushed the bills into the pocket of her apron then threw the pocketbook at Hazel's chest.

"Get your coat and get out!" she told Hazel. "If any of us ever sees you anywhere near here ever again, I promise you you'll go to prison. As it is, the money will cover most of what you've taken."

"Don't let them go!" Rose cried from the doorway. "You're crazy to let them go!"

"Look at him!" Leonie said, forcing the boy's chin up. "He's not more than twelve. How old are you, Hazel?"

"None of your business!"

"Fifteen or sixteen," Leonie said, her eyes narrowing.

"You're going to have to tell Mr. Rosen it didn't work." She watched Hazel's eyes widen and knew she'd guessed correctly. "And explain to him how you managed to lose the money."

"I don't know any Mr. Rosen." Hazel thrust her chin forward.

"Thank you, officer," Leonie held her hand out to him.

"You're makin' a mistake, miss," he said uncertainly, "lettin' these two go."

"I expect so."

"Well"—he shrugged—"it's up to you." He opened the back door and shoved Hazel and her brother out into the alley.

"It would be Lion's pleasure," Leonie said, "to give you lunch."

"I'll just put the fear of God into those two and take you up on that," he said, unsmiling. "Still say you're makin' a mistake."

"I know," she said faintly, feeling ill, turning to see Rose serving up another tray of food. "I'll take over now, Rose. Will you be able to manage out there on your own?"

"Next time," Rose said angrily, "let *me* hire the waitress. So I can fire her if it needs doing."

Leonie went back to the stove, mechanically stirring the soup as she tried to understand what Rosen was trying to do, and why. The incident frightened and sickened her.

"We'll have to see to some sort of screen for the lavatory window," she told Clark.

"I'll take care of it this afternoon," he said, glancing over at her. "You okay, Leonie?"

"Clark, I . . ." She couldn't answer, gave up, and picked up a cloth to dry the dishes he'd just finished washing. "We'll have to replace the bowls and salt shakers. Why the salt shakers?" she asked.

"You really think it was Rosen?"

"It was just a hunch. But judging from her reaction, I think I guessed correctly."

"It doesn't make sense."

"I think it does, actually. I suspect it may be how he drives out his tenants."

"Why would he want to do that?"

"It's some sort of blackmail. There's going to be more," she said ominously. "I can feel it."

That night, as she was bathing in the kitchen sink, she looked up to see eyes looking back at her through the slight gap in the curtains. She screamed, crossing her arms over her breasts, and the face vanished. Trembling, she drew the curtains tightly closed, then had to stand for several minutes holding herself until she was calm enough to finish washing.

In bed, she couldn't sleep, feeling she was being watched; seeing over and over the dark outline of the face in the window. The baby, as if also agitated, moved restlessly inside her.

She lay remembering the mission, the life without fear. Only the occasional attack from animals a threat. The children playing in the compound of the homestead, the men tending the fields, the women preparing the food.

I thought it would be my life, my future. I would go to England and study medicine, then return to continue Father's work; deliver the babies when there was some difficulty, treat the cuts and infections, live out my time on the homestead. No thought of marriage; it never occurred to me. Naive.

This place is fear, concrete and fear. It will crush me if I allow it. Thieves, and people who stand in the dark peering in through other people's windows. Cockroaches and penetrating cold that makes my bones hurt. The pavement jarring me at each step. Nothing green, nothing growing.

She ran her hand back and forth over her belly, attempting to soothe the small moving form within, whispering, "Sleep, sleep." Finally succeeding in calming herself sufficiently to relax into sleep.

Rose interviewed and hired a new waitress.

Alice was a pale blonde, appearing very frail but possessed of great stamina, imagination, and charm. She'd come from West Virginia only a few weeks before and was anxious, she said, "to get settled right in with a good job."

"This girl won't steal," Rose said firmly. "And she'll work hard for every penny. You can always trust the ones who look wiry. They've got spines of steel."

She watched Leonie push the hair out of her eyes, then heft the dough and pound it down on the floured pastry board.

"What's the matter?" Rose asked, lowering her voice. "You haven't heard a word I've been saying."

"It isn't over yet, Rose. Something more's going to happen. I can feel it."

"Nothing's going to happen. You're just tired. I'll stay this afternoon and help you get the food ready for tomorrow."

"You needn't do that, Rose. I know you've got your mother to look after, and dinner."

"I'll stay," Rose insisted. "I'll just help Clark finish, get the tables set up for the morning, and be back."

"Thank you very much."

Rose picked up the cloth and began drying a bowl, continuing to watch Leonie knead the dough, again wondering why it was she felt such an attachment to this too-tall, too-stubborn woman. Look at you, she thought. Beautiful and you don't care, don't even notice. Other people do, though. Too strong for your own good, as well. Because people like you don't have steel in the spine. More like a column of fire that can get out of control, burn you up.

"You should've had the two of them arrested," she said. "Two like that, they could wait for you one night . . ." She didn't go on, realizing she'd only further frighten Leonie. And Clark gave her a sharp, cautioning look as if to say: What d'you think you're doing? Hasn't she got enough problems? "I sure would've," she concluded weakly.

The following week, Mr. Rosen appeared at Lion's, insisting on seeing Leonie, making his way out to the kitchen despite Alice's protestations; looking at everything, everyone; taking note of the activity. Without invitation he went through to investigate the premises upstairs and down, before returning to confront an already furious Leonie, saying, "I didn't give you permission to have people living here!"

"The place is mine to do with as I choose for five years, Mr. Rosen. And the lease does not give you permission to come in here on a busy afternoon and upset my staff and scatter your cigar ash around. Not to mention going into my private rooms."

"Better read that lease again lady! I own this building and I could have you evicted right now."

"What do you want, Mr. Rosen?" she asked, feeling her anger threatening to go out of control. "Why are you here? What are you trying to do? You know perfectly well you've no intention of evicting the first paying tenant you've had in years."

"Don't be cocky," he said, tipping his cigar ash purposely on the floor.

"What do you *want?*" she asked again, filled with intense

dislike of this small, not terribly clean man with his malodorous cigar and lecherous eyes.

"I didn't give you permission to live here," he persisted infuriatingly.

"Mr. Rosen, *what* do you *want*?" She struggled to keep her voice down, aware of the dozen and a half people eating their meals in the next room; aware of Rose and Alice filling their own luncheon orders.

"You listen, I own this property. I can come in here anytime I want to make an inspection. Maybe get an inspector from the Health Department to come have a little look around."

Alice came into the kitchen again, set down an order slip, her eyes on Rosen. She picked up the slip, then a bowl, and moved to the stove to fill the bowl with stew, her eyes never leaving Rosen.

"All right," Leonie said. "Very well, Mr. Rosen. How much do you want?"

He smiled around his cigar, his eyes moving over her body as on their first meeting. "Got yourself a little loaf in the oven, huh?" He grinned around the cigar stub, looking at her middle. Clark, at the sink, picked up a bread knife. Rose, in the doorway, had her jaws locked so tightly her head was pounding.

"How much?" Leonie repeated, perspiring.

"Fifteen thousand."

"You're demented!" she declared, blood rushing into her face. "Six thousand." A voice in her head told her: You haven't any thousands at all. What do you think you're doing, bartering with this loathsome man?

"Thirteen."

"Eight."

"Eleven. And that's as low as I'll go."

"I'll give you nine and you'll take it. Now, kindly remove yourself from the premises before Clark goes at you with the bread knife."

His smile held as he turned to look over at Clark. But on seeing Clark's grim expression, the smile vanished. "Okay," he said, extending a forefinger, prodding her in the stomach with it so that a film of blood covered her eyes and she was tempted to snatch the knife from Clark and go at this vile man herself. "Nine," he said. "You've got two weeks to close." He intentionally tipped more ash onto the floor before sauntering importantly out through the restaurant, leaving in his wake the cigar's smell of burning hemp.

"That's Rosen?" Clark asked hotly, putting down the knife.

"My esteemed landlord," she said shakily, feeling that stubby finger pointing into her, feeling raped, violated; thinking she'd just made a commitment she couldn't possibly honor. "Clark, I'd like you to take over the serving for me. I have to go out."

"Okay, sure."

Rose, who'd swept up the cigar ash and was now standing looking questioningly at Leonie, opened her mouth to say something, then stopped as Leonie went into the office and returned pulling on her coat.

"I'll be back as soon as I'm able," she told Rose.

Rose watched her let herself out of the rear door, thinking: You're more in control than me. Because I couldn't've just stood there and let him touch me that way. I'd have killed him.

Leonie hurried over to Fifth Avenue to get the bus uptown, breathing hard, overheated, terrified she was about to lose the restaurant. They have to give me the money, she thought, boarding the bus, moving to a seat. They must. If I haven't got nine thousand dollars for him in two weeks, it will all be ended. Now, when it's just beginning to find its feet. Bill said five or six months. Another half-year would make all the difference. Oh, God! They've *got* to give me the money.

7

"I understand your position, Miss Benedict," Mr. Freeman said patiently. "But you must understand ours. We simply cannot give a mortgage of such sizable proportions to someone with so little collateral, a woman . . . I am sorry. I wish we could help."

"But surely the restaurant could be used as collateral?"

"Let me go over it once more," he said, "You have just over a thousand dollars cash to put up as a down payment. And you're asking this bank to give you an eight-thousand-dollar mortgage, using a restaurant that's scarcely an established business as collateral. Surely you can see how impossible it is. You're also, Miss Benedict, underage. And a woman. I'd be derelict in my duties if I allowed the bank to involve itself in such a venture."

"I see," she said unhappily.

"We might see our way clear to lending you five hundred or even a thousand dollars against the restaurant. But a mortgage is out of the question. Think about it. I'm sure you'll see the logic in our reasoning."

"I do see," she said, getting to her feet.

She arrived back at the restaurant in a state of total depression and went past Rose and Clark unseeingly, closing herself into the office, still in her overcoat, trying to think. Underage. Derelict in my duties.

She had no options left. The only person who could help her was Jimmy. She was going to have to ask or lose the restaurant. Lose everything. And taking his help meant giving herself.

She put her head down in her hands and cried silently,

thinking: Gray, I can't go any farther, I love you, but I can't, I have to do this—would you ever understand, it feels the most terrible betrayal, you of me, me of you. So many promises, words we gave to each other. I believed you, believed in your strength, your anger, the honesty. You said it was a marriage of convenience, talking about your First in English from Cambridge and the fear of finding yourself second-rate. First second-rate. Strong, such a big man, your size, your mind fascinating, your thoughts compelling, kaleidoscopic. You took me to the opera, the ballet, smiled distant smiles, held my hand, and everything in me gave itself to you, to your challenging questionings, your probing eyes, and the sadness of your eyes. I wanted nothing more than to be your life, have you in mine. I care for Jimmy, care very much, but it feels almost evil to sit here planning, hoping he'll accept the offer of my clumsy body in return for his money, his help. I have no choice, nothing left. You held me, your hands in my hair, saying, I like the way you look at me, Leonie, like your eyes when you look at me and the way you feel, so right, so perfectly right. And I hadn't any words, too filled with caring and pleasure, free to study the changing colors of your eyes, the shape of your mouth, and the message of your hands moving over me. I feel too young, too alone, too frightened, too disloyal to everything I promised. But choices—they give me none. Underage, a woman, with too little capital—it isn't fair, so unfair.

She got up, removed her coat, opened the sitting-room door, and beckoned to Clark.

"I'd like you to take a message to Mr. Newland. Would you do that for me?"

"Sure."

"I'll just write it now." Her hands trembled as she wrote the note, a dreadful feeling of finality overtaking her as she folded it into an envelope and returned to give it to Clark, who'd already donned his coat and was waiting to go. "Be sure to wait and see if there's an answer, Clark. Thank you."

"What're you gonna do?" Rose asked quietly, alarmed by the atypical inward curve of Leonie's shoulders, her look of fatigue.

"What needs to be done," she said, tying on her apron and going over to the icebox for the meat and vegetables for the next day's luncheons.

Rose came over and stood beside her at the table, almost inaudibly saying, "Don't do it! Nothing's worth it. You'll spend the rest of your life paying for it, one way or another. You don't have to give yourself away . . . not for this. There's room, you could come stay with me and Ma, Ange."

"You don't understand, Rose. It isn't just my living on the premises. The next time, it would be a Health Department inspection that would result in my having to spend a good deal of money to correct some trumped-up problem. And if not that, then a fire perhaps. Or the front windows smashed. I'm a woman, Rose. And I've defied that ugly little man. I'm a living thorn in his side. He's got to destroy me. I can't allow that to happen."

"Where did you go?" Rose asked, having guessed.

"The bank." She sighed. "I'm underage, have no collateral. I'm a woman, a bad risk. Oh, God, Rose! I think I could have borne anything, but not that he knew about the baby . . . did that."

Her eyes overran, and Rose put her arms around her, saying, "That little sneak Hazel must've figured it out and told him. That bitch!"

"I suppose Clark and Alice know now, too," she said, feeling soiled.

"I suppose," Rose said noncommittally. "It doesn't matter."

"I didn't think so . . . before. Now, it feels *shameful*. They've managed to shame me, Rose. And I feel it. Feel it . . . as if everyone knows and despises me. When that wasn't the way it was at all. It had to do with love, not shame."

"Why don't you go lie down for a while?" Rose said gently, disengaging herself. "I'll do the vegetables, the meat, so all you'll have to do is put everything in the pot."

"I'm sapping you." Leonie looked frightened and guilty. "You have so much to do as it is, without doing my work as well."

"You talk about love, caring," Rose said, "but you fight it when it comes at you. I *want to* help. You think I enjoy watching all this happen, knowing you're going to give yourself to that . . . that *dandy* so you can keep this place going? Oh, I know what you're doing. I just hope you can trust him."

"Don't put it that way," she whispered. "And Jimmy is completely trustworthy. He'd never hurt me."

"You hope!"

"I *know*, Rose. Just as I know you and Clark . . . I simply know."

"Go lie down for a while. Sometimes I think you're too stupid to live. But I'll stick by you. Go on."

Feeling cold, she roused herself to light the gas fire, then sat down again. Thinking of Rosen's finger poking her belly, she dug her nails into the palms of her hands, wanting to scream. She pushed off her shoes and sat back with her eyes closed, hearing Alice saying good night to Rose, hearing the chop of the knife on the cutting board as Rose prepared the vegetables. Thinking yet again how simple and uncomplicated life had once been, no more complicated than watching a butterfly make its way over the wildflowers. Now, obscene strangers had the right to make demands for money, to say fairly much what they liked, to push their filthy fingers into her belly. Bankers had the right to reject her for any number of reasons, but primarily because she was female. And that was why she was turned down. No other reason.

Rosen. He was *umstakatsi*, an evildoer. At home, she'd have gone to the *inyanga* to have him exercise his considerable powers against this man. But here she was powerless to effect any defense against him, able to do no more than make word battle with him, trying to pit her mind's strength against his. And at this moment she felt completely robbed of her strength. Her feet and legs swollen, breasts heavy and sore, her belly beginning to round out noticeably. She longed for a bath, to be able to run a tubful of hot water and stretch out in it, longed to feel completely clean. A bath, then a long sleep. Impossible. She had to sit and wait for Jimmy, in need of him now. Relying on him. Hadn't he offered? Surely he wouldn't refuse now, would he?

She tried to think objectively about him. He was very attractive. Tall, elegant, a bit old at times and somewhat jaded for his years, yet capable of surprising sentiment. Offering marriage. There was something about the curve of his mouth, the shape of his hands, that suggested a powerful sensuality. And he was sweet, his affectations quite endearing. She could quite readily imagine herself performing love acts with him. Had she never known Gray, she'd most likely have given herself freely to Jimmy. Of course, now there was no question. Except, where?

Not here, she thought, looking around. Not here.

"How much cash do you have?" he asked, a leather-bound notebook on his knee, pencil poised.

"About fourteen hundred dollars."

He made a note of that.

"And Rosen will take nine for the building?"

"Yes."

He wrote that down, then was silent for several minutes, going over the figures in his notebook. He sat tapping his pencil against his thumbnail, then looked over at her.

"You're asking me to help?"

"That's right. I am."

"The bank turned you down."

"Very politely."

"You sound so bitter, Leonie." He looked surprised. "Truth is perhaps not the panacea you thought."

"Are you going to be cruel, Jimmy?" she asked softly. "I've never suspected you of cruelty."

"I think"—he looked again at his notes—"with a cash down payment of three thousand, there should be no problem raising a mortgage on the six-thousand-dollar balance."

"I haven't *got* three thousand dollars."

"I'm well aware of that."

"Could we make some legal arrangement whereby you would undertake to secure the mortgage and I would repay you monthly with the understanding that once I've repaid the money, the building would then be mine?"

"And what," he asked, facing her, "would I benefit?"

"Jimmy"—she could feel the pulse throbbing in her throat—"I have four more months before the child will be born. But," she said meaningfully, "if you can bear it . . ."

"A business arrangement?" he asked somewhat coldly.

"If you like."

"You must have a very low opinion of me."

"On the contrary, I have the very highest opinion of you. I trust you."

"Offering yourself to me like so much raw meat."

"It wasn't my intention to make it sound that way."

"I don't know." He looked past her at the wall.

"I will be completely faithful to you," she said. "And once the child is born, I will be available to you whenever you like."

"I despise all this!" He jumped to his feet, throwing down his pencil and notebook. "I'm not in the business of buying women, Leonie! Nor of making financial transactions contingent upon the return of certain favors. When I offered to help, it was out of caring, not out of any devious desire to strike bargains."

She wet her lips, understanding how deeply she'd hurt and offended him. "Jimmy," she said quietly, "I need your help. I haven't anything to offer you but myself. I *want* to do this. I'm being very clumsy, in every way, these days."

"Don't you see how . . . *bald* this is?"

"I do. And I apologize."

"I love you," he said. "Making love to you under these conditions, these *terms* . . . I'm not at all sure it's something I care to do."

"Does that mean you will not help me?"

"I didn't say that!"

"Then what *are* you saying? For God's sake! Don't make me beg you!"

He resumed his seat on the chair and leaned toward her.

"I'm not a child, Leonie," he said earnestly. "I'm thirty-two years old. I'm also not so desperately in need of a woman that I'll allow one I care for as much as I do for you to sign herself away on the dotted line in order to have her. Nor am I so stupid as to blindly enter into a business venture without protecting my own interests, financially. If I make this arrangement with you, there are certain stipulations. I'll charge you exactly the same rate of interest as the bank would. I'll also hold the title to the property until such time as you have satisfied the mortgage. Finally, you will not undertake any further ventures until that mortgage is satisfied. I think you've been unrealistic all the way down the line. You do have a good business sense, but you've a great deal to learn. And I'm going to teach you. You will listen to what I have to say and you will implement my suggestions, unless you can provide me with first-class reasons why those suggestions aren't viable. In other words"—he paused to take a breath—"until such time as you've repaid the mortgage, I will act as your silent partner. Once the mortgage has been paid, I will sign the property over to you and you'll be free to do whatever you wish. As far as all the rest of it goes, I'm going to have to give it some thought. Will you accept those terms?"

Chastened, she nodded, asking, "How long will I have to repay the money?"

"As long as you need, as long as it takes."

"And you have criticisms of the way I've been running Lion's?"

"No, damn it! I have none!"

"I haven't eaten since breakfast," she said quietly. "Would you take me to dinner?"

"Certainly!"

She smiled and got up from the settee as he jumped from the chair looking angry and disoriented.

"You said some time ago that I'm young, Jimmy. Now, it seems, you've forgotten that I am. Don't be angry with me. Please?"

"I'm not angry. Yes I am. Let's go out! I need time to collect myself."

"I do trust you," she said. "Trust *me*. I will honor my obligation to you. Financially," she stressed. Silently adding: in every way.

He calmed down during dinner, regaining his sense of humor. By dessert, he was back to being recognizable.

"There's going to be a war, you know," she said.

"Very likely," he agreed.

"Will you go away to fight?"

"I doubt it. For one thing, I don't think Wilson's about to rush us into it. For another, I'm a bit too old. And for a final thing, I'd prefer to die in my bed rather than on some battlefield. I haven't all that much idealism left."

"I see."

"You think I'm an unpatriotic coward."

"Of course I don't."

"What, then?"

"I think you're very sensible. Why should you want to fight? Wars are monstrous."

"It's still early . . ." He consulted his pocket watch.

"Take me home, would you?"

Looking disappointed, he signaled to the waiter.

In the taxi she said, "I think you misunderstood, Jimmy. I want to go home with you." She kissed him on the mouth, then turned to look out the window for the duration of the ride.

He found himself in the impossible position of being unable to refuse. She'd somehow regained control of the situation.

It felt strange walking through the front door of the house on Tenth Street, and she accompanied him up the stairs hoping they wouldn't encounter Jenny Barnes They didn't. He held open the door to his apartment, and she entered wondering why she was surprised at what she saw. Why

TIMES OF TRIUMPH 75

shouldn't he have fine taste in furnishings as well as clothes? Why shouldn't he like beautifully executed watercolors and Oriental carpets?

"It's beautiful," she said. "Really very beautiful."

He took her coat and hung it away, asking, "Care for something to drink?"

"Thank you, no. May I use your bathroom?"

He poured himself a brandy, then sat down on the sofa to wait for her. His entire relationship with her ranged back and forth, in and out of his comprehension.

She unpinned her hair, watching herself in the mirror. Thinking: I am betraying you now, Gray; vows, promises I made, believing them to be for a lifetime.

For the first time ever, Grayson couldn't work, simply couldn't write at all. In disgust and despair, he gave up and paced the floor of his room at the club; then went out to walk through St. Jame's, trying to sort himself out.

A letter the previous week from Ingles, the detective, had informed him that they'd been able to ascertain that Leonie had been a passenger on the *Lusitania* and had disembarked in New York. Beyond that, they were completely unable to trace her. Gray had urged him to continue with the investigation, then spent his free time trying to read several recent publications he'd undertaken to review for *Punch*. Finding himself bewildered and mildly repelled by Kafka's *Metamorphosis*, he abandoned his effort at reviewing the book. But he was oddly moved by Proust's *À La Recherche Du Temps Perdu*, working through the French with the aid of a dictionary. The title alone struck a sympathetic chord, so that he found himself dwelling upon certain of his own recollections of times past, shrouded in a heavy feeling of bereavement.

Idiot, he told himself. Bloody fool to go off and leave Leonie alone with Gus. He should have known Gus would do something as senseless and damaging as sending Leonie off to America. He berated himself endlessly, free to do so because of his continuing inability to work.

Bored and tired of his own company, he accepted the invitation of a friend from the London *Times* and went with him to the music hall to see the latest rage, Marie Lloyd. The audience was plainly captivated. Gray couldn't understand why. The lyrics to all her songs, especially "A Little of What You Fancy Does You Good," were racy, suggestive, sending the audience wild. But she seemed to him nothing more than a small dark-haired, too-buxom woman looking and sounding anything but attractive. Clad in a mid-calf, far-too-low-cut beaded white dress with a ludicrously outsized hat festooned with ostrich feathers perched atop her head, she used a ruffled parasol to underscore the risqué lyrics to her songs.

Throughout the performance he made unwitting mental comparisons between the coarse little woman onstage and Leonie. Marie Lloyd emerged grossly underdressed, overstuffed, and completely devoid of any genuine charm. He excused himslf directly after the performance on the pretext of a just-remembered late-evening rendezvous and returned to his room at the club, glad to take up his Proust and his dictionary.

He then accepted an offer to interview the foreign secretary, Sir Edward Grey, and went along, doubtful of his ability to translate whatever conversation they might have into a viable piece.

He studied the man as they talked, his high forehead and deepset eyes, thin mouth and large nose, squarish jaw and look of intelligent sadness; seeing upon Sir Edward's face the lines of history writing themselves. Why print an article, Gray wondered, when a photograph of this man would tell all?

They discussed the European situation and the fact that the Serbian premier's trip to Petersburg begging rifles and cannons and the Tsar's promise to supply them had set off a multinational arms race.

"The Tsar," Sir Edward said, "has more emotional sense than political. An observation"—he smiled—"you made in that piece you wrote after your interview with Sazonov. A fine fellow, Sazonov. But that little bit of work has seen our defense expenditures increase by almost twenty million pounds."

The entire interview was lost to Gray. He returned to the club to face himself in his mirror, staring at the image of an oversized, too-old rugger-playing holder of an English First from Cambridge. Going to gray, going to seed. "You stupid ugly bastard," he told the mirror. "Give it up and forget it."

He couldn't write. His thoughts refused to coalesce.

In desperation he arranged an assignation with a certain young woman whose favors, although costly, he'd enjoyed in the past during the early part of his marriage to Gus.

He dined at her house in Eaton Square and found himself relaxing for the first time in months, enjoying both Clarissa's sense of humor and the tasteful appointments of her house.

With a glass of fine claret and a cigar, he sank gladly into the silk-cushioned, heavily perfumed luxury of her bedroom to watch her performance of disrobing—one he'd often enjoyed in the past; one, this time, that smacked too strongly of contrivance. But a second glass of claret together with Clarissa's nimble fingers deftly removing him from his clothes succeeded for a time in pleasantly distracting him.

Yet, once started, nothing seemed right. The quality of her skin seemed wrong. Her breasts too small, too hard. A certain concavity of her thighs bothered him, and a slight but inescapably too-female odor assailed his nostrils. Her body was engaged, her mind plainly elsewhere. He found himself all at once angry—with her, with himself, with the shabby quality of this confrontation.

"Feel something!" he insisted, alarming her with his abrupt change of voice and manner. "Do you feel anything? Have you become so adept at these performances that you have no real feelings left?"

"What's possessed you, Gray?" she asked, her hand moving toward the pull cord to summon her maid.

"Don't do that!" He stopped her hand. "I'm not about to harm you."

He lifted himself slightly away from her, looking down to where they were joined. The pleasure, the release, were there. But Leonie's presence in his mind was preventing it from happening. Taking hold of Clarissa's hands, he held them over her head, stifling her protests as his mouth ground into hers. Her body squirmed beneath his, and the more she moved, the harder he bore down on her, closely watching her eyes until they altered and her movements matched his.

"*Feel!*" he whispered, as a startled cry emerged from her throat.

"Oh, my God!" she moaned, her hands twisting beneath his grip, her body straining to meet his.

"*Feel!*" he hissed, freeing her hands to lift her closer from underneath, holding her riveted to him until she began making an animal mewing noise. He held her hard, watching her hands twitching above her head as if he still had possession of them; then let it all go as she groaned and she felt the pleasure he was determined to give her.

She lay sprawled across the bed, watching him dress, following him with stunned eyes, bruised lips, asking, "Will you come again?"

He looked over at her, at her glistening body and very red

nipples, then extracted several notes from his billfold and placed them on the dressing table. "Come again," she said, her hand closing around his wrist. "It won't be necessary to do that." She indicated the money.

"It's *absolutely necessary* to do that," he said, releasing his wrist from her grip.

Arriving back at his room, feeling tired and not satisfied as he'd hoped he might, he stood for a very long time staring out the window, deciding.

James heard the bathroom door open. Several seconds passed. There was a movement in the doorway, and he looked over to see Leonie removing her dress. He put down his glass, stood up, took a step, then stopped. What he'd wanted for months, but now he wasn't sure. She untied the ribbons of her chemise, her hair falling forward. Then she lifted her head, unfastening the chemise, baring her breasts, and stood looking at him. She watched him come across the room, his face coming closer to hers, then closer, until his mouth covered hers.

He looked bewildered as his mouth left hers and his hands closed over her breasts. But it would be all right, she thought. His hands were good. She had far more feeling to offer him than she'd suspected. Sighing, she put her arms around his neck, returning her mouth to his. Tasting the brandy on his tongue, feeling a wild urgency as her entire body responded to his hands caressing her breasts.

"I want you, Jimmy," she whispered, dizzy with pleasure as his hands circled her breasts around and around. "I do want you. Please don't let it matter, the baby."

"Come in here," he said hoarsely, leading her by the hand into the bedroom. "Come with me."

She went, going weak in the knees when he stopped her and put his mouth to her breast, his tongue touching against her nipple, his lips sucking at her. She felt treacherous deriving such soaring pleasure from his actions, when, in engaging herself this way, she was betraying someone she believed she loved to the exclusion of all others. But she closed her eyes to better savor his tongue, first on one breast, then the other.

Her hands unsteady, she fumbled with his shirt studs. Impatient now, anxious. He took over, still regarding her with bewildered eyes as she attended to her own clothes, shedding them with all possible haste, to stand shivering, waiting for him to finish, waiting for him to slowly study the swell of her belly, whispering, "It doesn't matter. You're beautiful," as he lined his long, lean body up with hers, pressing into her. Her hands were suddenly greedy for the feel of his skin, traveling from his shoulders the length of his back to his buttocks, molding herself to him while she opened her mouth on his neck, breathing him in, filling her hands, her senses with him.

Having waited so long wanting her, he was torn between a desire to move directly into her and satisfy all the weeks of craving, and a need to examine every inch of her, relishing the satiny texture of her skin, the hard curve of her hips, the gratifying little mound of her belly, her long muscular thighs and large round breasts. Intoxicated by her bold, somehow knowing yet innocent caresses and gasping responses to his delicately investigating hands. Encouraging him by whispering, "Yes, yes. Touch me here, here. Yes." She enveloped him, wrapping herself around him with such force he was fearful of harming the baby, but she whispered, "It's all right, yes," catching hold of his hands to kiss his palms, his fingers, before placing them over her breasts and directing them down over her, guiding his hands the length of her body, closing her thighs around his hand finally, moving steadily beneath his searching fingers, eyes heavy-lidded. She caressed her breasts as his hands made her writhe, made her straddle him, whispering to him to come into her, come. "So good ... I didn't realize ... yes."

He moved blindly into the magnetic heat of her body, lost to sensation, urged into frenetic performance by her low-throated cries, lost to love and grinding lust. Until it was ended and he lay at her side with his head upon her breast as her hand gently stroked his hair and she whispered, "It's so good to hold you. You're sweet, Jimmy, so sweet, and wonderful inside me, wonderful. Your hands and the way you touch me. Wonderful."

"I love you," he said, shaping her belly with a careful hand.

"I wish I could say it to you, mean it the way you do. But I do want to be with you, touch you, have you inside me. Not just because of the other, Jimmy. I need someone." I'm sorry, Gray, she thought. So sorry. But I must live. "I will be able to make love to you for perhaps another month. But after the baby is born . . ." She left the rest unsaid, surrendering to the spiraling pleasure created by his fingers stroking between her thighs. I must live. And Jimmy will take care of me, help me. It's only fair. . . .

8

In late March, Jimmy bought a Model T and excitedly invited Leonie out for a day in the country.

"Now that the weather seems to be breaking, I thought you might enjoy seeing a bit of the countryside.

"Where will we go?" she asked eagerly.

"I thought up along the Hudson."

"I'll pack a picnic. Bless you!" She smiled. "The sight of a bit of greenery will do me a world of good."

On the Sunday morning, she laughingly admired his driving outfit of hat, goggles, and duster as he helped her into the car.

Her first viewing of the countryside was enormously reviving, restorative. And when they stopped to eat at the roadside overlooking the river, she attacked the cold chicken with renewed appetite, eating so much she found herself suddenly sleepy.

"Have a nap," he said, covering her with the blanket he'd brought along, urging her head down on his shoulder.

Yawning, she closed her eyes and slipped almost instantly into a more peaceful sleep than she'd had in months. He sat with his arm around her, relishing the weight of her head on his shoulder, the warmth of her body against his. Inhaling deeply, satisfyingly, he enjoyed the clean country air, the scent of crushed grass; thinking that in just a matter of weeks now he'd be able again to make love to her. The baby was due in only six weeks or so. Another few weeks after that, she'd told him, they'd be free to go to bed together.

She slept for over an hour and opened her eyes to see his face directly above hers. Jimmy, she thought, you are so very dear. And none of your disguises or props can effectively camouflage the sensitivity and caring I've come to know in you. She lifted her hand to touch his cheek, and he gazed down at her, drawn to the shape of her mouth, to the slight parting of her lips, lowering his head to kiss her. A moment of exquisite caring. Then she sat up, saying, "I think we should start back to the city now."

He went to crank the car, and she watched, thinking she had to be mistaken. It was too soon. Perhaps she was mistaking the signs. But by the time he was seeing her through the front door of the restaurant, she knew it wasn't a mistake. The baby was coming, and far earlier than she'd expected. At least six weeks earlier. Perhaps the jolting automobile ride had forced the child to present itself prematurely. Whatever the reason, though, there was no doubt it was coming.

She lit the gas fire in the bedroom, went downstairs to bathe at the kitchen sink, then carried a pot of hot water upstairs with her, setting it down by the fire while she placed a thick layer of newspapers on the floor at the foot of the bed, an old sheet over top of them. She got out the small bath she'd purchased and set it, too, before the fire. Then two more trips back and forth from the kitchen for hot water. She arranged towels and blankets near the fire as well as a diaper, some pins, and a new set of infant's undergarments. She hadn't yet bought a crib or the remainder of the clothing the baby would require, so she'd simply have to improvise for the present. Her progress was halted more and more frequently by the pains.

Satisfied at last that she had everything she would require, she removed her wrapper and gripped the post of the footboard, prepared to ride it out. Able to think only of Gray as she shuddered her way through what seemed to be hundreds of contractions that came and went, arriving closer and closer together. Hours passed. The pain built in intensity until her body was running with perspiration, her hair saturated, and she was biting her lips to keep from crying out. The pressure increasing, there was a sudden gush of fluid down her legs, and she knew it would be very soon now.

She found herself drifting with the pain, going in and out of focus; remembering the evening she'd sat with Gray before the fire in the sitting room of the Kensington house, playing chess. He'd been teaching her, a glass of port on the table within his reach. And he'd said in an undertone, "You are sunshine, filling every room you enter with a light that blinds me. How can you bear it here? You belong somewhere else, somewhere . . . A bad move," he'd said, as she'd moved her bishop into dangerous territory. "I shall have to check you now." His eyes had fastened to hers, holding her with them so that her body had turned to warm liquid.

The pains grew worse, coming closer and closer together, until she could no longer stop the cries that emerged from her throat as the pressure forced her down to her haunches, one hand still wrapped wetly around the bedpost, the other reaching up between her thighs to feel the crown of the baby's head beginning to emerge. Shuddering with the pain as an overpowering need to push took hold of her, she strained, pushing until her lungs threatened to explode and her head was pounding. Tears poured down her face, her nose streamed. Pushing again. Then again. The head coming out slowly. Another deep breath, another monstrous push, and the shoulders were through. She was sobbing uncontrollably as all in a rush the infant slithered into her hands, and she cried harder, then laughed, hearing its thin protesting cry, as, shaking badly, she cut it from its cord and wrapped it in one of the blankets. She held the baby steady with her free hand, as, moments later, a final wrenching contraction presented the afterbirth.

She collapsed on the floor and lay for several minutes, unable to move. Then, gathering the last of her strength, she poured warm water into the small bath and carefully cleaned the baby before drying her, fastening on the diaper, getting her dressed and wrapped in a fresh blanket. Her legs barely able to hold her, she got up and placed the baby in the center of the bed, as, shuddering now as if palsied, she folded the newspapers up over the sheet and removed them to a corner of the room to be discarded later. Then she bathed herself from the second container of water. Finally done, she crawled up onto the bed to retrieve the baby.

"Leonie, Leo," she whispered, fitting the baby to her breast, crying noiselessly as the infant began to nurse. It's a girl, Gray, as I knew it would be.

The baby safe within the circle of her arm, still tugging at her, she closed her eyes and plunged into an exhausted sleep.

She was upset to find herself very ambivalent about the baby. Certainly she loved her. But there was a small well of resentment inside at having her waking and sleeping hours disturbed by Leo's crying demands to be fed, changed, picked up, held. Her work at the stove was interrupted a dozen times a day, so that she had to leave the kitchen and get the baby, hold her to her breast as she served up the meals with her free hand; beyond caring who knew about the baby or who saw her frantically offering her breast to that pinkly gaping mouth in order to silence her.

Some moments, when she nursed or bathed her, she felt herself ready to weep with love for this helpless, utterly dependent being she'd pushed from her body. At other moments, she was so angry—at anything and everything—she was afraid to go near Leo until she'd taken the time to collect herself and pull the unreasonable anger back into control. How, she asked herself, could she be angry with Leo when Leo was simply the end result of Leonie's own mistaken assumptions? She'd believed that Gray had been her destined mate, and she was now responsible for the by-product of that assumption.

Sometimes, when Leo lay across her knees, glutted with milk, Leonie stared at her with revulsion, seeing not an infant but a huge white slug that took its nourishment, its daily growing strength from Leonie's flesh. She'd put the baby in her basket on the kitchen floor in an out-of-the-way corner and attend to her bread-making or the next day's food, glancing over every so often at the sleeping infant, alternating between love and resentment.

Business was improving. They were serving between twenty-five and thirty breakfasts daily, thirty-odd lunches. But because of the additional burden of the mortgage payments, her bank account hung suspended at fourteen hundred dollars. And Bill's remarks did nothing to alleviate her frustrations.

"The restaurant's holding its own nicely," he assured her. "You ought to be really pleased with yourself. I wouldn't've believed a woman could do it."

"My being a woman hasn't *anything* to do with *anything!*" she barked at him.

Stung, he returned to his books. She snatched up her knife and hacked away at the beef.

What further surprised her was Jimmy's immediate attachment and devotion to Leo. He never failed to arrive without some soft toy or piece of clothing for Leo. And it was he who lifted her from the crib when Leonie was filled with irritation at her cries and couldn't, for a moment or two, trust herself to go near the infant. He seemed mesmerized by Leo, fascinated by her size, her features, the very fact of her existence.

"She simply wasn't real to me before," he said, sitting contentedly with the baby in the crook of his arm, tracing her pale eyebrows with his thumb. "I've never experienced anything quite like the feeling I have for this baby. Why are you so angry, Leonie?"

"You're so complacent!" she accused. "So filled with platitudes. She doesn't arouse *you* from your night's sleep or make her constant demands upon *you*. So it's quite a simple matter for you to come by four or five times a week to play with her and sit here asking me why I'm angry. I haven't had a decent *bath* in *months!* I . . ." She wanted to stop complaining about irrelevant matters, but the instant she started speaking again, she raced right back down the same track. "I feel as if I want to tear the skin off my body, as if I'll start screaming and never stop. I'm trying not to feel as I do, but I can't seem to help it." She stopped pacing and stood with her hands fisted, staring at Leo, her chest heaving. "*Give her to me!*" she cried, overwhelmed by guilt as she lifted the baby into her arms and burst into noisy tears. Starting to pace again, holding Leo tightly against her breasts, she whispered, "I do love you I do. I didn't mean it. I don't know what's wrong with me." Stopping in front of a bemused Jimmy to say, "I'm sorry, Jimmy. I'm so sorry. Perhaps I'm going mad. I'm sorry."

It was taking everything she possessed—both physically and financially—to run the restaurant. From five in the morning until five in the afternoon she was back and forth from the kitchen to the sitting room, trying to cook the meals, serve them, tallying the daily receipts, entering the receipts and expenditures in the book Bill had set up for her, writing out the market orders, which Clark and Alice now both collected daily, making up the deposits for Clark to take to the bank each afternoon, noting lists of items needing replacement. People, for no reason Leonie could think of, took occasional pieces of cutlery, napkins. There were broken dishes, staples to replenish, ovens to clean, coal and ice to pay for, a broken-down boiler that cost over a hundred dollars to repair. And no bathroom. The cockroaches vanished for three weeks, then reappeared by the dozens.

The restaurant needed dishwashing soap, towels, new trays, more dishes. The restaurant needed money, more time, more effort, new advertisements. The baby needed changing, feeding, burping, bathing. The baby needed money, airing, holding.

Rose said, "Wean her, Leonie. Start her on a bottle, and you'll be able to get some sleep. You're worn out."

"I can't! It isn't time yet!"

"What does your doctor say?"

"I haven't a doctor."

"You don't have one? Who delivered Leo, if you don't have a doctor?"

"I did."

"*You* did? *By yourself?*"

"That's right. It's traditional."

"Traditional. I'm speechless."

"She's not supposed to be weaned until she's three months old."

"You'll go mad long before then," Rose predicted gloomily.

"Rose, will you hold me? Please?"

Taking her into her arms, Rose said, "I never thought I'd hear myself say it, but why don't you let Jimmy move you out of here? You know he wants to, would in a minute. This place'd be enough to get anybody down, let alone someone with a new baby. You need help. Let him help you. You were right about him. He is a good man. And he loves you, Leonie." This'll never happen to me, Rose swore to herself. None of it. No man's ever going to lay me down, put himself into me, leave a baby in there, and go off. Not me. I won't end up like Mama, or you. Crazy, looking out the window all day, waiting to die. Or running in circles looking for a door that isn't there because you can't see where it was boarded over.

Leonie said nothing, simply held on for several moments, then freed herself and went to check the flame under the soup.

"I owe him too much already," she said, looking out the rear window at the rain. "It'll take me years to repay him for the mortgage."

"Okay," Rose said, letting it drop.

Her breasts ached from the weight of her milk. Her nipples cracked and split, then bled, so that nursing was agony. And there was insufficient time between nursings for the ointments and creams she used to have any healing effect. The internal bleeding went on and on, her insides contracting painfully. She lost the weight she'd gained while carrying the baby, but her body no longer looked or felt the same as it had. The sight of herself in the mirror only served to heighten her anxiety, and she tried every herbal remedy she knew to relieve it, but nothing helped. The final straw was washing her hair, then standing before the glass in her bedroom to brush it and seeing she'd lost quite a considerable amount of her hair. There were inch-long growths at her temples, her forehead. She lay down on the floor and wept miserably until Leo began to cry, demanding to be fed. Then, very close to the edge of her reason, she slowly raised herself from the floor and went to stand beside the crib, looking down at the baby, telling herself: You love her, you made her gladly, you love her, you must feed her, change her, hold her lovingly. It is not her fault that you've lost some hair, that your body feels unrecognizable to you, that your life's in bondage to a man you don't love as you feel you should, that your business won't again be your business until you've made good the tremendous financial obligations you now have. She forced herself to be gentle as she lifted Leo, set her down to change her, then carried her to the chair, where she sat and held her to her breast, noiselessly crying as the baby nursed and pain shot through her breast. Praying: Help me to love her, to love myself again. Help me, please!

Clark often forgot what he was doing, caught up in watching as Leonie, oblivious of everything but the baby and serving up the food, opened her clothes, exposed her breast, and held the baby to it. It was beautiful but awful, and he had to force himself to look away every time, wanting to watch because the sight of her breast made the breath catch in his throat, made his groin hurt. Looking away because he didn't love her that way. Busying himself with shredding lettuce for the salads with a vengeance, he concentrated on the girl he'd met, whose name, of all things, was Hazel. In a couple of years he'd marry her for sure. So he couldn't look at Leonie that way when he was just crazy about Hazel.

She set the bread under a wet cloth for its second rising, cut the flames under the soup and stew pots, returned the mixing bowls to the pantry, removed her apron, and exhaustedly went upstairs to stand staring in horror into the crib, seeing a cockroach crawling over the baby's face.

With a cry she plucked the insect off the baby, snatched

Leo from the crib, and stood with her in the middle of the room sobbing; at the end. Turning to look at the walls, the ceiling, her hands gripped the baby as she silently asked the walls, the ceiling: Why did you abandon me? Why have you left me to bear all this alone? You said you loved me, would always love me, and I believed you, *believed* in you. You were my credo, my personal theology, my every reason for being. *I believed you.* But you've left me to make my way alone, and I need to hold on, someone to hold and protect me. I don't want to hate you, not you, when I loved you so completely, so fully. But I will, I will hate you unless I find some measure of security.

She spent the night downstairs on the settee, curled uncomfortably on the too-short length of cushions, with Leo safely in her arm. And first thing in the morning, when Clark arrived, she sent him around to Tenth Street with a note for Jimmy. While waiting for Jimmy to come, she quickly prepared the breakfasts, slicing yesterday's bread for toast, placing a tray of eggs in the oven, watching the bacon to make sure it didn't burn, dishing up cups of fruit; working quickly, automatically, framing her words. She rejected whole strings of them, trying to find the right way to say what she wanted. All the prepared words deserted her though, at the sight of Jimmy hurrying through from the front, asking, "What's happened?"

Leaving Rose, who'd just arrived, to see that the food didn't burn, she went into the sitting room with Jimmy and closed the door, sagging against it as the words poured from her in a rushing stream.

"Bugs, and I can't bathe, I'll go mad if I can't bathe. I went up and there was one on the *baby!* Jimmy, I know you want to marry me. I can't do that, but *help* me! I've *got* to get *out* of here. People looking in the windows. I have to bathe in the kitchen at the sink. And I want to wean her, but I feel guilty. I can't stand it here! I simply cannot stay! I'll go mad. There's no separation, you see. I come in from out there, go upstairs, it's all still the same. Please! I'll do anything for you but I've got to get out of here!" She was crying, her words coming out in jagged spurts, her hands fastening to his coat sleeves. "Please, Jimmy! I can't *live* here!"

"What about this other man?" he asked very quietly.

"I can't, Jimmy!" She shook her head back and forth, the tears flying from her face with the motion. "*Please!* Haven't I kept my word, paid you faithfully every month, taken your suggestions? All of it. I know I haven't any right to ask, none really, but . . . an end. It has to end somewhere, somehow. I'm so tired, *so tired*."

"Everything's going to be all right," he said, enclosing her in his arms. "I'll rent another apartment, something large enough for the three of us and someone to help look after Leo. Until I make the arrangements, you and Leo will stay in a hotel. You can bring her here with you every day until we can get it all worked out, find someone to look after her."

Exactly what she'd wanted to hear. Overcome with relief and gratitude, she clung to him, unable to stop crying; sick with lack of sleep, giddy with the sudden loss of her fears. She hung on until she was finally able to speak, whispering, "Thank you, thank you. You won't regret it, I promise you."

"It needn't have come to this," he said, his hand soothingly stroking her hair. "But I'm not going to rub it in. Will you be all right?"

She let go of him, accepting his handkerchief, and nodded, wiping her face. "I'll be all right now." She looked at him, then threw her arms around him again, holding him with all her might, thinking: You once asked if I thought you a fool. I am the fool. Living on dreams and memories and far too much pride. "I do love you," she whispered, her face in his neck. "Very much."

In response, his arms tightened around her, then opened.

"I'm going to be late to the office. I'll be here at six to collect you and the baby, take you to a hotel. You don't have to say you love me, Leonie. It isn't necessary. I'm happy to have you whatever way I can. And I like being seen with you. Coming home to you and the baby . . . It's more than I'd hoped for. I'll be back at six."

He kissed her on the forehead, opened the door, and walked briskly out through the restaurant to the taxi he'd kept waiting.

Part TWO
1914-1918

9

Any other woman, he thought, would have married him. But not Leonie. She must love me, he thought time and again. It seemed incomprehensible that she could make love to him with the intensity and abandon she did and not love him. Kneeling naked before him on the floor, her breasts pressing against his knees, her hands curved over his hips as her mouth drew at him, carrying him headlong into a state of madness. When it was ended and she was gazing up at him, he lifted her to her feet and sank, in turn, to his knees, holding her to his mouth and tongue until her body crumpled and she lay gasping on the carpet, her hands opening and closing against the air. She climbed fully dressed over his lap, her hands freeing him from his clothes before lifting her skirts to reveal her nakedness underneath, her knees pressing hard into his thighs as she lifted and fell again and again until she lay collapsed against his chest as if in a faint.

And in the midst of this most extraordinary pleasure, when he whispered, "I love you," she answered, "Yes, yes, yes," and bent with him, opened to him so totally he felt himself involved in something beyond reality. Her tremendous, ever-present hunger created a corresponding rapacity within him, so that their time together was filled with heat and motion and peaks of pleasure attained in an atmosphere so thin and rarefied, he felt lost, completely adrift; everything once familiar cut away, gone. She was compelling him, indirectly, to live through his senses, making all his previous experiences seem tepid, unadventurous.

Sometimes she frightened him with her insatiable appetite, her strength and durability. And her capacity to leave their bed and the next morning appear in the restaurant kitchen cool and capable and completely in control as always left him wondering if she was entirely human.

When he expressed concern at the possibility of her becoming pregnant, she simply smiled and said, "It is taken care of." He didn't dare allow himself to imagine just how she might be taking care of it. The images his newly fecund imagination created were too bizarre to deal with.

While, of an evening, she pored over the restaurant's books, he sat with the baby, indulging himself in the pretense that Leo was his child. He'd never been happier or more at sea, and tried his best to leave well enough alone, resigned to graciously accepting whatever Leonie was willing and able to give. He did wonder, very occasionally, if others mightn't think him something of a cuckold for so gladly giving so much to someone who seemed to be with him, at best, only halfway. The rest of her held in abeyance for this shadowy figure named Grayson, who had somehow managed to capture her love and loyalty, even in the face of his absence and of tremendous adversity. He found it impossible to formulate any clear image of this man he knew was a year younger than himself, a journalist of some considerable repute, in possession of what was apparently a lofty degree in English from Cambridge University, a chess-playing seducer of his wife's cousin. It wasn't a good image, even blurred as it was. And he tried not to succumb to the temptation to further question her, knowing it could do neither of them good.

"I would like," she said, lying with her arms folded under her head, "to one day open a second restaurant. And then perhaps a third, and a fourth and a fifth."

"I can't see any reason why you shouldn't," he said. "In time."

"It's been a year, you know, since we opened. And we're finally making a bit of a profit. If we continue to grow, I'll be able to double my payments to you, perhaps even triple them, and repay the loan. If I wasn't a woman, I could go to the bank tomorrow and they'd give me the capital to open a second place."

"I don't understand you," he said, leaning on his elbow to look at her. "You're just coming out of the rough, and already you're thinking of taking on more. Why, for God's sake?"

"Why not?"

"What're you after, Leonie? Is it power?"

"Power? I don't think so. I haven't any particular wish to

exert my strength over anyone else. I simply wish to do what I know I'm able." She let her hand trail over his chest, then moved closer as he lay back, resting her head on his chest, closing her eyes, enjoying his hand tenderly shaping her breast. If I loved you, she thought, if I could really love you, if only. *Why* can't I love you? I can feel so strongly how much you love me, and it seems so dishonest, so wrong of me to take all you offer when I can't make myself care for you in the way you deserve.

"Just because I'm cautious," he said, "doesn't mean I don't believe in your capabilities, you know."

"Oh, Lord." She sighed. "Two years or so ago I was free, Jimmy; running across the space of my world, childishly believing it would be forever. Suddenly, here I am in another world altogether, my African heritage no longer valid because I've become an American in order to live and survive here. Here, with a child, a business, responsibilities. And you, of course. I owe you more than I can ever say. But some moments, I stop and stand very still, wondering how all this happened. Perhaps you're right. Perhaps Lion's is something more to me than just a business that provides food and shelter for Leo and me. Maybe it does have something to do with my personal power. Whatever it is, I know I want to go on with it, build it into more."

"Let's have a look at the figures again in a few months' time. Then we'll talk about the possibility of opening a second place."

"Yes, all right."

"There's something I've been meaning to talk to you about," he said. "I want your promise you won't be offended."

"What is it?"

"You're to see a dressmaker and have several new dresses made. You've been wearing the same few things as long as I've known you."

"Clothes aren't important to me."

"If you're going to learn the rules, Leonie, learn them all. This is an important one. Good clothes create a good impression. And whether you like it or not, you need to make a good impression. And keeping that in mind, I've decided you should come out from the kitchen, hire someone else to do the serving. I think it would be appropriate if you, as the proprietor, greeted people and saw them to their tables. It'd add a touch of class to the place. If you're to take on the role of hostess, you're going to have to look like someone with a future, not like a parlor maid on her free afternoon."

"I see," she said. "New clothes. Anything else?"

"One other thing. Move Rose up, give her more money, and let her oversee the waitresses, the kitchen. You might shift Clark, let him do the dishing up, handle the order slips. That lad'll do well with responsibility. If we're going to be thinking of opening a second restaurant, you're going to want to have people ready to move into new management positions. You've been lucky with Rose and Clark. You'll need them when the time comes to open the second place. Lastly, to encourage loyalty and keep morale high, give all the staff bonuses at Christmas. A week's pay."

"Raises, bonuses. There isn't the money to do it," she argued.

"Money makes money, Leonie. Use your capital. Invest it where it'll do the most good. Create loyal, happy employees, and you'll have a solid foundation to build on."

At Christmas, Clark, Rose, and Alice were duly given a week's wages as a bonus and two days off. Rose was given a two-dollar-a-week raise and the task of hiring another waitress as well as a new kitchen boy. Clark was given a dollar raise and advised of his new duties. Both were pleased. To Alice, Leonie also gave a dollar raise and the job of overseeing and training the new waitress once she was hired.

On Christmas Eve, at Leonie's invitation, Rose came to the new apartment, bringing an exquisite hand-knitted dress with matching leggings for Leo, a shawl for Leonie.

"What would you think," Leonie asked her, "of Clark's managing a new location?"

"I'd think he's awfully young," Rose said guardedly.

"I grant that."

"But I think he'd do just fine. Would you consider taking on my brother, Ange, for Clark's job, now that Clark's going to be serving?"

"I trust your judgment. I can't see why not, if you think he could handle it."

"Oh, Angelo's never going to amount to much more than a salad boy or a dishwasher. But he'll do his best. I don't know what'll happen once Mama goes. He depends on her and me for everything."

"Is your mother not well?"

"She's *never* been well. She won't last much longer now."

"That's very sad."

"No," she said calmly. "It really isn't sad. She and Angelo, they're the type of people who fasten onto someone and live their entire lives through that person. It makes me sick just thinking about it."

"But what about you, Rose?"

"I have almost everything I need. I'd rather die than have to have a child."

"But, Rose . . ."

"That doesn't mean I think badly of you or anything like that," she said. "It only means I don't want any of it for myself. Men . . ." She shook her head. "What do I need them for?"

"I don't know, Rose. *Do* you have a need?"

"Would you consider renting me the rooms at University Place?" she asked out of the blue.

"Of course I'd consider it. But not until I can afford to have a proper bathroom plumbed in. I wouldn't *allow* you to go through what I did there. And what about Angelo? And your mother?"

"Sooner or later, Ange's going to have to learn to make his own way in the world. I've been looking out for him since he was a baby. It's about time he started doing for himself. And Mama? She'll simply die."

"You surprise me."

"Why? Because I know my mother's going to die?"

"No. Because you put it so flatly, make it sound so final. I've always thought that one's spirit continues to live on in some fashion."

"I don't believe in ghosts," Rose stated.

"We create our own ghosts, Rose. We make them out of old memories, disappointments, bits of conversation."

"You still think he'll come to you, after all this time?"

"I think it. But I no longer believe or expect it. We're getting awfully gloomy." She clapped her hands as if to physically break down the perimeters of the mood. "It's Christmas. Let's not be morbid. Jimmy's late. Probably doing all his shopping now, having saved it until the last possible moment."

"Will you marry him?" Rose asked.

"No. Let's have some sherry!"

"I'd better be going. Ma's expecting me and Angelo to take her to midnight Mass."

"But that's hours away!"

"It'll take me a while to get over to Brooklyn. There's dinner to do. I've got to feed Ma, then get her cleaned up and dressed. Could I just have a look at Leo before I go?"

Rose followed her to the baby's room, thinking how much older Leonie seemed now. Only twenty, yet she seemed a good deal more. It showed in her carriage, her intonation, her eyes, and in those areas where Jimmy's influence could be readily detected: her clothes, her expanded decisiveness, her knowledge of the business. From last year to this, she'd learned everything there was to be known about running a restaurant. And what little remained Jimmy was painstakingly teaching her.

If I could have someone like Jimmy, Rose thought, accepting Leo into her arms, I might be happy. Someone to help me without wanting to change me, someone to love me without asking for things I can't give. But you can't trust men, she thought, lifting Leo into the air to make her laugh. You can't trust them. Look what that Englishman did to Leonie! Not even a letter. Not one word. None of them were any good, men.

"She's getting so big." She laughed as the baby pulled at her hair. "And so beautiful."

"You really wouldn't like one of your own, Rose?"

Returning the baby to her crib, she said, "There'll always be some friend or another with a baby. That's enough for me."

Later on that night, before going to sleep, she and Jimmy kissed a final time, then separated. "Happy Christmas, Jimmy," she whispered.

"And to you, my love."

The words struck her like a blow.

My love, are you dead? Or wounded, lying in the mud of some trench? Or are you safe, preparing to partake of your Christmas dinner with Augusta? Do you think of me ever? Wherever you are, Gray, I wish you well.

Learning that Augusta and her new husband had died while trying to get back to England from a vacation in Italy triggered Grayson to make his move. After a condolence visit to Gus's family and an embarrassingly affectionate welcome by them, he went along to have a chat with a friend at the War Office. And a few weeks later found himself sporting major's insignia, off on assignment as an official observer at Ypres, arriving on the fourteenth of April 1915.

What struck him strongest was the short distance from England to the battlefields. A matter of seventy-odd miles away, in London, life went on much as usual. Dinner parties, the theater. The only perceptible difference at home was the daily increasing number of men in uniform. But here, everywhere he looked was evidence of death.

With the spring thaw, the ground had turned to a sea of mud and he had to wade knee-deep into the thick, heavy stuff en route to the command observation post.

"How on earth do the men maneuver through this?" he asked.

"Ask Sir John French!" came the rather bitter reply of the young lieutenant there to escort him. "They're dying by the bloody thousands," he said. "God knows how many we've just trod upon."

For a week he made his observations, talked to the lads in the trenches, surprised to find the morale as high as it was.

"We're just doin' our bit for the guvnor," he was told by more than one boy who didn't look old enough to be bearing the weight of his heavy pack. "It's only right, i'n't it?"

He moved through the trenches, sharing cups of foul-tasting tea with conscriptees as well as the officers, deeply disturbed by the seemingly slow-motion efforts of the combined British and French forces to turn the enemy's western flank.

A week and a day after his arrival, the German artillery advanced and poisonous chlorine gas was used. A shift of the wind brought the gas over the heads of the majority of the troops, carrying it full into the faces of the four men on the observation post. Grayson had the presence of mind to cover his mouth with his handkerchief and throw himself to the ground, but his inhalations were sufficient to have him returned to England and hospitalized.

For no reason he could think of, no explanation he could find—nor could anyone else offer him—he lost the hearing in his left ear. He also coughed considerable quantities of blood for several weeks until the medications seemed to take hold and put an end to the bleeding, although not to the coughing.

When he finally emerged from the hospital some seven weeks later, he was deaf in one ear, warned off smoking for life, possessed of severely scarred lungs, and released from his War Office duties.

Discarding his notes, unable to write beyond the maintenance of a journal, he accepted the offer of an editorial post on the *Times* and took on the job of dealing with the inflow of material from a number of foreign correspondents.

By Christmas of 1915 his hair had turned completely gray. The detective, Ingles, had gone off into the army. Left with little hope now of finding Leonie, Grayson resigned himself to his present life and spent Christmas eve with Clarissa in order to reassure himself that he hadn't lost everything in his brief tour abroad.

He felt aged beyond measure, hardened in many ways, softened in numerous others. And moved into a small flat in Chelsea, where he spent the majority of his evenings either writing letters to Leonie that were destined never to be sent, or gazing into the coal fire remembering her. He formulated dozens of plans for going to America, finding her. None of them feasible. With the war, it was exceedingly dangerous to travel by ship unless necessary. The German submarines were sinking almost anything that came within their sights. The telegraph was restricted to only the most important messages. And where might he send a letter? Miss Leonie Benedict. Somewhere. In America.

He tracked Churchill's career with interest, studied the pieces from the foreign correspondents with editorial objectivity, and slowly redetermined his values, rejecting much of what had once seemed most desirable—money, career, status—learning instead to appreciate the alarmingly brief span of one's lifetime and the importance of loving. He felt as if he'd spent all his allotted share of loving during a few brief summer weeks in 1913 with a girl whose every detail was etched so permanently in his mind that he knew he'd never be satisfied until he found her and saw her, if only once, again.

In the meantime, he acquired the habits of someone older, slower, more gracious. Time and loss cleared both his mind and vision. He did his job, dozed by the fire, lived through each day; waiting out the war.

"Is she African, your new maid?"

"Don't call her that!" she said sharply. "She's *not* a maid. Amy's a person who works for me. Calling someone a maid. It leaves her no dignity at all."

Amy was about twenty and very black. The moment she had come through the apartment door, Leonie had felt a sense of rightness about her. Unlike all the others she'd interviewed since Leo's nanny had left to get married, the others who'd asked about wages and rooms and days off, Amy had asked first thing if she might see Leo.

"She's having her nap just now. But you're welcome to look in."

"I can tell a whole lot about the child just by looking," Amy had said confidently, accompanying Leonie to the bedroom, where she'd lifted Leo's hands to look at them, then spent several minutes studying the sleeping toddler's face before turning with a smile.

"That's a fine, strong little girl," she'd said when they'd returned to the sitting room. "I like strong, independent children. Need to be that to make your way in this world."

"When would you be free to start? And would you be available only days or could you live in?"

"I'm needin' a place to stay," she'd answered with admirable directness. "Just came down from Buffalo and I'm about out of money. I could come right away, right now, today."

"Splendid! I know Leo and Jimmy and I will be very happy having you here."

"Where you from?" Amy had asked, plainly puzzled.

"Africa."

A smile. The first Leonie had seen in years that had had any significant meaning. The same smile she'd seen, upon acceptance, on the face of every new Swazi friend she'd ever made.

"May I ask how much you were paid at your last job?" Leonie had asked.

"I was a cook, the last place. Paid me four dollars, and I had Thursday afternoon free."

"One afternoon a week?"

"Don't need no time at all. If you're needing me."

"I'll give you six dollars a week. And you'll be free evenings as soon as Leo's down for the night as well as Saturday afternoon and all day Sunday. Have you family here in the city, Amy?"

"Go no one here," she'd answered, trying to absorb an offer of six dollars a week and all that free time. "Got no one at all. Came from nowhere, ain't going nowhere."

"Well, you're here now."

"How you say that baby's name again? Lay-o?"

"That's right. Her name is the same as mine. Leonie Benedict. We call her Leo."

"This Jimmy, he ain't your husband?"

"Does that disturb you?"

"Don't disturb me none. It disturb you any?"

Leonie had laughed. "I hope you'll be happy here, Amy."

10

Rose let herself into the apartment, calling out, "It's me, Mama. I'm home. Ange won't be home for supper. He's going to a ball game." She glanced over at the figure by the window, then set the bag of groceries down on the table. "How can he go to a ball game when it isn't baseball season?" She laughed and shook her head. "Never thought of that before. Don't know why. Summer and winter, Ange always off to the ball game, when there's no ball game to go to. He's probably got a girlfriend." Removing the groceries from the bag, she pushed past the curtain, opened the icebox, and put the meat inside. Tying on an apron, she said, "You have a good day, Ma? See anything interesting on the street?"

She carried the bowl of vegetables to the table, put it down, and turned to look over to the window, noticing the curtains were lifting, flapping.

"Ma?" She walked across the room and bent around to look at her mother's face. She let her breath out very slowly, dropping to her knees to let her head rest on her mother's lap. Thinking: We're both of us free now, Mama.

"Since Rose's mother died, she's been very anxious to have me rent her the rooms at University Place."

"That sounds like a good idea."

"I can't ask her to pay rent, Jimmy. It wouldn't be right. And besides, I couldn't let her live there without a proper bathroom."

"A suggestion?"

"Please."

"Have a plumber come in and do the work, then let Rose

pay you ten or fifteen dollars a month until the work's paid for. That way both of you will be happy."

"You're wonderfully logical and clever." She grinned, kissing him on the nose. "I'd never have thought of that."

"I think I've found a place that would do nicely for your second Lion's."

"*Jimmy! Where?* Tell me about it!"

"On Fifteenth Street near Irving Place. The building's for sale. The place is already fully equipped. All it needs is some sprucing up, a bit of cleaning and painting."

"And what will the arrangement be this time?" she asked, knowing he'd already fully investigated all the possibilities before even mentioning the place.

"It's larger, for one thing. So you'd be able to accommodate more people. I think University Place is stable enough now to hold its own, cover your mortgage payments and staff salaries, without going into deficits. You tell me your cash status and I'll tell you what sort of mortgage we'll go for."

"What's the asking price?"

"Fourteen thousand. I'm fairly certain they'll accept an offer of eleven thousand, five hundred."

"That's a great deal of money, Jimmy. How will I carry such heavy payments?"

"I will now," he said, "give you another brief lesson in economics and public reasoning. You buy the building, open a second restaurant. People see the new place and think the first restaurant must be doing awfully well if you can afford to open a second. And since they personally have never given Lion's a try, they decide it must be a good place to eat if it's already expanding. So they come in, have a meal, find out it's better than good, and go away promising to come back. They also mention to their friends they had a good meal, liked the place, isn't it nice, haven't you been there yet. Clientele established.

"You use the revenue—the projected income—from the second restaurant to cover your running costs, the mortgage, what-have-you. Among other things, it's called 'goodwill,' Leonie. You're not just establishing a second business, based on a successful first, you're also establishing a reputation for quality food, good service, and so forth. You see?"

"I do. But there's no guarantee that's how it'll go."

"You only get guarantees with life-insurance policies. And even then, if you bother to read all the small print, you'll find all sorts of exclusions. You want an empire, my love, you have to be prepared to take risks. Big ones."

"I could put up twenty-five hundred dollars," she said, thinking that would leave very little capital in the Lion's account.

"What sort of working capital will that leave you?"

"Less than a thousand."

"Make it two thousand you put up. I'll put in an additional twenty-five hundred, and we'll go for a twenty-five-year seven-thousand-dollar mortgage. I'll prepare a codicil to my will to incorporate the new building, as well as drawing up new papers for both of us to sign protecting your interest in both places."

"What do you mean, a codicil?"

"If anything should happen to me, Leonie, without a properly executed will, you'd find yourself in a great deal of difficulty. I've taken all the precautions necessary to protect you. I gave you my word that once the mortgage was paid, University Place would be yours. But how would the courts know that? Some hell of a lawyer I'd be if I didn't put my promises in writing."

"You're not going to die," she said, finding the conversation suddenly distasteful.

"Don't be stupid! We're all of us going to die sooner or later. I have certain responsibilities, obligations. I've simply taken sensible steps to ensure they're fulfilled."

"You honestly think people will patronize the second place simply because it *is* the second place?"

"Bet my boots on it! Human nature. Curiosity. Envy. Why don't we just try this place for lunch? I've heard about it. That's all it takes, Leonie. Once they come through the door, you've got them. We've just got to get them to come through that door."

"When may I see the building?"

"I've made an appointment to take you there tomorrow at eleven. That'll give you time to see it and get back to the restaurant before the rush. The other thing I wanted to talk to you about has to do with suppliers, Leonie. If you're going to have two restaurants to run, it makes sense to set up supply agreements directly instead of going to the markets every day. You'll have to figure out what each restaurant requires and set up standing orders, have the produce and what-have-you delivered directly instead of wasting valuable time going to fetch it. You'll also get a break on the price by buying in bulk."

"How do you know all this?" she asked.

"Simple. I asked. Make sure you get at least three estimates on that plumbing job, too."

"Jimmy," she said slowly, "you're not trying to take it all over from me, are you?"

"I thought I would. I thought I'd just grow myself a mustache and play Simon Legree, oust you and the baby into the snow while I take over the family business. Great to know you trust me so implicitly."

"It isn't that I don't trust you. But lately you seem to be giving me very little room in which to make my own decisions."

"The decisions are all yours to make. I just want to be sure you're making them with some understanding and knowledge to back you up. It was pure blind luck the way you started Lion's, Leonie. The odds were a thousand to one against you. But somehow you managed to pull it off."

"Somehow," she scoffed. "Your money."

"You're wrong," he said seriously. "Not that I'm minimizing the effects of a strong capital base. But a restaurant's a very special sort of enterprise. It has to do with chemistry, and instinct. And you've got both. You're going to get your empire one day. All I'm doing is making sure you know what to do with it when you get it."

Mr. Freeman at the bank was more than happy to offer Jimmy a mortgage on the Fifteenth Street property. And beamed benevolently at the two of them, saying, "Why don't the two of you come to dinner one evening soon? My wife, Anne, is very interested in meeting you, Miss Benedict." Leonie looked up, surprised. "It seems she and several friends have been meeting once a week for lunch at Lion's for several months now, and she thinks most highly of it."

"I would like that very much," she said with a smile, wondering if this invitation was all part of what Jimmy had been trying to explain to her.

"Good! I'll let you know which evening."

Outside the bank, as they prepared to go in different directions, Jimmy said, "Didn't I tell you? Success breeds all sorts of things, including new rules. The next time you go to that bank for a mortgage, woman or not, you'll get it. Without my signature. On your own strength."

"The rules of this game are nonsensical," she said.

"You play by them until you're so well and truly ensconced that you're then able to create your own. By which time, what you do will be aped by dozens of others." He opened the taxi door for her, saw her inside, gave the driver instructions and a folded note, and said, "I'll see you at dinner."

She caught hold of his hand, saying, "I am grateful, Jimmy. For all of it. Thank you."

He ducked his head down to kiss her quickly, smiled, waved, and flagged down another taxi to take him back to his office.

Leonie recognized Anne Freeman at once, having seated her regularly at the restaurant. A petite, very erect woman she looked to be in her late forties or early fifties, and was undoubtedly older than her husband. Not a beautiful woman, but one possessed of such large features that her looks were arresting, somehow compelling. She was possessed of a deep, rasping voice that came as a surprise from someone of her diminutive stature. Leonie found herself unable to look away from the woman now, fascinated by a face that contained large eyes, a very wide mouth, a prominent nose, all set within a small oval. She was one of the most unusual women Leonie had ever seen, and she wondered why she hadn't previously taken note of just how unusual she was.

"I'm so happy to officially meet both of you," she said in a gravelly voice, offering Leonie a warm, solid handshake; unmistakable curiosity in her large pale eyes. Leonie was attracted to her, partially because she was obviously aware of her effect on people and seemed to derive a good deal of humorous pleasure in witnessing the reactions her face and voice aroused.

Jacob and Jimmy settled themselves with glasses of wine while Anne directed Leonie to sit with her on the settee, where, taking hold of both Leonie's hands, she studied them front and back, then kept hold of them while performing a similar close examination of Leonie's eyes. Not in the least bothered, Leonie sat without moving until Anne smiled again, asking, "How old are you?"

"Twenty-one come November."

"You are both infinitely older and a good deal younger. Your path is strewn with obstacles, but very straight. I've never seen hands quite like yours. I must warn you that there are those who, without the slightest hesitation, will tell you I'm a witch. A mad old witch. I'm opinionated, arrogant, and intolerant of stupid people. I don't frighten you in the least, do I?"

"A little, actually."

"Poo!" She laughed, releasing Leonie's hands. "The only things in life that frighten you, my dear, are the tasks you take upon yourself and later find nearly impossible to complete." We shall cross swords one day, you and I, she thought. And because of my arrogance and intolerance, I shall lose you. "Now"—she snapped her fingers, a startling, amusing gesture—"tell me where you come from and who you are."

Looking over at Jimmy to see amusement creasing in the corners of his eyes and mouth, Leonie proceeded to tell about her early life and how she'd started the restaurant; thinking that this woman seemed some rare form of bird, perhaps; sitting listening closely with her small head tilted to one side, her hands—apparently always restless—plucking and smoothing at the skirt of her fine wool dress.

As she talked, Anne absorbed the sense of this girl. Tall as any man, large-boned, with a tawny skin that served to emphasize the unusual amber-gold color of her eyes and the rather childlike bow of her upper lip. She itched to once more take hold of those big, long-fingered hands and examine them with the aid of a magnifying glass, but made herself listen in order not to miss the tale beneath the tale; determining there was a great deal that wasn't being said.

In the course of the evening, it came out that Anne's major outside interest was in the work of Margaret Sanger and that Anne had been one of the women who'd raised her voice loudly, publicly, over Mrs. Sanger's being jailed the year before.

"We're working to start a clinic for birth control," Anne said. "How do you feel about that?"

"I think it sounds a very good thing," Leonie said, suspecting Anne was going to attempt to solicit Leonie's time or money or both.

"Perhaps you'd be interested in helping?"

"I would, very much," Leonie said. "Unfortunately, we're about to open a second Lion's—as Mr. Freeman has probably told you—and I have almost no free time just now."

"Later on, then," Anne said, drawing over an embroidered footstool with the tip of her shoe, lifting both feet onto it.

"That's very pretty," Leonie observed.

Anne's foot nudged the stool back several inches as she said, "Did that bit of work during my pregnancy."

"You have a child?" Leonie asked interestedly.

"Had. Stillborn." For a second or two she appeared simply a very ordinary, rather ugly woman. Then she smiled and said, "You're not off the hook by any means. I'll be back at you again for the clinic."

"Hopefully, I'll have some free time then."

Later, as they were making their good nights and thank-yous, Anne again took hold of Leonie's hand, but wearing such a peculiar expression that Leonie was prompted to ask, "Are you all right? You seem rather . . ." She went silent as Anne raised her pale eyes and stared penetratingly at her for several long moments, her small hands grinding together before her like two tiny animals snapping at each other's heels. Then she blinked rapidly several times—so birdlike Leonie fully expected to see a membrane sliding down over her eyes—and said, "Money will be your undoing if you allow it. Remember why you do the things you do, and try not to lose sight of your reasons."

"I'm sorry," Leonie said, suddenly uncomfortable. "I'm afraid I don't understand what you're saying."

"One day," she said, with the same opaque gaze as that of the aged diviners of the Swazis, "you will gain great admiration and respect. You're a strong, clever woman. But you will pay dearly for that which you most value. Take care," her harsh voice cautioned, "not to be too independent. A time will come when you will be forced to seek sanctuary from the damaging effects of your own determination."

Feeling chilled, Leonie watched with amazement as Anne's face rearranged itself into a brilliant smile. She shook hands heartily with Jimmy, stating, "I like the look of you, the sense of you," then stood back smiling as Jimmy and Leonie made their way out of the Park Avenue apartment.

"What an odd woman!" Leonie said as they were returning home in the taxi.

"She's odd, all right. But she's got a lot of power with the right set. You want to stay on her good side, Leonie. That woman could single-handedly fill both restaurants every day with just a few words to her friends. She's powerful and not nearly so nonconforming as she'd like us to believe."

"Does that mean I'm somehow to find the time to work with the Sanger group?"

"That'd be too obvious," he said thoughtfully. "Let them woo you. They'll keep after you. At least that woman will."

"Why?"

"Why?" He smiled. "Because you're on the rise, Leonie. People are starting to know who you are. And the more you succeed, the more they'll be after you. Your affiliation with any group will someday guarantee that group's success."

"You're frightening me," she said, taking hold of his hand. "That isn't what I want, Jimmy."

"We'll see," he said, with vagueness. "We'll see."

One full day a week now Leonie worked with Bill, the bookkeeper, going over the figures, the projections; walking around with her head filled with numbers. The price of flour, eggs, butter, milk. Salaries, coal prices, the rising cost of staples. With an office set up on the second floor at Fifteenth Street, invoices to check, bills to approve for payment, applicants to interview, she found herself with too little time to do the cooking, the bread-baking. She made arrangements with a bakery on Eighth Street to prepare the bread to her recipe and supply the restaurants daily. Then, working with Rose, she hired two cooks and spent three weeks teaching them how to do the soups and stews, writing the lists of ingredients on small cards to be kept at each of the restaurants.

With the bread now provided and the cooks preparing the food, she was free to oversee the activities of both restaurants, make certain the waitresses were immaculate and gracious to the customers, check on the quality of the food and service, and satisfy herself that there was a minimum of pilferage by the customers and no stealing being done by the staff.

Alice was managing University Place, supervising the two waitresses out front, and keeping a close watch on the cook and Angelo. Rose and Clark were co-managing Fifteenth Street, supervising the four waitresses, the cook, busboy, and dishwasher.

Leonie had managed to repay more than half the mortgage on University Place and was constantly going over the books in an effort to find some previously hidden way she might accelerate the payments. She wanted to own the place outright, wanted the title in her hands, in her name. Not because of any lack of faith or trust in Jimmy, but simply because she wanted it. She did daily battle with her impatience, knowing it would be unwise to take too much of Lion's working capital in order to satisfy a personal desire. In time, all of it would come to her. She merely needed time to be slightly more accommodating to her needs.

At home, Leo, at two, was into everything, chattering away in her amusing American accent. Leonie frequently caught herself wondering what Gray's response might be to his American child. This little girl who ran about the apartment on daily lengthening legs, dragging things out of closets, refusing food, refusing toilet training. This child with her father's gray-green eyes and strong chin. His features hinting out at Leonie each time she saw Leo's face in sleep.

When she found herself thinking this way, she felt nearly sick now with guilt at her disloyalty to Jimmy. Jimmy. Devoted, attentive, reliable, loving. Clever, intuitive, creatively cautious. She gave him everything she could. Everything but what he most wanted: her complete love. And the guilt she felt at being unable to love him sufficiently too often threatened to reduce her to something like helplessness. So she pushed it away, telling herself she was living up to her obligations, honoring all of them as best she could.

For his part, he simply loved her. Looking at the insistent light of her eyes, he frequently thought: I love you more than my own life. And if I made a declaration to that effect at this moment, you'd wrinkle your forehead and look sad and guilty, believing I was expecting you to make a like declaration. When the truth is, I'm happy to remain as we are. Just as long as I can be with you, with Leo; just as long as I can feel your warmth, hear your almost soundless breathing in the night.

11

Two days after President Wilson proclaimed a state of war with Germany, Angelo hurried to volunteer for the army. And so did Clark. Leonie, deeply upset, begged Clark not to be foolish.

"Have you any idea at all of what you'll be fighting for?" she asked him. "Have you?"

"Our country's at war," he said, immovable. "I've got to do what's right."

"Clark!" she cried, frightened and exasperated. "They'll *kill* you! And you won't even know what it is you'll be dying for."

"Of course I know what it's all about," he insisted. "To keep Germany from taking over the world."

"It has to do with Serbia, Clark. And Italy, France, and Russia. You won't listen, and we'll lose you."

"I'll be back!" He grinned. "Can't kill me off that easily."

And off he went, returning a few weeks later to present himself at the office in uniform, ready to go. His face shining, abrim with excitement—looking precisely like a recruiting poster—he said good-bye to everyone, coming at last to Leonie.

"Will you write to me, Clark?" she asked. "Let me know where you are and how you're getting on?"

"Sure I will. You can bet on it!"

"Don't be brave, will you? Don't try for glory. Just do what you're supposed to and get through it, then come home to us. We love you." She embraced him, then held him away from her, carefully memorizing his face; stricken, in advance of the fact, by his loss. Thinking: None of us will ever see you again. You won't come back.

He saluted her, then was gone.

Desolated, Leonie said, "Come out, Rose. Walk with me for a bit, will you?"

Once outside, she linked her arm through Rose's, saying, "Let's walk over to the square. I'd like to see the trees."

Rose walked along at her side in silence, thinking about Angelo, convinced he'd finally found his niche. He'd take to military life, she was sure, as if he'd been born to nothing else. And would probably spend the remainder of his life as a soldier.

"What are you thinking?" Leonie asked.

"About Angelo. And Clark. The differences between them. Ange has waited all his life for something to happen that he'd understand. And it finally has. He's a born soldier, someone perfectly suited to taking orders. But Clark's not like that. He's got more imagination, more drive, more sensitivity. I think Clark'll hate the army. Right now, he's all just caught up in the patriotism, the excitement of being 'manly' at eighteen."

Rose, at twenty-five, seemed to have arrived herself at a new plateau. Her hair, worn less severely these days, framed the perfect oval of her face, accentuating the whiteness of her skin, the startling depths of her luminous black eyes.

"You've grown beautiful, Rose. Are you happy?"

"Very," she lied. "Are you?"

"At moments. Three years ago I wouldn't have believed I'd ever be happy again."

"Three years ago, we were working like fiends to get the restaurant cleaned up and ready to open. Seeing that sign in the window changed my whole life."

"Did it?"

"I thought I'd work for years in some factory or other, then marry eventually because I was so tired of working and there was nothing else to do. Have a lot of kids. End up like Mama."

"Aren't you ever lonely, though, Rose?"

"At times," she admitted. "Sometimes I think it'd be nice to have someone come visit in the evening, talk. It gets awfully quiet."

"He won't come back," Leonie said. "We'll never see him again. And I'll spend the rest of my life remembering Clark at random moments, remembering all his ideas and suggestions, his tremendous enthusiasm, his sweetness. The way he'd blush. Oh, *God*, Rose! Its a never-ending process of losing all the people you love most. Is that the price that has to be paid, do you think?"

"He'll come back."

"No." She shook her head, wiping at the tears with the back of her hand. "He won't. And it hurts. It hurts so terribly. As if I were losing a child of mine. It isn't fair that he should go off to his death, not even nineteen yet, not even really knowing why he's going."

"I don't know what to say to you," Rose said, distressed.

"Give me a few moments." Leonie squeezed her arm gently. "I'll get past it."

"How is Leo?" she asked, awkwardly attempting to shift the conversational direction.

"Strong-willed, rude, beautiful. She adores Jimmy, calls him Uncle Jimmy, but I know she thinks of him as her father. And it worries me."

"Why?"

"Because should her father ever come to us—not that I believe any longer that that's very much of a possibility—she'd have to transfer those feelings to the one who rightfully deserves them."

"Are you *crazy*?" Rose asked. "How can you *say* something like that? As far as Leo's concerned, Jimmy *does* deserve those feelings. You couldn't expect her to just one day stop caring about him and switch over to someone else, someone she's never laid eyes on before. Whether you think it's right or not, whether you like it or not, she loves him and she always will. He's the only father she's ever *known*, Leonie! And if that mysterious, romantic Englishman does one day miraculously happen to turn up, don't be surprised if she calls *him* uncle!"

"You hate him," Leonie said, a little cowed by Rose's ferocity. "How can you hate someone you've never met?"

"I don't hate him," she said impatiently. "I just can't believe how stupid you can sometimes be!"

"I'm capable of great stupidity, Rose."

"I think you're just feeling sorry for yourself because you couldn't single-handedly talk Clark out of going."

"Perhaps I am."

"And you're still," she accused, "thinking about that man showing up here after all this time! I don't mean to upset you or be cruel, but I just can't see what good it does you to be thinking of someone you haven't seen hide nor hair of in over three years. I can promise you *I* wouldn't still be thinking about him."

"It's so hard, Rose. Someday, perhaps, you'll be better able to understand why. One person who touches you, touches your life and leaves marks, memories, feelings that simply refuse to die. Someone who loves you just as you are, with no wish to change you, to whom you feel an instinctive desire to give the very best of yourself."

"I can't for the life of me see why you think I have to fall in love and be miserable in order to understand. I understand well enough right now."

"Of course you do, Rose." She smiled. Thinking: It will happen to you one day. No matter how hard you struggle against it, it will happen. And then you'll admit to possessing an entirely new understanding of just how very hard it is to let that person go away from you completely.

"You wouldn't provide me with any nasty surprises, would you, Jimmy?"

"What kind of nasty surprises?"

"Like getting up and going off to war."

"Never. Anyway, they wouldn't take me even if I wanted to go."

"Why?"

"I had consumption years ago. It's very doubtful they'd want someone with my medical history."

"You've never told me that! Were you very ill?"

"Two years of nonending boredom," he said dismissingly. "At seventeen, I was hardly in the right frame of mind for constant bedrest, too many fresh eggs and enough sunshine to put me off it for life."

"Two years?"

"It was *boring*."

"Oh, Jimmy." She hugged him with welling emotion, holding him close. "You minimize so many important things."

"What possible importance can something that happened all those years ago have now?" he asked, stroking behind her ear.

"It just does," she insisted.

"Any word yet from Clark?"

"Only one letter, from Saint-Nazaire in France. He said the crossing made him miserably seasick. But so were most of the others. Hellos to everyone. And that's all. I miss him terribly. None of the men I've interviewed have had one-tenth his insight or imagination."

"You talk about him as if he's dead."

She didn't say anything for a minute or two, then asked, "What do you think of my purchasing some Liberty Bonds? One of Anne's friends has been after me."

"I think it's the patriotic thing to do."

"Be serious! As an investment, what do you think of it?"

"You're certainly not going to *lose* money investing in them."

"How much do you think I should invest?"

"What's your cash situation right now?"

"University Place is showing a good, steady profit every week. We're still working to break even at Fifteenth Street. Another few months and we'll make it. We're ahead close to five thousand dollars."

"Don't go in for more than three."

"That much? I was quite sure you'd say a thousand or so."

"No, I think it's a wise move. Go for three."

"If I do, it means at least another year before I'm able to repay you the balance of the mortgage on University Place."

"Is there some sort of hurry?"

"No," she said quietly. "Not really. What was it like, having consumption?"

"I told you. Boring. A lot of coughing and spitting into little cups. Eggs by the gross, sunshine, and lying flat on my back month after month."

"Where did you get all that sunshine? Surely not around here."

"Switzerland. A private sanatorium near Klosters."

"You must have been terribly lonely."

"Just bored." He smiled. "Bored, bored!"

"And you recovered completely?"

"I'm not contagious, if that's what you're asking."

"You know that's not what I'm on about."

"A little weak in the lungs, that's all."

"Why do you smoke, if that's the case?"

"Why breathe?" he said equably. "It's all risky."

He wasn't really sure where he was or what he was doing there, sitting shivering at four-thirty in the morning with a tin cup of something that was supposed to be coffee, didn't taste like coffee, didn't taste like anything he could put a name to. But it was hot and he was freezing. Sitting huddled against the cold, not hungry, not wanting to eat. The others all along the line were eating, crouched the way he was. Their faces all seemed so dark, their eyes unnaturally large and glowing in the darkness.

A lot of them had already finished eating and were cleaning their guns. Slowly, moving slowly. Hands wiping back and forth, back and forth. Everyone listened to the silence, waiting. He looked at the boy over there, sitting with a cup in one hand, helmet off, picking lice from his hair. It made Clark itch, watching. As if he had the things now too and they were creeping around under his uniform, between his thighs. His skin crawled. He looked away, watching the sky, waiting for daylight. The dark-turning-light strange, everything slow, strange.

They came with rations, letters from home. He got rations, no letter. He polished his gun. Waiting.

He thought he could smell the dead men. He was sure that was what it was. Bodies over there somewhere. Rotting. In the wet. Everything was wet, you couldn't get dry. He went blank a lot, thinking about sitting at home in front of the gas fire; feeling warm, not itching, not constipated from seizing up in every muscle each time the firing started. During the shelling, curled into a tight ball, he made his body small, small so none of the fragments could reach him. Then, when the shelling was over and they were supposed to relax, he couldn't relax, couldn't even crap. Little pebbles. His whole body knots, hard knots. His head was full of knots, too.

If he risked lifting his head to look around, he wouldn't see anything over there. Nothing. Where were they? What were they all doing here? How did this have anything to do with defending the good old U.S.? It wasn't supposed to be like this. Was it?

Everything stank, everybody smelled. Every so often he'd try to smell himself, wondering if he stank, too. Probably. He nibbled on a piece of hardtack, his eyes shifting as if they weren't part of him and moved all by themselves. Even his eyes felt dirty. Could your eyes smell bad? he wondered.

He thought about a bath. A steaming hot bath with soap, the water right up to his chin. Saturday-night bath, getting ready to go out, take Hazel to the moving pictures, then to the ice-cream parlor. Chocolate ice cream. And a bath. Putting on clean underwear, dry socks.

Back a while—it seemed quite a long time but he couldn't be sure now about that—when they'd gone up there the first time, he'd seen all those bones, skulls. All over the place. Nearly got himself killed, so busy trying not to walk on those bones. As if those guys were still alive and not dead, not already bones lying all over the ground. He thought all the time about the skulls, all those bones out there.

He watched the sunrise, blinking a lot; trying to get rid of the feeling that his eyes were dirty. Watching the sun like watching a moving picture, he turned his head to see the others were watching it, too. Then, forgetting them, he just watched. Coming up over there, fat and pale like a plate being pushed up over the edge of a counter. He thought of the restaurant, remembering, smiling. Rose and Leonie, Alice and Martha. Angelo. Wondering what division he'd been sent to, Angelo.

There was an order, and it came to him from somewhere far away. Like an echo, he heard it repeating inside his head. He straightened slowly, all those knotted muscles aching, hearing the order. Moving, but he couldn't stop seeing the pictures in his head now. The bath. Seeing himself in the bath, whistling, scrubbing with the soap, and the lather. Hot water, warm.

The gunfire seemed to be coming from far away, too. More echoes, they weren't even anywhere near him. And it felt good, better to stand up, stretch himself so all the muscles eased a little. Somebody said his name. Like a whisper. But he was thinking about putting on his best Saturday-night clothes, brushing his hair, whistling. Taking Hazel to the moving pictures. Leonie and Rose at the restaurant. Saying his name, whispering.

He was careful not to step on any of the bones—Jesus, it bothered him, the bones—looking at the ground, all the bones getting in the way of his Saturday night. Then somebody knocked into him, knocked hard, and he jerked his head up to say what d'you think you're doing knocking into me that way, but he'd tripped or something, and whoever'd knocked him it hurt and Jesus he'd tripped and how did the ground I'm falling it hurts look out don't fall on the

"Let's talk about it," Rose said.
"I knew he'd never come back. What is there to talk about?"
"A lot."
Leonie stood up from her desk and turned to look out the window. "When is it going to end?" she wondered aloud.

"They've been fighting over there for three and a half years. Do you know"—she looked back at Rose—"I read an item in the *Times* the other day that said they estimate over five million have died so far? Five million. That's almost the entire population of this city, Rose. Five out of every six of the people out there on the streets dead."

"When are you going to hire someone to replace him? You can't keep on doing his job as well as everything else."

"They go off singing. It simply astonishes me," she went on, not hearing Rose. "*Singing*. As if on their way to a Sunday-school picnic." She sat down again. "You're right. I am tired. I really must hire someone. Rose, do you ever feel that part of what you're doing is absolutely right and the other part absolutely wrong?"

"I don't know what you mean."

"Can you understand if I try to explain how guilty I feel about Jimmy? This constant feeling that I'm using him, that it's immoral of me to take advantage of his kindness, his intelligence, his love, when I simply cannot return him the love he should have. It's so dishonest. And I try to tell myself it works well for both of us, he derives what he needs from our being together. But surely he deserves something more, something better. I *am* tired."

"Come downstairs and have lunch," Rose said. "And maybe you should go home after that, take some time for yourself."

"You're not answering me."

"I don't see any point in answering. I think you're wrong, that's all. And I don't want to argue about it. Because we will argue if we try to discuss it."

Rose, she thought, was beginning to have the look of an aging virgin. A certain tightness about the lips, a certain too-pristine aura about her. "You should take a lover, Rose," she said quietly. "You need to stop fighting all those strong feelings inside you and let someone touch you, untie you."

"For God's sake, Leonie! I don't *want* a *lover!* And I'd prefer not to be touched."

"Everything about you quietly shouts out for it," she said, leaning across the desk toward Rose. "You're as bad in your own way as I am in mine. I've made all sorts of compromises because I'm unable to live untouched. And you've refused to make any at all for fear of it. Have you noticed how Alice seems to shine since she married? She no longer looks so frail, so waiflike."

"I can't say that I have."

"Liar." Leonie smiled. "We all need the contact, Rose. One way or another. People aren't meant to live alone in small cells, never meeting, never touching. *You* weren't meant to live the way you do. You have such passion, Rose. It shows in so many ways."

"Oh, my God, *passion*! I think you're coming unhinged." Rose blushed, smiling involuntarily, so that Leonie laughed and reached across the desk to take hold of her hand.

"You know it's true," she said gently. "It isn't something to be ashamed of. So few people have passion. So few." She let go Rose's hand, her eyes drifting. Gray had passion. Jimmy has intensity, a capacity for deep caring. But Gray, you had such passion. And it's that I miss so terribly, cannot free myself from craving. To be swept away, caught in colliding passions. Knowing without having to put words to any of it.

The telephone rang, and her eyes pulled back into focus. "Why don't you go along and have your lunch?" The telephone rang again. "I think I will go home." She put her hand out to lift the receiver as Rose stood up, asking, "You're sure?"

Leonie nodded. "I'm sure. I'll see you in the morning."

Jimmy said, "I'm feeling a little seedy, just wanted to let you know I'm on my way home."

"What's wrong?"

"It's probably nothing. Something I had for lunch that isn't sitting too well."

"I'll come home, meet you there."

"You don't have to. I'll take a nap. I'm sure it's just a bit of indigestion."

He said good-bye, and she looked at the telephone for several seconds, then got up. It wasn't like him to complain of not feeling well. Not like him to complain of anything. And there seemed to be something going around, some sort of influenza. Several of the waitresses and one of the busboys were off ill. Which was why she and Rose and Alice had been working nonstop, to fill the gaps. And hadn't Amy mentioned that a number of Leo's friends hadn't shown up at the park the last day or two?

Jimmy looked awful, pale and feverish, a sheen of perspiration on his face.

"When did this start?" she asked, sitting down on the side of the bed, touching the back of her hand to his forehead.

"It's probably nothing."

"*When,* Jimmy?"

"A day or two," he admitted.

"You've got a fever. What else bothers you besides the upset stomach?"

"It's so silly," he argued, hating being fussed over.

"It isn't silly. You're ill. If you won't tell me what's bothering you, how am I to help?"

"You're going to brew up a few of your potions, are you?"

"This isn't the time to be witty. If you'll tell me what's wrong, I'll be able to make something that will ease you."

"I ache," he said wearily, abandoning his halfhearted effort at humor. "As if my bones are swelling. And it's freezing in here."

"I'm going to prepare something for you." She fixed the bedclothes snugly around him. "Try to rest. I'll be back in a few minutes."

Out in the kitchen, as Amy watched, she put pinches of this and that into a small pot, then added water and several other things to another.

"Don't like the look of him one little bit," Amy said. "What you making there?"

"I'm preparing an infusion, with sallow bark and gentian root. For his fever. This one"—she indicated the second pot—"is to soothe his stomach. Camomile, juniper berries, wormwood."

"Smells good anyway," Amy said. "What's he got?"

"I don't know. It seems to be a combination of things rather than any one. Don't let Leo go in to him, will you? I wouldn't like her to contract whatever it is he has."

"You think it's catchin', then?"

"I really don't know. But it doesn't make sense to take chances."

He took a mouthful of fever reducer, swallowed a little of the herbed tea, then pushed the cup away, making a face. "It's awful!" he complained.

"It'll *help* you, Jimmy. Please take a little more. You're being so childish."

"Leave me be, Leonie. I just want to sleep."

Throughout the remainder of the afternoon she kept returning to the bedroom to look in on him. He slept heavily. The air around the bed was thick and fetid. Distractedly she dined with Leo and Amy in the kitchen, then saw Leo off to bed and went to stand looking down at Jimmy, her hand on his forehead, trying to think what more she could do. If this had been going on a day or two, perhaps he was already at the worst of it and by morning would emerge from the fever and go past it.

She prepared a bed on the chaise in order not to disturb him. And sat up reading, unable to go to sleep, for several hours, looking over regularly to see if there was any change. She fell asleep finally with the book across her chest, to be awakened just after three by his coughing. A clotted, congested cough that didn't wake him but simply broke the pattern of his sleep every few minutes.

Getting up, she went out to the kitchen, filled a pot with water, added some acacia, rosemary, and saffron, and when the mixture had come to a boil, carried the steaming pot into the bedroom and set it down close to the bed so that he might breathe in the medicinal fumes.

It didn't help. The coughing continued, and she listened, growing more and more concerned, wondering at his being able to sleep through the proliferating spasms. She sat holding cold cloths to his face, racking her brain for further remedies, becoming very worried as the night progressed and the cough seemed to alter, turning liquid, and his breathing became more labored.

He seemed to be shrinking before her eyes, curling in around the fever and the cough, and she kept changing the cloths, freshening them, until, glancing over at the window, she saw it was dawn. And Amy was at the far side of the bed shaking her head doubtfully, saying, "We best get a doctor. He's lookin' bad. And I don't like the sound of that coughing one little bit, neither."

"The name of his doctor's in his diary. Over there, on the dresser. What is it?" she asked aloud, trying to think of his name. "I can't remember. Something like Bryson or Brian."

"Benton?" Amy asked, trying to decipher Jimmy's cramped handwriting.

"That's it. Ring his number, ask him to come."

Amy went off to telephone, and Leonie changed the cloth again, noticing as she did that he seemed to be becoming hotter. The cold cloths weren't helping. Leo, in her nightgown, appeared in the doorway, asking, "What's the matter with Uncle Jimmy, Mummy?" and Leonie nearly shouted at her, "Go to the kitchen, Leo! Amy will give you breakfast."

Seeing Leo's face closing down in readiness for tears, Leonie at once felt guilty and softened her voice. "Uncle Jimmy's not feeling well, darling. And you really mustn't come in here. Go on to the kitchen and have your breakfast. You'll see him later."

Looking dissatisfied, Leo turned away.

"Can't get no answer," Amy reported. "I'll get Leo started eating, then try again."

"Oh, Lord," Leonie whispered, watching Jimmy's eyes moving beneath their lids. "You're so ill, so feverish, and none of my medicines are helping you. I don't know what to do for you, Jimmy. I'm frightened."

Unable to think of anything else, she kept applying the cold compresses to his forehead, watching his face closely as if she might find some clue to a remedy there.

Near eight, he opened his eyes and struggled to sit up, saying, "I've got to go to the bathroom."

"I'll get you a pan," she said.

"No!" he said loudly, mortified by the thought of it. "I can manage."

But she had to help him into the bathroom. Then, at his insistence, she remained outside, hearing him retching. She covered her ears with her hands, suffering for him, knowing he'd hate it if he thought she could hear him.

At last, looking and moving like an old man, he came out of the bathroom and allowed her to help him back to bed, where, almost the instant he was settled, he was overtaken by another coughing fit.

"My damned bones hurt," he said, curling up on his side. "Dizzy."

"I'll fetch you some broth."

"Don't want it," he murmured, his eyelids fluttering closed.

She went for the broth anyway, but he was having another coughing spasm when she returned, and by the time it had passed, he'd once more fallen into that odd deep sleep and she decided it was best to let him rest. She asked Amy to try ringing the doctor again, then sat down with a fresh bowl of cold water and chipped ice, applying the cloth to his forehead once more.

Amy took over while Leonie went to bathe and get dressed before going down the hall to look in on Leo, who was sitting on the floor of her room holding one of her dolls on her lap, shaking her finger at it, and in a voice too ominously reminiscent of Leonie's saying, "Don't you bother Uncle Jimmy now, you hear? Don't you bother him!"

She looked up expectantly at Leonie, round gray-green eyes questioning. Leonie knelt down on the floor in front of her, saying, "You're a good girl. You're such a good girl." Gathering Leo into her arms, suddenly overwhelmed by emotion; holding Leo tightly to her, breathing in the fresh-washed scent of her hair, the softness of her cheek, her good health.

"Can I see Uncle Jimmy now?" she asked hopefully, automatically patting her mother's cheek. A gesture she made quite frequently that never failed to fill Leonie with the most desperate kind of loving, a mix of the most potent feelings that surged through her and made her feel helpless, strong, certain, unsure; everything. A flood of feelings, a high wave of caring.

"Perhaps a little later," Leonie answered. "You play very quietly now, and Amy will be out in a few minutes. She'll read to you, if you ask her, I'm sure."

"I'm very quiet," Leo said proudly, disengaging herself to retrieve her doll.

And just as Leo's affectionate gestures filled Leonie with caring, her ability to detach herself always brought Leonie up hard against the reality of Leo's separateness. They might always come together only at odd moments.

She returned to Jimmy, to hold his hand and apply a newly cold cloth to his forehead, more afraid with each passing minute. Especially when, after trying repeatedly, Amy reported, "Still nobody answering that doctor's telephone."

"Ring Mr. Freeman, Amy. Ask him to recommend a doctor we might call."

Amy went off, and a few minutes later Leonie could hear her voice as she spoke to someone on the telephone.

Jimmy's mouth was terribly dry-looking, his lips splitting from his openmouthed efforts to breathe. When he awakened again near midday, she urged him to try to swallow just a little broth. He did, and at once began retching, his eyes streaming, heat radiating from him as he collapsed against the pillows.

"All right," she said softly. "Lie still then while I straighten the bedclothes for you."

Leo laughed—a crystalline, bubbling sound—in her room, and Jimmy smiled. "Love the way she laughs," he said, then slid back into sleep.

At three in the afternoon Amy came in to say, "Finally got on to this other doctor. He says he's got too many people to see already but he'll come soon's he can."

"We need him *now*," Leonie said frantically as Jimmy began coughing violently. A spasm that lasted almost ten minutes. Amazingly, he slept right through it, while Amy and Leonie helplessly watched his hands tighten on the bedclothes, his chest heaving, his entire body shaking as he coughed and coughed and coughed. Then once again was still.

"His breathing don't sound no good to me," Amy said.

Leonie couldn't speak for a moment, then said, "I'm so worried," glancing over at Amy as Jimmy made a rasping, gurgling noise in his throat. She turned to look at him. His mouth hung open. A thin whisper of sound emerged from his throat. Then silence.

She sat rigid, waiting for him to take another breath, her own mouth open as if that might help him breathe. Nothing happened.

"He's passed on," Amy whispered. "He's gone." She sounded surprised, even mystified.

"That can't be!" Leonie argued, unbuttoning his pajamas to put her ear to his chest, her hand to his throat. Nothing. Silence. She sat up, her eyes huge. "Take a breath, Jimmy!" She pushed at his chest. "*Breathe!*" She pushed again. Then again. "Jimmy, *breathe!*"

Amy put her hand on Leonie's shoulder. Leonie jumped, her eyes fastening on Amy's.

"You can't do nothing for him," Amy said. "He's gone."

Leonie blinked several times, then wet her lips. "You'd best go wash your hands. Carefully. No. Take a bath before you go to Leo. I'll be along in a few moments, to tell her."

Amy backed away silently.

She continued to sit on the side of the bed holding Jimmy's hand, trying to make herself accept the fact that he was dead. So quickly. Dead. She smoothed his hair, then refastened the buttons on his pajamas, expecting every moment he'd open his eyes, take a deep breath, come back.

You're still here, still in your pajamas, still in bed, still warm—it isn't real of course it isn't . . .

She laid her head down on his chest, almost believing he would, as he always did when she rested her head on his chest this way, sit up and say something silly to make her laugh.

12

Three of the waitresses, a busboy, and one of the cooks died. Many of the war plants shut down, telephone service was cut in half, the draft call was suspended in several cities. People were panicked. The newspapers were filled with rumors, outlandish theories, long lists of dead as the influenza epidemic spread to forty-six states. None of it meant very much to Leonie. She drifted through Jimmy's funeral in a state of total disbelief, numbed, frozen, unable even to cry.

Leo was inconsolable, constantly in tears, her grief in no way lessened by Leonie's adamant refusal to allow either her or Amy to leave the apartment. Leonie herself went out for the groceries, milk, newspapers, whatever was needed; positive Leo and Amy would be safe so long as they didn't leave the apartment and no one else was allowed to enter.

On the occasion of each subsequent death, the restaurants closed. And Leonie sat alone in the office with Rose after each of the funerals, doing nothing more concrete than simply getting through time, waiting for the epidemic to be over. Or for something to penetrate the stifling curtain of her grief.

"I can't cry, Rose," she said after the last of the funerals for the employees. "I want to so badly, and I can't. How is it I could manage tears for Clark yet seem to have none for Jimmy?"

"It's the shock," Rose said.

"Shock," Leonie repeated.

She was solicited to buy more Liberty Bonds and absently committed half of Jimmy's estate, some thirty thousand dollars, to the bond drive; with vague ideas in mind of one day using this money for Leo's education, for the purchase of a farm where she and Amy and Leo might go to live. But not now. One day. Later, when she was able once again to move properly and blink easily and swallow without feeling she was going to choke.

She read the *Times* each day, noting particular items: that the cost of living in New York had risen seventeen percent between July the year before and now; that the first Chicago-to-New York airmail trip had been completed in one day; that Eugene V. Debs had been sentenced to ten years' imprisonment for violating the wartime espionage and sedition law; that a book of poetry, *Love Songs*, by Sara Teasdale, had won a Pulitzer Prize; that a new book by one of Leonie's favorite authors, Willa Cather, *My Antonia,* had just been published. She made notes to herself, then lost the notes; lost in a blackness nothing seemed to penetrate.

Until one afternoon when she looked across the desk at Rose and her vision seemed to clear as she realized Rose looked paler than usual, looked in fact quite ill.

"You're ill, Rose!" she said, abruptly emerging from the trance in which she'd been living since Jimmy's death. A voice awakened in her head to cry out, I won't lose you! Not you, too. "I'm going to get a taxi, Rose. Take you home."

"I don't feel too well," Rose acknowledged. And allowed Leonie to put her into her coat and lead her downstairs into a waiting taxi. The driver helped, and Leonie felt tearfully grateful to him; astonished to discover that her ability to shed tears seemed to be returning.

"Your friend doesn't look too good at all," he said sympathetically. Thinking: Your friend's beautiful. So're you. But she's different, beautiful.

When they arrived at University Place, Leonie asked him to wait.

"I'll have to charge you extra," he said apologetically, looking over at Rose again; worried about her. A woman he didn't even know.

"That doesn't matter," Leonie said. "Just wait, please."

"Sure thing. You go ahead. I'll wait as long as it takes. You want some help?"

"No, thank you." She glanced over at him in surprise. "I'm able to manage. But thank you."

She managed to get Rose upstairs to bed, then summoned one of the waitresses away from her duties. "You're to keep these cloths cold, change them every few minutes. If she asks for anything to drink, give her only tea with just a bit of honey and lemon in it. I'll be back as quickly as I can. I'm going after some things I need. If you're nervous about being here, cover your mouth with a cloth or a handkerchief. Just, please, don't leave her on her own. For any reason."

"I won't leave her," the girl promised.

"I'll be back as soon as I can, Rose," Leonie said softly, taking hold of Rose's hand. "Lie quietly and try to rest. I'll be back to look after you. Rose?"

"All right," Rose responded thickly, her eyelids heavy-looking.

"What is your name?" Leonie asked the girl.

"Faith, Miss Benedict."

"Faith." A good omen perhaps? "Stay right here with her, Faith."

"I will," Faith said solemnly.

She climbed into the front of the taxi, sitting down beside the driver, saying, "I must find a place with exotic plants."

"You mean like palm trees and that kind of thing?"

"Yes, exactly."

"You'll want the Bontanical Gardens," he said. "In the Bronx."

"The Bronx? Will it take us awfully long to get there and back?" she asked agitatedly.

"I'll do my best, but it'll be a couple of hours at least."

"All right. There's nowhere else nearer?"

"Not that I know of."

He had a face that reminded her of Clark's. Not his features so much as his expression, his alertness; a certain tall, lanky ease about him.

"My name," she said, "is Leonie Benedict. May I ask yours?"

"Dennis," he answered, concentrating on his driving. "Dennis Riley."

"Dennis, if you can take me there and bring me back in less than two hours, I will give you twenty dollars."

"Mind if I ask you a question?" He looked over at her.

"Not at all."

"How come you need exotic plants?"

"My friend has the influenza. If I can obtain certain roots, leaves, I may be able to make infusions, preparations that will help her."

"Are you a nurse or something?"

"I'm not a nurse," she answered, her body urging the car

forward faster. "I simply know a bit about herbal medicine. She's my dearest friend, you see."

"My baby sister died of it," he said, his facial muscles contracting. "The two of us, we were the last of the family. I've got this feeling, though, it's not going to bother me." He looked over again at her to see if she thought he was crazy.

"No," she agreed, "it probably won't."

"It won't get you either," he said.

"No," she said again.

"But it got somebody in your family, huh?"

"Someone I was very close to . . . fond of." The tears were coming. She refused to allow it. Not now, I won't, can't cry now. Jimmy. There is such a dreadful gaping emptiness in my life without you, without your laughter.

"Is it okay with you if I smoke a cigarette?" he asked.

"Do you enjoy them?"

"They kind of relax me."

"May I try one with you?"

"Sure thing." He gave her a cigarette, took one himself, struck a wooden match somewhere—she didn't notice where, saw only the flame—and lit both their cigarettes.

She drew on it and felt instantly dizzy, rolled down the window and threw it out. "I'm afraid it doesn't agree with me." She took several deep breaths before closing the window. "Tell me, Dennis," she said, "why haven't you . . . ?"

"How come I'm not over there, right? Every woman gets in my taxi asks me that. My kid sister, she was only nine. And there was nobody else to look after her. I would've gone. But they said I'd better stay around, look after her. Which was what I really wanted to do. Now . . ." He shrugged, puffed on his cigarette.

"I know," she said, falling with him into silence, thinking: Little sisters, lovers. Thousands and thousands of people dying. But not Rose. I will *not* let you go! Not like Clark and Jimmy, not like Claire and Wanda and Elsie, the three waitresses she'd seen perhaps only half a dozen times. And Jimmy. Oh, Lord, Jimmy, I never thought you'd die. I should have loved you more, argued less, been far less niggling about my declarations of caring. I deprived you in so many ways, my thoughts clinging to Gray, who may very well be as dead as you, as Clark, as this young man's little sister.

"You own those restaurants?" Dennis asked. "You're the one?"

"That's right."

"I don't know why, I thought you'd be a whole lot older. Just from things I've heard, read. You know?"

"I know," she said, aware of a strange quality to their words, as if the interior of the automobile were somehow amplifying and, at the same time, muting what they were saying.

"Lot of people've started wearing little masks over their faces," he said conversationally. "The other day, I went to the dentist"—he laughed suddenly and shook his head—"and there he was wearing one. As if that would help."

She nodded mechanically.

"I like to talk," he said. "If it's a bother to you, I'll be quiet."

"No, no. It helps make the time pass more quickly. How much longer before we get there, do you think?"

"With luck, another fifteen minutes. What're you going to do, if you don't mind my asking?"

"I'm going to vandalize a few plants. If I'm able to find what I want."

"Done a lot of things in my time, but I sure never have raided a botanical garden."

"I doubt if it's illegal," she said, wondering if that was true.

"Shouldn't think so." He puffed again on his cigarette, then threw it out the window. "You're really worried about her, aren't you?"

"I love Rose," she said without inflection. "I won't let her die."

Rose, he thought, is lucky to have a friend like you. Rose is beautiful.

While Dennis kept a lookout, she hurried to pinch a few leaves here and there and to cut several lengths of root from a number of plants with the help of Dennis' pocketknife. Then, wrapping everything in her handkerchief, they rushed to the car and started back to the city.

"Get everything you need?" he asked conspiratorially.

"I hope so."

He drove as fast as he possibly could and got her back to University Place in just under an hour. When she opened her bag to give him the promised twenty dollars, he said, "Just pay me the fare. I really couldn't take it."

"But you must! We agreed."

"I couldn't," he said, refusing to accept the bills. "I'll tell you what. You buy your friend Rose a big bunch of flowers and tell her they're from Dennis. I hope she makes it through."

"Dennis," she said slowly, "would you be interested in a new job?"

"What kind of job?"

"I'm not quite certain, and I can't stop to talk about it now. But will you come round to the office and see me in a few days' time?"

"Okay. Where is it?"

"The second floor of the Fifteenth Street Lion's. Ask anyone there. They'll direct you to me."

"Okay."

"And thank you for everything. I won't forget you."

"You're sure there's nothing else I can do?"

"Nothing I can think of just now. But do, please, come to see me."

"Don't forget to get Rose those flowers!" he called after her.

She made a hasty telephone call home to tell Amy, "I'll be staying here with Rose. Please don't worry. And *please* don't go out. May I speak with Leo for a moment?"

It struck her odd hearing Leo's voice over the telephone, as if she'd never before heard Leo's clear, very unchildlike voice.

"It's me, darling. I'm staying to take care of Auntie Rose. Please be a good girl. I know you're bored, but all this will be over soon, and then you'll be able to get out, go to the park again. Lots of places."

"Is Auntie Rose going to die like Uncle Jimmy?"

"*No* she is *not!*"

"You promise?"

"I can't promise you that, Leo. But I'm hoping she'll be all right. You say a little prayer for her, all right, darling?"

"When's Uncle Jimmy coming back?"

"Darling, you know he isn't coming back. You know that."

There was a long pause. Then Leo said, "Are you coming back?"

"I'll be home just as soon as I'm able. Now, you're not to worry. I'm just fine and I'll see you perhaps tomorrow."

She thanked Faith and sent her off with money for a taxi. Then she went over to have a look at Rose. It was the same as it had been with Jimmy. She was pale, her eyes sunken, face shiny with perspiration, her forehead very hot to the touch.

"How are you feeling, Rose?" she asked, gingerly perching on the side of the bed.

"Dizzy. Feels as if my bones are hurting."

"I'm going to leave you on your own for just a few minutes while I go down and prepare something for you to drink. Will you be all right on your own, do you think?"

"I'll just close my eyes."

I won't let you die I will not I refuse to let you die.

While the infusion was cooling to a drinkable temperature, she carried up a basin of water she'd heated, with leaves and herbs. Rose opened her eyes, asking, "What are you doing?" as Leonie began gently removing her from her nightgown.

"I'm going to bathe you, try to bring down the fever."

"But you *mustn't!*" Rose protested, modesty for a moment prevailing over the sick swimming in her head.

"Don't be difficult, Rose. I'm going to help you. You needn't think of being embarrassed." She smiled, taking hold of Rose's hand while she pulled the sleeve of the gown down over it. "We're both women."

A deep red flush traveled up from Rose's neck into her face. But she felt far too ill and too weak to fight. So, shivering, she suffered Leonie to remove the nightgown, keeping her eyes tightly closed against the whole humiliating scene.

"You shouldn't feel uncomfortable," Leonie said quietly, wringing out a cloth, then starting to bathe her. "You're lovely, Rose. Really very lovely. That nice young man—the taxi driver—was very taken with you, asked me to buy you flowers from him." She herself was so taken by the fragile beauty of Rose's body that she bathed her quite automatically, admiring her very white skin with its tracings of blue veins, the small round breasts with surprisingly full, very pink nipples; narrow hips, slim legs. What a pity, she thought, to hide such loveliness beneath so many layers of misleading, not especially attractive clothes. The feeling was similar in many ways to the one she experienced each time she attended to Leo's bath.

She looked up to see that Rose had averted her face in an effort to conceal the tears making their way down her cheeks.

"Don't cry, Rose," she said in that same quiet voice. "Isn't it soothing? This will help you, take away some of the heat. I can't lose you, Rose. I can't. I'd have no one. Please don't suffer it so. I love you. I derive no pleasure from your suffering."

"I'm trying not to mind," Rose said weakly.

"Don't think about it. Let yourself be peaceful. Think of how cool your skin feels as it dries. Doesn't it feel better?"

Rose nodded, eyes still closed.

"I'll be finished in just a few more moments, then I'll fetch you something to drink. And after that, you'll sleep."

It wasn't just having someone see her without her clothes—although that was distressing enough in itself—it was her body's shocking reaction to the tender stroking motions that moved up and down her arms, across her shoulders, over her breasts, and down her belly, the length of both legs. Her body quivered, experiencing—beneath the layers of fever, dizziness, nausea, and pain—a decidedly sexual pleasure. No one had ever touched her in this fashion, so intimately. She'd never conceived of a pleasure so piercing. Being bathed was an erotic experience she wasn't equipped, in any way, to handle.

When it was done, finally, Leonie left Rose's nightgown off and simply drew the bedclothes up over her. This, too, was a shock. She'd never before known such a sensation of physical freedom, sensual pleasure. It seemed as if it should be wrong, yet she luxuriated in all the new sensations, actually feeling considerably better as a result.

"I'll want to bathe you again later," Leonie explained. "And you'll feel far more comfortable without that bulky gown."

Rose thirstily drained the cup Leonie held to her mouth, then plunged into sleep.

Leonie settled in the armchair in the corner to keep watch, and woke with a start late in the evening. She got up to take a look at Rose, and satisfied there was no change, returned to the armchair and slept again, rousing herself near dawn to again bathe Rose and urge her to drink another cup of the infusion; arguing her into submitting to a bedpan. Rose cried unhappily throughout, but was so weak she could scarcely lift her hands.

The fever, by midday, was worse. Her hair clung wetly to her face and neck, her body shuddering as Leonie bathed her. Faith came up with a tray for Leonie, asking, "How is she?"

Leonie shook her head, afraid to risk putting Rose's condition into words.

"Thank you for this," she said, accepting the tray, not in the least bit hungry. "You're very thoughtful, Faith."

"We're all very worried about Miss Manero. You'll tell her, won't you, that we're all thinking of her and saying prayers?"

"I will, yes."

Feeling stiff from having slept in the chair, she perched on the edge of it while she made herself eat the meal Faith had brought up.

Before leaving for the day, Faith came again with a cup of hot coffee for Leonie, asking if there was anything else she could do.

"You might take this tray down with you when you go. And ask the last out to make sure everything's properly shut down, locked up."

"Yes, Miss Benedict." She set the coffee down, retrieved the tray, and went on her way.

Sitting drinking the coffee, her eyes on Rose, who slept now without moving at all, she thought about Dennis Riley, deciding she'd offer him Clark's job. And perhaps see about moving Faith up, making her a manager. Her mind moved here and there, touching this and that, never settling.

Another few weeks and she'd be twenty-four. She felt decades older. Her eyes were stinging from lack of sleep. She was in need of a good hot bath; in need of Jimmy. She thought of Gray, wondering, as she did so often, what had become of him. And, of Augusta, too. Poor Gus, trying so hard to turn me into a proper young lady. You'd be horrified, Gus, at my status now. Unwed mother, businesswoman, practical nurse. You'd blanch at the thought of seeing another woman's naked body. But then, you never really did care very deeply, Gus. Not the way I care for Rose, or, back then, for Gray, the way I did try to care for Jimmy. I've lived almost a quarter of a century, been in America five years. Five years of wondering, hoping, continuing to believe.

Rose. Small and pale. You'd begin crying again were you awake to realize I've left your body open to the air, hoping to heal it, save you. You'd suffer the torments of hell at being exposed to the air and my eyes. Yet all I see, Rose, is your beauty, the miracle of the fact of your life. And I won't let you go. I won't.

Late the next afternoon, the fever broke. The angry flush of color ebbed from Rose's face and chest, leaving her once more coolly white, her features relaxed, her sleep turning restful. Leonie bathed her a last time, returned her to her nightgown, and left a willing Faith to spend the night on the sofa downstairs.

"If anything happens, anything at all, telephone me at once."

"Yes, I will," Faith promised soberly. "You have a good rest, Miss Benedict. I'll take care of everything."

She laid her hand against Faith's cheek for a moment, searching the depths of the girl's eyes. Then she collected her coat and bag and left.

Faith stood, still feeling the touch of Leonie's hand on her face, watching her move away through the restaurant to the front door. No one had ever managed to make her feel needed, respected, cared for just with the touch of a hand. But Leonie had.

13

Although she'd have argued it at the time, she went slightly mad after Jimmy died. And using everything he'd taught her, as well as everything she'd learned, she put up the remaining half of his estate as collateral and purchased a third property on Thirty-fourth Street and then a fourth on Fifty-seventh Street. As Jimmy had predicted, Mr. Freeman at the bank seemed predisposed toward her now and was most accommodating, although she was obliged to put up the entire half—which would eventually amount to thirty-two thousand dollars—against the two properties that, in themselves, were only valued at twenty-seven. She didn't care. She arranged that thirteen thousand in cash would go directly from the estate—once it cleared probate—toward the mortgages, and the balance on both properties would be set up under two twenty-year mortgages.

Working closely with Bill, she further arranged to have Lion's lease the properties from her in order to separate her personal assets from those of the company. Then, all these arrangements implemented, she and Rose set to work hiring staff, training two new cooks, overseeing the redecorating of the new locations.

Rose said, "You *seem* to know what you're doing. I just hope to God you actually do!"

"I do," she answered, on the run, always in motion these days. There was the dressmaker to see about the waitresses' uniforms, the suppliers to talk to about a still better price on larger bulk orders, invoices to review, checks to sign, books to study. Work to be done. She couldn't stop, didn't want to. It had become vitally important to maintain her momentum.

As soon as the estate cleared probate, she returned to the bank for another visit with Jacob Freeman, asking to use the now-paid-for properties on University Place and Fifteenth Street as collateral in order to free the cash remaining in the estate. She planned to use this money to establish two more restaurants—both rentals. She had Bill working full time. Rose and Alice and Dennis were all run off their feet attempting to simultaneously supervise the existing restaurants while interviewing prospective employees for the two new places.

"What's she trying to do?" Dennis asked Rose, emerging from Leonie's office after an exhausting three-hour conference session.

"She's doing what she knows how to do best: running restaurants. Does it bother you?"

"It doesn't *bother* me," he said. "It sure makes me tired, though, trying to keep up with her. You know, I asked her the other day something about the projected expenses at Thirty-fourth Street, and just like some kind of machine she rattled off all the employees' salaries, the weekly cost for meat and produce, the monthly overhead including coal, ice, gas, and the cleaning lady. It was absolutely fantastic! Just like a machine."

"She knows what she's doing," Rose said again, privately doubtful; not of Leonie's ability to run six restaurants—or even sixty, but of her reasons for this somehow crazed flight into expansion.

Nevertheless, within weeks of opening, each of the locations was doing capacity business. It was as if Leonie's personal determination was some sort of magnet drawing people in.

She knew she was dangerously overextended, that if any of the restaurants should, for some reason, begin seeing a decrease in revenue, she'd be in serious trouble. But she felt she had to take the risk, and watched the books, looking at the end-of-week figures, gratified to see they were staying very nicely in the black.

Bill just shook his head and kept on making his entries, understanding the financial reasons why she was succeeding but unable to see the logic. Like some sort of Pied Piper, all Leonie had to do was open the door to a new restaurant and the people poured in after her. She was written up in several of the newspapers, interviewed by *The Wall Street Journal*, pursued by people with causes, people wanting money, people simply after the prestige of being seen publicly with her. She didn't have time.

One night a week she met with the cooks from all the locations and went over the old recipes, discussed new ones; reading from one of her many notebooks, she'd point out that on such and such a day the stew had been oversalted at Fifty-seventh Street, the salad underdressed at University Place, one of the waitresses impolite to a customer at Twenty-third Street.

"I'm not spying on you. Nothing like that. I'm simply trying to impress upon you that we have a standard to maintain. If you're unable to taste when you've put too much seasoning into the food, have one of the waitresses or busboys do the tasting for you. But, please, don't serve doubtful food to the customers. They're not there to be experimented upon."

Once a month, general staff meetings were held at Fifteenth Street. All the waitresses, busboys, kitchen boys, cooks, cleaning and office staff were expected to attend. And from yet another notebook she'd point out that one of the trash barrels at Fifty-seventh Street had been overturned and the garbage left standing in the alley, thereby attracting a great number of flies, many of which got into the restaurant and proved quite an annoyance to the customers. At Thirty-fourth Street, a female patron had complained about the lavatory being dirty. And at Twenty-third Street the eggs in the eggs Benedict the previous Wednesday had been poached too long, so that the yolks were solid.

"Do better, please," she said simply. "Or we're out of business."

Rose said, "I don't know how to explain this, but something strange is happening."

Looking up from the notes she was making, alarmed, Leonie asked, "What?"

"There's no more turnover in personnel. We haven't hired or fired anyone in months."

"You frightened me." Leonie smiled, relieved.

"It frightens *me*." Rose said. "It isn't natural."

"Of course it is," she said mystifyingly. "The staff is happy, well-paid, their opinions requested and valued. Why should they leave? Or, for that matter, do anything to jeopardize a job he or she likes?"

"Well, it certainly makes my life easier," Rose conceded.

"It gives me more time to keep an eye on things. But I honestly don't understand it."

"Don't worry about it, Rose." Leonie patted her hand, her eyes returning to her notes. "It's perfectly all right. The way I want it."

"Talk to me for a minute," Rose said, causing Leonie to put down her pen and look up questioningly. "I remember not so very long ago a conversation we had about living touched, untouched."

"I remember."

"Are you substituting all this"—Rose waved her hand toward the door, the staff outside—"for something you really need?"

"Not any more than you are," she hedged.

"Don't do that! *Talk* to me! I know you Leonie. It's getting on for five years now. We've been through a lot together, you and me. It won't go away no matter how fast you run, no matter how many hours you put in here six days a week. Are you planning to make Lion's do for you for the rest of your life, and live without what you told me that day—and I know for myself—you have to have"

"How am I supposed to answer that? I can't possibly."

"You can," Rose insisted. "Because you know."

Leonie sighed and laced her fingers together on the desk in front of her. "I feel guiltier than ever," she said finally. "All that time, Rose," she said hoarsely, "and I never said, 'I love you,' the way he needed to hear it."

"Don't be a damned fool! Jimmy knew you loved him."

"Do you really think so, Rose?" she asked with disarming hopefulness.

"Of course I think so. He was a happy man, with everything he ever wanted. You don't have to hit someone in the face with it twenty times a day. You, of all people, ought to know that. You're the one who's always telling me what a pinched-up old maid I'm turning into. You're the so-called authority in that area. I know how to eat." she smiled. "And I know how to cook. Remember?"

"You're a skinny old stick, Rose." Leonie smiled back at her. "I love you."

"I love you, too. And if you don't watch out, you'll wind up a skinny old stick yourself. Take a lover if you have to."

"You do surprise me!"

"The hell I do. If you can say things like that to me, I can sure enough say them back to you."

"I'll compromise." Leonie laughed. "When *you* do, *I* will."

"I knew it was hopeless."

"Come to dinner tonight. Leo would so much like to see you." Her eyes returned to the notebook, and Rose knew the conversation was over. She got up and went back to her own office, to sit for several minutes staring out the window, imagining making love to some man. To Dennis. Feeling the blood rushing up into her face, the heat at the tops of her thighs, she turned away from the window and reached for the telephone to order additional bowls for three of the locations. Breakage with six restaurants was running high.

The image of herself as a desiccated old woman was far too real, and Leonie frequently found Rose's words coming back at her, filled with inescapable truth. She was running, unsuccessfully, from both her guilt and her despair. It had taken Jimmy's death for her to realize just how little compromise had actually been involved in their relationship, and how much true feeling. He *had* been a happy man. And she had been far happier than she'd either realized or admitted. So that her guilt was doubled, compounded by her multiple failures. She'd continued to hold parts of herself in reserve, going on the unshakable conviction that Grayson would, somehow, someday, return into her life.

Now, to her sorrow and chagrin, she found she no longer believed that. Whatever reasons he might have had, the truth was they'd had a few weeks of intimacy once upon a time and she'd distorted their time together, their conversations, beyond all reasonable limits. She had no doubt that his love had been sincere. She believed, rather, that his need for position and security was stronger. Most likely he'd resigned himself to his life with Augusta.

She received invitations out, primarily from the Freemans, and much of the time declined, using the pressures of the business as an excuse. It was the same excuse she gave for not championing Mrs. Sanger's clinic in Brooklyn. She donated money, but she hadn't any time; although her evenings dragged unbearably once Leo was down for the night and Amy had either gone out in her best going-to-church dress or retired to her room with a book. Time, on these evenings, was something of which she had far too much. And night hours seemed endless as she lay on her half of the bed she'd shared with Jimmy. His absence now was as potent as his presence had been. She didn't know what else to do, so she threw herself into the business completely, blanking her mind to the loneliness, the renewed feeling of isolation, the returned longing for fresh air, green grass underfoot, and the scent of fresh running water.

She filled one notebook after another with columns of figures, recipes, comments on the various locations, random ideas, half-formed thoughts. And when not occupied with one of the notebooks, went over and over the books until the columns of figures began to blur, becoming meaningless. Lion's was a success. Money was flowing in, accumulating in the various accounts. There was nothing she needed, everything she needed. Some vital, unrecognized part of herself had died with Jimmy. And she wasn't quite sure how to live, simply live, without him.

She continued investing her personal money in Liberty Bonds, believing that at four-and-a-half-percent interest she was investing wisely and protecting herself and Leo as well as the company from any unexpected reversals.

She went often, without plan, to the movies; to sit in the dark and watch the screen, feeling, somehow, Jimmy was with her. She was able to laugh and cry viewing the films as she was unable to do in her life.

She read the *Times* from front to back every day.

She began going shoeless at home and at the office, shaking her head with a smile when she heard that Anne Freeman had recently given a party where everyone was asked to discard his shoes at the door. Jimmy, she thought, would have liked that. It seemed she had arrived at a point where she could finally defy certain social customs.

She discovered how wrong she was one Saturday afternoon when she brought Leo to Fifteenth Street for lunch. She was delighted by the way Leo behaved herself and responded to the cooing ministrations of the staff. As they were leaving to walk home, Leonie came face to face with Anne and several of her friends.

"We were just coming to have lunch." Anne's smile began but never took shape. She looked into Leonie's eyes, then down at Leo, then once again at Leonie, saying to her friends, "You go along in, girls. I'll join you in just a moment."

Her friends continued on into the restaurant while Anne remained on the sidewalk, waiting until they were out of earshot. Leo was tugging impatiently at Leonie's hand, anxious to go, saying, "Come *on*, Mummy."

"Just a moment, darling."

One gloved hand lifted and hovered in the air as Anne said, "She's yours, of course."

Unable to speak, Leonie nodded.

"You think you're clever enough, strong enough to fly in the face of the rules," her rasping voice said. "But one day, when you least expect it, it will all catch up with you. And whether or not you survive will depend entirely upon the same strength that will have put you in jeopardy in the first place. You *are* clever," she said, her eyes now on Leo. "She's a very well-kept secret. You needn't worry." Her head, birdlike, jerked up, her eyes again on Leonie's. "I won't discuss it. You will no longer be welcome in our home though," she said, her eyes as impenetrable as steel. "And be careful of your pride," she warned, her hand fluttering in the air. "Any fool with a womb can produce a bastard."

"She is *not* a secret. I am *not* a fool and she is *not* a bastard."

"She *is* and you *are*." The opaque eyes looked a final time at Leo. "*Both* of you will pay. But not at my hand. I wouldn't take on that responsibility. If you'll excuse me, the girls are waiting."

She carefully sidestepped past Leonie and went on into the restaurant.

"Who's that lady?" Leo asked, tugging again at Leonie's hand. Receiving no answer and sensing her mother's upset, Leo twisted up her face and began to cry. Unsteadily Leonie bent to lift her into her arms, patting her, whispering into Leo's hair, "You will *not* pay. She's no one, darling. No one."

Jacob said nothing. Throughout their next meeting, she kept expecting him to take advantage of one of the many openings that occurred. But he made no reference to her meeting with Anne. His manner, as always these days, was deferential and interested. Finally she asked, "Would you prefer I do my banking elsewhere?"

"No, of course not," he said quickly, then looked down at his desktop, aligning several papers. "The bank is happy to have Lion's business." He paused, then went on. "I'm sure it was unpleasant for both of you. I see both sides. However, I prefer not to become involved."

"Does that mean you approve or disapprove?"

"I'm not here to sit in judgment of your actions. I'm here to advise you on financial matters."

"I see," she said. He'd made himself very clear.

"You needn't worry yourself," he said in a lower voice. "Anne is not a spiteful woman. She wishes you no harm. Nor do I." He looked at her with unhappy eyes. "I know it hasn't been easy for you, Leonie. But . . ." He shrugged.

"I understand. Thank you."

What bothered her most was Anne's calling Leo a bastard in Leo's presence. She kept remembering Jimmy's words to her that first Christmas, when he'd warned her of what she'd be inflicting on that as-yet-unborn child.

It's here now, Jimmy, she thought, hurt for Leo and for herself. But I won't fall into that same trap again. Leaving my shoes off is as far as I'll venture to go. Because the next time around, whoever it is might not be quite as scrupulous and basically kind as Anne Freeman.

The incident did serve one very real purpose, though: it put an end to the temporary madness. Everything seemed to shift back into perspective, and she was able to relax somewhat, spending more time with Leo, the quality of that time much improved. It showed in Leo's better behavior, in her willingness to climb up on Leonie's lap and allow herself to be hugged and petted.

"You know what?" Leonie asked her at least twice a day.

"I know." Leo invariably laughed.

"What do you know?"

"You love me. I know."

"Sometime I might surprise you and say something else. Then what'll you do?"

"Can we ask Aunt Rose to come over?"

Mildly disappointed at the shortness of Leo's attention span, she sighed and said, "Aunt Rose is busy this evening."

"How d'you know that?"

"She told me, darling."

Aunt Rose, she said silently, is in love and doesn't know it.

14

As it had done when the Lusitania was sunk, the Monday, November 11, 1918, edition of the New York *Times* ran a four-line headline. Leonie sat at the kitchen table with her morning coffee reading each word slowly, trying to determine what, if any, personal meaning they might have for her.

> ARMISTICE SIGNED, END OF THE WAR!
> BERLIN SEIZED BY REVOLUTIONISTS;
> NEW CHANCELLOR BEGS FOR ORDER;
> OUSTED KAISER FLEES TO HOLLAND

The war is over, she told herself. Rose would be pleased. Angelo would be coming home. What else? she wondered. Was there more? There didn't seem to be. The epidemic was still continuing. Business was down and she'd postponed making a commitment on the location Jimmy had scouted out prior to his death.

Dennis was doing even better than she'd hoped, managing two of the restaurants; and paying a great deal of not-unwelcome attention to Rose, who seemed to be reluctantly blossoming as a result, although she consistently expressed doubts about the difference in their ages.

"I'm five years older than he is," she said, looking perplexed.

"What does it matter?" Leonie said. "As long as you enjoy one another's company, your ages are irrelevant."

"I can't help it. I *am* five years older."

It seemed as if it should be wrong to derive as much pleasure as she did from Dennis' you-can't-refuse-me invitations to drives in the country, to dinner, to the moving pictures. She went along, questioning the impulse inside her that wanted to resist him. Something that insisted she be vigilantly aware of her five years' seniority. Except that Dennis seemed, somehow, to have assumed complete control of the situation and appeared not in the least bothered by her reluctance, her self-conscious overawareness of their age difference, her flustered reactions to his compliments. He was pursuing her—it felt—with a vengeance. So that she was suspicious of his motives, doubtful of his sincerity, unwilling to trust that other something inside her that too eagerly wanted more compliments, more flattery, more attention, more of almost anything. She was living in a state of total confusion.

Until an evening in December when they found themselves alone in her sitting room after a dinner she'd prepared and, as always, feeling awkward, she made an oblique reference to their age differences and he became angry.

"Why're you always *talking* about it?" he demanded. "Seems like every time we start enjoying ourselves, right in the middle you've got to suddenly remind both of us that you're twenty-seven and I'm only twenty-two. To tell you the truth, Rose, I'm getting kind of fed up with it. If you don't want me coming around, just tell me and that'll be the end of it, with no hard feelings. But if you do want me here, then leave go of this stinking age stuff! It's getting me down. And things are bad enough all over without that."

"People are bound to look at the two of us and know you're with an older woman," she argued.

"If I don't care about it, why do you?"

"I don't know why."

"Well, just you listen here to me," he said, pacing back and forth in front of the settee where she sat anxiously grinding her hands together, loathing this confrontation. "I liked the look of you that first time when you were sick and Leonie hired my taxi to bring you home here. And whether you believe it or not, I'd've come calling on you even if she hadn't offered me the job. But you've got some idea in your head that the only real point of my spending time with you is because I've got the job and I'm working to keep in everybody's good graces. Isn't that a fact?"

"No. That's not a fact."

"Aw, come on, Rose." He stopped in front of her and bent down, bringing his face close to hers. "You're a crummy liar.

Every time you try, your face gives you away. You know that's what you think, so why don't you admit it?"

"Well, maybe I do." She sat back slightly to remove herself from his worrisome proximity.

"What're you scared of?" he asked, aware of her efforts to evade him. "What is it you think I'm going to do to you anyway?"

"Nothing. I'm not scared of you." She surreptitiously wiped her damp palms down the sides of her dress.

"Never seen anything like it!" he exclaimed, running his hand over his hair. "Sitting there looking at me like I was Jack the Ripper or something. If you're so all-fired scared of me, why're you spending so much time with me?"

"Because . . ." She wet her lips and tried again. "I do enjoy your company."

"I like the job," he said, as if addressing some unseen audience. "I really do. I've got all kinds of thoughts, ideas about it. And about the future. Now that the war's over and the men'll be coming home, there's bound to be a boom. And once this epidemic's out of the way for good, business'll pick up again. Leonie will want to keep expanding. It's exciting." He looked over at her. He had an almost overwhelming desire to pin her down, stop her talking, quiet her with his hands, his mouth, his body. But she'd go wild, he knew, if he came at her that way.

Getting a grip on his anger, he dropped down in front of her and took hold of her hand, keeping hold of it even though it couldn't have been plainer she wanted to withdraw it.

"I'll be twenty-three in a couple of weeks," he said, appreciating the softness of her skin, the delicate bones underneath, the dampness of her palm. "So"—he smiled persuasively—"that only gives you four years' edge on me. I've been on my own since I was seventeen, you know. And I've had my share of women. Now, don't *do* that!" he said, refusing to release her hand. "You're not a kid, Rose. You know what it's all about. I'm not going to force you into something you don't want. But I think it's something you do want. Unless I'm crazy and I've got all the signs wrong."

"I won't give up everything I've worked for," she said, painfully aware of his hands. One holding her captive, the other unconsciously stroking from her wrist to the tips of her fingers, sending shivers through her. She wished he'd let go.

"Nobody's asking you to give anything up," he said, lost.

"Oh, but you would if . . ."

"If what?"

"Nothing. Never mind."

"Sometimes, when I'm in bed at night, I imagine how you look with your hair down, without all these stiff old-woman clothes, how you'd be if you just relaxed a little and stopped being so edgy all the time when we're together. I'd enjoy looking after you, Rose."

"What does that mean? I don't need looking after."

"You know what I'm talking about," he said meaningfully, his eyes on her mouth. "Ever kissed a man, Rose?"

She looked like a trapped animal suddenly, her eyes searching the room. "Stop it," she said. He was making her feel inadequate, clumsy, ashamed.

"Hold still for just one minute and see if you don't like it." His hand cupped her chin.

She wanted to get up, run away, hide somewhere, disappear. But she had to stay there, cornered, as his face came too close and she couldn't breathe and his mouth touched against hers.

"Terrible? Was that so terrible?"

"Leave me alone," she said hoarsely. "Let me go, Dennis."

"I just this minute decided not to. You're burning like you've got the fever again."

"Dennis!"

"Marry me. I'll move in here with you. It's cozy. Plenty of room for the two of us. I'll look after you."

"No!" she cried frantically. "Someone your own age. I can't . . . Don't make sport of me. Please!" She yanked her hand free, shrinking against the back of the sofa. "It's cruel."

"Okay. Just let me ask you something."

"What?"

"Don't you really want to know? Aren't you curious?"

"I don't know what you *want* from me!"

"Yes, you do, Rose. I want to take down your hair, take you out of all those clothes, take you upstairs to your bedroom, and make love to you. Touch you, hold you, kiss you."

Her face turned crimson.

"Come on," he said. "Admit you're curious. Admit it's what you've been wanting all these months."

"Three months! And I'm nothing of the sort." What was he trying to do to her? "If I wish to take a lover," she said with forced bravado, "I will take one of my own choosing. I won't be forced."

"You want the truth, Rose? Here's the truth: you're not scared of me one bit. You're scared of what I might make you find out about yourself!"

"I know all there is to know about myself!"

"You do? Okay? What d'you know about this?" He placed both hands over her breasts.

She gasped and wrenched herself away, taking small desperate breaths. "How *dare* you!" she whispered, her voice failing.

"You know all there is to know," he chided. "All you know about yourself, Rose, is the surface, and the rest is a lot of suspicions about what you think you might be. Oh, I know what you're thinking now. Swearing to yourself you'll never have me here again. And how dare I put my twenty-two-year-old hands on your sacred twenty-seven-year-old body? I'm only human," he said more quietly. "I love you. Is that so hard to believe?"

"I won't be my mother, spending the rest of my life in a fourth-floor cold-water walk-up with a bunch of children to look after and a husband I never see. I won't be like that! I've got the life I want and I'm not giving it up!"

Tiredly he got up and sat down in the chair opposite, extending his legs and crossing them at the ankles.

"I guess I'm crazy," he said. "Wanting to make love to you. It'd be like trying to take hold of a porcupine. All sharp, stabbing needles digging into me, all fighting to get away."

"Why are you doing this?" she asked miserably.

"Look, you believe what you want. I love you. You hate it that you're older, hate it that you can't trust yourself to believe one word that comes out of my mouth. Okay. I'm sorry, but there's nothing I can do about what you believe, don't believe. I'm not out to change your life. Who ever said a word about any of that?"

She hadn't anything to say to this tall young man with the pale blond hair and light brown eyes sitting so loosely with his ankles crossed, his hand with a cigarette moving back and forth between his mouth and the ashtray on the table.

"Planning to die a virgin," he said with a trace of bitterness. "I can't promise any more than to marry you. I don't *have* anything else. It's the stupidest waste of a beautiful woman. I'll run along, I guess." He put out his cigarette and stood up. "You can believe whatever you like, Rose. I can't tell you more than the truth."

The silence began to grow lengthy as he stood waiting for

her to say something, and she battled again with wanting, not wanting.

"It's unfair of you," she said at last, "to make me feel this way."

"What way is that?" he asked, looking innocent, understanding exactly how she felt.

"This way."

"I have no idea what you mean. But I'd like to hear about it, though."

"You're right," she said almost inaudibly, agonized.

"Right about what?"

"Don't *do* this!" she begged.

The last thing he said to her before they went upstairs was, "I swear I won't hurt you. I swear I won't."

You will, she thought. Some way or another, you will hurt me. And then I'll wish I'd never known you, never allowed you to stir my feelings, my curiosity.

She kept her eyes tightly closed as Dennis undressed her. Standing rigid in her undergarments as he moved away, she ventured to open her eyes to see he was lighting the gas fire. Quickly shutting her eyes again, she remained motionless, hands clenched at her sides, jaws so tightly locked together her head ached; jumping with a start when his voice whispered in her ear, "Don't you care at all for me, Rose?"

She had to open her eyes then, nodding yes, made more fearful at the sight of his naked chest. When had he removed so many of his clothes? He was more substantial than she'd supposed. Broader, more solid. Her eyes now couldn't leave his body. He put his arms around her, and she was rigid once more, as his mouth came down over hers. Soft, very soft. She felt like crying.

"Open your mouth, Rose. Put your arms around me."

Obediently, she lifted her arms, closed her eyes, opened her mouth. The air gushed out of her lungs in shock and sudden pleasure as his tongue moved over her lips, into her mouth, sparred with hers; his hands slipping down her sides, coming to rest on her hips. His mouth on hers was hypnotic, deeply thrilling. When he moved his head away, she couldn't seem to focus, couldn't quite catch her breath, couldn't collect her thoughts or protest as he adeptly stripped her to her skin, directed her to the bed, put her down, put himself on top of her, his mouth once again covering hers. It felt good, bad, good. His skin so warm. She was touching him without realizing she was doing it. Her hands, too, it seemed, were possessed of a curiosity; one that sent them timidly traveling over his shoulders, across his wide back. Good, yes. He pulled her to a sitting position so he could remove the combs from her hair, smiling in satisfaction as her hair spilled thickly down over her shoulders, covering her breasts, her arms. Easing her back again, he lifted aside her hair to place his hands on her breasts—electrifying—touching her nipples maddeningly until they turned to small stones; kissing her while his hands played upon her breasts. Then he shocked her still further by kissing her breasts as he'd kissed her mouth, so that the air emerged from her throat in a hiss and she wanted to wind her fingers into his hair and pull hard, pull down; her mind and body sent mad.

"It isn't terrible, is it?" He smiled at her as his hand moved boldly down her belly and in between her thighs, so that she tried to keep her thighs together, but he said, "Don't! I know how to make you feel wonderful. And you want it, you know this is what you've wanted all along. Feel that, feel that!" Insisting, his mouth came closer to hers, his eyes boring into hers as he touched her in a way that made her want to scream. "It's the best thing in the world," he said, his mouth talking into hers, tongue darting out to touch her lips again, again, his knee cautiously insinuating its way between her thighs so that she was forced to open, forced to lie exposed totally to his hand, his probing fingers. "Sometimes the first time for a woman hurts. Just trust me," he said, positioned now between her thighs. "If you think only of being hurt, that's what it'll be. But if you think about how this feels," he coaxed, fingers slippery, sliding back and forth making her writhe, making everything inside her twist down like a clock spring, "it'll just be good, so good. Small, you're so pretty. Skin so white, so white. Wet, ooh!" He kept talking, kept touching, all the while slowly moving forward, distracting her until he'd succeeded in partially penetrating her body. Telling her to, "Look, I'm almost all the way inside of you, and it feels good, doesn't it? Look!" She looked, her eyes gaping. What? You my God putting all of yourself inside of me and oh Jesus my God what's happening to me that I can even want yes want to spread myself know if I can.

Her head fell back as he lifted her, holding her steady as he rocked back and forth, back and forth, gaining until he lay immersed in her, smiling beatifically, whispering, "I'll give you the finest feeling in the world, Rose, the finest. Isn't it good?" His hand kneaded her breast. Every muscle in her body seized, contracting in anticipation of something. What? All of her centered entirely upon the fact of his swollen presence inside her and a frenzied sense of dislocation. His body butted against hers, the motions making her want to scream all the more. All of it a monstrous assault on her senses. But he was right. Pleasure. Terrible pleasure. She was actually lifting higher, spreading more as he collided faster, then faster with the source of a potential pleasure looming closer and closer, her fingernails digging into her palms. Then he cried out her name, thrusting fast fast, then stopped; laying himself heavily down upon her, panting.

"Is it ended?" she asked in a shamed whisper.

"Not yet. Not nearly. I'm just resting for a moment."

She lay still, trying to imagine what "not nearly" could possibly mean. A minute, two, three. Then he withdrew himself from her and it hurt, shocking. A sound tearing from her mouth, hurting.

"It's all going to be just beautiful," he promised. "Turn, turn." Lifting open her legs, he started to caress her as he'd done before, his fingers slipping, sliding; kissing her wildly as he pressed and stroked and rubbed and searched her inside, outside, until she didn't care who he was or what or if he did love her as long as he took her to this feeling, *this feeling*. "That's it, sweetheart," he whispered, "that's it, Rose," he crooned, bending his head to suck, tugging at her nipple as she went over the edge of Rose and screamed. Her body racked by convulsions. Pressure in her head, her groin. Everything throbbing, shuddering on and on, until she pushed away his hand and lay twitching, struggling to breathe.

"Didn't I tell you?" He smiled, returning his lips to her breasts, his hand languidly caressing the length of her inner thigh. "Don't you worry. I'll look out for you, Rose."

Just words, she thought, beginning to regain herself. You say them so easily, too easily. You'll hurt me. I know sure as God you'll hurt me.

15

She was hurrying to get dressed to go out to dinner, and running late, having spent over an hour trying to smooth out a disagreement between one of the waitresses and the cook at the Murray Hill restaurant. A conflict of personalities. Dennis had telephoned to say, "A little visit from you would do the trick, settle things down." So she'd stopped at the restaurant before coming home. The three of them had sat in the kitchen with cups of coffee, and talking quietly, had managed to get the problem solved. The problem having consisted entirely of the fact that the cook didn't like the waitress's handwriting, couldn't read her orders, and therefore got them wrong.

"Why don't you print?" Leonie suggested. "That way both of you will be satisifed."

That simple. But it took well over an hour to return the two to a state of friendliness. Then she'd rushed home to oversee Leo's dinner and bath before finally starting her own.

The invitation from Cavanaugh hadn't come as a surprise. Being senior partner in the firm, he'd offered to take over Lion's legal work after Jimmy's death, and she'd accepted. He was a soft-spoken, meticulously mannered man in his early forties who expressed much sadness at Jimmy's death and from time to time spoke of him fondly and with amusement, as of a departed son or brother. Leonie liked him, liked his old-world graciousness, his way of speaking of his late wife—who'd also died in the epidemic—and of his grown son living in California with his wife and three children. He spoke regularly about taking the long train ride out there to see them but invariably allowed the pressures of business to delay his trip.

They'd been working over the final details of the lease for the new Forty-seventh Street Lion's when Arthur cleared his throat, looking not in the least sure of himself, and asked if she'd care to have dinner with him.

"I'd like that." She'd smiled.

Relief had visibly washed over him like a sudden cool breeze on a very hot day. She decided he was shy. But she'd certainly never seen anyone quite so nervous at extending a dinner invitation.

Now she was late, something she very much disliked to be. Being on time had always been a matter of principle, and it upset her to think of Arthur's being kept waiting while she fussed. The image was too much the typical female one to be easily dismissed.

She was at the point of pinning up her hair when Amy knocked at the bedroom door, then opened it to say, "There's a gentleman here asking to see you."

"Not Mr. Cavanaugh already! He can't be this early!"

"Not him." Amy came over carrying a card. "I don't know this one. But he says it's important. He's waiting."

Her hands in her hair, she glanced over at the card, prepared to tell her to have him call at the office during business hours. Her throat going dry, a quiet rushing in her ears, she slowly extended her hand to take the card, running her thumb over the embossed lettering as she stared at it, breathing as if she'd just run up three or four flights of stairs.

"He's waiting," Amy repeated. "What you want me to say to him?"

With shaking hands she reached for her dressing gown and pulled it on, then went to the bedroom door, stopping with her hand on the knob, her eyes closed. Trying to calm herself. She couldn't stop the interior fluttering and knocking, the feeling very close to panic that had taken hold of her. She opened the door and stepped into the living room.

He looked very much older. Gray streaked his hair. Older, sadder. Yet the same. Just the same. He looked up and their eyes met. Neither of them were able to speak.

She was even lovelier than he'd remembered. Tall and formidable, radiating strength and power. He'd forgotten how powerful she was, how aristocratic in her bearing.

"*Gray?*" Her voice emerged high with emotion and surprise.

"It took me rather longer than I'd thought it would," he said quietly, the sound of his voice penetrating her head and body, seeming to echo inside her.

Leo, in her nightgown, came to the doorway to look first at her mother and then at the man over there holding his hat with both hands. They both looked funny, she thought, standing at opposite sides of the room, staring at each other.

Leonie reached for her daughter, saying, "This is Leo. Leo, say hello to Mr. Marlowe."

As she'd been taught, Leo walked across the room, extended her hand to him, and said, "How do you do?"

"I do very well, thank you." He smiled at her. "And how do *you* do?"

She giggled. "You're funny!"

"Say good night now," Leonie said, feeling there were too many people in the room. "Amy, please return Leo to bed. And ring Mr. Cavanaugh for me, tell him I'm terribly sorry but something important's come up and I won't be able to keep our engagement. Give him my apologies and say I'll ring him at the office tomorrow to explain."

"Yes, ma'am," Amy said, eyeing Gray as she shooed Leo back to her room.

He followed this interchange, thinking: How in control you are! And what a splendid little girl! You've changed so, become somehow more of what you were; yet less, too.

"She's beautiful," he said.

"Look at us!" She laughed, a nervous little sound. "Squared off like boxers in a ring. Do take off your coat! What am I thinking of? Will you stay for a bit?" She moved forward with her hand extended to take his coat. He opened his arms and she went into them with a sigh that shook her entire body as she closed her eyes and stood inside the circle of his arms with her head resting on his shoulder, stunned by his reality, his presence here.

He could feel her hair against his cheek, her substance within his arms, but couldn't quite make his mind accept that it was actually happening. He had a childish-feeling desire to cry.

"I thought you were dead," she whispered. "I thought I'd never see you again."

"They couldn't find you," he explained. "I hired detectives at once, as soon as I learned Gus had sent you away. But they had no success at all. I thought I'd go mad. The frustration ... I kept them hard at it until the war. Then, with that ... it put a stop to everything."

You didn't abandon me after all, she thought. I knew I wasn't wrong to believe. I *knew*.

She removed herself and took his hat and coat, set them on a chair before leading him to the sofa, where they sat gazing at each other, their hands joined.

"This time round"—he freed one hand to lift a strand of hair from her cheek—"it took them no time at all. Less than a month. I'd settled in to wait, you see. Then they rang to say they'd managed to locate you. So easily. I've read all about your success. It's simply wonderful! I am ... so proud of you."

"You didn't receive my letters."

"I knew you'd tell me you'd written." He looked pained. "I knew you'd say it, and I knew I'd feel just as angry as I do. Where did you send them?"

"To your office."

"Gus, of course. God, I'd've given anything on earth to have had a letter! I wonder how she did it."

"How is Gus?"

"She died. She and her new husband. Returning from their honeymoon abroad. They got caught at the start of the fighting."

"I'm sorry to hear that."

"I understand," he said, "that your daughter's father died this past year in the epidemic. I was sorry to learn of it. She must miss her father."

"Jimmy wasn't Leo's father. And she's always known that he wasn't."

"I did know that the two of you weren't married. I was trying, I'm afraid, for a bit of diplomacy there that didn't quite come off." He looked dismayed.

"Leo's your daughter," she said quietly.

"Mine? My daughter?"

He couldn't speak for several seconds, trying to absorb that. Then found himself furious with Gus all over again. "That makes it all the worse!" he exclaimed. "Sending you away that way. I hit her." He looked down at their joined hands. "I wanted to kill her."

"All that's over now," she said.

"But it must have been awful for you. I kept thinking of how you'd been when you arrived from Africa. The way everything startled you. And your reaction to the noise. I'm sorry. I'm sorrier than I can say."

They were silent for several seconds. Then he said, "I've disarranged your plans for the evening. But it seemed more sensible to come directly here than approach you at the office."

"My plans aren't in the least important. Not in the least. You were absolutely right to come."

"Have you dined? Will you come out, dine with me? I do so want to talk with you . . . such a lot to talk about."

"Will you be staying in New York long? Or must you return?"

"I left the Ambassador's office some time back, worked on the London *Times* through most of the war. I've had an offer here, you see, an editorial position on the New York *Times*."

"You'll be staying?" She felt as if she was soaring, rising into the sky.

"That was my plan."

"And is your family here with you?"

"There is no family."

"We sound so stiff." She smiled. "So formal. Trying to ask each other everything in the subtlest possible way, ending up sounding like pompous asses. I'll get dressed. There's some sherry in that decanter, brandy in the other. Of course, we both run the risk of going to jail now that the Eighteenth Amendment has been ratified. But I've no intention of throwing away perfectly good wines and spirits simply because a group of teetotalers . . ." She stopped. "I'm doing it again. Please do have something to drink. I'll be as quick as I'm able."

She told Amy, "I may or may not be home tonight."

"What's going on? Who's he, anyway?"

"That is Leo's father," she said, then held Amy tightly for several seconds. "I feel as if I'm dreaming. I can't make myself believe this is happening."

"That's Leo's daddy, huh? Isn't that something!"

"I must finish dressing. Would you give him a drink, Amy? Offer him a bit of cheese or something."

"Leo know that's her daddy?" she asked cannily.

"No. Not yet."

He explained that he'd arrived the day before, that he'd taken a room at the Astor, and that he'd already finalized all the arrangements for his new job with the *Times*.

"I came determined to find you if it took the rest of my life. I came hoping I hadn't lost you. I came because I had to. For some stupid reason, I expected you to look just as you did. But of course you don't. You're a beautiful woman. For just a moment, when you came into the room back there, I knew you yet didn't at all. As if I'd seen you once upon a time and I knew your face but hadn't any idea who you were. My God! I'm talking the most preposterous rubbish! Forgive it! I've been so keyed up."

"It's been more than five years, Gray. People change. You've changed. Your eyes seem less mocking. Your whole manner is altered."

"The war altered most of us. After the embassy, I was transferred over to the foreign secretary's office and was sent abroad too regularly for my liking. Never had the remotest idea what it was I was supposed to be doing over there. Observing the carnage, taking notes like some sort of ghoul. It all put paid to my prior beliefs and suppositions. One can't maintain lofty viewpoints, ludicrous ambitions, in the face of senseless deaths. But let's not waste time talking about me," he said impatiently. "You! You've accomplished such a lot! *Six* restaurants. And everyone seems to know who you are."

"You'll be staying, then," she said, wondering why she was having so much trouble accepting all this.

"How old is she?" he asked.

"She'll be five in March. She was deeply attached to Jimmy, took his death very badly. It's been a difficult year for her, especially with the influenza. I wouldn't allow her or Amy out of the apartment for months. It became frightfully tense. But the last few months have been far better."

"How did you do it," he asked, "get it all started?"

"Augusta. She gave me a thousand pounds. I used the money to start the first restaurant. Then used each successive restaurant as collateral against the next. She said Father had sent along the money for my maintenance and it was only right that I should have what was mine."

Well, he thought, you weren't totally unkind, Gus. At least you gave her something to go on with. Because there couldn't have been more than three or four hundred left of the money Dr. Benedict sent.

"Clever of you," he said. "I always suspected you'd do well at whatever you chose to do."

"No," she disagreed. "I was afraid to stop, to think about where it was I found myself. As long as I kept going, kept moving, there wasn't time to be frightened by the city—I was determined not to give in to that fear—or time to spend endlessly wondering what had become of you and why you hadn't answered my letters."

"You do believe that I tried?" he asked anxiously.

"Of course, if you say it's the truth."

"I don't know that I'd have had your kind of faith."

"It's always been much more than simply a matter of faith, Gray. I suppose it sounds simpleminded, but I made a commitment. I had to honor it as best I could. I loved you. After Leo was born, I started feeling as if I was coming to pieces. Jimmy was there. I needed someone. And he adored Leo. But I always felt so guilty, feeling it was a betrayal of the commitment I'd made to you. And then, after a time, it did seem as if I'd been mistaken, that the commitment had only been in my mind."

"You needn't explain. I'm scarcely in a position to question your actions."

"Was there someone for you?" she asked, still terribly nervous; despairing over how stilted and unnatural the conversation seemed.

"A few hours here and there that, afterward, never seemed worthwhile."

They both made a pretense of attending to their food, each trying to think of what to say next; neither of them able to predict where they might go from here.

"I have no appetite," she said finally, putting down her knife and fork.

"Nor I." He followed suit. "It seems . . . surprising, I suppose, is the word I want. Surprising to see you've adapted so completely to city life. I wouldn't have thought you would."

"I was determined," she said, "to make the best of it, better it, somehow; conquer my dislike, my fear. The city was somewhat of a personal enemy I had to learn to live with."

"There is something I've been . . . I have a small gift for you," he said, discomfited. Their conversation was staggering drunkenly, going here, going there. "I've had it quite some time. Since my trip to St. Petersburg."

"Russia," she said, as if the name were a clue to the underlying meanings of the conversation. "I can't imagine it."

"Shall we leave?" he suggested.

"Yes, I think so."

"Leonie"—his voice dropped as he took hold of her hand—"I don't know how to say what I want or even if I have the right to say it. All this is so difficult. Far more so than I'd imagined it would be."

"Yes," she agreed. "Perhaps," she said slowly, looking at their two hands, "if I come back with you to the hotel . . . we'll be able to talk to one another a little more easily."

Their stiff formality continued until they arrived at his hotel room. As he took care of their coats, she looked around, noticing he'd taken a suite. The door ajar over there opened into a bedroom.

"May I use your bathroom?" she asked, feeling she was about to offer herself with great premeditation to a total stranger she'd met on the street.

"Of course," he said, looking equally ill-at-ease.

She went into the bathroom and closed the door, and he sat down on the arm of the sofa, wanting again to cry, to cover his face with his hands and weep until the weight in his chest and the anxiety pulsing in his throat were eased. He got up and took several steps toward the door, turned, walked back to the sofa, stopped, turned, stopped. He'd forgotten the gift and went now to get it from his suitcase.

She avoided looking at herself in the mirror, afraid to look and discover her own face unrecognizable. What had happened to their ease with one another, their passionate inability to remain apart without contriving to find some way to touch? Strangers. I was still very much a child then, perhaps perceived you as I wished to and not as you really were. But there *is* a feeling, a sense of satisfaction in not having been mistaken. You did come. I wasn't wrong. Will we come together now to find, with considerable upset, that we no longer fit?

He stood holding the tissue-wrapped package in his hand, staring at her as she emerged from the bathroom. She looked different. It took him a second or two to realize it was because she'd unpinned her hair and was carrying her shoes. She appeared smaller, less formidable, more familiar.

She put down her shoes and he came over to give her the gift.

"A lion." She smiled at him. "How lovely! What sort of stone is this?"

"Chalcedony. I've carried it everywhere with me during the last five years, with the arbitrary notion in mind that as long as I kept it close by me, with every intention in the world of finding you and giving it to you, then you weren't lost to me. My single worst fear has been that I'd lost you."

She held the carving in her hand, watching it lose its definition as her eyes filled with tears, her throat closing painfully.

"You're upset," he said, shaken.

"No," she shook her head. Then, reconsidering, said, "Yes. But not just with you, with both of us. We're two completely different people now, Gray. I see so many differences in you, and I'm sure you must see them in me. Such a lot has happened. Deaths. I feel very much as if I want you. It does feel as if I do. But I'm . . . confused. Thank you for this." She opened her hand again to look at the carving. "I'll get a suitable chain, wear it." She opened her bag and placed the lion inside it, then put down the bag, wondering if his presence was arousing old memories or new desires. She stood waiting, thinking: How odd to find I no longer have quite so bold a nature as I once did. You will have to make the first gesture. I find myself unable to voluntarily bare myself to you.

He put his hand out to her hair. "You didn't have it bobbed," he said. "Like all the others."

"No," she said. "I always thought . . . I had a picture in my mind of the way it would be if . . . when you came to me."

"I know." He smiled. "It isn't at all as I thought it'd be either."

"We're fools," she said sadly. "Unbelievable fools. I want to kiss you." She moved slightly closer, and he lowered his head to kiss her, at once fired with longing.

"You're right," he said, holding her against his chest. "Fools. I love you, Leonie. Knowing you, loving you, changed everything. Why didn't you marry this chap, Jimmy?"

"I told you. And I didn't love him that way."

As if they'd established their mutual intention, they went into the bedroom. And made love gently, tenderly, as if respectful of unseen injuries. When it was ended, they lay looking into each other's eyes, continuing their rediscovery of one another.

"You will marry me," he asked, "won't you?"

"In time," she said. "We must first learn to know one another again. And of course Leo must become accustomed to you. I'll have to make arrangements to take a larger apartment."

"How shall I contribute?" he asked, eager to assume responsibility both for her and their child.

"I hadn't thought of that," she said. "I have quite a good deal of money now, Gray. I hope that isn't going to become a problem between us."

"I shouldn't think so."

"And of course I shall continue with the business."

"If that's what you wish."

"You mean that?" she asked. "You're aware of how much of a commitment I have to the business?"

"I think I am."

"I couldn't possibly stop now. I have to continue on with what I've started." She heard how she sounded and hated it suddenly, hated having brought business and the making of arrangements into bed with them. "Oh, Gray," she said, returning herself to him. "Five years. It was such a long time."

"It's all in back of us now."

His hands were familiar, she thought, their tenderness unchanged, the message they conveyed still the same. "I love you so very much." She sighed. "Are you fatigued?"

In answer, he came down over her again, starting to make love to her with the fire and urgency she remembered.

I will have another child, she thought. I can feel it, feel myself opening to accept it. And I will suffer the pain, deliver it from my body gladly. So long as I have you.

Part THREE
1928-1933

16

When she thought of her childhood, there were two events that always, immediately, came to mind. The first was the death of Uncle Jimmy. And the second was the arrival of the tall gray-haired man she was told was her father. Somehow, the two events were inextricably intertwined in her mind, although she knew—it having been explained many times to her—that Uncle Jimmy died almost seven months before her father came to America to find them.

For a very long time it didn't make any sense to her that her father could be someone she'd never seen, and not Uncle Jimmy, who'd always been there. And much as she liked her father and called him that, she couldn't help thinking of Uncle Jimmy as her father.

"When I left England," her mother explained countless times, "I didn't know I would be having you. And because of the war, your father didn't know you'd been born. I know it's very complicated and difficult to understand, but someday it'll all make sense to you."

In 1928, by the time she was fourteen, she understood quite a number of things, among them the fact that she'd been born illegitimately. She asked, and her mother told her the truth. But still it was an awful shock, and for several months Leo went about furious with both of them for lying to her—well, not really lying, but not telling the whole truth either—and for having her believe all sorts of things that just weren't true. During those months she refused to believe anything they told her and denied everything she'd been told in the past, going to Rose for confirmation of certain facts. Because Aunt Rose had always been truthful and didn't have any reason to change.

She loved Aunt Rose, loved her smart clothes and her high-heeled shoes, and the way she'd fixed up the apartment on University Place. She wasn't like Mummy, who never wore her shoes and half the time went around at home with her hair hanging all over the place and once even got out on the sidewalk on her way to the office before realizing she'd forgotten her shoes and had to come back up to the apartment to get them. And, naturally, Father had just laughed and thought the whole thing very amusing.

But Aunt Rose began acting strangely that year. So Leo slowly stopped going to her to talk, to look for answers. It had, Leo knew, something to do with Dennis Riley. Although nobody ever bothered to enlighten her as to what was going on. Something else that drove her crazy: the way they all talked among themselves and went suddenly quiet if she or Gray happened to come into the room. Even Amy stopped talking if she came upon her and her mother in conversation.

And if all that wasn't bad enough, she started having periods and she grew breasts almost between going to bed one night and waking up the next morning. And she'd be laughing about something, then start to cry, with no idea why or what was happening to her.

To be fair, she thought her mother was really nice about the way she'd made it an occasion to celebrate. They went out to lunch together and they talked and Leo came home feeling a lot better. For a little while. But then she was off, going up and down again, so things were just the same.

The only one who didn't go quiet if she walked into the room, or treat her like some kind of oversized baby, was Gray. But he was only eight and spent most of his time curled up in some corner or another reading, or playing for hours with a big box of tin soldiers Father had bought him the Christmas Gray was five. Little Gray listened well enough, but he never had much to say. And she knew it bothered *them* because she overhead them talking quite a few times, about how Gray was so remote and quiet, so undemonstrative. He wasn't shy or anything, and took himself off to the library all the time, or went out for walks alone without bothering to tell anyone he was going. There was some kind of quiet panic about once a month over Gray's being gone for hours and no one knowing where he was. But then he'd let himself in with the key he'd insisted he should have and stand there wondering what all the fuss was about.

Leo thought he was a little old man disguised as a too-tall-for-his-age eight-year-old.

They were all too tall, she thought. Except for Amy, who certainly wasn't short. Leo herself was still growing, and afraid she'd never stop, walking around all hunched over so nobody would notice she was already five-foot-nine and growing out of her new clothes after only a couple of months.

No one seemed to have time for her. Mummy was always rushing off to the office or opening another restaurant or campaigning for somebody or other. And Father was forever having late editions and deadlines. Or he came in the door waving theater tickets he'd got free from somebody at the paper and the two of them would dress and rush off for the evening, leaving Amy to see to the childrens' dinner and wish them good night.

Then, just when she was giving serious thought to doing something drastic, 1928 became the year of the third important event she'd always remember.

Leonie asked Rose out to lunch specifically for the purpose of enlisting her help in dealing with Leo. But, to her surprise, within moments of being seated in the dining room of the Waldorf, Rose silently began to cry and covered her eyes with a handkerchief.

"What is it?" Leonie asked, touching her arm. This was so unlike Rose it was hard to believe Leonie was actually seeing this happen. Rose struggled to control herself and finally managed to get out in a choked voice, "I don't suppose Dennis has been in to talk to you?"

"Not about anything unusual, no."

"Well, he will," she said bitterly, in her mind once more going over that terrible scene the night before. "Of course, he'll leave it until the last possible moment. But forewarned is forearmed. He's leaving."

"Leaving?"

"He's been offered a job with some big company. Won't even tell me the *name* of it. And that's not all." She paused, determined not to break down again. "He's . . . found somebody else." She couldn't meet Leonie's eyes and made a pretense of searching her handbag for something.

"Why don't you tell me about it, Rose? Perhaps I might help."

"There's nothing to help," she said in that same bitter tone.

"It's just so humiliating. We had a terrible fight about it last night. Terrible." The way they'd shouted at each other. And his voice, saying, "You should've married me when I wanted you, Rose. It's too late now. I'm sorry, but that's the way things go." Then pleading with him, begging him to reconsider, using any argument, any ploy she could think of. Sick with fear at the prospect of losing him, equally sick with shame at lowering herself to beg; the one thought going round and round in her mind: You did use me. I knew you'd hurt me. I always knew. "It's amusing," she said caustically. "He's going to marry Faith."

"Faith? That seems rather an odd match."

"It isn't so odd if you think about it. She's done very well for herself since she left Lion's. Oh, he'll use her to advance himself just as he used me. Anyway . . ." She cleared her throat, thinking of the way he'd thrown his things into the suitcase, leaving absolutely nothing behind but too much empty space in the apartment. She hadn't slept at all. "I just wanted to prepare you."

"I'm sorry, Rose."

"Don't be sorry. I should've known better. A thirty-six-year-old woman with a thirty-one-year-old man. Anyone with eyes could *see* he was younger. Faith is only twenty-seven, you know." It isn't only just that, she thought, hating the way she was sounding. It's me. And all the things I've done in the last year, trying to keep him with me. The awful things.

"First of all," Leonie said carefully, "I don't believe Dennis used you to advance himself, Rose. Nor do I think he'd use Faith that way. And as far as your difference in ages, I don't think anyone would have looked at the two of you and started speculating on that. I don't think anyone but you ever noticed. And, I don't mean to be unkind, but I don't think it was the age difference that really bothered you. There was far more to it than that, wasn't there?"

"I shouldn't have brought all this . . . I only wanted to warn you, let you know what's coming. Shall we order?"

She closed the door firmly in the face of further discussion. And throughout the meal, which Rose scarcely touched, Leonie couldn't help feeling uneasy. Everything Rose was saying and doing struck discordant notes. When Leonie finally did manage to get around to the subject of Leo, Rose seemed to come back into focus and listened intently.

"She's at a stage right now," Leonie was saying, "when nothing we say or do is right. I truthfully haven't any idea what to do. Sometimes I'd like nothing better than to throw her down across my lap and spank her silly. Other times I'm so filled with sympathy for her I can scarcely bear the distance she insists on keeping between us."

"Perhaps," Rose offered, "she might be better off away. At a boarding school or something like that."

"It's a thought. Although boarding schools have always seemed to me so . . . cold. A place where people who haven't time or love to spare leave their children. And that's not at all the case with Leo. We love her. She knows we do. But it's as if she simply has to torment us and herself, testing us at every possible opportunity. I'm afraid she'd take the idea of boarding school as being the ultimate proof of our lack of caring."

"She'll grow out of it," Rose said, her thoughts returning to Dennis; wondering where he was, what he was doing, if he was with Faith.

Seeing she'd lost Rose's attention, Leonie gave up and finished her coffee, thinking about her children. Leo, detached and emotional. Gray, indifferent and cool. And Rose, in this dreadful state.

How did we come to be here? she wondered. How did fourteen years manage to get by us so quickly? How did Leo come to be someone so removed from me? She again remembered Jimmy talking about Leo having to live in society as a bastard. But she hasn't lived as a bastard.

"I sometimes wonder"—she let her thoughts have voice—"if I shouldn't have stopped years ago, with six restaurants. When I think of where we are now . . . It's as if I've created something that's somehow managed to take control of me, when it's supposed to be the other way around. Eleven locations. All that business of incorporating, stock certificates, offices, secretaries, people coming, going, salesmen. And there you have Gray, happily going off to his job every day, not in the least bothered by the constant motion of all the others around him. Such serenity. It was the war, you know, that gave it to him. Back at the beginning, he was quite different. Quite different. But then, I suppose we all were." She stopped, realizing Rose wasn't listening. She continued her thoughts silently.

I think so often now of stopping, letting it all go. But I can't. It's a feeling of having created something that has an impetus entirely its own, a compelling power over me; the challenge, the pride in the responsibility. Is it misplaced? Am

I depriving my family, my children? I should be able to do both. Yet very often it seems I can't. I don't know. I couldn't quietly sit at home now and attend to meals, read. Not when every day there's the company, like a growing child, pulling at me, at my attention. I can't let it go.

"Why don't you take the afternoon off, Rose? Go shopping, have some time to yourself. You look worn out. Perhaps you should just go home and sleep."

"Yes," Rose said abstractedly. "If you really don't mind, I think maybe I will."

Leonie signaled to the waiter, then said, "I'd better be going. I've got a managers' meeting at three, to review the pension program and discuss changing the evening for the cooking class. I think I'd much prefer to go shopping." She smiled. "I'm not at all in the mood to sit and listen to a lengthy list of petty grievances."

"Why *do* you keep on with it?" Rose asked. "You don't need to. You've got Gray, the children, money. What are you doing it for?"

"For me," she said quietly. "For something in me that needs to keep on growing."

"Vanity," Rose said, mildly contemptuous.

"No, Rose. It isn't that and you know it. It's like a second family. A great, squabbling group of relatives. I know all their names, their husbands' names, wives' names, children's names. I know their likes, their dislikes, their little eccentricities. I care about every single one of our people. It's my homestead, my family group, the way it was growing up in Africa, surrounded by family; all working toward a common goal: survival, growth. I depend on them just as much as they depend on me. And I love it all, love them. You have a brother, Rose. I was the only child. All I ever wanted was to really belong on the homestead, to be black, have my earlobes slit, marry, and belong. I was a child then, of course. But the feeling of the family, Rose. It was so strong. My feeling for Lion's is the same. It would be like giving up sixty-odd relatives. I simply couldn't do it."

They left the hotel together and Rose said good-bye, then went off down the street, walking rather directionlessly. Leonie watched her out of sight, then took a taxi back to the office. She still automatically thought of Fifteenth Street when she thought of the office, and wondered if she'd ever become accustomed to the new, large quarters on Madison Avenue. They'd been in this new location for almost three years. Yet every time she came through the door, it was a shock to see the receptionist alone at her island, to continue on through past the two switchboard girls, then the four secretaries, and on into her own office. Directly next door was Rose's office. Dennis across the way, and Alice next door to him. Off the secretarial area was the bookkeeping department, where Bill had his office. And beyond that, the file room. There was a huge conference room beside the reception area, where this afternoon's meeting with the eleven managers would be held.

She knew they wanted stock in the company. And Cavanaugh had advised she offer them a half-share apiece, shares the company would have the right to buy back in the event of any manager leaving the company's employ; shares they did not have the right to sell to anyone outside the company, although they could be sold to other employees. The logistics of it all defeated her. She simply accepted Cavanaugh's advice on most legally related matters—from shares for the employees to the investment of her money and the maintenance of the pension funds. Although she did balk at some of his suggestions for investments, since a great number of his schemes had to do with the stock market, and she'd never been able to make very much sense of the market, so preferred not to invest. For the sake of friendship, though, she'd acquiesced to the point of allowing Arthur a free hand with twenty-five percent of the annual profits. The rest, he assured her, had been carefully placed in nonrisk high-yield investments. Real estate, utilities. She trusted him and paid little attention to his boyish tinkerings with the market. All men, it seemed, suffered an almost hypnotic fascination with the market. Even Jacob Freeman avidly advised her to buy this or that, quite often ringing her up with a "hot tip." She invariably smiled and declined, saying Arthur was doing a fine job managing the company's assets. She did wonder if Gray was also privately enamored of the stock market, but somehow never remembered to get around to asking him about it.

Although she'd refused to allow Lion's to go public—for no more specific reason than her desire to remain, however exhaustedly, in control of what she'd created—there was something Arthur explained to her as the current market value of her shares in the company. And according to his calculations, each share of Lion's stock was worth something close to three thousand dollars. Being the majority stockholder, with seventy-five percent of the stock, it meant that, on paper, Lion's was worth almost one-third of a million dollars.

"Of course," Arthur hastened to explain, "that doesn't include your personal real-estate holdings—the four buildings you now own and lease to the company, or the furnishings and fixtures of any of the locations. The figure's based on net annual yield."

Taking everything into consideration, he told her, Lion's was worth well over a million dollars. Using long-scale projections—dizzying her with his terminology—she could conceivably sell Lion's, right then and there, for a minimum of four million dollars. She simply laughed. To her, it was all columns of figures on paper and had nowhere near the meaning for her that simply visiting each of the locations and chatting with the staff had. That was something real, something tangible. The rest of it was a lot of legal double-talk she hadn't the interest or the energy to unravel. She had seventy-five percent of the shares. Rose had ten. Dennis had five. Alice had five. Bill had five. Now that Dennis was purportedly leaving, those five shares would revert to the company, and instead of having to give the managers five and a half of her personal shares, she'd use Dennis'.

All through the meeting, which was—as she'd predicted—a thinly disguised grievance session, she found herself preoccupied with thoughts of Rose. Something was wrong. Very wrong. And the more she thought about the whole luncheon, the more bothered she became. Until, surprising everyone, she got up and said, "I have an urgent matter to attend to. Alice will take over for me. We'll meet again the same time next week. Do excuse me."

She ran back to her office, grabbed her bag, told Imogene, her secretary, to "Ring home and say I'm with Rose," then flew to the elevator.

The last of the staff had just left University Place, and everything was locked up. Digging about in her bag, she found her set of master keys and let herself in, wondering if she wasn't being ridiculous. Rose was probably still out shopping, or perhaps sitting having a cup of tea upstairs. *But I have to be sure,* she thought, returning the keys to her bag and relocking the door before making her way through to the rear to knock at the sitting-room door. No response. She opened the door.

There was an air of disuse, emptiness about the room, an unnatural stillness. Dust motes hovered in shafts of late-afternoon sunshine from the rear window. She walked over to the staircase door, opened it, and feeling greatly apprehensive, went slowly up the stairs, calling out, "Rose? Are you here?"

She stopped at the top of the stairs, a shiver running the length of her spine as her eyes came to rest on the figure on the bed. For a few seconds she was incapable of movement, her eyes on Rose, her brain telling her: She's asleep. You'll wake her and she'll think you're mad, wondering what on earth you're on about. But she stepped up into the room, setting her handbag down on the floor before proceeding over to stand beside the bed looking down at Rose, eyes narrowed slightly, ears straining to hear.

Her breathing was too shallow, her sleep unnaturally deep.

She made a quick, fruitless search of the room, then took hold of Rose by the shoulders and shook her, loudly asking, "What did you take, Rose? Wake up! What did you take?"

Rose was a limp, heavy doll, her head lolling, hair coming unfastened as Leonie shook her.

Letting her go, Leonie searched the room again, looking for a bottle or container of some sort, something to give her a clue. Nothing. She tore downstairs to the restaurant kitchen, throwing open the pantry door, to find vinegar, soda, mustard. Anything that would upset Rose's stomach sufficiently to make her vomit up whatever she'd taken. She mixed everything in a cup, carried it through to the bathroom, then returned upstairs faced with the problem of how to get Rose down the stairs and into the bathroom. If she attempted to lift her, carry her down, she'd most likely fall attempting to navigate the narrow stairway and end up useless. Her brain working at a frantic speed, she dragged one of the blankets off the bed and spread it on the floor, then tugged and pulled at Rose until she was able to get her down on the floor. Wrapping the blanket around her, gathering the head end, she dragged the blanket and Rose to the top of the stairs, and bracing Rose's head against her calf, began backing down the stairs one at a time, wincing every time Rose's body thudded down another step. Finally managing to get to the bottom, she pulled her into the bathroom, where, with no regard whatsoever for anything but precious time, she unceremoniously tore off Rose's clothes and with a tremendous heave managed to get her into the tub. Then, maneuvering her around so that her back was to the side of the tub nearest Leonie, she held Rose's mouth open, poured in the mixture, and massaged Rose's throat to make her swallow. Satisfied the liquid had gone down, she slipped her arms through Rose's, joined her hands tightly together, and brought them sharply forward up into Rose's stomach. Something she'd many years ago seen her father do to a small Swazi child who'd managed to poison himself by eating the heads of a dozen or so newly blossomed buttercups.

Rose's mouth opened, and fluid gushed out. Leonie did it again twice. Then, fairly certain that most of whatever Rose had taken had been expelled, Leonie left her in the tub while she hurriedly prepared a pot of coffee and set it on the front burner of the stove.

Returning to the bathroom, averting her face from the sight and smell of the sour vomit, she stoppered the tub and began the cold water running full blast.

Starting to come out of her drugged sleep, Rose protested, trying to pull herself away from the rush of cold water. Leonie splashed the water into her face, saying, "Wake up, Rose! Why would you *do* this to yourself, you fool? This is so *idiotic*, Rose! *Come on!*" she shouted. "I'll be *damned* if I'll *let* you *die!*"

When she saw that Rose was past the worst of it, sitting slumped blue-lipped against the side of the tub, Leonie went for the coffeepot and a cup and began forcing the scalding coffee into Rose's mouth. "I hope it burns your imbecilic tongue out!" she shouted, managing to get about half a cup into her before putting the cup to one side, angrily grabbing a handful of Rose's hair, and pushing her head under the water; bringing her up spluttering, thrashing. "You're a *bloody* damned *fool!* I ought to *drown* you!" Leonie shouted.

She let the water run until Rose was up to her armpits in freezing cold water, and went on pouring cups of coffee into Rose's mouth, then dunking her in the cold water until, at last, Rose came sufficiently awake to throw out her hand, muttering, "Stop it!" But the instant Leonie stopped, Rose's eyes slammed closed and she at once slumped back into the water.

"You're not going to get a chance to get used to it!" Leonie said, pulling the stopper. "I'll be just as happy to deal with your having a good whopping case of pneumonia. But there's no way on God's earth I'll let you sleep yourself to death in this bloody bathtub!"

She pulled Rose out of the tub, held her up, and forced more coffee into her mouth, then began marching her back and forth the length of the sitting room until Rose's reflexes started to come back into play and she was moving of her own accord. And becoming very loud in her protestations, trying to push Leonie away.

A second pot of coffee later, Rose sat huddled in a corner of the settee with a cup of coffee in both hands, her hair tangled and wet hanging over her face, her dressing gown haphazardly covering half of her. Beyond caring, she sat staring stupidly into the cup, the gown hanging halfway down one arm, leaving her shoulder and breast exposed.

"You look *bloody pathetic*!" Leonie said furiously, unable to control the complete anger that had had her in its grip from the moment she'd realized Rose wasn't going to die. "You silly bitch! I simply cannot believe that someone as intelligent as you could do something so positively moronic! He's *not* the only damned *man* in the *world*!"

"You don't understand," Rose accused dejectedly.

"Of course not!" Leonie snapped. "How on earth could I *possibly* understand, having led the sheltered life I have? You're behaving like a self-pitying ass! I should have drowned you."

"I wish you had."

"I swear, as God is my witness, if you say one more thing like that, I'll strike you. I'll hit you so hard, I'll . . . Oh, Rose!" she said tiredly. "It's so stupid. You finally, at a very late date indeed, discovered sex. And now you're terrified because you've lost it."

"I love him."

"Rubbish! You love his penis! I never dreamed you were such a silly woman."

"How can you *talk* that way?" Rose was horrified.

"Good Lord, Rose! It's anatomy, having to do with the parts of the body. Not love. None of it has to do with love. Certainly not where you're concerned. Where Dennis was concerned, it did have very much to do with love. It wasn't *he* who used *you*, Rose. It was quite the reverse. And now, since you've very obviously lost him and are devastated at the thought of doing without, I suggest you learn to masturbate if you don't already know how. And before you open your mouth to start telling me how shocked you are at my daring to put words to all these sinister, secret acts we all know about but don't discuss, I want you to know you're coming home with me. I want you where I can see you."

"I don't care," Rose said, making an unsuccessful pass at drawing her dressing gown closed.

Exhausted and more upset than she'd had time to be at any point earlier, Leonie lowered her voice, saying, "I've never been the sort of person to go about telling people all I've done for them. Because I haven't done all that much for anyone, really. But this is the second time I've been frightened out of my wits that I was going to lose you, Rose. Here you sit, up to your eyes in self-pity because after all these years you've lost someone who was never anything less than attractive and most considerate to you. I'm not interested in whose fault it is that it's ended or in what shocking ways you've exercised your body. The fact is, Dennis came along and showed you a side of yourself you'd always been afraid to admit to. You like making love, it's something you need. Now Dennis is gone and you're convinced no other man's ever going to want you. Even if that were the truth—which I doubt very much—there's more to life than just men, more than having climaxes and a body next to yours in the bed. Right now, I need you. For Leo. You're the only one she'll talk to or listen to, and I need you to help her. You owe me that, Rose. I loathe having to put things in those terms. But you do owe me at least that much. You're coming home with me and you're going to stay until you've managed to regain a bit of perspective. And you're going to help Leo. There are all sorts of debts, Rose. We all of us have them. Lord knows, you've helped me any number of times, by being around when I needed someone to hold me, to talk with, to be a friend without passing judgments. I *need* you, Rose. I love you. You're a silly woman, and it's you who has the vanity, not I. Don't throw everything away on a wish to die in order to escape a bit of unpleasantness. I'm going to go up now and collect some of your things. Then I'll ring for a taxi and we'll be leaving."

"I'm sorry," Rose said tearfully. "I'm so ashamed. Of all of it."

"If only you'd talk to me, Rose. There's *nothing* two good friends can't discuss. Not even sex. Put it in back of you now. We're both too old for this nonsense."

Rose put down her cup and stood up, then touched her hair and went off to the bathroom for a towel.

After getting Rose settled into the guest room, Leonie summoned Leo and sat down with her in the master bedroom.

"There is something I want to say to you, Leo." Her manner was so intense, Leo felt afraid. "You are *never* to repeat what I'm going to tell you. Do you understand?"

"Yes." Leo wet her lips.

"Rose tried to kill herself this afternoon."

"Oh, Mummy!" Leo blanched, her eyes growing round. *"Why?"*

"Why isn't important. What is important is what you can do for her."

Leo nodded, listening closely.

"I know you find it difficult to talk to me just now. I also know you feel easier talking to Rose. For her own reasons, Rose is having a problem just now too. Perhaps the two of you can talk to each other. I love you, Leo. You know that, don't you?"

Leo nodded again.

"You weren't a mistake or an accident or something that *happened* to me. I *wanted* you. I want for you what makes you happy. Please, talk to Rose, let her talk to you. Divert her, encourage her to think of anything but her own problems. I think you're grown-up enough to be discreet. Do you understand what I'm asking?"

"I think so." Leo felt strangely elated. "I'll try. What did she do, Mummy?"

"She took poison."

"Poison?"

"She'll be all right. Your father will be home shortly, and I'd like to freshen up a bit. I'm going to trust you to use your own judgment, decide for yourself how you're going to handle the situation. I believe the two of you can help each other. Lord knows, I'm not doing terribly well with either one of you."

"Yes, you are," Leo said softly. "It's just that . . . I don't know . . . It's as if nobody ever *listens* to me."

"We listen, Leo. You simply don't approve of our responses. And I know we don't give you perhaps quite so much time as you need. That *is* my fault, and I'm very aware of it. But be patient with us, darling. Nothing is easy."

"I know, Mummy." Leo offered herself into her mother's embrace. "And I'll try. I really will."

"No one will ever ask more than that of you, Leo."

"I love you, too," Leo whispered, then disengaged herself, and feeling enlarged by her new responsibilities, went out to look in on Rose.

Leonie sat a moment longer, then, with a shuddering sigh, got up to bathe before Gray arrived home.

17

Rose moved into a small apartment in Gramercy Park. And, hating herself for it, thought constantly of Dennis, experiencing a stab of jealousy and anger every time she thought of Dennis and Faith together. She tried not to do it, but there seemed to be something inside her that had to keep going back and forth over the matter ceaselessly, so that she was grateful for anyone or anything that happened along to interrupt her compulsive repeated analyses of how and why it had all turned out as it had.

Angelo, on leave from the army, came to visit. Transformed from a plodding, unambitious boy into a staff sergeant who was decisive, relaxed, confident, he announced his engagement to the daughter of a fellow sergeant. Just as Rose had predicted years before, the army had given Angelo the direction his prior life had failed to provide.

Leo came often, sometimes staying the weekend. And Rose was glad of her presence, even sometimes entered into a private fantasy that Leo was her daughter. And when the two of them were out on the street together, she felt a certain pride in Leo's being with her, in Leo's slow but steady emergence from an outraged puberty into a glowing young womanhood. She looked very much like her mother, but her gray-green eyes and delicately pointed chin made her altogether less overwhelming than Leonie. Whereas Leonie's presence was commanding, quietly authoritative, Leo was simply tall and beautiful, with just the slightest bit of her mother's powerful aura.

Having come through her difficult phase, Leo had become very studious, determined to study medicine.

"Mummy wanted to be a doctor, you know," she said, "when she was growing up in Africa. Of course, that was a long time ago, and things were different then. But I'm going to do it. Lots of women are doctors nowadays."

"I'm sure you'll be a wonderful doctor," Rose said, quite easily able to visualize her in a white coat with a stethoscope around her neck, striding down the corridor of some hospital.

"I will be good," Leo said, reminding Rose of Leonie. Leo, in many ways, was very like her mother. While little Gray seemed the antithesis. Solemn, bookish, rarely given to conversation, an old-looking child with a passion for history and a distant look to his eyes. It was difficult to approach Gray, more difficult to talk to him.

Alone, Rose too often found herself envying Leonie's life. She had the children, and Grayson, the business, her political involvements; so much to occupy her, fill her thoughts. While Rose paced out the weekends idly plotting confrontations between herself and a deeply repentent Dennis, confrontations destined never to materialize anywhere but within the arena of her own imaginings; a fact that only served to heighten her frustration.

She wished desperately someone else would come along to distract her, love her, make love to her. She'd become addicted and felt she'd go mad if she didn't somehow satisfy her cravings. Sitting alone in the apartment, she whispered words to herself that seemed to epitomize everything foul and base she so desired; remembering that afternoon she'd tried to kill herself and Leonie had accused her of being in love with Dennis' penis. Just the word was sufficient to make her cringe at its awfulness, yet go wet with an aching appetite. It was all that way. Every word pertaining to the male or female anatomy was possessed of such a dreadful duality of personal meaning that she couldn't see the words "breast of chicken" printed on a menu without feeling a hot flush of embarrassment and lust spreading over her.

Catching sight of herself in a mirror, she'd stop and stare, hating her face, hating everything about herself, but most especially that segment of her brain housing her private knowledge of intensely meaningful double-sided words. She thought "breast," and at once was acutely aware of her nipples shrinking in anticipation of pleasure. She thought "penis" and contracted moistly, her entire body weakening, going submissively pliant. She went about with her insides roiling, fingernails digging into her palms, feeling like the worst sort of secret deviate, trying frantically to think of some way to occupy herself, take her mind off Dennis and her gaping need to replace him.

Leo, with surprising insight, said, "You spend too much time alone, Aunt Rose. What you ought to do is get out, be with other people more, find something new to do that you enjoy. Like painting, or needlework. A hobby of some sort. It isn't good for anybody to spend too much time alone. Except maybe little Gray, but he's different. Really," she added emphatically, "I know I feel awfully blue if there's no one around and I haven't got anything to do and I'm lonely or bored."

She hadn't done any knitting or crocheting in years, and was disinclined to take it up again now. It seemed too old-womanish. But, inspired, she enrolled for a course in the American novel at the New School; reasoning that she enjoyed reading the books Leonie passed along to her and the course might enlighten her reading.

To her relief, she found she liked the classes and began buying more books, following the recommended reading list given out by the instructor who intrigued and interested her. Her Monday and Thursday evenings now lent some more meaningful focus to her life, and she hurried home from the office those days, eager for what the evening would bring. She'd found a new challenge. His name was Peter Elliott.

Grayson was perfectly contented, perfectly happy. Not that there weren't problems, disagreements. And the difficult patch with Leo upset him badly, feeling, as he did, on a very tentative footing with her at the best of times. She was polite, even occasionally affectionate with him, but held herself away in a fashion that stated unequivocally that although he might have fathered her, it was Jimmy she'd always think of in that capacity. Grayson's role was, he was given by her to feel, only peripheral, his paternity merely a question of incident and not a matter of intimate familiarity. It seemed she placed blame equally upon him and Leonie both for the circumstances of her birth, and also for the fact that for the first five years of her life she'd been Benedict and not Marlowe—as she was now.

"It's her age," Leonie said often. "You take it much too seriously. She'll come round in time."

"Well," he said philosophically, "At least we haven't that problem with young Gray. If anything, he's as uninterested in us as he is in almost everything and everyone else. I think I'd prefer to deal with that than two of them, both filled with galloping animosity."

"Perhaps," she thought aloud, "when he's older, he might decide to come into the business, eventually take over."

"And you'll retire to that imaginary farm in Connecticut and spend your twilight years cultivating herbs and wildflowers."

"I'd like that," she said.

He shook his head. "You'd like it for a month or two, then you'd have to take up something new, something impossibly challenging, something you could shape into a meaningful form for yourself. I think your growing up in Africa had far more influence upon you than anyone realizes."

"Explain that, would you?"

"I'm not sure I'm able. It's simply a feeling I have, one I've always had. One speaks of a 'pride of lions.' I think of your endeavors as the 'lion's pride.' "

"You're an idiot," she said, placing a cold foot on his belly so that he groaned. "I think all men hate competent women."

"You're the idiot," he said, smiling. "Working yourself to death. You could just as easily delegate a bit of authority—"

"Leave it be," she said quietly. "I don't question your work, or the amount of energy you put into it."

"It's hardly the same thing."

"It's hardly different. Leave it be, Gray."

He let it go. And lay back with his arm folded under his head, smoking a cigarette, gazing at the ceiling. For no particular reason, remembering Gray's birth. How she'd sent Amy and Leo out for the evening to Rose. She'd have sent him, too, but he adamantly refused to go. "In case," he'd said, "something happens and you need someone." She'd insisted she needed no one. But he'd taken her completely by surprise by insisting just as strongly on staying. And he had, throughout the entire thing. She'd consigned him to the armchair in the corner of the room where he'd spent the next five hours feeling terrified, astonished, anxious, impotent as Leonie suffered pain he seemed to feel inside himself; able to do no more than bathe her face with a cool cloth and offer her encouragement for a moment or two before she shooed him back to his corner. Naked, her body running with perspiration, she clung to the bedpost, while he saw tremors shake her again and again until he thought he couldn't bear a single moment more of it. But she'd said, "This is right, the way it's supposed to be. There's nothing to fear." And then, before his eyes, she'd gone down on her haunches and delivered their son into his hands. At that point he'd been overcome by the miraculous aspects of the performance and lost all his fear, enveloped in a monumental cloud of loving as he continued to watch—holding the squalling infant in his hands—through to the very last. He'd seen it all, finally, and in the process freed himself forever of a vaguely disquieting anxiety that had always attended his thoughts of women and the birth process. From that point on, he'd felt joined with her by far more than vows and documents.

He smiled now, glancing over at her—she was sitting with her knees drawn up, writing in a small notebook—remembering how he'd looked at the infant after it was cleaned and fed and asleep in her arms, saying, "He looks awfully like Winnie Churchill," and Leonie had asked, "Who's she? One of your English ladies?" And he'd laughed until tears came to his eyes.

"What are you smiling to yourself about?" she asked, putting down the notebook.

"I was remembering your asking me 'Who's she?' about Winnie Churchill."

"You're a clot!" She smiled. "How was I to know Winnie wasn't a woman?"

"He'll be prime minister one day, mark my words. Did you vote?"

"Of course. Did you?"

"Of course. Who did you vote for?"

"Who did you?"

"Hoover. And you?"

"Hoover."

"I had a call from Jacob Freeman today," he said, leaning across to put out his cigarette. "Had another of his 'hot tips' for me."

"I didn't realize he got on to you with them, too. Have you been buying stocks, Gray?"

"Some," he said dismissively. "Have you?"

"Absolutely not. You know, I quite like the idea of a farm in Connecticut. Every so often, walking along the sidewalk, I stop and wonder what on earth I'm doing here, surrounded on all sides by concrete. Then I have to remind myself what it's all for."

"We're not going to get into another discussion of that," he said. "One near-argument is enough."

"You know," she said slowly, "rather too often for my liking, our conversations are ominously reminiscent of those I had with Jimmy. The two of you are very alike in quite a few ways."

"It simply proves you're consistent when it comes to men."

"Rubbish! It simply proves all men have single-track minds. I haven't found too many women getting themselves similarly caught on one thought."

"Except, of course, when it comes to thinking about men. And Rose is a prime example of that."

"Please, don't let's talk about Rose," she said wearily. "She's attached herself to this Peter Elliott, and I've an awful feeling it's going to be Dennis all over again. He's asked her to marry him and she's as adamant as ever she was in refusing. So now he's moved into her apartment and she's going about again with that guilty look of pleasure. She truly does defeat me. It's so terribly obvious that she's highly sexed. But she'd rather die, quite literally, than discuss it. The whole subject to her is equatable with bowel movements and certain types of surgery—simply not talked about. All very shameful and messy. I sometimes worry what's to become of Rose."

Peter was far more sophisticated than Dennis. He was also older, a divorcé, and well-schooled in the art of lovemaking. Rose very quickly became deeply involved and giddily turned herself over to him with abandon, keeping her eyes carefully averted from the sight of her own body, which was changing at a far faster rate than she cared to see. Her breasts were beginning to droop. There was a definite thickening around the middle, and more fullness at the tops of her thighs. But the external changes were far less startling than the evidence of her heightened sexual appetite. She wanted nothing more than to make love, and when she wasn't avidly occupied at it, daydreamed nonstop about the ways in which Peter stimulated her.

She still retained her self-disgust, a small voice in her head that mocked her animal groans and posturings and tormented her when she was away from Peter, leading her to think all sorts of negative thoughts about both him and herself. She was also obliged to spend an annoying amount of time trying to explain why she couldn't and wouldn't get married.

"I'd like to have a family, Rose," he said; "before it's too late and I'm too old."

It frightened her to death.

"I'm too old to have babies," she told him. "Far too old."

"That's not true," he argued. "I don't know what you're so frightened of."

"I am frightened," she admitted. "Could you just accept it and leave it at that?"

"I don't give up that easily."

"I'm not in the mood for talking," she said. And used the only means available to distract him, undressing in the middle of the living room, running her hands over her body until he gave up and took her right then and there, on the floor, not bothering to do more than lower his trousers. She wound her legs around him, closed her eyes, and sighed with pleasure and relief. She'd managed to deflect him again.

It was Peter, the elegant English professor who showed her everything, ultimately, about the dark side of her nature. And like a blinded rabbit caught in the glare of the headlights of an oncoming automobile, she remained frozen, trapped by the compelling horror of her own capacities.

He spread her out naked on the bed and tormented her with a feather, preventing her from moving away by keeping her two hands held tightly above her head. Then, when he'd taken her to the brink of climax, whispered things against her ear that made the blood pound in her head and turned her face brilliant red; insisting she say aloud what it was she wanted him to do. She did it, closed her eyes, and whispered, "Fuck me!" and he put her on her hands and knees and took her, she thought, like an animal. Which, she also thought, she'd become.

Then he pleaded, "Let me watch, Rose. It's so exciting. Do it for me."

What did it matter now? she wondered. And masturbated to orgasm while he stroked her breasts and watched. As a reward, he made her come again with his mouth. Then again by strategically positioning her and plunging into her, as if from some undefined anger, in what felt like an effort to break her in two.

He tied her hands and legs so that she lay spread upon the bed like a sacrificial victim, and then, leaning comfortably between her gaping thighs, closely watching her face and refusing to allow her to move at all, slowly dragged one finger back and forth over her, slowly, slowly, slowly, until she was weeping, begging him to finish it. But he ignored her and kept on until she was electrocuted with pleasure, her skin feeling as if it had split in a hundred places and everything inside her was leaking out through the innumerable rents in her flesh.

It went on for months. Until September of 1929, when, upon arriving home from the office one evening, she discovered he'd gone. All his things had been cleared from the closets, the bathroom, the bedroom, the living room. He'd taken nothing of hers, and had left a note saying, "You and I together aren't healthy. I don't like the man I'm becoming. And I can't like the woman I'm forcing you to be. I am sorry, although I know you won't believe it. And I love you, though I know you won't believe that, either. The thing of it is, if I don't go, we'll both end up destroyed. Peter."

Devastated, enraged, abandoned, she went into the bathroom, snatched up a razor blade, and slashed off most of her hair. The act expressed everything she was unable to say with words. Then, in a state of shock, repeatedly running her hand over her butchered hair—her hair Peter had so loved, complimented, admired—she went out and began to walk; finding herself at two in the morning on the Fifty-ninth Street bridge staring down at the water, summoning the courage to climb the rail and let herself over the edge. She was interrupted by a patrolman named Patrick Sheehan who knew the moment he saw her what her intention was and took her firmly, forcibly by the arm and walked her off the bridge before attempting to talk to her. She went along, docile and silent, unable to answer his questions.

"D'you have any identification on you?" he asked, looking at her hair as she shook her head.

"Is there somebody I can call to come get you?" he asked.

She shook her head again, her only conscious thought being to keep Leonie well out of it this time.

"What'm I to do with you?" he said, pushing his cap back on his head with the tip of his nightstick.

"Take me home," she said in a whisper.

He looked at his pocket watch and said, "I'm off duty now. I'll just phone in from the box over there"—he pointed, leading her along by the arm—"then I'll take you home. Where d'you live?"

"Gramercy Park."

"Thank the good Lord for that." He smiled. "A trip to the Bronx or Queens is the last thing on my mind this time of the night."

She stood shivering as he made his call, and he studied her, wondering what would possess a fine-looking woman like her to do whatever it was she'd done to her hair, then decide to throw herself off a bridge. He completed the call, again took hold of her arm, and said, "I'll buy you some coffee. You look half-frozen."

She wrenched herself away from him, her hand going to her hair, saying, "No!"

"All right, now," he said calmly, his hand solid again on her arm, "don't get yourself worked up. I'll let you give me breakfast. Can you cook?"

"In 1914 I was on my lunch break one afternoon and saw a 'HELP WANTED' sign in a window. That was one of the first things Leonie asked me." She smiled, remembering. How young we were, she thought. Oh, God! We were so young. She smiled. And Pat was captivated by the loveliness of her smile, the way it changed her face.

"And what did you answer?" he asked, directing her across an intersection.

Still smiling, remembering so clearly, she said "I think I said, 'I know how to eat.' Dear God, we were so young! I was so *young*!" She turned large, liquid eyes upon him. "Do you ever feel that way: that you were terribly young once upon a time and you woke up this morning to find yourself old and it was such a shock. An awful shock. Do you ever?"

"Oh, sometimes."

"Where are we going?" she asked, adrift, disoriented.

"Downtown," he replied. "Taking you home. What's your name?"

"Rose Manero."

"Patrick Sheehan. What sent you to the bridge tonight, Rose?"

"I'm tired. Tired of everything. Mostly me. Tired of me. Are you ever tired of you?"

"Wouldn't be natural if a person didn't get fed up with himself every now and again."

"Am I acting like someone who's crazy?" she asked, again fixing those dark eyes on him.

"A bit. I'm not bothered."

"I don't know how I feel," she said, dazed, his hand on her arm keeping her moving. "Are we going to walk all the way home?"

"Too far for you?"

"Twenty years ago, I often walked from Brooklyn, over the bridge to my job in Manhattan. The last five years, I don't think I've walked more than three blocks."

"Do you good," he said. "Clear your thoughts."

"It would take more than a long walk to do that."

"Seems to me, Rose, you want either to be crazy or dead. If it was me making the choice, I'd choose crazy. That way, you can always change your mind and decide to come back. You can't come back from the bottom of the river."

"I don't know what there is to come back to. That's the problem. I keep on making the same mistake over and over. Are you married? Do you have a family waiting for you somewhere?"

"I'm just an old bachelor." He laughed a soft laugh.

"I'm not drunk, you know. I haven't been visiting some bootleg place."

"Didn't think you had."

She stopped walking, pulling back against his hand so that he, too, stopped.

"Do I look like someone you'd care to make love to?"

"You're not going to proposition an officer of the law, are you, Rose?"

"I'm asking you a question. Would you?"

"I might," he said consideringly. "Depending on the circumstances."

"Why do you call yourself 'an old bachelor'? Are you so old?"

"Forty-four."

"I'm getting on for thirty-eight," she said, saying the numbers as if they represented decades and not individual years. "I lived with Dennis for almost ten years." She began walking again. "He wanted to get married. I kept saying no. He finally married someone else, someone younger. For a long time I kept imagining myself running into him in the street, or in some restaurant, and being very cool, very in control . . . of everything. Making him suffer. But I already did that."

"Did what?"

"Made him suffer. By saying no all those years. I had two abortions. Awful. *Awful!* My God, *God,* it was awful! He hit me. Said it wasn't my right to do that without even telling him, asking him. But I couldn't. I wouldn't end up like Mama. With the roaches in the sink and the water bugs, the silverfish. Then, today . . . When I came home from the office, Peter was gone. He said in his note we weren't healthy together. As if I had some kind of disease. It feels that way, sometimes. Like a disease. *Wanting.* A sickness."

"And so you cut off your hair," he said. "To punish yourself for the wanting."

She looked at him in surprise, then moistened her lips and said, "Yes, that's right. How do you know?"

"It's not hard to understand. Not a good enough reason to jump off the bridge, though."

"Why can't it just be a matter of two people giving each other what they need and being happy together? Why can't it just be that? Instead of wanting marriage and children and things I can't give, don't want to have to give. Why can't it be what I *can* give?"

"Maybe, Rose, it has to do with how much you can *take* and not what you're able to give."

"How?"

"Maybe it's that you find it easier giving. Takes a bit of learning how to take, knowing when enough is enough. We're almost there now." He guided her across Twenty-third Street. "Tell me," he said. "What do you do with yourself, Rose?"

"Do you know Lion's?"

"Of course."

"I'm vice-president of the company."

'That's very impressive." He took another look at her. Then laughed that soft laugh. "Your Leonie gave the boys downtown one hell of a time a few weeks back for that raid on the Sanger clinic, arresting those nurses and doctors."

"She's always supported Mrs. Sanger."

"And do you?"

"I don't take stands on things the way Leonie does."

"Sounds to me as if you do."

"Does it?"

"All that about not getting married, not having children, not wanting to end up like your ma with the roaches, all of that. Sounds like a stand to me."

"I've never thought of myself as someone . . . Just around the corner here."

"As someone what?" he prompted, interested.

"Someone with the right to take stands. Do you really want breakfast?"

"Feel like cooking?"

She thought about it. "I haven't eaten today. I'm hungry."

"Okay." He smiled. "So long as you don't mind if I take my boots off. The feet get tired after eight hours on the beat."

"Is it because you're a policeman?" she asked.

"What?"

"You understand so well. How is it that you do?"

"It's what I'm good at," he said simply. "Like you're too good at giving."

She smiled again, and he followed her inside.

18

The third week in October that year, Gray telephoned Leonie at the office. She knew at once, simply from the tone of his voice, that something dreadful had happened, and listened, fearing one of the children had had some sort of accident.

"The bottom's falling out of the market," he said a little breathlessly. "Everyone's selling, dumping their stock. There's a veritable panic on Wall Street."

"Gray," she asked quietly, "did you invest after all, darling?"

"Almost everything," he said, sounding ill. "I rang my broker. He said not to move. It was just temporary and would pass."

"Well, then . . ."

"This *isn't* going to pass, Leonie. I think you'd better get on to Arthur Cavanaugh and find out exactly what the company's status is. And your own, as well. People are going mad. I can't stay on the line. The entire editorial staff is going crazy trying to handle all the reports and calls. I just wanted to let you know, tell you to ring Cavanaugh."

He broke the connection and she sat staring at the receiver before putting it down. Then picked it up again and dialed Cavanaugh's number. His secretary said, "He isn't in just now. May I have him call you?"

She left her name, asked that he get back to her as soon as possible, then went down the hall to have a talk to Bill, the bookkeeper.

"What is our financial status right now?" she asked, wondering if Gray wasn't overstating the case simply because he'd invested unwisely.

"Oh, very good!" He smiled, inviting her to sit down.

"Could you give me a quick overall picture so that I'm able to understand, Bill? In simple terms."

"Okay." He got up and went over to the metal storage cabinet and came back with two heavy black ledgers and a large checkbook. "Anything wrong?" he asked, sensing her nervousness.

"I'm not sure. Just tell me what we owe, what's on hand, and accounts receivable. I'd like to make a note of the figures." She sat with a pencil and a piece of paper at the ready, waiting while Bill scanned the checkbook entries, then referred to the accounts-receivable and accounts-payable ledgers, jotting numbers down on a ruled pad. He ran a tape on the adding machine, then closed the ledgers and picked up the pad, saying, "Okay. Very roughly, here's how it looks. The figures on both sides of the ledgers are a little high, what with the end of the month coming up. But we've got about eighty-four thousand cash on hand in the bank. And accounts payable as of today of just over thirty thousand. Leaving an approximate balance of fifty-four thousand. Accounts receivable runs about six thousand. Nothing significant."

"I see," she said, looking at the figures she'd written down. "What are our monthly expenses overall?"

"Between twenty-five and thirty thousand."

"And our monthly income?"

"Between sixty and eighty."

"So, we've been running at a profit of between thirty and fifty thousand dollars a month?"

"Not quite. That doesn't take into consideration taxes, or extras like replacement of certain furniture and fixtures, Christmas bonuses, the pension-plan contributions, fluctuating costs on a lot of things."

"What about my personal accounts? What are the balances on my checking and savings accounts? Also, I'd like to know what there is in the investment and pension accounts for the company, as well as what's in my personal portfolio. Will you get back to me with the information?"

"An hour," he said, returning the ledgers to the cabinet, reaching for another set of books.

She went back to her office and sat down, trying to determine how, if at all, the stock market might affect her personally and the company. At that moment she couldn't see that she'd be affected at all. And over lunch, she related to Rose the details of Gray's call.

"What does it mean?" Rose asked, paling.

"I'm not completely certain. He seems to think the market's going to collapse altogether. Everyone's apparently caught up in some sort of panic, selling shares by the millions."

"Pat's got his entire life savings invested in stocks," Rose said softly. "Everything. My God! Does this mean he'll lose it all?"

"According to Gray, it does."

"But he could be wrong, couldn't he?"

"Don't upset yourself before you know what's happening, Rose. Wait until you've got some facts to deal with."

"What will happen to Lion's?"

"As far as I can so far tell, very little. Most of our working capital is safely in the Bank of New York. I've never believed in gambling in the market. Gray, though, says he's put everything of his into stocks. He sounded so upset. You haven't invested, have you?"

"Me? Oh, no! I've kept my money in a savings account at the bank. What about you?"

"The same. Except for a small amount I've allowed Arthur to invest." Talking about Arthur, she was suddenly very doubtful. Surely he wouldn't . . . She didn't dare allow herself even to think about it. She smiled over at Rose, saying, "Your hair's growing in nicely. What on earth possessed you to do that?"

"Self-pity. Anger. I'm not having an affair with Pat, you know."

"I actually hadn't thought about it. I mean, I have, but . . ."

"I know. We're friends, Leonie. We *talk*. I never seemed able to with Peter or Dennis. It was more like constant arguing. They said what they wanted. I said what *I didn't* want. And then we were off, going around and around, arguing about wanting, not wanting. Pat isn't like that. He's been on days for the last few weeks and we've spent almost every evening together. Just talking. About so many things. I've never had a man friend before. But we're . . . *easy* together. I discuss things with him I've never been able to talk about to anyone. You know what I mean."

"Yes."

"The one time I did try . . . you know . . . to get him interested, he said I should stop all that and just relax. And I actually can relax with him. Because I don't always have the feeling that, in the back of his mind, he's just waiting for the right moment to jump on top of me." Color flooded her face, but she kept her eyes on Leonie's. "Not," she went on, "that I wouldn't like that. Because I would. It's just not what he likes about me, I guess."

"He sounds like a fine man, Rose. Perhaps you'd like to bring him round to dinner one evening."

"Yes, perhaps. . . ."

By Thursday of that week, everyone knew disaster had struck. Greatly alarmed at being unable to reach Arthur Cavanaugh, she was on the verge of going around to call on him at home when Gray telephoned her at the office to say, "I don't quite know how to put this. I've just received a hand-delivered letter for you, from Cavanaugh. I think I know why he sent it here. In any event, you'd better meet me at home. I can't discuss this with you over the telephone."

"What's happened?"

"I'll tell you when I see you. There's one other piece of news, too, I'm afraid."

"Oh, Lord! What?"

"Jacob's committed suicide. I'm terribly sorry, Leonie. I know how very fond you were of him. It's a nightmare," he said. "Men are jumping out windows, putting guns in their mouths, leaping under trains. I'll meet you at home in an hour."

Trembling, she sat staring sightlessly at the top of her desk, trying to absorb the fact of Jacob's death, trying to understand why. She thought of Anne, and wanted to go to her, offer her something—help, sympathy. Had it not been for them, she'd never have succeeded as she had. She pushed her feet into her shoes, stiffly got up and walked out of her office. The place was abnormally silent. Lunchtime. Only Bill was hard at it, eating a sandwich brought from home as he worked at a ledger.

She looked in at him, noticing he'd lost most of his hair. Fifteen years ago, he'd had a headful of wavy brown hair. A thin young man newly armed with a diploma and eagerness, he'd worked for seven different companies, back then. Half a day here, a day there. For the last eleven years he'd been a full-time employee of Lion's. He'd grown a small paunch, married, had two children, lost his hair. He was highly paid, totally trusted, and happy at his work.

"I'm going home, Bill. Will you tell Imogene when she returns from lunch?"

"Okay. Anything wrong?"

"Everything, from the sound of it. I'll see you in the morning."

She opted to walk home, needing time both to prepare herself for what—judging from the tone of Gray's voice—was sure to be more bad news, and also to try to come to terms with the fact of Jacob's suicide. He'd killed himself, taken his life. Why? Men jumping out windows, putting guns in their mouths.

The *Times* that morning had reported on a nationwide stampede to unload stocks, but said the banks would attempt to support the market. It neither sounded especially hopeful nor looked very good, seeing the list of stocks, their loss in points, their depreciation. She walked along wondering: Will we lose everything now? Will it all come tumbling down around us? What will Hoover do? Can he do anything?

For the first time in years she found she was frightened. Things were happening over which she hadn't any control whatsoever. And these things would directly touch all their lives. Overcome by a stifling sense of helplessness, she made her way home dreading finding out what was in that hand-delivered letter from Cavanaugh; telling herself that whatever happened, she wouldn't panic. And she'd make some effort to contact Anne.

It was far worse than she could possibily have imagined.

"He invested all of the company's and your personal capital in the market," Gray told her, looking and sounding dumbfounded. "Every cent of it. There's nothing left."

"But he wasn't to invest more than twenty-five percent of the company profits, and not my personal funds. What about all the securities, the utility companies he invested in for me?"

"He put everything into the market. It's all gone."

"The company money, too?"

"Everything. And he's run off."

"Run off?"

"Gone. Saying he's sorry and all the rest of it. My God! He's *sorry*! Leonie, neither of us has any savings left. And I'm very much afraid this is only the beginning. I don't believe this is something that's simply going to blow over in a week or two."

"Everything's gone," she said, feeling ill. "Everything both of us have worked so hard for. I must think. I have to think." She began pacing back and forth across the bedroom, trying to align her thoughts. "I feel so frightened," she said, opening and closing her hands. "I've got to think this through."

"It's not as if we're destitute, by any means," he said with a bluff heartiness. "I've my salary, and you've the income from the restaurants."

"Gray, if a great number of people have lost all their money, there are going to be far fewer people paying to eat in restaurants. If people don't spend money to buy their breakfast or midday meal, but bring their food from home—or even go without—in very short order Lion's will be out of business. I've simply got to get this straight in my head. *Now.* Before anything further happens. We must be prepared for every conceivable eventuality. At least, as best we are able. There's no chance of your being let go by the paper, is there?"

"Very doubtful," he said consideringly. "I think they'll let the secretarial and junior staff go before they get to the point of cutting back on the senior editors. And that's unlikely. They've got to have staff to get the paper out."

"The thing to do," she said, pacing more quickly, "is to somehow keep everything going, cut down in areas where it won't show. We'll move the offices back to Fifteenth Street, save right there on that whopping great rental. We don't need all that space. Tomorrow I'll sit down with Bill and work out to the penny precisely what profit we realize on every meal we serve. I think if we reduce the portions ever so slightly and lower the price five or ten cents, we'll be able to keep going. Lion's has always been attractive because of good food at a very reasonable price. We're still among the least-expensive restaurants in the city. We'll just have to become even less expensive, without lowering the quality of either the food or the service. No one's to be let go. No one. But how am I going to tell them that Arthur squandered all their pension money? Oh, *Lord*! It's a bloody good thing he's run away. Bad enough to have thrown away all my savings, not to mention all the company profits. But the employees, their contributions. I'd like to kill him!"

She stopped pacing and stared at him. "We're going to move Gray! We pay far too much rent for this place. We'll save over four hundred dollars a month if we move."

"Where?"

"I have all my Liberty Bonds!" she realized excitedly. "And there's a good fifty thousand clear still in the company account at the bank. The banks! What do you suppose will happen now to them?"

"I think you should get down there first thing in the morning and withdraw everything you have. The whisper going round the paper is that the banks are going to start closing right, left, and center. If that does happen, you'll never see the money again. Withdraw it and we'll keep it somewhere safe until the banks have stabilized. Then, when everything has steadied, you'll be able to return your money to the bank without fear of losing it. And cash in the bonds. I think our only hope—all the way round—is to convert everything to cash and work strictly on that basis. How much do you have in the bonds?"

"Quite a lot, I think. Seventy thousand, at least. But what if they refuse to allow me to withdraw the money?"

"They won't. Not yet. It's still too early on."

"We'll *buy* a place, Gray, use some of the bond money to buy a house instead of simply throwing money away on rent month after month. We'll go up to Connecticut this weekend and find something suitable. We've got the car. I can't see any reason why we couldn't very easily travel back and forth each day. The train. Or the car. And I'd forgotten! There are the children's savings accounts. I must gather my wits about me, sit down, and make a list of just exactly what we do have left."

There was no answer when she rang the Freemans' apartment. She made a note to remind herself to try again the next day from the office.

First thing the next morning, along with Rose and Bill, she went to the bank to present the company statements, the children's passbooks, and after clearing her safe-deposit box, her bonds; requesting cash.

The vice-president with whom she dealt lifted his eyebrows, saying, "We don't have this sort of cash on hand, Mrs. Marlowe. It'll have to be brought up from downtown. That may take a bit of time."

"We'll wait!" she announced.

A little over three hours later, they left the bank. Bill, in his briefcase, was carrying $189,612.37. Of that, $8,812.37 belonged to the children; $81,000 was from the bonds. And the nearly $100,000 remaining belonged to the company. Bill was gray with fear at carrying such a large amount of money and kept looking around nervously as if fully expecting a gang of thugs to jump out of a doorway and relieve him of his burden.

In her handbag, Rose carried her lifetime savings of some twelve thousand dollars. She wasn't in the least nervous and sat in the taxi glancing over at Bill every so often, for some reason wanting to laugh.

Upon arriving back at the office, Leonie turned the briefcase over to Gray, who was waiting to collect it. Arrangements had already been made to store the money in a safe place for the present. That done, Leonie instructed Rose to inform their landlords that they would be vacating the premises by the fifteenth of November. "Make all the arrangements for the move. And get Alice to help you. When you've done that, I want you to contact the staff at all locations and advise them there will be a general meeting here on Monday after-hours. I expect *everyone* to attend. Anyone who fails to be present needn't return to work Tuesday morning. I also want you to prepare a list of all the furnishings here that are dispensable. Then arrange to have them sold. We're going to turn everything we possibly can into cash. Take as many of the secretaries and operators to help you as you need."

She and Bill then closed themselves into her office with the full set of books and began working out the profit margins.

Friday night, Leonie and Grayson had a family conference with Leo, Gray, and Amy to advise them of the move out of the city and of the various other changes that would be implemented. To everyone's surprise, it was little Gray who was most upset, angrily demanding to know, "What am I going to use for a *library*? And where am I going to go to *school*? And what am I going to do in *Connecticut*? And where am I going to go for *walks*? What am I going to use for *museums*? And *art galleries*? *I won't go!*" He then burst into tears and stood red-faced and bleating, waiting for answers.

For one of the few times in his life, he went into the embrace Leonie offered him and clung to her, sobbing. "I'll *hate* it! I'll have nothing to do and nowhere to go! Don't make me go! *Please*!"

"There'll be lots of things for you to do, darling," she told him gently. "They have libraries and very fine schools and lovely places to walk. You'll see. You might find you even prefer it to the city. It's lovely and quiet and you can hear the birds, walk on grass, Gray. All the things you've never been able to do here, living in the city. There isn't a choice involved, darling. It's something we've got to do."

He was, she thought, almost as inconsolable as Leo had been when Jimmy died. It was a little gratifying to know he was capable of such strong, positive feelings. She stroked and patted him, enjoying this rare opportunity to hold his little boy's body in her arms as Leo asked, "Are we going to be poor now?"

"We've never been *rich*!" Leonie answered sharply. "Not in the sense you mean it. And we're certainly not going to be poor. We're just going to be . . ."

"Careful," Grayson finished for her. "We're all going to be very sensible and very careful from here on in about how we spend our money. Amy," he asked, "how does all this sit with you?"

"Don't make no never-mind to me," she said. "Ain't nothing here I'll miss all that much."

The property on Round Hill Road in Greenwich included a guesthouse, a triple-car garage with an apartment over it, and three acres of land. The house itself was large, with eight rooms, and in excellent repair. Their offer was accepted that same afternoon by the wife of a broker who'd jumped to his death from his office window two weeks earlier. They drove back to the city in somewhat higher spirits, although, privately, Leonie felt bothered at profiting from someone else's loss. But little Gray grudgingly admitted he thought it "might be nice."

The move was accomplished very quickly, the children enrolled in school, and arrangements were made for the installation of a wall safe in the master bedroom. That done, Gray placed the cash inside and closed the thick steel door with an audible sigh of relief. Thereafter, one or the other of them carried in the cash Lion's required each week to pay rentals, expenses, salaries, and general overhead. And the weekly receipts from all the locations traveled out with them in the same fashion.

The employees, at first loudly dismayed and upset over the loss of their pension money, soon quieted down to hear what Leonie had to say.

"First of all, I know it's highly unorthodox, but I'm going

to advise every one of you who has money in the bank to remove it. Hide it away somewhere safe and pay in cash for everything from now on. The banks, it seems, are going to fail just as the market has done, and I should very much hate to see any of you lose your savings.

"Secondly, we've always given a fine meal at a fair price, and we'll continue to do so. But we're going to try for far less waste and more savings, slightly smaller portions and a lower cost per meal. As for your pension money, bear with me. Let's get through this. And once we do, you have my word that I will restore that fund if it takes every last cent I have to do it. I know you've all worked hard and contributed to the fund in good conscience. Bill has complete records of all the contributions, and Lion's guarantees to undertake to reestablish the lost funds. I'll leave it up to you to decide if you wish to continue contributing. Under the circumstances, I think it would be unfair of me to insist upon it as a company policy.

"I will not close one location! We will stay open, and we will, as we've always done, serve the best-quality food in the best-possible fashion. We are a family. If one of you has a problem, we all do, and I want to know about it. The only way we can possibly survive is to work together—without petty squabbles—and be conscientious in our efforts. I want to thank every one of you for being here today. I know it means being late home to your families, delayed dinners, and rides, for many of you, on crowded subways. They say there are going to be hard times ahead. No matter what happens, every Lion's location will remain open. Are there any questions?"

No questions.

Rose asked if she could move back to University Place.

"I don't want to waste my money on rent. And I also don't need anywhere near the hundred dollars a week I'm being paid. I want to go on quarter salary starting right now. And Alice has asked to go on half salary. We've talked it over and we both agree."

Speechless, Leonie embraced her.

"The guest cottage is empty, Rose. You're welcome to it."

"I think I'd prefer to stay in the city, near Pat. He's very down now. But thank you. Maybe we could come up some weekend."

"Anytime. Leo misses you."

"How are the kids liking it there?"

"Leo's fine. Gray's complaining a good deal less, settling in."

"I miss them," Rose said.

"We're going to make it through this, Rose. Or bloody well die trying."

19

Gradually, "TO LET" signs appeared here and there. There were fewer automobiles on the streets. Factories went over to half-time. Weeds began to grow in the crevices of unfinished buildings. There were long lines of depositors standing outside all the banks, jostling for places in line. And Pat told Rose, "Every cop on the force wonders every week if we're going to have a payday. Things look black." The New York Bank of the United States failed. And a million people—one-sixth of the city's population—lost their savings.

Gray, upon occasion driving into the city, while stopped for a light, found himself being solicited by well-dressed young women. Out-of-work secretaries.

The newspapers became thinner and thinner as advertising became less and less. And as he'd predicted, the secretaries and junior staff at the paper were let go. The billboards, one after another, went blank. Doormen disappeared from office buildings, and no one was in the elevators.

Elmer Davis, a reporter friend of Gray's, said, "I looked up at the sky the other night and saw a sixty-story city empty above the twentieth floor. And I thought to myself: these buildings will stand empty for decades and our descendants will compare them to the pyramids and the great structures of the Roman Empire, architectural monuments to an age of faith. They will never be of use to anyone, save the artists of some future Romantic movement who will find inspiration in the ruins of the never-completed Empire State Building at Fifth and Thirty-fourth."

And A. W. Mellon, the secretary of the treasury, publicly, blithely stated, "It will purge the rottenness out of the system.

High costs of living and high living will come down. People will work harder, live a more moral life. Values will be adjusted and enterprising people will pick up the wrecks from less competent people."

Infuriated, frustrated, Grayson took to writing his journal once more. He simply couldn't trust himself to talk rationally, without anger, about someone like Mellon who believed in the survival of the fittest and that traditional American charity would take care of those in distress.

Hoover organized "Buy Now" movements to combat slipping prices. And for a few months the country appeared to be in good shape, with more goods being produced each week than had been turned out in a month before the war.

But by the spring of 1930, if a "MEN WANTED" sign appeared, police had to be called out to hold back the crowds seeking jobs. And farm prices kept dropping. Hoover studied the still-declining stock market, the reports of failed banks, and set up the President's Committee for Unemployment Relief, which consisted of three thousand local groups working to see that no one went hungry. Leonie took charge of one of the groups and began staying through the week in the city, returning home to Connecticut only on weekends. She donated as much as Lion's possibly could afford in the way of food, to the soup kitchens; asking for volunteers from her own staff to help man the kitchens, serve.

It shattered her, one evening, to find herself dishing up soup to Dennis Riley, who, upon accepting his bowl, raised his head to say, "Thank you," then closed his eyes as if he'd been stricken a blow at recognizing her.

She summoned over one of the girls to take her place and went to sit down with him, asking, "Are things very bad, Dennis?"

"I was one of the last they hired, so one of the first they let go. And Faith's pregnant, not working now. We're using up our savings."

"I am so sorry, Dennis. What will you do?"

"I've been out all day every day trying to find work. Anything. There's nothing to be had, Leonie. I'm just one of thousands of guys all telling their wives they're going out for an interview, then standing on street corners panhandling nickels and dimes. I don't mind so much for me. But Faith, being pregnant . . ."

"Dennis, I haven't got a single opening anywhere. Not even for a busboy or a dishwasher. But I do have an empty guest cottage. And if it wouldn't offend you, Amy could use a hand with the heavy work around the house, shoveling the snow, odds and ends. You might do a bit of driving for us now and then. I'd like to help. You always worked very hard for the company. I don't want it to sound as if we're offering charity, but we've only been in Connecticut for a few months and there's far more work running the place than I'd imagined there would be. Especially since I've been staying in town and only going up on weekends. Very often Gray stays in as well, which leaves Amy and the children alone up there. I'd feel a good deal better if I knew there was someone around to keep an eye on things, help out."

She discreetly turned away to give Dennis time to recover himself. Finally, his voice clotted, he asked, "How's all that going to sit with Rose?"

"Rose doesn't run Lion's or my life! I love her dearly, but she doesn't make my decisions. Whatever problems you had, had to do with the two of you, not with me. I was sorry to have you leave the company. I'm sorry to find you now in this predicament. I'm offering you what I can. There's no money. The cottage is very small and not terribly warm. But there's food and shelter and work to do, and you're welcome to it."

"I know it'll make all the difference in the world to Faith. She's been so worried, and trying to keep me from knowing. Bless you," he said. "You won't be sorry."

"It's very little, Dennis."

"No, no! It's everything! Everything! If you don't mind, I'm going to run right home now and tell Faith."

"Meet me at Fifteenth Street at four o'clock Friday afternoon. I'll arrange to have Gray collect us there with the car."

He shook her hand and went hurrying out, his overcoat flapping open. She sat a moment longer wondering what was happening to the world. Everything was rushing backward at a terrifying rate. But there was little time to dwell on it. She was too busy running the company, working with the relief group, and campaigning for Roosevelt's reelection as governor of New York; confident, as was Gray, that Roosevelt would, in time, seek to run for president.

When, in November, he was reelected with a record majority, Gray declared it was the first hopeful sign in a very long while. But his elation was short-lived. On February 27, 1931, The *World* closed down, putting out their last issue. And it seemed, talking to newspaper friends who were now out of jobs, that the Depression was nowhere near the end Hoover had so optimistically been predicting.

When she arrived back at the office one afternoon, there was a message for Leonie. She went out to ask Imogene, "Who left this message?"

"I did, Leonie."

"Who called?"

"Some man. He didn't leave his name. He just said to tell you Mrs. Freeman died last week of a stroke and was buried Friday before sundown. I'm sorry."

"Oh, Lord," she said, starting to cry. "So am I."

Excerpts from Grayson's Journal

5th March, 1931

Germany and Austria moving toward possible merger. France menaced by proposed amalgamation working for discriminatory import quotas, unfavorable currency-exchange rates, rail rate increases, closed markets.

9th April, 1931

Austrian bank system beginning to collapse as bills held by foreigners are being presented for immediate payment. We are witnessing what will be a worldwide entry into the Depression.

L. driving herself very hard, constantly fretting over the business, working with Bill at the figures. One has to admire her almost fanatic adherence to promises made.

7th May, 1931

Frederick Sackett, U.S. amb. to Germany, today arrived in Washington to report to Hoover that Ger. chancellor, von Bruning, says Ger. facing economic ruin. Also a letter for Hoover from President von Hindenburg saying: "The need of the German people has reached a climax that compels me to adopt the unusual step of addressing you personally. . . . All possibilities of improving the situation by domestic measures without relief from abroad are exhausted." More simply, they are begging for help. We haven't any to give them.

21st May, 1931

Situation worsens everywhere—Austria, Central Europe. All the banks are tottering. Hoover quoted as sighing, "It's a cruel world," upon receipt of further bad reports. How frightfully profound!

1st June, 1931

European banks failing one after another. Wholesale executions of dissidents reported in Hungary; pogroms in Poland; British troops firing on Indian mobs; one coup after another in Latin America. Monstrous series of political assassinations moving Japan toward possible civil war. Foreign buying here almost completely stopped.

17 June, 1931

Gr. Brit. has gone off gold standard. Seventeen other nations following suit. Rumors of suppressed mutiny in Royal Navy. More Amer. banks failing. Everyone becoming critically disenchanted with Hoover. A pity. A fine man in the right office at the wrong time.

L. working passionately for Roosevelt, who we expect will announce his candidacy for pres. early next year. Leo has asked to help L. now she is home from college for summer. Gray always to be found in crook of second branch of maple near guest cottage. With a book. Or in the garage apartment—empty, disused, foully dirty . . . we must put the place to some good use—playing elaborate games with his soldiers. Strange, unpredictable little chap. But he's settled in well.

20th June, 1931

Hoover has proposed international moratorium on war reparations and war debts. His first important act to try to break international financial panic. It won't work.

26th July, 1931

Panic worse.

30th September, 1931

305 banks closed. Leo has returned to college, Dennis driving her to Bronxville and back each day.

12th October, 1931

522 more banks closed. People are hoarding. A rare treat these days, L. and I attended opening of new Elmer Rice play *Counsellor-at-Law*. Fine bit of work woven round beauty-and-the-beast fable. L. looking very tired these days, thinner.

26th December, 1931

Family outing—via complimentary reviewer's tickets—to attend opening of *Of Thee I Sing*. Marvelous. Leo singing all the way home. In enviably high spirits, happy and pulling down splendid grades. She'll do it! L.'s daughter all the way.

Rose was surprisingly sympathetic to the news that Dennis and Faith were occupying the guest cottage and that Faith had given birth to a little boy.

"Whatever went wrong," she said expansively, "was at least fifty percent my fault. And probably more. I'd like to send them something I've made for the baby. Do you think they'd be offended?"

"I think they'd be thrilled. How is Pat?"

Rose did something she hadn't done in quite a long time: she blushed. And Leonie knew instantly they'd become lovers.

"I take it he's very well indeed," Leonie couldn't resist teasing.

"I'm very happy." Rose laughed. "Very happy."

It had happened when she'd least expected it. Pat had come by at two-thirty in the morning, rousing her from a sound sleep. She'd run downstairs barefoot in her nightgown to open the front door and let him in, anxiously asking, "Is anything wrong, Pat?"

"I've been tramping back and forth along that beat all night in the miserable cold asking myself what am I waiting for. Asking myself. I didn't have an answer."

"Come into the kitchen," she urged. "It's very cold out here. I'll put on some coffee. Are you hungry? Have you eaten?"

"Hold on a minute, Rose." He grabbed her arm, stopping her. "Don't go rushing off. Let me say what I came to say."

"All right," she agreed, standing with one foot resting on the instep of the other, trying not to shiver, a little afraid.

"Walking out there, seeing people sleeping in doorways looking like bundles of rags, Rose. Dragging a poor immigrant woman away from the window of the bank. God knows how long she'd been there! Screaming she wanted her money, they had to give her her money. It's so damned bleak. And I'm walking thinking I don't have the heart to make some devil move from that doorway because he'll just go to sleep in some other one. Asking myself, what am I waiting for. Almost two years now, we've been sharing a lot of meals, drinking a lot of coffee, talking the nights away I don't know how many times. I want you, Rose. Right now, right this minute. If I don't touch you, don't have someone to hold on to, I'm going to go crazy. Maybe I'm already crazy. Look at me, keeping you standing here shivering while I'm making speeches. I want to spend the night. Will you sleep with me, Rose?"

"I'll make you some coffee. You can take a good hot bath."

"You're not answering me!"

"I *am* answering you. I'm saying I'll make some coffee, something for you to eat while you take your bath."

"Is that yes or is that no?"

"It's yes," she said, and stood on tiptoe to give him an openmouthed kiss that made him think he'd been a champion fool wasting all those nights. She took a step away, smiling, saying, "I'll put on the coffee."

He said, "People are dying, Rose. In the doorways, on the sidewalks."

"I know, Pat," she said, understanding fully his meaning. "I know."

She sat beside him in bed with a cup of coffee and watched him eat, then set the tray and her cup aside, lifted her nightgown off over her head, directed his hand between her thighs, and opened her mouth over his. Two years of demoralizingly attending to her own needs, and otherwise abstaining, now seemed an agonizing length of time to have gone untouched. He thought she was what he'd always suspected: hotly potent.

Without further preliminaries, she sat astride his lap and he ecstatically closed his hands over her breasts as she began to quiveringly rise and fall, lifting more and more quickly so that within less than two minutes she was moaning softly, her small hands gripping his shoulders as he removed his hands from her breasts, held her hard by the hips, and with a startled cry, finished.

They rested a few moments, then began again.

He said, "Oh, sweet Jesus, you're beautiful!" put his hands over her breasts again, his face between her thighs, and kissed her into oblivion.

She said, "Lie still!" and put her mouth on him. He cried.

Near dawn, before they went to sleep, he held her tightly against his chest, asking, "Are you going to wake up in a few hours' time and decide now you hate me, Rose?"

Puzzled, she sat up. "Why do you say that?"

"Isn't that the way it's always been? Then you build from there until you're hating yourself for being with whoever you're with, and hating them, too, for wanting to be with you?"

"You've thought it over and decided that that's how I am?"

"I've stayed away from touching you all this time because I didn't want to lose you, have you hating me the way you did those others. I like to make sure the woman I'm with knows who I am and is with me because she *wants* to be. Not because she hates the both of us and can't stop."

"I'd never hate you, Pat. You've never demanded anything or been angry with me because of something you wanted that I couldn't give you."

"But that was before. This changes everything."

"No it doesn't. It doesn't change anything. I'll keep on feeling the same way I've always felt about you."

"And how's that?"

She looked surprised at his asking, as if he should have known.

"I love you, Pat," she said simply. "I thought you knew."

He smiled rather sadly. "I don't read minds, Rose. And you can't be in love by yourself. You've never said you love me."

"You've never given me a chance to say it. We've always talked about other things, things that didn't leave any room for talking about love."

"Well," he said, circling her breast with his fingertips, "maybe we'll make some room for talking about it."

"Let's go to sleep," she said, slipping down against his chest. "We talk too much."

Leonie and Bill sat at his desk going over the books.

"How are we doing?" she asked him.

"Just about breaking even most weeks. Getting a little bit into the red. I think we're going to keep on slipping bit by bit more and more into the red."

"I intend to keep the company going. And I want to install good strong wall safes in all the locations, have each restaurant keep a close tally of receipts and expenditures. Fridays, you and I will go round to collect from the restaurants, fill pay packets for the staff, enter the receipts into the books, and bring the balance of the money back, keep it in the safe here."

"It means the managers are going to have to do more bookkeeping."

"I don't think any of them is going to mind a bit of extra work as long as the restaurants stay open."

"There's something more," he said, removing his wire-frame glasses, tiredly pinching the bridge of his nose.

"What?"

"You're getting low on cash reserves. The only way I can

see to make up the deficit and give us some running capital is to take a mortgage on one of the four buildings you own."

"I'd hoped it wouldn't come to this."

"I don't see you've got any choice."

"All right." She sighed. "Make arrangements for a mortgage on the Fifty-seventh Street property. It's the biggest, so it should bring in the largest sum."

Depressed, she got up and returned to her own small office, to stand looking out the window; telling herself it was just a mortgage and not the first sign of the end.

It seemed impossible to walk five blocks without seeing a breadline operated by a church, hospital, Salvation Army unit, rescue mission, fraternal or religious order. Men stood in line in all kinds of weather and ate their beans, or stew, or soup in full view of passersby. There was hardly a single block of New York that each day didn't see at least one family numbly sitting on a couch on the sidewalk, while upstairs, their apartment door was being bolted with an eviction notice posted beside the lock. People going by put nickels and dimes in a pot or a saucer sitting on the family's kitchen table.

Early in 1932, led by Father James Cox of Pittsburgh, the "hunger marches" began in earnest. Gray telephoned Leonie to read her the United Press release of Father Cox's statement in Washington.

"Listen to this," he told her, feeling the same aching sickness he'd known standing on a slight rise watching boys of seventeen and eighteen struggling forward through thigh-deep mud. He read, " 'The United States is not the firm of Herbert Hoover, Limited. I am the mayor of Shantytown. That is a town in the heart of Pittsburgh, in the shadows of the skyscrapers owned by one of the richest men in America—Andrew W. Mellon. The men in my town want work but can't get it. So they live in huts and hovels. If the Pilgrim Fathers came here today, would they be satisfied? They came here to give us a country. Now it has been taken away. Who owns it now? The Andrew Mellons.' " He stopped reading and held the receiver to his ear, feeling a terrible anger and sadness.

She cried. She sat with her head in her hand, the receiver against her ear, and cried. "What can we do?" she asked him. "What should we *do*?"

"I didn't mean to upset you," he said apologetically. "I simply wanted to share it with you."

"I know. And I'm not sorry you did. I just feel so bloody *helpless!*"

The night courts for New York were handling five hundred percent more convictions for panhandling, and expecting it to become worse. Only half a dozen Broadway shows were playing. More than fifty theaters were dark, with the last attractions that had played there in 1929 or 1930 still on the marquees. And each of the few playgoers found himself being asked for coins two or three times on every block.

In the South, farmers began cutting off the fronts of cars for which they couldn't afford to buy gas, attaching mules, and holding what they called Hoovercart races.

Rudy Vallee, invited to sing at the White House, was requested by the president to sing something to make people forget their troubles and the Depression. Vallee sang, "Brother, Can You Spare a Dime?"

20

It was in 1932, during her second year at Sarah Lawrence College for Women, when Leo began to see the people around her, and in particular, her mother and father, with some genuine measure of objectivity. And viewing their actions with her newly clarified vision, listening to them talk, learning of their personal sacrifices, she came to the realization of how deeply she loved them both. She knew that her mother's money was slowly being used up to keep the restaurants going, to keep the staff employed. But what really brought it home to her was one day innocently asking, "What's happened to your rings, Mummy? You never wear them anymore."

And Leonie, looking at her denuded hands, smiled and said, "I've sold everything."

"You sold it all?"

"I'd hoped to pass them along to you, all the things Jimmy gave me, and your father. But I'm afraid the money was needed."

Leo knew, without having to be told, that her mother's jewelry—although there hadn't been a great deal of it—had been of very fine quality, and whatever money she'd received for it had gone directly into Lion's.

Both her mother and father were wearing clothes a minimum of three years old. And at home Leonie gave up shoes altogether. Leo wondered if she intended making do indefinitely with those she had, and felt guilty when Leonie insisted she and Gray have new school clothes.

"We don't need them, Mummy," she argued.

"No," Leonie said firmly. "You *do*. Please, darling, don't make us self-conscious."

Self-conscious? Leo thought that was an interesting way of putting it. She and Gray all togged out in new clothes while their parents wore the same old ones. But she didn't argue, because there were certain areas where Leonie wouldn't allow argument. Still, this in no way diminished Leo's discomfort at knowing her parents were doing without all sorts of things in order to maintain a certain life-style for the children; not to mention supporting Dennis, Faith, and their little boy, Charlie. Of course Dennis worked hard around the place and was an awfully nice man, an awfully kind one. But it was Lion's and her mother's almost herculean strength that seemed to be holding everything together.

On an afternoon during her vacation, she accompanied her mother into the city to lend a hand at the office, and as they were walking back from University Place to Fifteenth Street, they were approached by a small group of bedraggled children asking for pennies.

As Leo watched, her mother stopped, dropped down to their level to take the hand of the nearest child, asking, "Are you hungry?" as her eyes moved slowly over the faces of the children. They all nodded. She stood up, keeping hold of the one child's hand, saying, "Come. Come with me." And as if entranced, they followed her back to the restaurant. Leo hurried to help as Leonie instructed two of the waitresses to join several of the smaller tables and align the chairs. Then, very formally, she invited the children to be seated. Their eyes clinging to Leonie, they all sat down. And Leonie, Leo, and the two waitresses began serving trays of food to the children exactly as they'd have done to paying customers.

It made Leo hurt inside. After the children had said thank you and gone on their way, she had to say, in a voice husky with emotion, "They loved you, Mummy. They never took their eyes off you."

"Nothing is worse than hunger, Leo," she said, linking her arm through her daughter's. "Especially when it shows on the faces of small children. Thank you for helping, darling. You did beautifully."

Leo saw more and more of the same. Groups of children, old customers who stopped Leonie in the street. She treated them all with respect, according them the dignity they'd lost. She gave away time and love by the armload while each week taking a little more money from the wall safe of the Round Hill Road house in order to make up the deficits.

"What will you do when it's all gone?" Leo asked, helping both parents write out envelopes for a massive mailing in Mr. Roosevelt's behalf.

"I'll worry about that when it happens."

At twelve, little Gray was taller, possessed of a voice in the process of breaking, but otherwise relatively unchanged. Still silent, still private and bookish, he created ever-more-elaborate plans of strategy in the attic with his batallions of soldiers. Or he sat on the floor with a pillow by the fireplace, reading. He said little, seemed to have made no friends at all at school, and still, at least once a month, vanished for long mysterious hours.

Leonie was fretting over having to mortgage a second property.

Gray was fretting over Leonie's thinness and pallor.

Amy was fretting over the entire family.

The number of unemployed reached thirteen million in 1932. National wages were sixty percent less than in 1929. The Reconstruction Finance Corporation was established in late January with two billion dollars at its disposal to advance loans to failing banks, to farm-mortgage associations, to building-and-loan societies, railroads, and insurance companies.

On the first of March, the Lindbergh baby was kidnapped from his parents' home in Hopewell, New Jersey, and the resulting outrage in public opinion forced adoption of the death penalty in federal kidnapping cases.

The same month, a gathering of five thousand jobless men marched on the River Rouge plant of the Ford Motor Company in Dearborn, Michigan, wanting work. The police were waiting and ordered the marchers to disperse. The men kept coming in the face of tear gas and fire hoses, turning suddenly into an irate, screaming mob. The police ran for their lives. Mr. Ford's private police force then opened fire with heavy machine guns, resulting in the deaths of four men, the injury of several dozen. A few days later, the dead were buried and men marched again, wearing red armbands and carrying signs saying "Ford Gave Bullets for Bread."

Wheat prices dropped to a new low of thirty-two cents a bushel. More than two dollars less a bushel than in 1920.

On May 20 Amelia Earhart became the first woman to

cross the Atlantic in a solo flight when she landed near Londonderry, Ireland, after a flight of thirteen and a half hours.

In June the National Convention of the Republican Party met at Chicago and renominated President Hoover on the first ballot.

A week later, Leonie took a mortgage on the Murray Hill property.

On June 27 the Democratic National Convention met in Chicago Stadium, with Roosevelt, John Nance Garner, and Al Smith vying for the nomination. Leonie was in Chicago as a member of the New York delegation. Her first major trip outside New York since arriving there nineteen years earlier.

In the garbage dumps of Chicago the hungry were scavenging for what they could find. The smell was sickening, as were the great swarms of summer flies falling upon the heaps of refuse as soon as the garbage trucks pulled away. People attacked the garbage, dug in with their hands, devouring whatever was left of old slices of watermelon or canteloupe. They washed and cooked discarded onions, turnips, potatoes, cabbages, carrots; sometimes they cut away the rotting parts of meat but more often scalded it, sprinkled it with soda to kill the taste and odor, then ate it. They made fish-head soup, chicken-claw soup.

Leonie saw and heard about this, and more, asking to be shown around the city; determined to face every aspect of this view of humanity at its lowest ebb. All too aware of the possibility that she might soon enough find herself scavenging—in different fashion—for pennies in order to keep her promises.

The tension among the delegates was running very high. Although Roosevelt was the frontrunner as the convention got under way, he didn't have much strength. Fearing that the two-thirds rule of Democratic conventions might defeat Roosevelt, two of the prime candidate's movers, Ed Flynn and Jim Farley of New York, tried to change the two-thirds rule to a simple majority. There was a fierce outcry which resulted in Roosevelt issuing a statement that he and his forces had no intention of changing the rule. He did not attend Chicago. But Al Smith did. Smith had beaten Roosevelt in the Massachusetts primary by three to one and had also made an excellent showing in Pennsylvania.

At the stadium, as John E. Mack began his nomination speech, Al Smith, clad in evening clothes, came in and stood listening. At the mention of Roosevelt's name, he was overheard—by a considerable number of people—to say, "I can go back to the hotel and listen to that on the radio." And he walked out. Leonie hoped the stupid gesture had just cost him some delegates.

The speeches went on and on through the hot night, and it wasn't until well after four A.M. when the first ballot was taken. Roosevelt received 661 out of 1,100-odd votes. It didn't look as if he'd get a two-thirds majority. The delegates balloted again, and he gained some new votes as states began deserting their favorite sons. Leonie was convinced it was due to Smith's little display at the outset.

She wanted Roosevelt to win as she'd never wanted anything in her life, believing absolutely that if anyone alive was capable of altering the country's present course, it was this man.

The delegates had been up all night, and it was light outside, but they decided to try another ballot. The situation, Leonie knew, was desperate for Roosevelt. If his position didn't improve on this or the next ballot, he'd start losing strength. Talking among the other delegates, she was disgusted to discover that no more than one in five of the Roosevelt delegates was actually voting for him. She went from group to group arguing, talking, trying to rally some spirit of unity.

There was a strong element of unreality about all of it, she felt, and had to keep reminding herself of the people she'd seen fighting over the refuse at the dumps, the men who'd attacked the garbage truck as it had tried to empty its load.

She shared a cup of watery coffee with a fellow New York delegate and even accepted a puff of his cigarette as they waited for the ballotting to begin again.

"Hell of a thing," her companion said, "isn't it? We don't get a majority pretty damned soon, we're up the creek."

"We're going to get it!" she said with such ferocity that he looked at her for several long moments in surprise. Then he chuckled and said, "You're a pistol, sweetheart! A hot-damn pistol!"

The third ballot didn't materially improve Roosevelt's standing.

The sun had long been up, the heat of the day beginning. The delegates, now a sorry, rumpled-looking lot, adjourned and staggered off to their hotels, leaving the nomination still hanging in the balance.

Back in her room at the Congress Hotel, Leonie telephoned Gray to bring him up-to-date. Then she bathed and lay down to nap for a while.

And while she slept, all kinds of bargaining went on. Bird of Virginia said he'd swing his votes over to Roosevelt if he could be U.S. senator from Virginia. Roosevelt now had Virginia. A call to San Simeon started William Randolph Hearst working on the California and Texas delegations to swing votes Bird's way. Since Garner of Texas as a presidential candidate was practically Hearst's single-handed creation, Hearst was successfully able to exercise his power.

By the time Leonie had returned to the stadium, rumors were spreading that Texas and California would switch from Garner to Roosevelt, with Garner getting the vice-presidential nomination. The fourth ballot began. And when McAdoo called out, "California came here to nominate a president of the United States. It did not come here to deadlock this convention. California casts forty-four votes for Franklin D. Roosevelt," Leonie clutched her fellow delegate's hand, both of them shouting and laughing. They'd done it! Roosevelt was going to get the two-thirds majority and carry off the nomination.

On July 2 Roosevelt addressed the delegates. "I pledge you, I pledge myself, to a new deal for the American people." He said, "Let us all here assembled constitute ourselves prophets of a new order of competence and of courage. This is more than a political campaign; it is a call to arms. Give me your help, not to win votes alone, but to win in this crusade to restore America to its own people."

Leonie got to her feet, applauding wildly. The delegates sang "Happy Days Are Here Again" as Roosevelt waved with one hand and with the other clutched his son's arm for support and left the platform. He was going to do it—set the world on its feet again.

Excerpts from Grayson's Journal

12th August, 1932

Very worried about L. Working night and day at campaign headquarters, dashing back and forth to office, home, back again. No doubt Hoover will be defeated. Certainly no question with L. enlisting volunteers from everywhere to help in the campaign. Even Leo, Rose, and Amy doing their share. Still, too much of a strain on her, what with worries about the company and a third mortgage pending.

18 September, 1932

"New Deal," catch phrase of campaign, picked up and used everywhere. Thought Gray would enjoy evening in the city. Not much success. L. horribly fatigued but will not slow down. Can't continue on this way very much longer. Something's bound to crack.

4th October, 1932

Long talk with Leo, who feels as I do. But impossible to get L. to stop long enough to listen. Scarcely see her these days. She's slept at home twice since early September. I wonder does she sleep at all.

8th November, 1932

Election night. Landslide victory for FDR, carrying all but seven states with 472 electoral votes to Hoover's 59. Am working on final copy for early edition. L. to meet me here upon her return from election headquarters. Using three-line lead:

> ROOSEVELT WINNER IN LANDSLIDE!
> DEMOCRATIC CONTROL WET CONGRESS;
> LEGHMAN GOVERNOR, O'BRIEN MAYOR

The end of dear old Jimmy Walker. No surprises anywhere down the line.

The celebrating was loud and drunken, and suddenly Leonie felt far too worn out to stay. She got her hat and coat and made her way out to the street, taking a deep breath of the cold night air as she turned, starting across town toward Gray's office. She'd surprise him by being earlier than promised for a change.

She'd take a long weekend, she decided, go home tonight to Greenwich, sleep late in the morning; spend tomorrow, Friday and Saturday with the children, attend to some long-delayed projects, devote some much-needed time to the family. She walked along making plans, trying to determine how much longer the company would be able to hold out before the last of the money would be gone. Business had picked up slightly in the past few months, but not nearly enough to cover the thousands she'd poured in in the last two years to keep the company afloat.

I really must rest, she told herself, alarmed by the question of what would happen to the company if she were suddenly incapacitated.

She started walking a little more quickly when she became aware of footsteps echoing hers. Coming out of her thoughts, she looked around, realizing with a stab of panic that the streets were deserted. It was after three in the morning. Gray was putting the finishing touches to the five A.M. edition, not expecting her much before four. Stupid of me! she thought. Why didn't I take a taxi?

The footsteps broke into a run, and she whirled around to see a giant figure in a voluminous overcoat and some sort of hat racing toward her. She hadn't any time to react, no time even to open her mouth to cry out. The figure leaped upon her, sending her staggering backward into the mouth of an alleyway. A tangle of hands as she tried to push him away, but she was tired, not thinking clearly, and a stunning blow in the face and the tremendous weight of her attacker brought her to the ground. As her head began to clear and she understood what was happening, that it wasn't just her handbag he was after, she started to fight; trying to get him off. She cried out, and something was shoved into her mouth and held there as the huge figure wedged himself between her legs and began tearing at her clothes. Summoning the last of her strength, she made one final monumental effort to free herself and was rewarded by a blow to the side of her head that sent her into something like paralysis; so that she could do nothing but lie there as a voice whispered in her ear and things were done to her. Everything was a slow-motion film. Then there was a blinding flash of white light that turned instantly black.

When she regained consciousness, she was lying naked except for her stockings, her clothes hanging in tatters from her body. She was trying to sit up when a light burst into her eyes, blinding her, and a voice was saying, "Holy Christ! I think it's Mrs. Marlowe," and she struggled to stay awake, sensing someone was going to help her, but it was all pain, and she was sliding away from it, from the light, going.

At four-thirty Gray received the call at his desk, where he was sitting drinking cold coffee, waiting for Leonie. He slammed down the receiver, ran out of the building to his car, and drove to Bellevue, where he was told to wait. "You'll be able to see her in a little while." He was also told that the patrolman who'd found her happened to be a friend of Pat Sheehan's and had recognized her. Otherwise, it might very well have been days before they'd have been able to identify her and notify him.

"Whoever did it," the patrolman came over to tell him, "took her coat, her bag, her shoes. It was a damned vicious attack. I'm real sorry."

Bitter-tasting fluid was rising into his throat, and he kept moving up and down the corridor while he waited, afraid to think what "damned vicious attack" might mean. It was the single worst hour of his life, waiting there to learn what had happened to her.

Finally the resident on duty came out to say, "She's got a lot of bruises, some peculiar cuts, and a pretty bad concussion, but she'll be all right. Did the officer tell you all of it?" he asked hesitantly.

"All of what? I don't understand."

"She was assaulted, too," the doctor said quietly. "Sexually."

"Oh, my God!" He had the feeling the floor was dropping away from under his feet, the walls and ceiling tilting.

"C'mon over here and sit down." The resident directed him to a bench. "I'm sorry," he said. "She put up a fight and got pretty badly roughed-up for her efforts."

"Hurt how? For God's sake, don't *mince* words! Just *tell* me!"

"I'm trying to tell you," the doctor said, somewhat exasperated. "It's a little hard to just dump in your lap."

"Look," Gray said, "Just tell me."

"She's cut up," he said, looking as if something foul had permeated the atmosphere. "Mostly about the breasts."

"I'd like to see her now."

"A few more minutes."

He wouldn't have known her, and wondered how the patrolman had been able to recognize her, but was nevertheless deeply grateful that he had. Her face was horribly swollen; one eye completely closed, bruised black with a deep crescent of dark red underneath; an ugly purple bruise across her right cheek, her lower lip split. She was awake and taking deep rasping breaths, her lips moving.

He held her hand, trying to prevent his shock from showing on his face as he forced a smile and said, "You've seen better days, old girl." Then, hearing how imbecilic he sounded, horrified by what had happened, imagining the damage he couldn't see, he put his head down on the edge of the bed and began to cry. He felt her fingers touching his hair, heard her whisper, "It's all right, Gray," and was filled with a consuming rage, wanting to go out and search the streets, find the man who'd done this, and kill him with his bare hands, beat him to death.

He told the children she'd had an accident, confided the truth only to Amy and Rose, and asked everyone—at Leonie's request—to stay away. She wanted no visitors.

After eight days in the hospital she was well enough to go home, but clutched Gray's hands, looking panic-stricken, saying "I *can't*! I know we haven't the money to spare, but I can't have the children see me this way. Please, let me stay in a small room somewhere until I'm fit to be seen."

So he rented an inexpensive room at a small, clean hotel in the Village and took her there. Explaining about the accident, he was given a week's leave and moved into the hotel with her for the next nine days. For the first two days she walked unsteadily back and forth in the cramped room, talking nonstop in a half-delirious monologue, partly in English, partly in what he believed was Swazi. She refused to allow him to see her without clothes or to touch her, but insisted he sleep with her in the bed.

Sensing the wisest thing he could do would simply be to listen and wait, he did just that until the afternoon of the third day, when she stopped pacing and talking and turned to look at him, her face softening as she seemed to recognize him for the first time. Tears pouring down her cheeks, she came over to the armchair and sat down on his lap, winding her arms around his neck, hiding her face against his shoulder.

"I need desperately to make love to you," she sobbed, "replace him with you inside me. But I can't until I properly cleanse myself. I feel so . . . *fouled*, indescribably filthy."

"You want your herbs," he guessed. "Tell me what you need. I'll get them for you."

Her arms tightened around his neck as she kept on whispering. ". . . his *slime* inside me. It's vile, *vile! I* never imagined I could feel as I do, Gray. Like a monstrous disease." She sat back from him abruptly, asking, "The company? Who's taking care of things?"

"Rose is looking after everything," he said, easing her back against him. "You're not to worry about any of it."

"He was enormous," she whispered, shuddering. "A huge figure, pounding down on me. I thought he'd simply take my bag, strike me perhaps. But not . . . that. Gray"—her arms were like a vise around his neck, her face buried in his neck—"huge . . . he was huge. And it hurt so terribly, hurt."

"It's all right," he said again, stroking her soothingly, rocking her. For hours, her voice whispered on and on, telling him everything he wished he hadn't ever had to hear. Until, very suddenly, like a child, she went to sleep mid-sentence. He carried her to the bed, and unable to resist a need to know, opened her dressing gown to look at her. Gaping, drymouthed, sickened at the scabbed injuries in the process of healing. They'd leave scars. Deep, permanent ones. His hands shaking uncontrollably, he closed her gown, tucked the blankets around her, and went out to try to find the things she'd told him she had to have.

He slept badly that night, tortured by the vision of her body that came to him over and over until he had to get up out of bed and sit out the balance of the night in the armchair, smoking one cigarette after another, watching her restless sleep.

The next day she closed herself into the bathroom for several hours while she repeatedly flushed her interior with a liquid mixture containing extract of cotton root, ergot, and crushed mistletoe berries. Finally satisfied, she bathed twice in scaldingly hot water, then for the first time risked facing herself in the mirror on the back of the bathroom door.

There was very little swelling left in her face, her eye now encircled by a ring of pale violet, the bruise on her cheek fading. She lowered her eyes to look at everything she'd avoided seeing until this moment, having only touched with her fingertips the edges of the encrusted slashes.

I am always going to carry these marks, she thought, refusing to look away. For the rest of my life, every time I remove my clothes I will see these reminders of what was done. Why? *Why?* Gashes across both breasts. Like stars. The tip of one nipple gone. And bisecting her body from her throat to her pubic hair, a deep slash. Several cuts at the tops of her inner thighs.

Stepping away from the mirror, she again looked down at herself, holding out first one arm, then the other, once more examining both breasts, then her legs, running her hands over her buttocks and down the backs of her thighs; whispering as she took her hands over her body again and again. Then a final time, confronting the mirror. Telling herself: It will be all right. The mixture would destroy any seed that might have taken root inside her. It would kill the seed, bring it away in a premature flow of blood. By tomorrow it would begin, and then this much, at least, would be ended.

When she came out of the bathroom and saw the deep concern and tension cutting lines into Gray's forehead and at the corners of his eyes, she understood how he'd suffered with her, and went onto the bed determined to ease them both.

She opened her dressing gown and said, "I know you've seen. Can you live with it? They said I could, in time, have grafts. But the grafts would simply form scars of a different pattern."

"Can *you* live with it?" he asked, daring to trace with his fingers the jagged cuts and slashes marring the perfection of her skin.

"I don't know. I'm going to try." She grasped his hand, bringing him closer to her, urgently whispering, "Replace him in me. Take him away!"

But her responses were frozen, her body wouldn't perform, remaining as dry as the plains soil before the spring rains. "I am so ashamed," she whispered from between stiff lips as she got up off the bed and went into the bathroom, closing the door with a small click.

He sat up and lit a cigarette, feeling nauseated. She was gone for quite some time. He finished the cigarette; the bathroom door opened, and she came back to the bed, saying, "It will be all right now."

When he touched her, she was wet.

"What did you do?" he asked, almost afraid to hear.

"You know," she answered, guiding him into her. "But this time, I couldn't bear to have you see." She stiffened for a moment, her fingers digging into his back, then forced herself to relax and accept him.

"You're not enjoying this, not the least little bit," he said after a time.

"Don't stop, please. I'm not *able* to enjoy it. *Understand*, please! That's why we have to do this. So that I'll be able to enjoy it again. I love you. Don't stop!" If you stop I'll die. Inside, I will close forever, knit shut like the walls of a tomb.

It was the only time ever he failed to derive any pleasure whatsoever in making love to her. Dutifully, feeling as soiled as she claimed to, he performed. And when it was done, she cradled his head to her breasts, whispering, "I'm sorry, I'm sorry, I know it was awful for you, I'm so sorry."

He bathed, dressed, went out for food, and came back. They ate in silence, her exposed wounds between them like barbed wire.

She said, "You feel I've used you."

"No. I feel I could commit murder. It's ugly, Leonie. Is this the way it's to be?"

"No, no," she said quickly. "It won't. I promise you." She knelt beside him on the bed, examining his eyes. "Tell me you love me," she said. "Do you love me?"

He put his arm around her, her hair feeling cool. "I love you, Leonie."

"If you do," she whispered, "make love to me again." *I am so afraid, so afraid, so afraid.*

Before they slept, she stroked him the length of his body, promising, "It will get better, it will. I love you, love you."

In the early morning, when she got up to go to the bathroom, blood ran down her thighs. She stood a moment looking at it, then exhaled slowly and continued on into the bathroom.

21

The nightmare came night after night. Footsteps pounded along the pavement, a figure hurled itself at her, knocking her backward. But the surrounding walls were mountains, the pavement hard-packed earth. And she had a blow gun, spat poison-tipped darts again and again into impervious flesh. The figure kept coming. Naked, she tried to scramble up the gravelly foothill, but her ankle was grabbed, she was slowly dragged down, small sharp stones scraping her naked flesh as her hands searched in vain for something to hold on to.

She woke up screaming, and once awake, couldn't get back to sleep. So, after assuring Gray she was perfectly all right and he doubtfully returned to sleep, she spent the nights downstairs in the deep armchair beside the fireplace, staring with stinging eyes into the blackened remains of the previous evening's fire; wondering how much longer the company could hold out, how much longer she could go without sleep, when the nightmares were going to leave her. Her bones seemed to be moving closer to her skin so that she was very aware of her skeletal framework whenever she looked at her hand or noticed the knob of bone at her wrist.

It wasn't only the actual attack that haunted her, but a loss of faith, a loss of belief in her own safety. She knew it was asinine, but she'd believed that because she cared, because she was trying her best to help remedy the situation, she was therefore rendered safe from the anger of those less fortunate. And what had begun years and years before as an initial determination to best the city, conquer her instinctive fear and dislike of it, now had turned back to dislike and fear. Every hour she spent in the city was an hour she spent in danger. It did no good telling herself she was being irrational, that she was well out of harm's way. Every time she found herself alone on the sidewalk, even in the middle of the day, she was in the eye of her personal storm of fear.

What she wanted now was time to herself, time for the family, time to attend to her home and her garden, time to heal all the wounds. But there was no way she could possibly take it. The company was still alive, due almost entirely to the steady flow of cash emanating from the Round Hill Road wall safe. And with the last of her four properties mortgaged, the number of dollars remaining in the safe was shrinking weekly. She'd have to begin closing locations soon, if something didn't break to the good.

On top of all that, she invited little Gray to come into the city with her one afternoon to see the office, visit the various locations. She hoped he'd be interested, that he might get caught up in the warmth and family spirit. But he was bored, painfully polite to the employees who made such a wholehearted effort to be friendly. Her disappointment, she knew, was disproportionately great, but everything seemed to strike her at an emotional level of late, and this was simply another blow of a softer order.

Leo, in her third year at college, was deeply involved in her premedical studies, working to pull off the highest grades possible in order to be eligible for the Yale Medical School, her dream. She seemed to move through the house in a fog of facts, apparently unaware of her mother's anxiety or her father's daily growing concern for her mother.

So it came as a surprise to Leonie when Leo approached her one evening when Gray had taken little Gray to a baseball game, to say, "I know things aren't going very well, that we're running out of money. I've been giving it a lot of thought, and I can wait to finish college for a year or two. You can use the money for the company."

"Oh, darling"—Leonie smiled tremulously—"it must have been very difficult for you to make that decision. There's no need for it, Leo. I know you'd like to help but, truthfully, those few hundred dollars simply wouldn't make very much of a difference. But I thank you. I do thank you."

"I'm worried about you," Leo admitted nervously. "We're *all* worried about you. I know you spend half the night every night down here. And I've heard you scream. It terrified me the first few times. Gray, too. Now it's as if we're all sleeping but we're waiting for you to scream. Then we wake up for a few moments, know you're up and on your way down here, that whatever it is is over and we can go back to sleep again. It's all *wrong*! I want to help, to do something. I don't want anything more to happen to you. And I'm afraid something more *will* happen."

"Nothing's going to happen to me. I'm simply going through rather a rough patch just now."

"And what happened election night?" Leo asked. "Why weren't we allowed to come see you? Oh, I know Daddy says there was some kind of accident. But I'm not a kid anymore. I'm old enough to be told the truth. It wasn't just some 'accident,' was it?"

"No," she admitted, for a moment jarred at seeing herself sitting opposite. A mirror image of twenty years before.

Leo picked up the poker and jabbed at one of the logs, creating a brief burst of sparks, replaced the poker, and sat gazing thoughtfully into the fire.

"I remember the afternoon you told me Rose had tried to kill herself by taking poison. I remember that so well. It was the first time I really felt you didn't think of me as a child but as someone capable of understanding, being grown-up enough to accept certain responsibilities. I'm almost nineteen." She turned to look at her mother. "When you were nineteen, you were running a restaurant. You had employees. And you had me. Don't you think I'm old enough to know?" Before Leonie could answer, Leo looked again at the fire. "It's been almost three months since whatever happened happened. Maybe I'm trying to make you put it into words because I think I've known all along. It's just"—her eyes returned to her mother's—"that I want you to trust me enough to want to tell me about it. Don't you understand? I want to *share* it with you. I'm not a little girl anymore. I'm a grown woman. I love you. You're the most important person in the world to me. And I've learned not to be jealous of the time you spend on other things, other people. So why won't you let me be a part of you in the way that I'm able? I know perfectly well life isn't all good times. I've seen you sell your jewelry. I've seen you going for the last four years without buying so much as a new slip. When are you going to *trust* me, Mummy?"

"I have a bottle of sherry hidden away," Leonie said. "Shall we have a glass?"

"Yes, all right."

Leonie got up and walked out of the room. Leo watched

her go, thinking: We're separate and I can look at you, study you like one of my textbooks, and admire you for being beautiful, for moving like someone never really meant to wear shoes; admire your thoughts and your kindness and a certain way you look at me sometimes that makes me want to cry because you're looking love at me. So why do you refuse to allow me to return your feelings? I want to share it all, the good and the bad, and the love, too.

They sat sipping the sherry, both watching the fire, Leonie's voice very low, uninflected, relating what had happened that night. As if telling a story about something once upon a time that happened to a princess who lived in an evil land, not anything that had touched her directly. Yet it was real and somehow more horrific because of that unemotional, flat quality to her mother's voice.

At the end, Leo was feeling a cold terror and a dreadful anger. That something so terrifying should have happened. To *my mother*, she thought. Not someone I've never met, some stranger. My mother. She could see it all far too clearly. The night, the dark. The overwhelming exertion of force. Her face twisted suddenly, imagining herself as her mother, feeling her thighs being wrenched open, and the pain.

Leo continued staring into the fire, finally saying, "So that's why you scream. I knew. But I didn't know. Oh, I *knew*. When I was little, I always thought of you as being so big, so strong. I suppose I've gone along thinking that. We all have, I believe. It's so awful to think of someone . . . It makes me think of you altogether differently now, somehow. Strong, as always, but weaker, too. Because you are real and capable of being hurt. It sounds as if I don't care, the things I'm saying. But I *do* care. It's just that I'm not sure how to say what I mean."

"You needn't say it, Leo. I understand."

"*Do* you?" Leo moved away from the fire to sit on her knees facing her mother. "*Do* you?"

"I've been frightened quite a number of times in my life, darling. For all sorts of reasons. Large fears, small ones. It's inevitable, in the course of a lifetime. But now, now I'm afraid much of the time. And I loathe feeling this way. I tell myself it will go soon, time will take it. But I've always had rather an impatient nature—at least as far as I, personally, am concerned. I want it to go more quickly than it is. Because I'm afraid, and because you sense it, you now see me differently. I've never tried to establish myself in your eyes as someone beyond pain, Leo; someone inaccessible, untouched by the things that affect others. It's been your image of me, perhaps. And maybe, unwittingly, I've contributed to that because I've never been able to bear being idle. One seldom thinks of terribly busy people, people always on the go, as fearful people. I grew up with a man whose every moment was allocated, who couldn't abide wasting a single moment of what he believed was too short a lifetime. I'm no longer totally positive of my actions. And that, too, gives you the feeling that I may be arriving at the end of my energies. I know. It's the same feeling I have myself too often these days."

"That's some of it," Leo said. "But not all. I don't understand why, with all that's happened, you keep driving yourself, why you refuse to stop—even for a few days—to give yourself a chance to rebuild your energies."

"I'm afraid to stop," she said candidly.

"You'll collapse if you don't."

Leonie hadn't any response to that. She set her empty glass down on the side table and looked at her hands, at the bones in her wrists, thinking: I deluded myself. Wanting so desperately to hurry past that numbing fear. I've simply managed to hold it at bay, because there isn't time now to deal with it. Telling myself I'll deal with it later, when there's time, when other problems don't have precedence. But I'm not succeeding. And you know it. Certainly Grayson knows it, because our acts of love have become like rituals performed from habit, containing less and less pleasure for us both. I feel those mountains moving closer.

Leo rested her folded arms on her mother's knees, saying, "Stop now, for just a little while. For me, because I need you. For all of us. I'm begging you to stop, Mummy. You're making yourself ill. I can see it. I'm the one who's going to be a doctor, remember? I wouldn't have much of a future in medicine if I couldn't see symptoms that're staring me right in the face. You're so thin. It's terrible. And your hands tremble." She closed her hands around her mother's wrists. "Look! They're trembling. *Please*! If you could only see the way Daddy looks at you when you're not aware. It's the way we all look at you. Amy, too. Even Dennis and Faith. We all see it! Let Rose take over for a while. She'll be happy to do it. I think she'd like the chance to show you she *can* do it. A few weeks isn't going to make much difference to Lion's. But it will to you."

"Soon. In a few months. When we're past this crisis."

"Now!" Leo said impatiently. "Now! Or you won't *be* here in a few months! No one can go without sleeping, working twelve and fifteen hours a day. No one, Mummy! Not even you. Is it that you *have* to be in command, running everything? At least explain to me why you can't stop!"

Is this how I was? Leonie wondered. Fierce and filled with conviction, positive of my viewpoints?

"Just a week," Leo kept on. "One week. Stay home and rest, eat properly, sleep, get some fresh air."

"Soon," she promised. "Very soon."

"All right." Leo sighed, releasing her mother's wrists. "All right."

"Don't get angry, Leo. There are things you fail to understand. The most important right now is for me to be there. As long as I'm at the office every day, it means we're still going forward. If I should suddenly stay away, it would affect everyone. It's a matter of morale. And it isn't at all easy to keep up one's morale when you see people fighting over rotting garbage and are faced with the possibility that you might soon be one of those determined to have that scrap of maggoty meat. I'm going to go up to bed now. Are you coming?"

"In a little while."

"You're not wrong, darling. We're each of us right in our own way. But one can't start something then leave it at a critical juncture and entrust others to maintain it. I know Rose could take over beautifully, and that she'd be glad to do it. But right now, I've simply *got* to be there. They're the rest of my family, Leo. And each of those people has an importance to me that it would take me months to explain to you. But they've all pulled together in the best possible way to keep it all going. Because *I've* demonstrated my good faith in *them*. I'll still be here for you, darling. I'll always be here for you. I have no intention of dying." She smiled, running her hand over Leo's hair. "It would be inconvenient just now."

"I suppose," Leo said, her voice laden with irony, "I'll probably wind up just like you."

Leonie laughed. "Put up the fire screen when you come up, will you?"

"I will."

Leonie went up to bed. Leo continued to sit before the fire, idly stabbing at the remaining bits of burning wood with the poker, feeling both frustrated and oddly reassured. Smiling wryly, thinking of her mother's words. I have no intention of dying. It would be inconvenient just now. And you won't either, she thought. You damned well won't, either.

Rose, Alice, Bill, and Leonie sat in her office reviewing the previous month's figures.

"We're juggling money around like a circus act," Bill said. "Just barely covering ourselves."

"It doesn't look like it's going to get any better in a hurry," Alice said glumly. "Banks are closing all over the place."

"Once Roosevelt is inaugurated," Leonie said confidently, "he'll start getting things back under control. I know it."

"But what do we do until then?" Rose wanted to know. "It could be months."

"Maybe if we closed one or two locations—" Bill began.

"We will *not* close! I'll think of something."

"Rose and I have been talking," Alice said. "And we've made up our minds. We'd like to lend the company our savings. It's almost twenty-two thousand dollars."

"I can't accept it!" Leonie said unhappily. "For all any of us knows, you might never see one penny of that money again. I couldn't accept the responsibility for depriving you both of your life savings."

"Take the money!" Rose said quietly but firmly in a voice that wouldn't allow argument. "We've both talked it out every way till Sunday and we know exactly what kind of chances we're taking."

"Twenty-odd thousand could carry us for quite a few months if business continues to hold up," Bill said. "It could make all the difference."

"I've only got a few thousand left," Leonie said. "When that's gone, and the twenty-two thousand is gone, we'll be right back to this point again. And you'll both have lost all your money."

"The only other alternative we have is to close a couple of the restaurants."

"No! I gave my *promise* we'd stay open, that no one would lose his job."

"Then you'll take the money?" Alice asked.

She got up from the desk and turned to stand looking out the window at the rooftops, the sky; feeling so tired. Deeply moved by their faith, but overwhelmed by the burden of responsibility. Risking their futures. Was that it though? Or was it a matter of investing in something larger, something for the common good? The money could conceivably see them through to the end of the Depression and on into the start of better times. Still, there were no guarantees Roosevelt would pull the country out of this. Oh, but he will! she thought. He will. He's the only one who can give us what we all need: hope.

"All right." She turned from the window, looking at each of them in turn. "I accept your offer with my deepest gratitude. I only hope to God we're not all suffering from some common delusion. But I insist on a note, with interest, against the company. I will repay every cent."

"We know that," Rose said, thinking how unlike herself Leonie appeared, her height serving to emphasize her thinness, and the tremor in her hands she couldn't quite conceal. "Neither of us is concerned about your repaying the money. We know you will."

"I, um, have a few thousand put aside I'd like to add to that," Bill said. "I feel the way Rose and Alice do. The wife and me, we talked it over and she's with me all the way. It's not a whole lot, about forty-five hundred. But it should help."

Leonie nodded, her throat too constricted to speak.

The three of them collected their various papers and returned to their desks. Turning again to the window, Leonie let her head rest against the glass and noiselessly wept.

Excerpts from Grayson's Journal

4th March, 1933

Splendid inaugural speech. "The only thing we have to fear is fear itself." FDR has closed every bank in the Country until he can decide which deserve federal support, which will be allowed to go under. He's asking Congress for emergency power. "As great," he said, "as the power that would be given me if we were in fact invaded by a foreign foe."

6th March, 1933

FDR has ordered 4-day bank holiday, put an embargo on gold, declared there will be prison penalties for those hoarding gold, bullion, or currency. L. and I making arrangements to collect all the cash, reestablish accounts, in accordance with new regulations.

12th March, 1933

First of FDR's "fireside chats" on Sunday evening, promising re-opening of banks.

13th March, 1933

Banks reopening today. L. and I established new accounts. She seems somewhat better, although alarmingly gaunt. Nightmare continues to recur. But the responses are better, for us both. Lovemaking no longer quite the horror it was. Thank God. Leo hovering over her mother, even little Gray displaying concern. I refuse to dwell on or project negative possibilities. Too frightening.

31st March, 1933

Civilian Conservation Corps (CCC) created by Reforestation Unemployment Act to alleviate unemployment and initiate reforestation program. Business starting to improve very slightly, Lion's too. L. burns, almost literally. As if possessed of an interior fire. Her skill at manipulating money exceptional. Constantly with Bill going over books and figures. Her skin hot to the touch always.

19 April, 1933

Embargo placed on all shipments by executive order FDR. In effect taking us off gold standard.

12th May, 1933

Agricultural Adjustment Act created the AAA, restricting production of certain crops—to be determined by farmer—and pays farmer bounty for uncultivated acreage. Lion's continues slight upswing. Unemployment coming down fractionally. Congress today passed Federal Emergency Relief Act, with five-hundred-million-dollar appropriation. L. looking very frail. I admit to being afraid.

18 May, 1933

Tenessee Valley Act passed, establishing TVA with purposes of controlling Tennessee River floods, instituting another reforestation program, and developing rural electrification. L. the same.

27th May, 1933

Federal Securities Act passed, requiring registration and approval of all issues of stocks and bonds. Lion's has stabilized, accounts balancing. No further outflow of personal cash.

2nd June, 1933

Lion's has realized its first profitable week, on its way to a second. L. has promised—after loud family conference—to stop at the end of this week for a week's stay at home.

Lion's checking account sank to just under two thousand dollars, and Leonie was about to consent to the closing of two locations when the daily receipts began to show a very slight rise. With everyone holding his breath, they waited down the weeks, watching the gradual increase of business.

By the end of May, Bill looked up from the previous week's figures and smiled, saying, "It looks like we're holding our own." Leonie had to sit down. The trembling in her hands, throughout her body, was so fierce she couldn't remain upright.

"Let's not be overly optimistic," she said. "We'll want to keep watching very closely for the next few months to make sure there isn't a sudden reversal."

The following Thursday, before her scheduled week off, in the middle of another meeting with Rose, Alice and Bill, she found herself suddenly unable to draw a deep breath. A stabbing pain in her chest, a shooting pain in her left arm, she felt nauseated, sickeningly dizzy, and went to stand by the open window, flexing the fingers of her left hand, opening and closing her mouth in an effort to fill her lungs. Rose, coming around the desk to see what was wrong, took one look at Leonie's completely purple face, at her heaving chest and told Alice, *"Call Gray!* Tell him to get here *right away!* Bill, get a cold cloth and some smelling salts!"

Leonie continued to stand in front of the window, hearing only a thunderous roaring in her ears. Then she turned her head slowly to look at Rose, wanting to say something, feeling her legs go dead, her body turn to smoke. Her eyes rolled back into her head and she slithered to the floor as if boneless.

Determined to keep her wits about her, Rose dropped down to lift Leonie's head onto her lap and loosen the top of her clothing, stopped for a moment by the scars all across Leonie's chest. When Bill came back, she placed the cold cloth across Leonie's forehead, telling Bill, "You'd better go out," as she opened the bottle of smelling salts and passed it back and forth under Leonie's nose.

"Gray's coming," Rose told her as her eyelids fluttered open. "You should be in the hospital, Leonie."

"No!" She grabbed hold of Rose's hand, her eyes imploring. "If I go into a hospital, Rose, I'll never come out! I must go home. Gray will take me home. Whatever happens, swear to me you won't allow me to be taken to hospital!"

"All right. Hush. I knew you'd do this to yourself," Rose said with mixed anger and fear. "But you wouldn't *listen.*"

"Take care of everything." Leonie dragged air into her lungs, the pain in her chest spreading. "I trust you."

Oh God! Rose thought, unable to do more than hold her hand, stroke her cheek. You let this damned company devour you. "Nothing's worth this," she said despairingly. "Nothing."

"Rose . . ." Her voice was a whisper, almost inaudible, tears creeping from beneath her tightly closed eyelids, her hand thin and cold. "I'm so ashamed, Rose," she whispered, her face contorted with pain. "I've wet myself."

Rose sat, cradling Leonie's head in her lap, praying for Gray to hurry and get there. Praying that Leonie wasn't going to die.

You look like an old woman, so thin. Shivering like some poor sick animal. Gray, hurry up! I'll never understand you, not really.

"He'll be here soon," she said, then bent herself around Leonie, crying, "I love you. Everything will be all right. He'll be here and you'll go home." *Hurry!*

22

"You've had a heart attack, Mummy," Leo said fearfully. "I *know* that's what it is. I know all the symptoms. You shouldn't be *here*. You should be in the hospital."

"Leo, *listen* to me!" Her hand drew Leo closer. "Listen very carefully, will you?"

"I'm listening."

"I will not go into a hospital," she said in a whisper. "If I do, I know I'll never come home again. I can't tell you why or how I know that, you simply must trust that I do. I'm going to tell you how to prepare some medications, infusions. Are you listening, Leo?"

"I'm listening."

"Foxglove," she said. "I'll tell you how to find it, where. You must be very sure that it's not a new plant, and you must wear gloves to touch it. Collect a good supply of the leaves. Then I'll tell you how to prepare them."

"Mummy! This is—"

"*Listen!*" Her hand tightened around Leo's arm. "Listen and learn! I know exactly what I'm doing. You go into the fields nearby. You'll find it, I've seen it growing. A tall plant. Two to as much as four or five feet tall, with a stout stem, rather downy. Are you listening?"

"Yes."

"The leaves grow alternately. You must be very, very careful to collect the older, lower leaves, and whatever you do, wear gloves! If any part of the plant touches your skin, you could become very ill. The flowers are of no use, only the leaves. You understand?"

"Yes."

"All right. Take along a bag of some sort and mind you remember the gloves. When you return, come to me and I'll tell you what to do next." She released Leo's arm and lay back, closing her eyes. Every beat of her heart sent waves of pain and nausea through her.

"Go on, Leo!" she whispered. "Trust my knowledge!"

Leo located the wildflower book on the shelf in the living room next to her father's several dictionaries and carried it with her through to the rear of the house. Foxglove, digitalis. Frightened by the cautionary notes about the plant, she studied the picture. But Mummy knows, she told herself, pulling on her mother's heavy gardening gloves. She's always known how to prepare teas and medicines to get us over colds and stomach aches, everything.

"What are gonna do in that getup?" Amy asked, watching her.

"I'm going to the far field to collect come leaves Mummy's asked for."

"Whole thing's crazy," Amy said. "That woman gonna kill herself, and you all gonna let her!"

"*Amy!*"

"I'm just worried," Amy said, pulling at her lower lip, something she did only when deeply in thought or very upset. "Looking the way she does. Can't even stand up or go to the bathroom without somebody helping."

"She's going to be all right," Leo said with more conviction than she possessed. "You go up and stay with her until I get back. Where's Gray?"

"Off to the tree, reading."

"Okay. Stay with her, please."

Amy wiped her hands on her apron and turned to go. Leo went out the back door, then hurried inside again to pull on her rubber boots. Satisfied, she left the house, walking beyond the boundary of their property and on, into the high grass of the field beyond. Slowly scanning the plants, she looked back and forth from the book to the wildflowers growing in the field.

She wondered how her mother had managed to convince her father to go in to work. Absolutely incredible the way she could talk anyone into doing something he started out believing impossible. But she'd done it. And he'd gone. Now he kept telephoning every hour or so to ask how things were, and she and Amy had been taking the calls, assuring him everything was all right. Everything *isn't* all right! she thought angrily, frightened. She should be in a hospital but she's upstairs in bed and I'm out here like some kind of idiot looking for a plant. But I've got to believe it'll work, because she says: Listen and learn, Leo! And all my life, when she's taken hold of my attention, made me listen and see, she's shown me something new, something exceptional, I'd never before noticed. Like those wild violets she found growing between the cracks in the sidewalk.

"*Leo!*"

She turned to see Gray running clumsily through the tall grass, and was suddenly scared. Did it mean something? She stood waiting for him to catch up, her heartbeat so fast she could feel it in her throat.

"What?" she called to him.

"Where're you going?"

"Getting something for Mummy!"

"I want to come with you!"

Relieved, she waited for him. And when he caught up, she pinched his arm hard, saying, "Don't *ever* do that again! You scared me to death!"

"Sorry." He rubbed his arm, looking unjustly accused. "I only wanted to come with you. Why've you got all that stuff on?"

"Because I don't want to get poisoned."

"*Poisoned?*"

"Mummy said I could be if I touched the plant with my bare hands or let it touch my skin."

"What plant?"

"This one." She showed him the picture in the book.

"I'll help you look."

"Okay. But make sure you don't touch it. Just tell me, and I'll do the collecting."

The sun was very hot as they moved slowly through the grass. Butterflies fluttered over the flowers. Grasshoppers leaped out of their way as they trod on the grass. There was a pervasive humming in the air.

"Leo?"

"What? Did you find it?"

"No. I just wanted to ask you."

"What?"

"Is she going to die?"

"No!" she said crossly. Then, seeing she'd upset him, said, "No," again, more softly.

"She *looks* like she's going to die," he said, pushing the hair off his forehead.

"Aren't you hot with those knickers and that sweater?"

"Some. I don't mind. How come nobody will tell me what's happening?"

She stopped walking and looked at him. "Maybe because you never seem very interested in what's happening, Gray. Always in the attic, or over in the garage with those stupid soldiers. Or in that damned tree with some book or other. Half the time you never open your mouth except to eat. I don't think anybody knows if you care one way or another."

"That's not fair!" he protested, looking stung. "Sure I care. She's *my* mother, *too*, you know!"

"Nobody'd ever know it from the way you behave. You're like someone who rents a room from us or something. Anytime they try to hug or kiss you or do something they hope will please you, you act bored, like you'd rather be in the attic or out in the tree, or off on one of your mysterious disappearing trips."

"I can't help it," he said, all seriousness. "That's just the way I am. I don't ask you to be different from the way you are."

"Maybe not," she said, starting to search again, moving forward. "I don't know, Gray. Couldn't you even *pretend* to like the things we try to do for you?"

"But I *do* like lots of the things we do. I *never said* I *didn't*. *You're* the one saying that."

"It's your attitude, Gray. Oh! Nuts! I thought that was it, but it isn't."

"What's my attitude?"

"Indifference. What's inside your head, anyway?"

"Lots of things. *Lots* of things."

"Like what, for example?"

"Well, I love them just as much as you do, for one thing!"

"Do you, Gray? Really?"

"'Course I do! Gee, you sure make me sound like I'm strange or something." He began idly collecting some of the wildflowers, fashioning a small bouquet as they went along. "I'm going to be a politician one day," he said. "Or maybe a general. Or possibly a history professor. I haven't decided. But it'll be one of those three, for sure." He bent to pick some more flowers, then pointed, saying, "Is that the one?"

She looked over to where he was pointing and exclaimed,

"Good boy! That's it! You stay here while I go collect the leaves."

Unruffled, he continued to gather the flowers, discarding some, keeping others. Thinking maybe she'd like them. He'd ask Amy to give him a vase or a jar, something to put them in and he'd take them up, put them on the dresser where she could see them.

"Come on, Gray!" Leo called, beckoning to him. "Let's go back now!"

As they ran, puffing, back through the overgrown field, Leo asked, "Where do you go, anyway, when you take off and just disappear?"

"Oh, places."

"What places?"

"Just alone places. To think."

"Maybe you will be a professor," she said, the boots slowing her down. "You sure remind me of enough of mine."

Amy said, "It's Miss Rose, wanting to talk to you."

Leonie held out her hand—again appalled at the sight of it—and took the receiver.

"I thought you'd want to know. Luncheons were up again today. Bill's working on the figures right now, and he says it looks like we'll see a little more profit this week."

"That's wonderful, Rose."

"How *are* you?"

"By the weekend when you come up, I'll be much better."

"You're not thinking of getting *up*, are you?"

She laughed, a weak, unconvincing sound. "I couldn't if I wanted to."

"Don't you dare even *try*!" Rose ordered. "For God's sake, get better! I'm worried half crazy about you."

"Don't be worried, Rose. Just take care of business. I'll see you Friday evening." She handed the receiver back to Amy.

"*Friday!*" Amy snorted. "I've known you a lot of years and always thought you was peculiar. Now I know for sure you're plain crazy! I'm gonna go fetch you up some broth. You move, woman, I'll put my fist upside your head!"

"I love you, Amy." She smiled. "You get meaner every year."

"And you just getting stupider. I'll get the broth, and when you've done with that, I'll sponge you down. Hot today," she said at the door. "Gonna be a hot summer."

She lay looking at the ceiling, the reflected sunlight casting leafy patterns. Thinking: I can't possibly die. Not now. I'm not even thirty-nine years old. I won't die! We're just starting to come through the hard times. It's the wrong time to be dying. But, Lord, it hurts! What was it Father said? "There's an inner knowledge of the rightness of time. And I know I've arrived at the end of my allotted measure. I'm not angry and I'm not afraid. A bit regretful, though, because there's so much more to be done. But not for you, Leonie. Not here. You'll make your way somewhere else. Someplace new, where'll you'll be able to grow."

I never had the sort of dreams other girls did. Like Gus. Thinking she'd shape me into the ideal debutante, to be presented at court, then come out and be deluged by the attentions of eager young men. I couldn't share her dreams. All I ever wanted was my freedom, to move without constriction, to run if I felt the need. To love, have love. What happened to those simple needs? How did I come to be a city woman with brick walls my chosen confinement?

Almost twenty years. Rose has been with me nineteen years, Alice eighteen, Bill seventeen. The newest employee Lion's has been with the company six years. Not one of them has left us. Not one has complained or done anything but his best. Is that what it's all for?

Jimmy. Clark. And Gray. The children. My family, my families. I have no wish to die. None. Acts performed from necessity, not out of vanity, as Rose once accused. Necessity turning to pride, in my accomplishments, my friends, my children, my husband. A home within the boundaries of the homestead. The animals running free, killed only with discretion. For survival. To sustain the families.

She was asleep when Amy returned with the broth.

"Just a few drops," Leonie cautioned. "More than that is dangerous. That's right." She watched Leo place two drops of the liquid in the herb tea. "Perfect. You've done beautifully, Leo." She held the cup to her lips with both hands, steadily drinking down the hot mixture. Then she returned the cup to Leo and sank back against the pillows, exhausted by the slightest efforts.

"Little Gray's here," Leo said in an undertone, causing Leonie to open her eyes.

"I got these for you," he said shyly, holding a vase filled with carefully arranged wildflowers, their scent bringing sunshine into the room.

"They're lovely, darling." She smiled as he carried the vase over to the dresser. "Come give me a hug." She held her arms out to him, wondering if this once he mightn't suffer her embrace with some measure of gladness.

Looking miserably embarrassed, stains of color upon his cheeks, he approached and placed himself within her arms. "I'm sorry you're ill," he said, feeling he'd melt with the heat of his discomfort. "I hope you'll feel better very soon."

"Thank you." She held him a moment longer, knowing he hated it but unable to release him. "It was so thoughtful of you. They're beautiful."

"Don't be sick," he whispered, his cheek against hers. "I hate it."

"I know," she whispered back. "I rather hate it myself."

He stood away from her, their hands joined. "Would you like me to read to you?" he offered. "I will if you'd like."

"Perhaps later this afternoon?"

"All right." His fingers slipped out of her hand and he dashed away.

"I feel it already." She sighed. "I know it will work."

"Amy says she's coming up to bathe you," Leo said. "Why can't *I* bathe you?"

"I'd prefer it if you took the afternoon to yourself, darling. You've spent the entire morning on me. Take some time to yourself now."

"You don't *want* me to, do you? Why?"

"Leo, I haven't a modest bone in my body. It isn't anything to do with that. It's simply that Amy and I are of an age. We're comfortable together."

"You don't want me to see you. Isn't that it?"

"Yes."

"But why?"

"You needn't face all the medical horrors in just one day, Leo. You've got years of it in front of you as a doctor. You go along now, ring up some of your friends."

"Okay." Leo backed down reluctantly, wondering what she meant by medical horrors. Something to do with that man who'd attacked her. Was there more than she'd been told? "I guess," she said, "I'd probably feel the same way if it were me."

"Makes my teeth hurt just looking at you," Amy said, squeezing the sponge into the enamel basin, her eyes on Leonie's body. The scars crisscrossing her now-shrunken breasts, her mutilated nipple, her rib cage too clearly defined, her protruding hip bones. The bruises on her arm and leg from when she'd fainted in the office. "We're gonna fatten you up good. That stuff working at all?"

"Oh, yes," she said dreamily, her eyes closed. The absence of pain a narcotic of its own. "I feel so much better. I won't die," she whispered, unaware she'd spoken aloud.

"Damn right you won't!" Amy said, putting down the sponge, needing both hands to turn Leonie over onto her stomach. "What you thinking of anyway, talking about dying? Scaring us all this way, now here you are actin' like you been smoking dopeweed or something."

"What's dopeweed?" she asked faintly.

"You know! That dope them folks smoke in cigarettes."

"Cannabis." Leonie smiled into the pillow. "I'm falling asleep. That feels so good, Amy."

She sank into the most peaceful sleep she'd had in months. A deep, dreaming sleep that seemed to last a very long time. The dreams were brilliantly colored, overlapping; gradually changing, growing darker, until she was hearing those pounding footsteps again and she was being pursued through the tall grass in blackness, panting as she ran. Then she crouched upon a small rise while behind her huddled all the children. She fought, failing. She was thrown down, down; never landing. Pinned by the weight of air alone to the driving body of a huge faceless being whose repellent presence within her body, whose whispering in her ear made her scream soundlessly; twisting in her futile efforts to escape, succeeding only in driving him deeper into her, so that her womb was penetrated, torn, and he was thrusting higher, destroying everything she needed to continue living. She was terrorized as his movements accelerated, knowing he would pour himself into her, befoul her in the vilest possible way. She felt the sudden spasm, and despair, as, acidlike, semen spilled into her lacerated interior, destroying her.

Her cries brought everyone running, crowding into the bedroom, where Grayson, first to arrive, was already holding her, talking softly as she came awake. Her eyes were sunken, enormous; her entire body shaken by fierce tremors.

"I'll get you more of the medicine!" Leo ran off.

Deeply frightened, little Gray clung to Amy's hand, watching his father trying to calm his mother.

"Is she dying?" he asked Amy in a whisper, echoing the question Amy was asking herself.

She gave his hand a smart tug and led him away, saying, "You come on down with me, help me get the trays ready for your mummy and daddy. She's gonna be hungry now she's been sleepin' so long."

"*Is* she?" He snatched his hand away, his mouth quivering.

Amy looked at him in surprise, this little boy who never showed any feelings, any caring. "You gonna cry, child?" she asked, unable to stop and immediately angry with herself for inadvertently provoking him.

"No! 'Course I'm not going to cry!"

"Do you a power of good," she said, continuing on down the stairs. "Ain't no sin I know of, cryin'."

Leo hurried past them up the stairs, carrying a small round tray, leaving the scent of fear in her wake. Gray turned to watch her go into the bedroom, then went along down after Amy, following her into the kitchen.

"You fetch me the trays," Amy said, still annoyed with herself. "And get me a coupla those napkins from the sideboard, too!"

He got the trays and napkins, all the while saying: Please don't die, please don't die—over and over inside his head until all the words ran together and were just one long wish, an awful dread. Don't die please don't.

She drank the tea containing the drops of digitalis, then sagged against Grayson, whispering "Thank you" to Leo.

Gray waved Leo away and settled Leonie more comfortably against him, lifting the long mass of her hair over his arm. She seemed so frail, yet her weight against him was a comfort. You do have substance, he reassured himself. Take one breath after another and mend, let us help you to mend.

"I should have told Leo to wake me," she said. " I went too long without the medicine. If I forget, will you remind her? Every few hours. Lord, I'm so weak! I loathe it. Have you had dinner, darling? You look tired."

"The children ate with Amy. I thought I'd wait, have a tray up here with you."

"Yes," she said, feeling the dreamy lassitude overtaking her, easing her as the pain subsided. "Good. Any news?"

"FDR's started the recovery program, promising a million jobs by the first of October. Several bills went through yesterday, a hundred-and-fifty-million-dollar allocation to the wheat growers. We're going to pull out of it now."

"What else?"

"You want every column, don't you?"

"Naturally." She touched his face in an instinctively affectionate gesture, then started to withdraw, sickened by the sight of her hand.

"Don't take your hand away. Why do you do that? Half a dozen times in the last few weeks you've started to touch me, then pulled back your hand. Why?"

"I can't stand the look of them, my hands."

"There's nothing wrong with your hands," he said, perplexed. "It's your imagination."

"They look like ... claws ... some sort of animal."

"What nonsense! You have wonderful hands. Strong, capable hands."

"Why is it they looked so ... *deformed* to me?"

"You're ill, darling. I expect everything appears slightly off to you now."

"Perhaps that's it. I'm actually hungry. That's a good sign."

"Gray begged to be allowed to come read to you after dinner. Would you be up to it?"

"He's been so dear. Did you see the flowers he gathered for me?"

"I did, yes."

"I'd adore to have him read to me. You'll tell him?"

"Leonie," he began, "about what happened ..."

She looked at him questioningly.

"I never ... I know it wasn't your fault. But what worries me ... Do *you* know it wasn't your fault?"

"I don't follow." She looked at him blankly.

"I can't help feeling you're blaming yourself. Because you were there on the street alone. Because it was an unwise decision and we both know it. You should've taken a taxi."

"I know!" Her hands clenched. "I *know* it!"

"You made a mistake," he said gently. "But you seem unable to forgive yourself for the mistakes you sometimes make."

"But it shouldn't have *happened*! It was so stupid of me, so unforgivably *stupid*!"

"Tell me!" he said.

Her eyes widened; she opened her mouth, then closed it.

"Tell me," he said again. "Tell me the dream, and why you scream."

She shut her eyes. "I didn't know him, Gray. But he knew me. Followed me from ... He'd been waiting, he said. Waiting."

"Go on."

"No." She shook her head.

"You've got to, Leonie. Because it isn't any of the rest of this . . . this . . . It isn't something purely physical that's making you so desperately ill. You and I both know it. I can feel it every time I touch you. Every time we try to make love, I'm aware of it."

"He *hated* me, Gray!" She could feel the horror welling up again. "Someone I'd never known! *Why*? I've never harmed anyone . . . tried so hard . . ." She stopped. He held her, waiting for her to go on, knowing she would.

"All the time it was happening," she whispered, turning her face into his neck, "while he was holding me down, tearing at my clothes, I couldn't move, as if . . . paralyzed . . . and his voice went on and on . . . saying how much he hated me, people like me. . . . I'd suffer the way he had, the way he was suffering. . . . I can't!"

"You're not to blame. Don't you know that?"

"But you don't *know*!" The pain was starting to threaten again in her breast.

"Please, tell me," he coaxed.

"He said wherever I went . . . whatever I did . . . for the rest of my *life* . . . Just remember, he said . . . someone is out there with . . . with a piece of you, a private *piece* of you. . . . Then he did it, held my breast and *did* that! And I couldn't move, couldn't . . . He cut . . . then put his *mouth* . . . all the blood all over his mouth. Mine. Licked his mouth." She was trembling, shaking her head back and forth against his shoulder as if to physically wipe her head clean.

"It's over," he whispered. "Tell me the dream and let it go!"

"Yes. The dream." She freed one hand to wipe her eyes and nose, gripping the handkerchief he gave her. "I'm an animal," she said, able to let go of him now. "Some sort of animal, running on all fours through the grass. And he's coming. I can hear him. I can't stop, because if I do and he catches me, once he's done with me he'll kill my . . . I don't know what they are. Pups or cubs. I don't know. I only know he'll kill them. Then I'm caught and . . . it happens. And while it's happening, I know when he's done with me he'll kill them. Then he finishes and he's going to go after them, I know that's what he'll do, and I wake up. Screaming."

She held the handkerchief over her eyes, letting her head fall back.

Gray looked at the long, vulnerable line of her throat, trying to make sense of it, fit all the pieces together. Without really knowing why, or what he was doing, he lowered the nightgown over her breast and looked at her. She opened her eyes and watched him anxiously.

"What are you doing?" she whispered.

"Tribal ritual," he whispered back, and opened his mouth over her breast, touching with his tongue the strangely puckered flesh where they'd stitched together her nipple. He sat up and held his palm over her breast and said, "Look at me! There's no blood."

"Gray?"

"*I* have pieces of you I carry about with me. So do Leo and Gray. You're no less than you were. Not at all. I have to have you here, Leonie. Life without you would be desolate for me. Those years during the war, I've never known such utter emptiness. In every conceivable way. I know what it means," he said, holding her with his eyes, the green dominant, as if lit from within. "Fighting to keep it all intact. You endangered your life. Yes, it was stupid. Frightfully stupid. But it was a perfectly human mistake. And the dream is about you and Lion's. Because you've managed to combine the attack with your fears for the company. It's *all over* now, Leonie! The company is going to pull through. And you're going to be fine. You've got to let it all go and concentrate simply on getting well. Nothing else."

"You've become an African," she said, a smile taking shape.

"Call it anything you like. After all these years, I think I finally understand your medicine. Look at your hands!" he said, taking hold of her wrists and raising them. "They're perfectly fine, rather oversized *hands*. That's all." He let go of her wrists and smiled. "I've never insisted you perform according to my order, because I've always respected your endeavors, your intelligence. Now, I'm insisting. Let Rose handle matters, and Alice, Bill. For the next six months, your place is here, at home. After that, you'll work again."

"I am tired," she admitted. "I do want to rest."

"You've earned it," he said quietly. "Don't you think?"

"I suppose so. Hold me for a bit, would you?"

She sat up, and he put his arms around her.

"I love you, Leonie. It doesn't matter, any of the other. I promise you it doesn't."

Rose called a general meeting, put her proposal to a vote

and received unanimous approval. Then preparations got under way. All the arrangements were kept highly secret so that no word would get back to Leonie. Two buses were hired. The cooks from each of the restaurants worked all Saturday afternoon. And Sunday, midmorning, the first week in September, they set out.

Leo said, "It's a gorgeous day, Mummy. Come, get dressed, and take a walk with me!"

Leonie put down her book, and looking at Leo's eager expression, smiled, asking, "You think I'm up to it, do you, doctor?"

Leo laughed and went to the closet, throwing open the door to pick through her mother's clothes. "You're really going to have to get some new clothes," she said, rejecting dresses one after another, finally lifting down an old pale pink crepe de chine she'd always loved on her mother. "Wear this," she said, laying it across the foot of the bed.

"Isn't this awfully fussy for just a walk?"

"I love you in that dress," she said, searching for shoes.

"What are you doing now?" Leonie craned to see.

"Trying to find some shoes."

"Oh, please, not shoes! If it's as gorgeous as you say, I couldn't bear them. I'll do without."

"Okay." Leo closed the closet door. "I'll be right back," she said, running down the hall to her room. "Wear your little lion!" she shouted. "I love it! And I want you to make sure you leave that to me in your will!"

She stopped for a moment, hearing her mother laughing, then quickly brushed her hair, so excited she could barely catch her breath.

"Let me brush your hair for you," she offered, returning to watch her mother—her back carefully turned to Leo—wearing only a thin teddy, step into the dress. "You look so well, Mummy."

"I'm afraid I'm still a bit wobbly," Leonie said, fastening the tiny covered buttons at the front of the dress.

"Come, sit down." Urging Leonie down on the bench in front of the dressing table, she lifted her mother's hair to fasten on the necklace, then began drawing the brush through the waist-length hair, saying, "Mine's nowhere near as nice and thick as yours is. I'm jealous. I want you to know that."

"You're up to something," Leonie said suspiciously, looking at Leo in the mirror. "You're all flushed."

"Oh, I've just been rushing around," she lied blithely, paying close attention to the brushing.

They held hands going down the stairs, and Leonie stopped halfway down. Gray and little Gray and Amy were standing in the front hall, looking up at her expectantly. Little Gray's face was shining, his hair wet-combed. Amy in her best go-to-church dress. Grayson in trousers and shirt, sports jacket.

"Something's going on," she said, continuing down with a smile. "And you're all in it together."

"Come on." Grayson held his hand out to her.

"You're making me horribly nervous with all this pomp and circumstance," she said as little Gray took her other hand. Amy opened the front door and held it.

"Close your eyes, Mummy," Gray said. "It's a surprise. You've got to close your eyes."

She looked at him, puzzled.

"Do it, darling." Grayson tugged gently at her hand. "Humor him."

She closed her eyes and allowed them to lead her out onto the porch, then felt them let go of her hands, and opened her eyes, her breath catching in her throat as she saw all the people gathered on the lawn, a crowd of smiling faces. All of them. Rose and Alice and Bill; Imogene, the secretaries, the switchboard girls; every waitress, busboy, manager, and cook; the two cleaning ladies, Dennis and Faith—everyone. They were all there, their hands beating the air; smiling, clapping their hands together.

She wanted to smile, couldn't; turned and put her arms around Grayson's neck and laughed, crying while he held her, saying, "We thought you might enjoy a picnic, darling, with the family."

She laughed and cried harder, overwhelmed.

Rose, standing with Pat near the steps, thought how lovely Leonie was; as lovely as the first time she'd seen her, standing leaning on a broom, looking up at the sky. She watched, as Leonie unwound her arms from Gray's neck, took a deep breath, and turned, smiling; sniffing back the tears, lifting her chin as she extended her hands—as if she might, with that gesture, embrace them all—and came slowly down the steps.

Part
FOUR
1937-1946

23

During her first session with Dr. Birkell, Leo missed at least half of everything, and later had to look at Anson Conroy's notes to see what she'd missed; relieved to find it wasn't quite as bad as she'd thought. But she'd been so distracted by Birkell's voice, his aura of knowledgeable authority, his atypical patience with the class. And his left hand. His hand. Her eyes kept returning to look at it, while none of the others seemed to take any special notice. The net result being she felt foolish and ashamed at not being better able to control her . . . what? Curiosity? She didn't know what to call it.

A few weeks later, when he invited her to come out for a cup of coffee, she was convinced the point of the invitation was to quietly reprimand her for that lapse in medical etiquette. So she was taken aback when he began, without preamble, by saying, "Tell me who you are. I want to know about you."

"But why?"

"You've got one of the primary essentials of a good doctor: curiosity. The rest of them, with all that studied nonchalance, pointedly refused to notice." He smiled. "You're honest. That's good, too."

"But I thought it was so horribly rude of me. I came tonight prepared to apologize."

"Don't do that," he said, placing his hand on the table in front of her. "Ask me about it, if you want to. I promise you, I don't mind a bit."

She looked at his hand, then at his eyes, then again at his hand. Thumb and forefinger, then a smooth ridge of scar tissue running across the top of the palm, the faintest swellings where the other three fingers had been.

"How did it happen?" she asked, turning his hand over to study the palm.

"Car accident. A young kid full of bootleg hooch. He ran into us coming down the wrong side of the road, then kept going. The car took fire. Luckily, another car came along, smashed the window on my side, got me out. Penny was already dead, but I didn't know that, and severed the fingers trying to get back inside to her."

"When?" she asked.

"A long time ago."

She looked up finally, releasing his hand.

"Penny was my wife," he explained. "You have extraordinary eyes. Angry eyes."

"I'm terribly sorry," she said inadequately, unsure of herself with this man.

"It was a long time ago," he said again.

This man. Very tall, very large, with hair that had once been black but had since turned silver-gray. Blue eyes with startlingly black perimeters to the pupils. In his middle forties or so.

"Are you going to specialize?" he asked.

"I haven't decided. I'm torn between general surgery and obstetrics. I'll probably do the surgery. Although I like the idea of having a general practice, being the old family doctor." She smiled.

"Not quite the white-haired, wire-framed-glasses type." He returned the smile.

"No. Maybe that's why I like the idea."

"We're heading into a war," he said, closely watching her eyes. "Are you aware of that?"

"I come from a family that takes copies of all the local and New York papers every day. And when I say copies, I mean two of each."

"Tell me about your family," he urged.

"I'd rather not. This doesn't feel quite ... comfortable."

"My turn to apologize," he said, his deep voice filling her head. "The last thing I want is to make you uncomfortable."

He knew just exactly how her body would be. The flesh very solid, tight to the bone; long limbs, and skin of a texture that defied description. Everything silken, oiled, supple, young.

"I really don't know why I'm here," she said, looking

around the coffee shop, thinking of the extra hours she'd have to put in tonight for the time she was spending here. All the notes to prepare.

"I've become a little heavy-handed in my old age." He smiled again. "Forgotten how these things are done. I was hoping you might come out to dinner with me one evening."

Her eyes returned to his as his meaning penetrated her brain, and she viewed him now as a potential lover, finding the idea endowed with considerable appeal. Sooner or later she was going to have to take the step. Why not with him?

When she failed to respond, he asked, "Does the idea, my being a one-handed former surgeon, put you off?"

"I don't feel sorry for you!" she said sharply. "I don't do things out of pity."

He raised his eyes, and she again felt foolish, realizing he hadn't been seeking pity but simply stating cases.

"Why *do* you do things?" he asked.

"Because . . . Because they're there to be done."

"You're one of three women who've managed to make it through to the fourth year without dropping out to get married or switching over to some less-demanding course. And I understand you're to do your internship here. That's quite something. Are you battling everyone in general or someone specific?"

"I'm not battling anyone," she answered. "And if you know such a great deal about me, why did you ask?"

"There's always more," he said easily. "You interest me. Very much. I'd like a chance to get to know you better."

"Almost every man I've met has told me that, or something close to it," she said warily. "They've also told me, in considerable detail, just how beneficial sex would be for me. For my skin, my general outlook, all of it."

He laughed and lit a cigarette, offering her one, which she refused.

"I have no intention of telling you any of that. I'm also not going to tell you how beautiful you are, since I'm quite sure you've been told that, too, ad nauseam. But suppose now," he continued, holding her eyes with his, "I said I'd like to marry you, that I've wanted to make love to you since the first time I saw you; that I'd like to live with you, have children with you, that I'd like to meet your family, be a part of you. How would you respond to that?"

She let her breath out very slowly, reaching, as she did, for his pack of cigarettes. She lit one and went on looking at him through the smoke, at last asking, "Are you in love with me?"

"I'd like to have you let me be."

"Why?"

"All sorts of reasons. You're going to be a fine doctor. I'd like to share in that, for one. You'll probably produce beautiful children. And I'd like to have a family before it's too late. More?"

"You don't know me," she countered.

"I've spent months learning you," he said, unruffled. "I know most of what's relevant."

"This is absurd!" she decided, nevertheless intrigued.

"Is it?" he challenged. "If I invite you back to my apartment, will you say no?"

"Now?"

"Right now."

"Why?" she asked again, trying to imagine how it might feel to have that sadly mangled hand moving over her body.

"Perhaps it'll strike you as too tangential, not to the point, even irrelevant," he said, putting out his cigarette. "But when they started burning books, putting people into camps, I had a sudden sick intimation of what the world's about to face. If I were twenty years younger . . . I'm too old. And too many people are going to die. Before it all starts exploding in our faces, I'd like to know a little happiness again. I sound like a fanatic, no doubt."

"No," she disagreed. "For the first time, you're making sense. You're sounding like my mother and father. I understand exactly what you're saying. It terrifies me. Because no one's going to believe what's happening until it's too late. My younger brother's just waiting to be old enough to fight."

"How old is he?"

"Seventeen."

"And he wants to go off to war?"

"When Gray was little, all he ever did was read books on military campaigns, or about history, and make up incredibly complicated maneuvers with a set of tin soldiers Daddy bought him the Christmas he was five. He told me years ago he was either going to be a history professor or a general. I believe him."

"If he has any of your intensity, I think I'd believe him, too."

"I'm not intense. I'm just . . . I don't know. Tired, in a lot of ways. I've spent the last four years fighting off almost every man I've met; having them picking away at me, at my motives. Trying to show me up as inferior or inadequate because I'm a woman, demanding to know what I think I'm trying to prove by being a woman in medicine. So many of the professors, your associates, treat us with barely concealed contempt because we none of us women deserve to come as far as we have. Why *shouldn't* I be a doctor?" she demanded hotly. "And why should I have to constantly explain myself when none of the men do? I'm tired of it!"

"I'm not challenging your right to be in medicine," he said. "I'd like to help."

"Isn't this just a new and different way to try to pin me down and prove how inadequate I am?"

"*You* don't think you're inadequate. Why should you assume that *I* think it?"

"Because it's all I've had coming at me for so long, I've learned to expect it."

"You impress me," he said candidly. "Your anger especially. I realize I'm old enough to be your father. Does that bother you?"

"Look . . ." She wet her lips. "All of this is making me . . . Are you serious?"

"About what?"

"All of it, everything you've said."

"Oh, very."

"Well, all right," she said. "All right."

"Now I'm a little lost."

"All right. I'll come with you. To your apartment. I'm going to have to sooner or later. I might as well."

"You're making it sound hideously final."

"It is final. Once it's done, I can't ever be the same."

"Feeling that way, are you sure it's something you really want to do?"

"Are *you* changing your mind now?" she asked.

"No. I'm just wondering if it's merely an act of defiance on your part, or a matter of some genuine interest."

"Let's say both."

She'd been prepared for something shattering, some sort of assault, and wasn't in the least ready for the feelings he aroused in her; the sweetness of his kisses, or the boldness of his caresses. He held her over top of him, whispering, "Skin, your skin. And the softness right here," his hand turning against her upper thighs, causing her to open expectantly, holding herself motionless as his fingers parted her, moving importantly.

"What am I supposed to do?" she asked frantically, feeling a pulsing desperation generated by his searching caresses.

He laughed very softly, continuing to stroke her, whispering, "Nothing. Not a thing. Just let me love you."

It went on and on like swimming floating his body the sea pulling her into motion as he drew from her mouth she held herself poised in amazement at his slow entrance into her effortless painless holding her gently locked to his rhythm introducing her to pleasure she wanted to prolong forever remaining afloat impaled on this sea rocking his hands securing her rocking until she was overtaken by spasms waves of pleasure engulfing her so that she was only distantly aware of the sighing sounds he made as she rested afloat her face in his neck until like a sea swell subsiding it was calm again. And then they both laughed.

It wasn't until they were on their way to Greenwich that she wondered how her family was going to react to this man she'd married in such haste. A man the same age as her mother. She was so consumed by anxiety she chain-smoked all the way there, perspiring heavily, convinced they'd denounce both her and Adam as well as the marriage. Turning up unannounced with a husband in tow. She glanced over at Adam. He looked as self-possessed as always.

"I'm nervous," she said.

"Tell you the truth, I'm kind of nervous myself." He gave her a pale smile.

As it turned out, their arrival was anticlimactic. Leonie met them at the front door exclaiming, "Thank God! I've been trying to reach you since last night!"

"Why? What's happened?"

"Gray's gone! Packed his things and left a note. The dean rang me from Choate yesterday afternoon. Come in! Do come in!" She hurried into the living room, saying, "He's gone off to England. To join the RAF. Your father's been on the telephone for hours, trying to find out where he left and how. It's mad! Completely mad!"

"I'd like you to meet Adam," Leo said, doubting there'd be any more appropriate time.

"I'm sorry." Leonie smiled distractedly, coming across the

room to shake his hand. "This has been so upsetting. Forgive me. How very nice to meet you."

"Adam and I are married," she said, watching her mother's face. "We thought we'd come down, surprise you."

She loved her mother for the way she managed to turn a handshake into an embrace, breaking into a beautiful smile, saying, "I'm happy for you. Both of you." She then hugged Leo before saying, "I'll just go up, get your father. We'll celebrate." She went out quickly, leaving Leo and Adam standing there staring at each other.

"How," he asked, sitting down in one of the armchairs, "did she do that?"

"I think I'd better go up, too. I'll be right back."

She rushed out, and he sank back into the chair. It had been the most gracious display of spontaneous welcome he'd ever seen anyone make.

Leonie said in an undertone, "I simply cannot believe she's done this! He's not at all the right sort of man for Leo."

"What sort of chap is he?" Gray asked.

"Haven't any idea," she said. "Just that he's not the right sort. Not at all. And I couldn't begin to tell you why."

"Silly nit, rushing headlong into a marriage with someone she scarcely knows."

"Well, for God's sake, don't come over all angry with her. It isn't up to us to make Leo's decisions."

The conversation over dinner was entirely about Gray.

"He's bound to get in touch with you," Adam said, trying for an optimistic note.

"The most idiotic damned thing to do!" Gray declared. "The RAF! And they'll take him on, too!" He shook his head, furious with both his children. Gray for being so reckless. Leo for being reckless, too, but in a different fashion. Two headstrong, impulsive children bent on living dangerously.

"He'll be all right," Leo said. "Gray," she explained to Adam, "has been mysteriously disappearing since he was about eight. He always manages to turn up perfectly all right sooner or later."

"I think it might be a good idea if we headed back to New Haven tonight," Adam offered.

"Nonsense!" Leonie said. "I've had Amy prepare the guest room. We scarcely see Leo these days. And we're certainly not going to miss out on an opportunity to get to know her husband. Gray and I do go to bed rather early, but please don't feel you have to follow. Have another drink, put another log on the fire. We'll see you in the morning."

They exchanged good nights. Amy cleared the table. Leo and Adam drifted into the living room.

"Mummy had a heart attack about four and a half years ago. It's why they go to bed so early. They don't actually go straight to sleep. They read. And talk. They'll be up for hours now, discussing Gray. How could he *do* that? It was so thoughtless."

"Tell me about your mother's heart problem," he said.

"There's not a great deal to tell. She refused to go into the hospital, had me prepare a number of infusions and so forth, medicated herself. She's been perfectly all right since, but Daddy insists she rest when she's at home."

"What sort of infusions?" he asked.

"An extract of digitalis."

"Are you serious?"

There were times when his questions created an instant and immediate anger in her, like asking her to qualify an already-serious remark.

"My mother grew up in Africa," she said evenly. "She knows more about herbal medicine than most of the doctors I've met know about medicine period. I can assure you she cured herself."

"Why are you getting yourself so worked up?" he asked complacently.

"Why must you always ask for an explanation of an explanation?"

"A good doctor—"

"Oh, Jesus!" she snapped. "Don't sing me the good-doctor song again! I don't think I can take it." *This isn't going to work, it'll never work, what am I doing here with you? I don't even like you.*

The following afternoon a telegram came from London: "JOINING RAF STOP DON'T WORRY STOP LETTER FOLLOWING STOP LOVE GRAY."

"Bloody marvelous!" Gray said, exasperated, waving the telegram around. "Now, tell us something we don't already know!"

"He'll be all right, darling," Leonie said, watching Leo and

Adam walking outside. They appeared to be arguing. "I don't give them a year," she said.

"Six months," Gray wagered, coming to stand beside her at the window. "Is that what you're crying about?"

"All of it," she said dismally, noting the way Leo was using her hands for emphasis. "The lot."

24

Once on board the plane, he knew everything was going to work perfectly, according to his plan. He strapped himself in, then sat back to enjoy his first flight, again going over what he'd do upon arriving in England. He had the money he'd taken from his savings account—he'd taken only part of it, just over three thousand dollars—and the room he'd booked at the small hotel in West Kensington. And while he was waiting for his eighteenth birthday, he'd take advantage of this free time to visit the galleries and museums, see as much as possible before presenting himself to the recruiting office—or whatever they called it.

He hadn't any doubt they'd take him. Although it had been difficult deciding between the army and the air force. But he preferred the challenge of the air force, believing the world had moved into a new era of warfare. The army simply wouldn't offer his imagination the same stimulus the air force would. And since it was perfectly obvious to him that the States wouldn't get into the war for some time yet, he'd get himself into the RAF and be trained, primed to go when Germany made its inevitable declaration of war.

He did worry about his mother's reaction to what he was doing, and hoped she wouldn't be so upset she'd have another heart attack. That was the only thing that might have stopped him going: the fear that he'd be responsible for making her ill. But after thinking it through dozens of times, he finally had to decide that just wasn't going to happen.

Father, of course, would be furious. Gray could just hear him saying, "You've gone too bloody far this time, chappie!" in that amazingly theatrical-sounding voice he used when he was so upset it was all he could do to control himself. He'd stand there, his head tilted with his good ear presented so he wouldn't miss anything, red in the face and eloquent as hell, sounding just exactly like Nigel Bruce.

The minute he arrived, he'd send them a telegram, then write a letter explaining. They'd be mad, upset for a while, but they'd get used to it. And as long as they didn't know specifically where he was, they couldn't come after him or make him go home.

Feeling relaxed, he got out his copy of *The Decline and Fall of the Roman Empire* and read steadily until he fell asleep.

He sent off the telegram, then hired a taxi to take him to the hotel in West Kensington, where he lay down, thinking to take a nap, and ended up sleeping for thirteen hours. Waking up ravenous, and anxious to write the promised letter, he took a bath, shaved—for the third time that week—dressed in fresh clothes, and made his way out to the street. He bought some fish and chips and created something close to a riot of laughing derision by asking for a napkin.

"A napkin?" The girl behind the counter stared at him with remarkably unblinking fishlike eyes while half a dozen men standing in the queue hooted with laughter and made lewd remarks.

"You know," Gray said, "to wipe my hands on. A napkin."

" 'E means a serviette, luv," an older woman behind him said, turning to glare at the men, saying, "Off wiff it, you louts. Don't pay 'em no mind, dear," she told Gray. "Bunch o' layabouts!"

He was given something stiffly resembling a napkin and escaped out of the place carrying his vinegar-damp newspaper package of fish and chips and walked along eating, looking at everything and everyone, wishing he'd ordered double portions. He was still hungry when he crumpled the soggy newspaper and pushed it into a dustbin.

After purchasing some airmail stationery, he went into a second fish-and-chip shop and emerged with a double order, which he ate very quickly, keeping his package of envelopes and paper tucked up under his arm.

Aside from that nonsense about the napkin, the city didn't seem at all strange to him. In fact, there was a definite familiarity about everything, as if he'd been here many times before and was returning home after a considerable absence. He felt exceptionally comfortable and relaxed, and went into a pub, ordering what the fellow next to him did, a pint of Guinness, then stood drinking the stuff down, thinking he could easily acquire quite a taste for it. But exercising his usual caution, he finished the pint before retracing his route to the hotel, where he sat down in the small lounge to write his letter, advising them of the post office where they might address their letters to him. Then, feeling pleased with himself—the letter safely posted—he returned to his room to make a list of things he wanted to do the next day. Making lists and keeping notebooks was a habit he'd acquired from his mother; although he'd have argued that, had anyone suggested it to him.

"Clever little sod!" Grayson swore, passing the letter back to Leonie. "Knows damned well we're not about to fly over there and wait about for him to come collect his post."

"It's a very sensible letter," she said, returning it to its envelope.

"Hardly a *sensible* thing to do, is it?" he demanded, tossing his book to the floor, where it landed with a surprisingly loud bang.

She was thinking about Clark, about the feeling she'd had when he'd gone off; that foreboding. It chilled her, making her shrink down under the bedclothes. She wouldn't think about it. There was a general staff meeting tomorrow afternoon. Rose wanted to talk about new uniforms for the waitresses, and several other things. Leonie was due to have a long sit-down with Bill and review the books. She wasn't in the mood for any of it, didn't want to have to think at all, about anything. Not about Gray, or Leo's suddenly marrying so unsuitable a man, or about Grayson's anger.

When he was afraid, he got angry. When he was upset, he got angry. The anger was a cover for all the caring raging away beneath the surface. He was a man who said little, thought long and carefully before he spoke, then sounded angry as he delivered his words; much of the time completely unaware of how potent and even intimidating his anger could be to those who didn't know him as well as she did.

He put out the light and lay glaring into the darkness, until he felt her move close against him. And then much of the anger dissipated itself and he slid down to fit her into his arms, saying, "Sorry to go on so, darling. It's just such a dangerous thing for him to have done, reckless."

"Knowing Gray," she said very quietly, "he had every bit of it planned down to the last detail. He's not reckless. You know he isn't."

"He might at least have discussed it with us."

"Why?" she said calmly. "We'd simply have refused to hear of it."

"That's absolutely right," he agreed.

"And then he'd have found some other way to do what he wanted." She slid her hand up inside his pajama top.

"Your bloody hand's freezing!" he complained, turning more toward her. "We've got to see to a new furnace. Another winter with that old monster in the cellar and they'll find the lot of us frozen to death in our beds."

"I don't want to talk," she said meaningfully. "Not at all."

He sat up and quickly threw off his pajamas, then stretched out again as she lay down over top of him and remained without moving for several minutes, her hand smoothing his shoulder as her eyes became accustomed to the dark. She thought about how their lovemaking had undergone a very definite change since the upsets with the children, how he invariably approached her these nights as if she was constructed of too-fragile substances and might, very easily, be damaged in some irreparable fashion if he didn't exercise the utmost caution in handling her.

She lifted her head to look at him, able only to discern a faintly reflected light from his eyes before turning her head slightly to kiss him, running her tongue over his lower lip.

"You've been smoking," she accused him.

"I had a cigarette," he admitted. "I needed it."

"That's as sensible as my leaping into ice water."

"We weren't going to talk," he reminded her, his hands covering the backs of her thighs.

"That's right," she said, "we weren't."

She moved down somewhat so that she could feel him pressing hard at the apex of her thighs, kissing him again, her hips revolving against his; wet where he pressed into her. His hands moved up her sides, signaling, so that she raised the upper part of her body and he put his mouth to her breast, but so delicately she could scarcely feel it. She wanted more, wanted to feel the recognizable gentle ferocity of his passion, the storm he could become, sweeping her up into him.

She sat away, then turned suddenly, using her mouth and hands to convey what she wanted him to know. He sighed, murmuring something she couldn't decipher, and she teased him with her tongue, feeling a corresponding interior twisting in anticipation of pleasure; going on until she knew if she continued he'd finish in her mouth, and he disliked that, preferring to end inside her. Sitting up, looking at him through the darkness, she touched the tips of her fingers to her mouth, then reached for his hand and placed it firmly over her breast, squeezing his hand around her breast so that for the first time in weeks she was able to derive a definite darting pleasure.

"I'm not going to die if you make love to me," she said, keeping her hand over his on her breast. "If I haven't died yet, I'm certainly not going to now."

"But it's—"

"You're making me feel like an invalid, Gray. Must I be more graphic?" She withdrew her hand from his, but his fingers remained in place, gently pressing inward as his other hand came up under her hair and over the back of her neck, urging her once more down on top of him as he kissed her hard, their teeth colliding as his tongue thrust assertively into her mouth; rolling over with her so that their positions were reversed and he was now on top. His hand insistently stroked down her belly, up between her thighs. She bent open her legs, he came down, stabbing forward, making her gasp at the suddenness, holding still for a moment before extending her legs to lock them around his, whispering, "Yes! God, yes!" her hands directing him.

She could go away into feeling instead of having to lie in fearful suspension, wondering if they'd ever see their son again, or if Leo had made the most frightful mistake, or if she'd outlive Gray, or any of the dozens of other doubtful possibilities.

For the first time in years he thought of Clarissa, of that evening when he'd plowed her body, wanting her to be Leonie and not the underendowed, somehow flimsy fascimile she'd been; trying, with his body and through his superior strength, to transform someone he cared for only slightly into someone for whom he cared completely. He'd never made love to Leonie in quite this fashion—with abandon, without regard for all the intimacies of their daily life together. He was disregarding his perpetual fear of losing her again, not to another life or some other man, but to a death with which she seemed, at times, to live too closely. What she was showing him now was the loss—never mind whether temporary or merely transitional—of fear and her determination to take hold of the moment, just as she'd taken firm hold of his hand, and draw from it every possible measure of pleasure and pain.

He thought of how he'd promised himself that if he failed to find Leonie, he'd return to London to marry Clarissa. Because she was the only other woman with whom he felt he had a positive identity. Someone who respected the perimeters of his willingness without feeling compelled to invade the more private areas of his mind in order to securely establish herself there. Clarissa had been growing into a woman of some wisdom. And he'd observed the gradual transformation, realizing he'd grown to care for her far more than he'd imagined possible; all of it stemming from that night when he'd insisted upon her allowing herself to feel. She told him once, soon before he left London after the war's end, "You've spoiled me for what always was a very lucrative enterprise, so long as my feelings remained safely separate. I'm a little frightened of where I find myself." Where, he wondered, had she eventually managed to find herself?

With Leonie, now as at the beginning, it had always been feeling; intense, ungovernable feeling pouring from him into her. He cherished the vulnerability of her secret self, her tremendous determination and drive, her ability to give herself utterly, withholding nothing. This prompted him to commit himself, in every way, because the sight of her alone was sufficient to fill him with pleasure and a boundless optimism and gratitude that she'd elected to love him.

His senses charged almost beyond bearing, awed as ever by her tumultuous responses, he kept on until she was seized—as if jolted by an electrical current—and studied her at the peak of passion, overcome by tenderness and caring; blindly loving the heat and fluid rhythm of her body, blindly submitting to her.

When it was done and he lay collapsed on her breasts, listening to her decelerating breathing as well as his own, she held him, he thought, with a corresponding tenderness, whispering, "I love you. So very much. Tell me he's not going to die over there. It's what I feel, can't escape feeling, since they rang us from the school."

"He's *not* going to die!" he said, looking and sounding furious as he sat up and switched on the light. "He's bloody *not* going to die!"

In the unrelenting glare of the light, his eyes moved over the scars he was never aware of in darkness, the damage she'd had, since it happened, managed to make him forget. The sight of it now made something inside him ache miserably, so that he wanted anew to run out, comb the city streets, find the man and barehandedly kill him. Slowly.

"Why do you look at me that way?" she asked, too sated to draw her legs closed, although his expression made her want to, made her aware that her body was no longer the unblemished, healthy entity it once had been.

"It frightens me just as much," he said, his eyes traveling over her. "But you indulge yourself, brood. Are you aware," he asked, the gentleness of his hand cupping her ruined breast belying the ferocity of his expression, "that the two of us spend very little time together? You're spending your life nursing Lion's along as if it's some sort of invalid child, putting in far more time than is needed."

"And you don't?" she countered softly. "With your deadlines and headlines and all the rest of it? Off before the sun's barely up to catch the seven-fifteen. And sometimes, only sometimes, mind you, managing to catch the seven-oh-five home."

"There's not much point to my coming home to sit about chatting with Amy, is there?"

She was filled with dread, suddenly; anticipating he was about to deliver some sort of ultimatum; finding herself tautly suspended, waiting. But his hand continued to caress her, his eyes moving over her body until he sighed tiredly, saying, "I hate sharing you. Every so often it catches up with me, takes me by the throat. Then I want to drag you off somewhere, keep you exclusively mine. Primal, caveman sort of mentality. It doesn't happen often, as I say. But when it does, and when you become the African, mystical and frightening, prophesying, I feel you've gone off somewhere without me, and that's when I'm struck by this desire to keep you mine, exclusively. And bugger the children, the business, all of it! It's unreasonable," he said, winding down. "I'm well aware of that. It's simply that I find myself caring more than I ever imagined I could, and frightened because I'm getting old and can't have all I want of you."

"Don't feel that way," she said huskily, drawing him down.

"I can't sort myself out well enough to tell you how hearing all that makes me feel."

"I love you, Leonie." His body went tight, hard. "I love you to the exclusion of everyone and everything else." Graphically, he demonstrated. She made a small sound and he asked, "Am I hurting you?"

"Yes. But no, no."

He understood and gentled himself so that this time was dreamlike slow thrusting into a dizzy euphoria crested by sighs, soft sighs of heightening pleasure displacing fear and aging and the drafty reminder of winter's presence just outside their small secure island.

It surprised Leo how easily Adam settled into married life, while she reacted with something very like shock every time someone addressed her as Mrs. Birkell. And when she was more correctly addressed as Dr. Birkell, she found she wasn't sure if it was her or Adam being referred to. Something about their both being eligible for the same title deprived her of a large measure of her satisfaction in attaining her degree. She'd always had an image of herself in hospital whites, hurrying down some corridor as Dr. Marlowe. Somehow, being Dr. Birkell was less.

She found she also minded living with someone else on so intimate a basis. Especially at those times when becoming a doctor seemed solely predicated on one's stamina, on how many back-to-back shifts one could cope with alertly before finally being freed to go off for a few hours' sleep. After coming off emergency-room duty for sixteen hours, she didn't want to make love or talk or do any of the things it seemed Adam expected of her. The laundry could go to hell, Hershey bars made a fine meal, even the brown-acid hospital-cafeteria coffee went down easily. Adam, apparently, had forgotten this aspect of the route to earning the right to be called "doctor." Or perhaps the gap in their ages signified differences in the system. It might have been different during his internship, his residency. She was invariably too tired to discuss it.

Among other things, there was the problem of the patients who, believing her to be a nurse, wouldn't allow her to perform her duties, saying, "I'll just wait for the doctor, dear," so that she was obliged to explain never-endingly that she *was* the doctor and there wasn't anyone else to wait for. And too often they countered, with narrowed eyes and considerable suspicion, by saying, "You're *not* my doctor."

"No, but I'm going to have a look at you today."

"You're a nice kid. You go on, dear, look at someone else. I'll just wait for my doctor."

I *am* your *goddamned* doctor! she wanted to shout.

The male interns sneered among themselves while Leo battled down her frustration and anger and got on with her work—wherever she was allowed.

Adam, attempting to be helpful, said, "Don't delude yourself that it doesn't happen to the men, too. Because it does. They're just taking a perverse pleasure in seeing it coming down on you because you represent the so-called weaker half."

"I'm no damned *weaker* than anyone! I've done shifts for Anson Conroy three times in a row because he was 'too tired,' and would I please, as a great favor."

"The system's designed to test you in all areas, Leo," he said, making a great display of fatherly/husbandly patience. "Not just your knowledge is under the gun, you know. Accept the system for what it is and ignore the rest."

"That's fine, except you don't have the patients you try to examine patting you on the head saying they'll just wait for the *doctor,* if it's all the same, thank you anyway."

"You're always going to run into that," he said philosophically, infuriatingly. "At least until there are a lot more women entering medicine. Which isn't likely to happen tomorrow."

"Of course not!" she stormed. "Not when they know they're going to have to put up with all this *crap*! Why should any sane woman volunteer herself into such a stinking system?"

"It'll happen," he said. "Eventually."

Platitudes, she thought. I don't need that from you. What *do* I need from you? You haven't any idea what I'm talking about.

She was called to take an arterial blood sample from a woman up on Six who'd just had a cesarean section. She went along to the room with a tray of equipment and needles, to be met with glaring hostility by the woman's husband, who hovered doubtfully over her, preventing her from properly accomplishing this relatively simple task. The woman's veins and skin were good. It wouldn't be at all difficult to draw the sample from the left hand. But the husband kept asking questions, wanting to know, "Are you a nurse, or what?"

"I'm a doctor," she answered, selecting a needle.

"What kind of doctor?"

"An intern."

"That means you're a student."

She chose not to answer, swabbing the woman's hand in preparation for drawing the sample. The woman lay watching in somehow serene silence, obviously accustomed to her husband's exercising of doubtful power.

Just as Leo was about to insert the needle, he asked, "What're you doing there, eh?" so that she slipped, the needle grazing the woman's skin.

Straightening, keeping hold of the woman's cool hand, Leo said quietly, "Would you mind stepping out into the corridor until I've finished taking this sample?"

"Why should I? What for?"

"Because you are interfering, making it difficult for both me and your wife." She looked full in the woman's eyes, wanting support; seeing a strange expression overtaking those eyes as the woman said, "Go on, Jack. The doctor asked you to wait outside."

He hadn't expected it. Neither had Leo. He left. And the two women smiling at each other, Leo quickly drew the sample, placed a bandage over the woman's hand, and recovered the tray.

"Don't let him bother you," the woman said encouragingly. "He blows a lot but it's just because he worries about me. He didn't mean any harm."

For a few seconds Leo loved her. For her tolerance, her understanding, her having taken a stand—however minimal. She said, "Thank you," sensing her own inadequacy, picked up her tray, and went out past the distraught husband, who called out, "That was awfully fast, wasn't it?"

She continued on her way, pretending she hadn't heard. If she'd risked answering, she'd have said something that ultimately would have served only to do herself harm. Because she was subject to the reactions and whims of the patients and the families of the patients in this hospital. Any one of them could, with a few well-placed words, see her out of the hospital and on the street with nowhere to go. And she wasn't about to jeopardize everything she'd struggled to achieve.

Horrified and literally sickened, she discovered almost a

year to the day of their marriage that she was pregnant. And for a change, she coerced Anson Conroy into taking over her night shift so that she could go home at a reasonable hour and think about this, talk it over with Adam; filled with doubts about the possible outcome.

"I don't want to stop at this point to have a baby," she told him. "I can't. Not now."

"But we agreed we wanted children."

"I know that. And I do. But having one now will delay me for at least a year. I can't *have* a baby *now*."

"I assumed," he said, distressed, "you'd had yourself outfitted with a diaphragm."

"You *assumed*?" She could feel her temper building. "Why," she asked, controlling her voice, "would you assume a thing like that? *I* assumed you were taking care to protect me. It never occurred to me that you weren't."

"It looks as if we've both made a little mistake." He smiled, as if he'd made an enormously funny joke.

She hated him, could hardly bear to look at him, but forced herself to. "All right," she said evenly. "The 'little mistake' has been made. What do I do about it?"

"You want to abort?" he asked, looking appalled.

"I am *not* going to have a child I *don't want*. Obviously, since we're living on 'assumptions,' I'm going to have to be more careful in the future. But I'm not going to have this child!"

"I won't have you going to some backstreet quack," he warned.

"Then do it for me!" she said coldly. "You put it in there, you can take it out!"

He wanted to hit her, but refused to allow himself to strike her. "You're asking me to put my entire career in jeopardy," he said stiffly.

"Oh, for God's sake! Who's going to know? Do you think I'm going to go skipping merrily through the hospital announcing to everyone that my husband performs weekend abortions?"

"I can't!" he argued, his eyes begging her not to insist on this. "Aside from everything else, I don't happen to have two good hands, Leo."

"I see," she said barely audibly, her throat pulsing. "I see."

She turned away and went into the kitchen—the only room, aside from the bathroom, where she had any measure of privacy. She leaned against the stove trying to decide what to do, knowing now the marriage had been a mistake, wrong in every conceivable way. A year, and she wanted to escape the claustrophobic, enforced intimacy, the demands upon her time and body, the utter lack of communication in almost every area. What was the point of their being together? she asked herself, staring at the pilot light. I got more sleep, accomplished more, when I was alone. I didn't have to listen to someone snoring in the night beside me, or contend with having to make love first thing in the morning when it was the last thing I wanted. I had no stacks of laundry, no accumulations of dirty dishes left awaiting me; none of this. I *hate* this! My God, I hate it!

He came to the doorway, in a subdued voice asking, "What can I do, Leo? Tell me what you want me to do."

"I've told you," she said.

"But I can't. Ask me anything else. There *must* be something else."

"Nothing," she said without inflection. "Absolutely nothing. I'll call the hospital, contrive some family emergency." She moved past him and went into the bedroom to get her suitcase from the closet. "I shouldn't be gone for more than two days, or three."

"What are you doing?"

She stopped, her hand on the dresser, and looked over at him wide-eyed, saying, "I'm going to someone who will help, without forcing me to listen to excuses and sob stories, or demanding explanations of my explanations. Someone who cares about me simply because I'm me and not for any other selfish reason. This was a mistake, Adam. A terrible mistake. I'm sorry. I know not all of it is your fault. I am guilty of assuming just as much as you did. Not about the same things, but that doesn't matter."

"Another man," he said suspiciously.

"You fool!" she said, filled with contempt. "You stupid fool!"

"Where are you going, then?" he demanded.

"Home. *Home*! What I should have thought of in the first place, instead of asking you to violate your oath, jeopardize your career, perform a fairly simple procedure with your one and two-fifths hands."

"Bitch! You bitch!"

She looked up at him as she snapped closed her suitcase. "You know I'm not, Adam," she said sadly. "But you'll spend the rest of your life telling everyone I am because you're afraid, using your injured hand as an excuse for too many failings. Like fat people or Negroes or Jewish people using their fatness, their Jewishness, their being a different color as their reason why, their rationale, for someone's disliking them, or for their failures. It can't be anything as simple as a conflict of personalities, or a quality about someone that grates on the other person, or an inability to care deeply about someone else. It has to be that visible something that everyone can see. I feel so embarrassed, so juvenile; going home to my mother because I can't deal with my husband. If you'd just said something instead of calling me a bitch, I'd have stayed to talk it through. But I know now it's over."

Red in the face, groping for words, he watched her lift the suitcase off the bed, pick up her handbag, and walk out of the room. Let her go! he thought. Selfish bitch!

"I'll pick up the rest of my things, leave you the keys next week." She opened the front door and stood leaning tiredly against it for a moment. "I really am sorry, Adam. I think we should have just kept on making love. We didn't have to get married for that. You thought marriage was what I wanted and expected, and I thought it was what you needed. We'd probably have lasted a lot longer without it. The sex part was wonderful. I really am sorry."

She telephoned from a public box to let them know she was coming.

"Is something wrong, Leo?" her mother asked.

"Everything."

"Your father will pick you up at the station."

See how you love me! Leo thought, close to tears as she hung up and reached for her suitcase. No unnecessary questions or demands for explanations I can't make. Just acceptance and caring. Maybe it's something only mothers—certain mothers—give you.

25

He was trained to pilot the Battles, then the Blenheims and light bombers, and after putting in a request for additional training, the heavy bombers, in order to qualify for one of the eighteen squadrons of the Bomber Command.

He had his uniform, his training, a few routine missions, and very little to do. Everyone seemed to be hanging suspended, watching the daily newspapers, listening to the BBC reports of Hitler's various moves: first the invasion of Czechoslovakia, then the signing of the German-Russian nonaggression pact, and finally the invasion of Poland. Then tension replaced the bored suspension, and everyone waited until September 3, when France and Britain declared war on Germany while, that same day, Belgium declared her neutrality.

"It's very depressing over here," he wrote in a letter home early in January 1940. "Leave over Christmas, some of us went down to London, where they've been trying out what they call 'amenity lighting,' to relieve the blackouts. The effect is of trying to fix on a candle about seventy or eighty feet away.

"New Year's Eve in Piccadilly, we watched the old year out, courtesy of a flashlight somebody held on the face of a nearby clock. At the entrance to the Piccadilly Circus tube station, there was a party going on, complete with fancy hats and everybody singing 'Knees Up, Mother Brown.' It seemed pretty self-conscious and we all started drifting off after that, deciding to risk returning directly to base. Murder driving without lights, though.

"Feelings are running on the dark side, too. A good half of everyone I've met believes this one's going to last longer than the last. One fellow at the pub said he felt like he was waiting, indefinitely, in a dentist's waiting room. Although the general feelings is: We can't let old Hitler get away with it again, can we?

"England's certainly ready. The worst of what's happened so far is the number of people killed on the roads because of the blackouts. But they've got thousands of hospital beds all ready for the injured, and I read the other day in the *Times* that a million burial forms have been issued. That bothered me probably more than anything else so far. A *million!*

"It's the coldest winter here in forty-five years. A terrific amount of snow, just like home, except they're not really equipped to deal with it. I'd appreciate some of those heavy sets of underwear I left behind thinking I wouldn't need them and ..."

Leo, working a double shift at the hospital, was unable to get away until eight in the morning Christmas Day and drove down to Greenwich barely able to see the road, she was so exhausted; still feeling the aftereffects of her self-induced abortion as well as of the legalities undertaken to instigate the divorce.

She kept reliving the experience, going over the details, trying to get to the bottom of her feelings. Seeing herself following her mother's instructions, preparing the mixture, letting it cool. Then, feeling stark, feeling criminal somehow, douching herself with the surprisingly refreshing fluid. Thinking it was easy. Incredibly easy. But later, the pain awakened her, to send her staggering into the bathroom as the internal pressure built unbearably, and she couldn't help thinking she must have done something wrong, misunderstood the instructions somehow, because the pain was monstrous and surely it wasn't supposed to hurt as much as it did. Her medical knowledge and common sense deserted her as she climbed into the bathtub—it being the only logical place she could think of—to stand clutching her belly, her legs spread; the pain forcing her to crouch in the cold tub as, both fascinated and appalled, she delivered this unwanted child out of her.

It felt as if she'd killed something inside herself in the process. She remained crouched in the tub, racked by unimaginable pain, unable to look away from what emerged from her body; hating Adam and herself for causing this to happen. She struggled back to her feet to run the water, get rid of the evidence before cleaning herself. Sick, sobbing uncontrollably, hurt, she blamed herself for her naiveté, her lunatic haste in marrying, her pathetically bad taste in the choice of a husband. And blamed Adam for capitalizing on her innocence, and for his "assumptions." She felt self-maimed, damaged, and returned to New Haven weak, guilty, and totally determined to escape the marriage. Now it was Christmas and she had never felt less like celebrating in her life.

Amy had a cold and went about with two cardigans and a scarf, snuffling as she prepared the turkey for the oven. Leonie silently raised the thermostat, then went back to work on the rest of the meal, worried about Leo driving in this weather; worried about Gray, not having heard from him in several weeks. Never mind that the mails were fouled, slowed. There should have been a letter.

Grayson, sitting in the living room reading the *Herald Tribune*, looked at the tree every so often with an expression of mild dissatisfaction.

Nothing felt right.

Leonie had invited half a dozen of her new refugee friends to come for the day, explaining, "They've been through such a lot. No one should spend Christmas alone, even if they don't celebrate the holiday."

"I don't in the least mind," Gray had said calmly. "But one or two of the neighbors have made rather snide remarks, displaying the anti-Semitic underside to their sterling characters."

"What comments?" she'd asked, a flush of heat rising up from her throat.

"Nothing specific. You know, observations while one's collecting the post from the box. Having your group of 'friends' up for the holidays, eh, Marlowe? Ha, ha, ha. The slightest stress on 'friends.' All very subtle. Nearly let Bigelow have it across the back of the head with the shovel, snide bastard."

"Why is everyone suddenly hating Jews?" she asked now, coming into the living room to stand looking askance at the tree. "Why? As if it's some new vogue, as if *they're* responsible for what's happening to them. What have they *done*? If someone could just explain that to my satisfaction, perhaps at least I might be able to argue it intelligently. But I fail to see what crimes they've committed. I shouldn't have started," she said. "There's no answer, and I'll simply put myself into a temper and spoil the day."

"I've pledged to help White with his Committee to Defend America," he said, putting aside the newspaper.

"Money?"

"Money and some time. Not that I think anything's going to be resolved by debate. But Nye, Wheeler and Ford, Lindbergh—that group makes my blood boil. Say anything, do anything, but keep America out of the war. It's not our concern. Let the bloody Brits and Poles and frogs fend for themselves and leave us out of it! Immoral, the whole mess. And going to get messier, too."

"Have they honestly made remarks to you?" she asked, nettled.

"I shouldn't have said anything. I knew it'd upset you."

"You *should* have bashed that fool over the head with the shovel!"

He laughed and got up from his chair. "Do everyone a lot of good with a lawsuit on my hands," he said, putting his arm around her shoulders. "What time did Leo say she'd be getting here?"

"She didn't say, said she couldn't promise."

"I can't say I'm too happy about her driving down in all this snow."

"She'll be all right," she said automatically, knowing his casual observation was simply the visible tip of his considerable fear. He worried constantly about both the children. So much so, she sometimes felt she must be deficient in caring by comparison.

Leo could hardly keep herself awake and listened to the several conversations taking place across the dining table, finding the voices unnaturally loud and impassioned. A discussion revolving around politics—America in or out of the war?; religious discrimination; and details of personal experiences, ranging from the confiscation of property to physical, emotional, and spiritual abuse. She cared. About all of it. But she couldn't drag herself sufficiently far from her lethargy or exhaustion to actively contribute or even to listen with full attention. She found herself thinking of Gray, trying to imagine him in uniform. A flier. A pilot. She couldn't see it. Any more than she could see herself getting involved again with some man. The mere idea of an involvement, of having to share her life, her thoughts, her time, her body with another person was too enervating. She wanted, more than anything else, to go up to her old room and lie down, close her eyes, and sleep.

The long meal finally ended, everyone moved into the living room for coffee. She curled up on the floor in front of the fire, leaning against her father's chair, feeling his hand stroking her hair. She closed her eyes just for a moment and awakened at the sound of good-byes and thank-yous being exchanged in the front hall. The two Polish artists; the German professor and his doctor wife; the Czech husband and wife, both dancers—all Jews—embracing her mother and father, thanking them for a fine day before hurrying to catch the 8:05 back to the city and their various jobs.

The Poles had temporary jobs shoveling snow. The German professor, fortunately well-spoken in English, had been given a lecturing position at Columbia. His wife, her degree useless here, was studying in order to be recertified as a pediatric surgeon. The Czechs had luckily landed jobs as supers with the Metropolitan Opera and were taking classes six hours a day, hoping to find positions as soloists soon with one of the ballet companies.

Leo got up to say good-bye and apologize for failing to participate. They all turned sympathetic smiles upon her, understanding. Particularly the pediatric surgeon, who, in her halting English, said, "I am to work also, so I am knowing how it makes fatigued." Nice people, good people. Her parents' friends. She returned to the living room to sit on the sofa beside Rose, pouring herself a cup of tepid coffee, saying, "I feel awful. Why didn't somebody kick me or something, wake me up?"

"Nobody minded, sweetheart." Rose smiled. "You look worn out. Why don't you go on up to bed?"

"*I* mind," she protested. "It was . . . I don't know. I wanted to listen, hear what they all had to say. I miss half of everything that gets said these days. I think I will go to bed," she said uncertainly, covering Rose's hand with her own. "I'm bad company right now. Where did Pat and Daddy get to?"

"They're making turkey sandwiches."

"God! How can they be thinking of eating again so soon?"

Rose shrugged, and Leo studied her, noticing how the texture of Rose's facial skin had altered, softened. It now had that blurred, misted look certain older women acquired; a flattering, vulnerable softness that emphasized her eyes, the width of her mouth, her previously unconsidered sexuality. Rose was a powerfully sexual woman, Leo saw. It seemed to shine off her. And something about Rose's features, her expression, made Leo's lungs constrict, made her turn her face into Rose's shoulder.

"What's the matter, sweetheart?" Rose asked.

"I don't know," she answered, unusually aware of the delicate swell of Rose's breasts, her perfume, the silken quality of her skin where her shoulder rose into her neck. I envy you, Leo thought, surprised. I envy you so much. Because you're where I want to be, and I become exhausted just thinking about how far I'm going to have to travel before I can be where you are.

"You're just tired," Rose said consolingly. "When you're tired, everything's too much. I know how that feels."

"*You* never get tired! I've never, as long as I can remember, seen you anything but . . . perfect."

Rose laughed. "You just haven't seen me at the right moments, that's all. Like a Saturday afternoon at around three when I drag myself home and fall apart all over poor old Pat."

"Did Mummy tell you?"

"Tell me what?"

"About the abortion?"

"Not directly."

"She told me what to do. And I did it. At first, it didn't feel like anything. Nothing. But later. My God! I still feel it."

"I know," Rose said softly, so that Leo sat away and looked at her.

"Did you?" Leo asked.

"Twice. The first time, there was a woman. She kept her hat on the entire time. And the doctor. I think he was. But I've always wondered about that. He had an apron, like a butcher's apron. I sometimes dream about the two of them. Even now, after all these years. I think because none of it seemed real. Yet it was so real it was impossible to believe it was happening to me. Not to me. How could I be there, be naked that way with two strangers? A woman with a hat, and a man with a white apron. It couldn't be me. But it was. I was there."

Leo returned her head to Rose's shoulder, holding her tightly.

"I want to do something, Aunt Rose. Go somewhere, *do* something, get the answers I need; finish out my residency and then use it somehow. By the time I'm available, they're bound to be needing surgeons. And I want to . . . It's so unfair! That woman, Frau Doktor Liebmann. Do you know she wrote one of *the* definitive textbooks on pediatric surgery and they won't allow her to practice here? And her husband. He's an authority on medieval literature, but the most he can do here is lecture on contemporary German authors, without doubt the least popular course they've probably got at Columbia. The whole thing makes me sick, angry. I don't understand why. And now, today, Mummy tells me the neighbors have been making cute-nasty remarks to Daddy about the fact that we have Jewish refugee friends who come to visit. Then, if all that isn't enough"—she pulled away and lit a cigarette, sitting with her elbows on her knees leaning toward Rose—"Adam and I keep running into each other at the hospital and he makes an obvious point of avoiding me. So everyone knows, or thinks he knows, about us. I can't simply be left alone to do my work, I've got to justify myself one way or another. And spend whatever free time I do happen to have refusing stud offers. As if I'm some sort of pathetic brood mare whose entire disposition will undergo phenomenal alterations if I just lie back and let them fix me up right.

"I was hoping to talk to Mummy, but there hasn't been a chance and I've got to get back in the morning. Now they're out there making turkey sandwiches, probably speculating on what Gray's up to, discussing the pros and cons of Mother's working for Roosevelt's reelection committee. I sound like sour grapes, Rose. It isn't what I mean. I can't even *say* what I mean. There's just no time, not enough time." She stubbed out the cigarette, saying, "That's just making me feel sick." She looked penetratingly at Rose for a moment, her throat working. "I'll be twenty-six in a few months, Rose. Another year and I'll be an honest-to-God surgeon. I've been in school, working for that for ten years. Oh, Jesus!" She jumped up, took several steps, then stopped. "I'm sorry, Rose. I sound *insane*! Complaining to you. *Complaining*. I don't have the right. Tell Mummy I've gone up to bed, will you? I'm sorry, Rose. Truly." She paused to grab her cigarettes and matches, then ran out, leaving Rose sitting in stunned silence.

"Leo?"

She opened her eyes, blinking against the light, to see her mother sitting on the side of the bed.

"What time is it?" she asked, squinting at the bedside clock.

"Just after ten. I'm sorry I didn't have time to talk with you today, darling. It's been so hectic."

"It's all right." Leo pulled herself up against the pillows, lighting a cigarette. "You don't have to apologize to me, for God's sake. It was disgusting of me, falling asleep that way. Then ranting and raving at Rose. I don't know what the hell's happening to me."

"Shall we talk about it?"

"I behaved like an imbecile with Rose. She must think I've lost my mind."

"Of course she doesn't. You've had a trying time of it this past year. We all understand that."

"Don't laugh, but if I thought they'd take me, I'd join the army or something. Just to get away."

"I don't find that amusing," Leonie said quietly, waving away the cigarette smoke.

"I didn't intend it to be. I'll put this out," she said, reaching for the ashtray. "I know you hate it when I smoke."

"I don't hate it, Leo. I simply dislike it. And you haven't been an imbecile. We seem to be dealing in superlatives. I want to help, but you're not giving me any indication of how I might."

"Sometimes," she said slowly, "you have a way of making me feel so inferior, of showing me up for being too self-concerned, too. . . . I don't know. Everything. Just the way you keep on opening yourself up to everything. Refugees, causes, campaigns."

"And you?" Leonie smiled.

"Yes, *me*! In control, there you are. And I'm falling apart faster than the human eye can see. Why don't you say something about it, finally? I'm sure you have an opinion or two on the mess I've made of things."

"You're going to dig away at me because you're angry."

"Maybe."

"I'm no one's whipping boy, Leo. Not even yours. Don't mistake my caring for something else. Of course I have opinions. I thought the marriage was a mistake from the onset. He's a perfectly nice man, a little self-pitying, with a very pedestrian concept of marriage. What did you expect of him? You don't marry someone, Leo, because you think you can—after the fact—change him to suit your purposes. That's not the way things are done."

"And you think that's what I did?"

"Yes, I do. It wasn't he who changed, Leo. You did. I'm

not criticizing you. It's not easy to live with *anyone*, even under the best of circumstances. I think you're angry with yourself for making a mistake. I also think you're carrying it a bit far. It's odd," she said softly, "seeing myself in you. Years ago, I carried on just as you are now for being unable to sustain, without outside help, what I'd started. Perhaps it's simply being young. If you want to get away somewhere, darling, go. You're a grown woman. Surely you don't think we'd try to stop you?"

"Every time you're nice this way, understanding—not that you're not all the rest of the time—but when you're especially nice and especially understanding, I feel so goddamned guilty. It's just hideous how guilty I feel. By comparison. You know one of the things Adam liked best about me? The fact that you're my mother. That impressed the hell out of him. I want someone around who's impressed by *me*. That makes me sound as if I'm jealous of you, and I'm not. I'm totally proud of you. I admire what you've done. No, it's me. I hated being Dr. Birkell when all my life I'd planned on being Dr. Marlowe. Now, I'm finally Dr. Marlowe, and everything grates. No one can answer my questions. No one even seems to *understand* them. I'm spoiling your Christmas, and I feel so guilty. I feel guilty just talking to you this way. I want things I can't seem to have. I have things I can't seem to want."

"Perhaps," Leonie said carefully, "it would be a good idea for you to try to get clear away."

"I saw how you reacted when Gray went!"

"You're seven years older than Gray. And I doubt you'll be allowed into combat zones. I'm sorry you feel like my shadow. I don't know how to respond to that. Give me a hug," she coaxed softly.

Wondering at her own perverseness, Leo gave herself reluctantly into her mother's arms, at once deriving enormous comfort from being held, breathing in the faintly herbal fragrance that belonged only to her mother, recognizing the shape of her mother's body, its familiar warmth.

"Don't pay any attention to me," she murmured. "Tomorrow, when I'm driving back to the hospital, I'll go over everything I've said tonight and want to die for talking the way I have to you."

"Don't be so hard on yourself. I think I'm able to decide which things are critical and which are just the end result of your frustration. I'm going to go to bed now. Your father's rustling his pages very loudly. Do you hear?" They listened, hearing pages being turned, then laughed together quietly.

"I love you!" Leo's voice emerged thin. "You and Daddy ... Rose—you're the only ones who make any sense to me."

"We love you, too."

"Why didn't you ever tell me Rose had had two abortions?"

"Why?" Leonie stood up. "Because it was none of your business."

"Well . . ." Leo smiled, chagrined. "I guess that puts me in my place."

"What you share with other women, Leo, is between you and them. What I share with you has to do, much of the time, with my being your mother. One of the nicest parts of your being an adult is that I no longer feel I have to censor what you can be told. It wasn't any of your business at the time."

"But it's become my business now."

"In a way," Leonie said thoughtfully, "I sometimes think we're each mothers to the other. It's something women do for each other. It's what Rose has done for me countless times. And what I hope I've done for her. You need friends, Leo. You need them badly. It isn't Gray who's always been the private one. It's you. And I can't show you or tell you how to share yourself in that way. But I hope you'll find some friends. We all need them."

There wasn't much to Tewkesbury. It was just somewhere to walk around, have a pint at the local. Until a group was invited to afternoon tea one Sunday at Lady Browning's house. And bitching loudly among themselves, six of them—all Americans and Canadians, because she'd specifically asked for overseas boys—went along, all spit-cleaned and polished, to have tea.

Lady Browning appeared younger than Gray had anticipated, looking to be in her early forties. Upon hearing his name, she kept hold of his hand, studying his face intently, saying, "But I know the name. Of course I do. Could it be your father?"

"I'm sorry," he said. "Could who be my father?"

"He's your height, but darker than you, with odd grayish-green eyes, and a frightful temper."

"That's right."

She laughed delightedly and released his hand, saying, "We will talk. Don't hurry away, will you? We'll talk."

Lady Browning also had a daughter. With long red hair, skin as white as milk and as markless, and eyes of the most amazing red-brown color Gray had ever seen. She carried around a tray of sandwiches while a uniformed woman—evidently the housekeeper—brought in a full silver tea service. She asked among the others, trying to find out her name.

Hughes, one of the Canadians, said, "I think it's something like Pat or Jane. But I'm not sure."

None of them, it turned out, had any idea. The guesses covered everything from Penelope to Elizabeth.

Once tea was poured, Lady Browning beckoned, inviting him to sit with her on the loveseat, at once asking, "Are you in touch with your father?"

"The letters are a little slow back and forth, but we're in touch, all right."

"Splendid!" She smiled, holding her cup and saucer perched on a narrow kneecap. "When next you write to him, tell him you've been to tea with Clarissa of Eaton Square. Send him my very fondest regards and tell him I'll keep an eye on you."

"You and my father were friends?"

"Very good friends." Her smile widened. "I noticed," she said slyly, "you seem rather taken with Sam."

"Sam?"

"My daughter, Samara."

"Oh! She's very pretty," he said ingenuously. "Seems awfully shy, though."

"Sam isn't the least bit shy," she said in a confidential undertone. "She simply finds all this dreadfully boring. Thinks I'm a bit of an ass for asking you groups of boys round to tea. Says I overdo it. 'A bit much, Mother,' is how she puts it."

She had an exceptional smile, one that seemed to invite an exchange of confidences while at the same time hinting she was in possession of a special, perhaps even superior and privileged understanding of the more ambiguous subtleties of human nature. Gray liked her very much. He also strongly admired her slender legs and graceful arms.

"Do you mind if I ask how old Sam is?"

"Eighteen," she answered, amused by the irony of the situation. "But anything else you care to know about Sam, you'll have to learn for yourself."

"Okay," he said, devouring a watercress sandwich in half a dozen bites.

"How old are you, Gray?" she asked, giving him another of those dazzling smiles.

"Eighteen. Almost nineteen," he added quickly. She laughed and patted him on the arm before setting down her teacup and excusing herself to have a word with each of the others.

Samara didn't reappear that afternoon, and, considerably disappointed, Gray again shook hands with Lady Browning at the door.

"Come Saturday evening for dinner," she said in a whisper. "Just the three of us. You'll have a proper chance to meet Sam. And I expect you could do with a decent meal."

"I sure could," he agreed. "If there's a problem or anything, I'll let you know during the week."

"There'll be no problem," she said confidently, giving his hand a squeeze. "We'll look forward to seeing you."

He went away not sure if he'd fallen in love with the mother or the daughter.

"What does this last bit mean?" Leonie asked, passing over Gray's latest letter.

He read it, then laughed loudly, exclaiming, "I'll be buggered! No need to worry about young Gray! He's in the best possible hands."

"Who, dare I ask, is Clarissa of Eaton Square?"

"I'll tell you later," he promised. "In bed."

26

Squadrons of the lightweight Battles were flying regular raids in daylight along the entire front at the Meuse. Gray watched the groups going off on these raids, feeling envious. But when many of his friends failed to return, he was made sharply aware of the war's reality.

On May 10, eight planes were sent off to bomb enemy columns on the Luxembourg-Dippach Road. Only five came home. Hughes, the Canadian, was one of the ones who didn't make it back. Gray tried for a time to tell himself that at least one of the men—possibly even Hughes—had made it safely down and been taken prisoner or safely hidden by some arm of the resistance. But it was a doubtful fantasy, at best, and, more realistically, another shocking encounter with death.

The losses in the daylight attacks were staggering, as much as fifty percent, and the men tried to disguise their nervousness about going out on them. But by the fifteenth, with forty of the seventy-one light planes lost, the Battle squadrons were withdrawn from daylight attacks. Meanwhile, the eighteen squadrons of the Bomber Command remained uncommitted, sitting, waiting for word to go.

Then the change of government took place. Churchill appointed himself minister of defense, Sir Archibald Sinclair the new air minister, and Anthony Eden the new war minister. These changes caused a great deal of speculation among the men as to how they might directly affect them. There'd been whispers for quite some time about a plan of attack along the Ruhr, going after the oil plants and troop concentrations there. But apparently, the whisper went, there was considerable debate in the cabinet as well as between the ministries over the plan. So they continued to wait. And meanwhile, killed time; sitting at the ready, talking among themselves, Until the night of the fifteenth, when the first bombers were sent out to attack, finally, along the Ruhr. For two nights, with the most rudimentary navigational and aiming equipment, they flew over the area dropping their bombs, then headed home. Elated. They hadn't lost a single plane.

After that, it seemed they were rarely out of the air. And time accelerated at a dizzying rate.

When he was on the ground, he went as often as possible to visit with Clarissa, hoping to catch a glimpse of the elusive Samara, who, despite her mother's observations to the contrary, Gray was convinced was shy almost to the point of incoherency. She gave him occasional smiles—of a quality as dazzling and exquisitely piercing as those of her mother, without her mother's self-assurance, though—and a number of times walked with him through the overgrown garden, nodding or shaking her head in response to his comments and questions.

Over a period of months he was able to determine that she'd been attending Roedean but had hated it so thoroughly—for reasons undisclosed—that she'd succeeded in convincing her mother to bring her home and allow her to attend a nearby college, where she'd just completed her A levels and was now trying to decide what to do next. In the meantime, she periodically helped her father—whom she called Joshua—with his work in some mysterious organization she said was, "Secret. And not to be openly discussed, you understand," and grudgingly assisted her mother with the weekly teas for the overseas fliers from the nearby base.

"It's a bore, really," she said. "All a bit of bearding, actually."

She didn't make a great deal of sense to him. But being with her was more than enough to keep him happy. And she wasn't in the least averse to holding his hand as they walked through the gardenerless garden, or to exchanging hotly significant kisses in back of the potting shed. He loved her absolutely and hadn't any doubt that they'd eventually marry.

The mystery, though, of Joshua Browning's allegedly secret and highly dangerous activities piqued Gray's curiosity. And on an afternoon when Sam was off to London for the day, he asked Clarissa specifically what her husband did.

Her entire demeanor underwent a startling alteration, and

she looked all at once much older, less prepossessed, less commanding. She lit a cigarette, recrossed her legs, and looked probingly at Gray for several long moments before speaking.

"Since there's no doubt whatsoever in my mind that you're not a German spy"—she smiled grimly—"I see no harm in telling you. You will, of course, speak of it to no one."

"Of course," he agreed, more than a little intimidated both by the remarks and by her caution.

"My husband is a Jew, you see." She gazed straight ahead, drawing thoughtfully on her cigarette. "His family has been in England hundreds of years. Literally. Assimilated as can be, you understand. With an inherited title, the lot." She waved away her cigarette smoke before going on. "He's been working with the underground network since thirty-three, getting people out. Since the start of the war, they've gone deeper and deeper underground. So deep, in fact, you'd have to dig awfully far to substantiate anything I'm telling you." She turned to look at him again, smiling. A smile lacking her usual dazzle, just an expression of resignation and a certain very real sadness; an acceptance of the inevitable. It said far more, somehow, than her actual words. "He's a barrister," she explained. "A most successful one. It's a perfect blind, as it were. You'll have noticed he's never here. Sam and I constitute the major part of the beard."

"I don't understand."

"You're so very like your father in many ways," she observed with that same sad smile. "When I first knew him, he'd left some sort of ambassadorial post and was a quite wonderful writer. I remember," she said. "He was a press attache. In any case, one saw articles, pieces everywhere; everything one picked up had something by him. Then he stopped. It happened very suddenly, and I often wondered why. But he'd never discuss his reasons. About anything. Oh, he'd happily talk abstracts for days. Or about the war, then. About the direction certain politicians might take. But never about why he'd stopped writing.

"He was always, I thought, a deeply caring man. But someone who found it difficult, almost painful to expose his caring. And so he cloaked it in anger and questions and a ceaseless probing at the whys and wherefores of the people around him. You do put me in mind of him. Your directness. And a certain . . . power. It's difficult to articulate. I expect you're disappointed at not seeing Sam today."

He smiled, caught out, and nodded, saying, "I am, kind of. But I always enjoy visiting with you."

"Next time," she said. And deftly managed to so successfully reroute the conversation, it wasn't until long after he'd returned to base that he realized she'd never explained how and in what way she and Sam were the major part of that bewildering "beard."

She'd had enough of hospitals and decided to respond to several private practitioners who were seeking associates and/or partners. What she really wanted was to get overseas, be of some real value where it was most needed.

Her mother was again driving herself too hard, getting ready to open a Lion's in Stamford. And her father was working equally hard with William Allen White and his group, who were urging intervention in the form of arms for Britain. For the first time in years, her father went back to writing. He did an impassioned piece, thinking to submit it to one of the lesser journals; and was gratified when an associate at the *Times* asked to read it and subsequently submitted the piece for publication on the editorial page. Leo had clipped out the article and carried it around in her wallet, impressed and proud of her father's grasp of what was happening in the world. She searched the piece, reading and rereading it, for something that would allow her the same sort of understanding.

"... while Mr. Lindbergh is urging us to 'stop this hysterical chatter of calamity and invasion,' Germany is smashing through Belgium and Holland, murdering peaceable people in neutral countries; single-handedly attempting to destroy a race that for thousands of years has contributed their considerable talents and admirable diligence toward making both the best of themselves as well as endowing whatever community in which they've chosen to live with the benefits of those talents."

It still didn't tell her why, or provide answers to her questions. Her restlessness led her into the beds of quite a number of her fellow residents, who, having given up hope of ever seducing her, accepted her casual offer of her body with something she could only view as childish greed. She took what she wanted from the encounters, feeling it no longer mattered now, as it was only a matter of weeks before she'd be leaving the hospital, afterward feeling more disturbed and disoriented than before. For as long as they lasted, the sexual performances soothed something that felt critically damaged inside her. And that was good. Certainly there was no danger of another pregnancy. She'd secured not one but two diaphragms to protect herself. And felt positively whorish and premeditated inserting one or the other of them in advance of an evening out; hating whatever it was inside her that had done such a complete about-face, but unable to regain control of her appetite or her need to channel off some of her raging energies.

Ultimately she decided to share the practice of a G.P. in Stamford. She liked, first of all, the look of the people in the waiting room. Second, the nurse appeared to be a kind and caring woman who treated the patients with intelligence and understanding. And third, Aaron Grossman was so engagingly good-humored, obviously overworked, and basically, intrinsically good, treating her—she was sure—exactly as he'd have treated any man.

"You won't get rich in this practice," he told her at their interview. "But God knows, you'll get experience. Why you'd want to work in an office like this with your background and credentials, I can't begin to imagine. But I'll tell you straight, you'd be heaven-sent. And far be it from me to question you. I've been working with two surgeons, one at St. Joseph's and the other at Stamford. A surgeon right here would be nothing short of a miracle."

She liked him. She accepted his offer. and moved her things down from New Haven into a small apartment at the Pickwick Arms in Greenwich. To her parents, she explained, "I'm going to have odd hours, house calls, telephone calls coming in night and day. It'll be better all around if I know I can do all that without disrupting the household. Anyway"—she smiled—"I adore the Pickwick. It has so much character."

Aaron Grossman was tall, stoop-shouldered, balding. At forty, he looked fifty. He wore wire-framed bifocals, seemed to live on coffee, and displayed a touching adoration for his wife and three children; always relating some anecdote or another about what one of the children had been up to. He was witty, profound, and the sort of physician who inspired complete confidence both in his patients and in anyone else with whom he came into contact. Leo found herself fantasizing about meeting a man who'd embody the characteristics Aaron possessed. He was consistent, gentle, even-tempered, and very well-read. He was deeply, privately religious; in what Leo considered to be the truest sense. He exercised his beliefs in his daily contacts with everyone, treating people with the respect and dignity he felt they deserved. Working with him restored her basic belief in the rightness of her entering medicine. And she worked happily, treating scraped knees, cases of ringworm, cuts, ulcers, bronchial infections, broken bones, concussions, appendectomies, edema, colic, births, deaths. Anything, everything. He was right. She was getting all the experience, in every area, she'd ever need. Through an arrangement with Stamford Hospital, she was on call in the emergency room there two evenings and one full day a week in exchange for the use of their surgical facilities.

To celebrate the completion of her first year at the office, Leonie arranged a dinner party for the Grossmans and Leo at the country club. On the appointed Saturday evening, after meeting at the house and driving in one car to the club, they went into the bar, anticipating a fine time. The Grossmans, Leonie and Gray agreed, were a charming couple, unpretentious, wholesome. And the conversation flowed easily back and forth.

While having their drinks in the bar, Leonie slowly became aware of something happening, a faint undercurrent running through the place, conversations muting almost to silence. She looked over at Gray, seeing he, too, was aware of the alteration in the atmosphere. Leo, in conversation with Deborah Grossman about a problem their youngest seemed to be having with a slightly inturned foot, was unaware. But Aaron, his eyes connecting with Leonie's, wasn't.

It was all very subtle. The captain came over to have a word with Gray, quietly saying, "There seems to have been some mistake made."

Tensing, but keeping his tone light, Gray said, "A mistake?" knowing full-well what was coming.

"We've got your reservations, but someone's put it down for *next* Saturday."

"Change it then," Gray said smoothly. "There's a good fellow."

"I'm afraid there's a *problem*," the captain persisted, keeping his eyes averted.

Leonie placed a hand on Leo's shoulder, saying, "Excuse us just a moment," smiled, and signaled to Gray that the three of them should move out of the bar to further discuss this.

"What exactly is happening?" she asked very quietly, noticing a flush of brilliant color climbing into the captain's face.

"It seems"—Gray's tone matched hers—"we're about to deal with a 'mistake.'"

"We rang," she said, "to say there'd be five for dinner."

"But somebody wrote it into the book for next Saturday. Not tonight."

"Might I see the book?" Gray asked.

"Well, I . . . you see—"

"Ask the manager to step out here, would you?" Leonie asked with a smile.

"Oh, certainly. Yes." Eager to escape the man hurried off.

"They're not going to bloody *do* this!" Gray said from between his teeth.

"I think they are." She glanced back into the bar, her eyes again meeting Aaron's. "And I'm afraid Dr. Grossman's aware of what's happening. We've got to do something."

"They *can't* be this stupid!" he said furiously. "*Surely* they *can't!*"

"I'm afraid they can." Her heart was beating strangely, erratically, as if the anger had taken possession of her entire body, throwing all her systems out of gear.

The manager, oozing charm, danced toward them, smiling, saying, "So good to see you, Mrs. Marlowe, Mr. Marlowe. Henry tells me there seems to be some problem."

"Either we have a table for dinner," Gray said, carefully enunciating every word, "or *this club* has a problem. In fact, I think you're going to be in trouble either way."

The smile and the charm ebbing, the man looked at Leonie, then at Gray, plainly in a quandary as to how to handle the situation.

"Perhaps you'd enlighten me as to the specifics of the 'problem,'" Gray invited, holding one hand clenched behind his back.

"Well, you see, Mr. Marlowe, this *is* a restricted club . . ."

Leonie wanted to strike him, to do great damage to this place; burn it down; administer slaps in the face to all those smug, self-righteous people who belonged to the club. An unreasoning, unreasonable violence burned out of control, making her head ache suddenly.

"I wouldn't," she warned, putting her hand on Gray's arm as she addressed the manager, "go on with this, if I were you. Darling"—she turned to Gray—"why don't you ring up that lovely French restaurant in Westport, see if we can't get a reservation?"

Doubtfully, his eyes sparred with Leonie's.

Do it! she insisted.

All right! he gave in. But I don't like it one bit!

He walked across the lobby to the telephone.

"Are you aware," she said softly, "that my husband writes for the New York *Times*? And that a large number of the members of this club patronize my restaurants, are good friends? I'd like a direct answer: who instigated this 'problem' tonight?"

"Look," he said, abandoning the last vestiges of his professional charm, "I don't make the rules, Mrs. Marlowe. I think this whole thing is disgusting. But I only work here. The minute your party hit the bar, I got a phone call. What'm I supposed to do? I can't tell the members of the board how to think. I know it's stupid, but what can I do? I'm sorry. *Believe* me! You think I *like* having to pull a stunt like this on nice people like you and your friends? But you tell me! What'm I going to do? I seat the five of you in the dining room, and tomorrow morning I'm out looking for another job."

"Tell me your name again," she said, looking over at Gray, who was nodding, having succeeded in booking an alternative reservation.

"Charlie Gibbs."

"Charlie, how many times a week does this happen?"

"Oh, not all that often anymore. Word's out. You know."

"How can you have any self-respect, working under these conditions?"

Looking agonized, he said, "It's a *job*, Mrs. Marlowe. I've got a wife and four kids. Everybody's got to be somewhere. I really am sorry. Believe me!"

"You've insulted our friends, our guests. Not for any other reason than that someone in there"—she indicated the bar—"decided there were Jews on the premises. And they might possibly contaminate the place. I understand the Nazis carry out their orders in just this fashion. I'm sure it must make you feel splendid, knowing how much you have in common with them."

He literally lost all his color.

She walked away from him across the lobby to take Gray's arm, whispering, "Smile and think up some believable lie about the change in reservations."

"I'd like to go through this sodding place with a Sten gun," he hissed.

"And me," she whispered back. "Kill the lot of them! Smile, for God's sake!"

The evening quietly died. The Grossmans left early, saying they had to get the sitter home. And Leo stayed on at the house for coffee, demanding to know, "What the hell happened? What was all that whispering and signaling about?"

"They weren't going to seat us," Leonie said.

"Jesus Christ!" Leo exploded. "I knew it! I can't *stand* this!"

"By the way," Gray asked, "what were you telling that simpleton while I was ringing the restaurant?"

"Putting a bit of propaganda to work. By tomorrow they'll all be quaking in their boots, looking up and down the editorial page for the condemning column you're going to write, denouncing the lot of them."

He laughed, relaxing for the first time that evening. "Bastards!" He pounded his fist on the arm of the chair. "We're resigning, of course."

"Why *don't* you do a column?" Leo asked her father.

"There's no point, darling," Leonie answered for him, "in wasting our energies where they'll have no effect. We're not going to change these people."

"What did you say to that one, the manager?"

"He was only doing his job. One truly cannot hold him responsible."

"*Mother!*"

"He needs the job. He was personally most apologetic. I can't totally condemn him. Not with eight million people out of work."

"You're overcompensating. Nobody has to do a job like that!"

"We can't all be endowed with moral courage and integrity, Leo. Not when a job means food on the table, self-respect."

"Self-respect," she scoffed. "What about Aaron and Deborah? What about them? Doesn't it matter that grubby *jobholders* have the right to offend them? Never mind whether it's firsthand or second. I think you *should* write an article about it," she again addressed her father. "You damned well should!"

"This war," he said thoughtfully, "seems to be bringing out

every prejudice—racial and otherwise—anyone's ever possessed."

Lighting a cigarette off the one she was just finishing, Leo hotly exclaimed, "I don't understand either of you! What do you call this: turning the other cheek?"

"Don't provoke me, Leo!" he warned. "I'm in no fit mood."

"Oh, Daddy," she said tiredly. "Why the hell didn't you just punch him in the nose? I could see you were dying to."

"Because it would simply have served to aggravate an already difficult situation. Do you honestly think your Dr. Grossman would have thanked me for entering into a fistfight on his behalf? I think not. There are ways and ways, Leo. That isn't one of them."

"It's getting late," Leonie said diplomatically.

Crushing out her newly lit cigarette, Leo said, "What do we do next time we want to go out? Eat in?"

"Calm down, darling," Leonie said. "You can't accomplish what you want with anger."

"What then?"

"Reason, logic. Not anger. It only generates more anger. Then you've got wars being waged at every intersection."

"We already do," Leo said grimly. "It's all just cleverly camouflaged. What *do* you do about it, then?"

"Oh"—Leonie rested her head against the back of the armchair, looking thoughtfully at the ceiling—"there'll be a number of resignations, for one thing. Then there'll be a sudden surprising drop in the quality of the food at the club."

"How?"

"I know all the suppliers. A word or two, and they'll be receiving vegetables on the verge of going bad. The cuts of meat will have quite a lot of gristle. They may or may not get their bread and rolls on time. The milk and cream may be a bit off."

"And what does that accomplish?"

"It hurts them where they're most vulnerable," Leonie said patiently. "Their revenues. Loss of memberships, loss of customers in the dining room. Enough to worry them."

Leo got up, reaching for her bag. "I wish to Christ," she said, "I understood all this. I'll talk to you tomorrow. Thank you for wanting to make it a nice evening."

Now that school was finally out of the way for a time, Sam was far more relaxed and expansive and they spent all

Gray's free time together. They went to the cinema, or to the local to sit and talk, or exchanged lingering kisses and arousing caresses behind the potting shed until Sam was breathlessly aflame and Gray invariably broke away from her saying, "We really shouldn't be doing this!"

"Why ever not?" she asked, her eyes glazed, hands reaching for him.

"I want us to get married!" he said, surprising both of them.

She stared at him disbelievingly for several seconds, began to smile, then laughed and threw her arms around his neck. "I'd love it! I'd simply *love* it!"

"You would?" he asked, astonished.

"I thought you'd go off on one of your missions, get yourself killed, and that would be the end of it. If we're married, I know you'll have to come back. Let's go tell Mother straightaway!"

"Hold on a minute, Sam. I've got to think this through."

"You're not changing your mind?"

"No, no. I'm just trying to think how your mother's going to react to this. After all, you're just twenty. And I won't be twenty-one for a few more months."

"What possible difference could that make?" she asked, twisting a strand of hair around her finger, coiling and uncoiling it. A habit she had when nervous.

"Do you really know what you're doing, Sam?"

"I love you, if that's what you mean. You haven't said if you love me."

"I do. But . . . Well, what about your father? What'll he say?"

"Joshua?"

"That's right."

"He isn't my father. I thought you knew that."

"He's not? Well, who is?"

For an answer she gave him a hard kiss on the mouth, then grabbed at his hand, laughing, saying, "Come on! I'm dying to get back and tell her."

"She *is* your mother, isn't she?"

"Of course, idiot!"

Clarissa was anything but surprised, and said so.

"Is it all right, then?" Sam asked eagerly, impatiently.

"Go along and let me have a chat with Gray," she told Sam.

"We're *not* too young," Sam protested.

"Go along, Sam!"

Unwillingly, she went. Clarissa lit a cigarette, crossed her wonderful legs, and said, "It's all happened far faster than I'd anticipated."

"We've been seeing each other for over a year," he said, wondering if she'd say a marriage was out of the question.

"I'm aware of that." She smiled absently, then looked away, and he watched her hands as she smoked, noticing her fine bone structure. Bright red polish on long, carefully manicured nails. Flawless hands moving rather restlessly. Her full lips pursed thoughtfully. "I expect," she said at length, "Sam has told you Joshua is not her father."

"She told me."

"I haven't any idea actually who Sam's father is." She turned toward him. "Quite some time ago, I started to tell you a bit about what Joshua's constructed here. The long and short of it is, we were married almost nine years ago. The agreement was very simple. He would give Sam his name. And Sam and I would give him a very proper wife and daughter in the country to whom he allegedly returned on weekends. In fact, as you've seen, he is never here. What he does really hasn't any bearing on you and Sam. But I think it only fair you know who you'd be marrying. It says 'Father Unknown' on Sam's birth certificate."

"That doesn't matter. I don't care about that."

"I didn't think you would. But what about your family? Don't you think they might?"

"They won't mind either. I promise you. And anyway, I'm not marrying Sam's father. I'm marrying Sam."

"She isn't easy," she warned. "She's unpredictable, temperamental."

"I like those things about her."

"And I suppose," she said, "the two of you have no interest in a proper wedding?"

"We've talked it over. We'd prefer a civil ceremony."

"Then it's all settled, really, isn't it?" She got up and walked across the room to stand looking out through the French doors.

He thought how different she and Sam were. Sam was taller, rounder, less fragile-looking; exotic with her odd-colored eyes and red hair. Clarissa was small-boned, narrow, yet possessed of something that held her spine perfectly straight, set her chin defiantly forward; but as unpredictable as Sam. He wondered if it hadn't been difficult for so small a woman to produce so large a child. Then almost laughed aloud, realizing how stupid the thought was.

The silence lengthened as he continued to admire the narrowness of her back and waist, the sudden rounding of her hips. She reached across to put out her cigarette and turned, saying, "Go on, darling. There's no point to your sitting waiting to hear words of wisdom. I haven't any."

"You don't think we should do it," he stated.

"You're wrong. I'm happier than I could possibly say. Go along now."

Two weekends later, they got married. After a quiet luncheon at the house, Clarissa announced, "I'm going down to London. I'll be back tomorrow evening," and departed, leaving the house to them.

Sam, stretched happily naked on the bed, said, "One of the reasons I left school was this girl. She used to come into bed with me all the time. I hated it, but couldn't get her to stop; didn't know how, actually. I absolutely would not touch her, but she was quite content to touch me. In any event, she devirginated me one night before I realized quite what was happening."

"*Devirginated* you?" He stared at her body, his first complete viewing of her, temporarily forgetting what he was doing.

"You know. *Did* it. With her hand."

"What was it like? I mean, how did you . . .?"

"I was enjoying it, you see." She smiled, taking hold of his hand and directing it down. "Made me feel positively horrid after. And I had to put a stop to it somehow. Yes, right there. That's lovely. So I asked Mummy to let me come home. I hated it that it was another girl, you see."

"I think I do."

She moved closer to him so that their faces were about an inch apart, her body moving under his hand. "Actually," she whispered, "I think Mother's quite sure we've already done all this. I think she's always suspected I was rather too much like her, perhaps, for my own good."

"What do you mean?" He stopped her hand. "You've lost me."

"Oh!" Her smile disappeared. "I thought you knew, that she'd told you. About your father. All of it. Oh, dear!"

"Would you please just tell me what the hell all this is? I'm so confused I can't figure any of it out."

She sat up, looking on the verge of tears. "Mother was a

whore," she said softly. "I thought you knew, that she'd told you. A jolly expensive one. But a whore."

He was too stunned to speak.

"It's quite true," she said softly. "I've always known. She's never been anything but completely truthful. . . . You must understand. I love my mother . . . Oh, I feel dreadful. I've made it all sound so frightfully sordid." She covered her eyes with her hand, starting to cry.

Completely lost, he sat up and put his arms around her. "Explain it to me. Maybe I'm a little slow."

"Coming out with it that way," she cried. "So crudely. And she's not . . . I've made it sound . . ."

"Hey, Sam? I love you. And I know your mother's okay."

"She did it for me, you see." She uncovered her eyes. "Married Joshua so I could have a good name, go to Roedean. I *love* my mother," she said again fiercely. "She's the best person I know. Next to you," she added. "And she loves Joshua. Terribly. He's been very good to us."

"So that's how she knew my Dad," he said, at last making the connection.

Sam nodded. "But he was special," she said. "Not a client."

"You mean he didn't pay?"

"She wouldn't ever take money from him, she told me. She'd have married him, she said. They'd actually planned to, if he returned from America. But he never did come back. And then, she got pregnant. It was an accident. But she wanted to keep me. It made it very difficult for her, keeping me. She's *good*," she insisted tearfully. "And it doesn't matter, any of that. Does it?"

"No," he said soberly. "None of it matters."

They lay down together. He couldn't help visualizing his father making love to Clarissa. It was all too easy to imagine. Something about her mouth, her legs. He pushed it all away and turned to Sam.

27

The board of directors of the American Medical Women's Association tried right up until the day before Pearl Harbor to establish commissions for women doctors in the Medical Reserve Corps of the army and navy. Theirs and a number of individual requests—including Leo's—were rejected by the government in a statement issued expressing the hope that whatever additional physicians were required for complete mobilization would be drawn from the available supply of male physicians. Further, women doctors were informed that, if by chance, certain women specialists were needed, they would be employed on a contract basis.

Leo waited, hoping now that the U.S. was in the war, the government would alter its stance on accepting female doctors. But as 1942 came in and it was announced women could serve as physicians in the Women's Army Auxiliary Corps, and the AMWA rejected both contract surgeon status and medical duty in the WAACS as representing an inferior form of medical service, she lost hope. As a contract surgeon, one was offered low salary, low status, lack of both uniform and promotion, as well as no provision whatsoever for housing. The WAACS prohibited women from the combat zones and grouped women doctors with military units whose primary purpose was to fill jobs such as clerks, stenographers, and telephone operators. The AMWA's objections were based on the conviction that women doctors should not be forced to serve their country in a second-class capacity and so advised their sister members.

Finally, deciding to follow the lead of a mere handful of others, Leo wrote making application to the Royal Army

Medical Corps. And within six weeks it was arranged. She went in to tell Aaron that she'd be leaving. Sadly he embraced her, saying, "There'll always be a place for you here, Leo. You know that."

"I know. And I'll be back."

"God willing."

She knew her mother wanted desperately to ask her to reconsider, not go; but Leonie said nothing. So Leo went about cleaning out the apartment, getting ready to leave, wishing her parents had said what they really thought instead of simply wishing her well, observing she'd made a generous gesture.

It isn't generous, she argued with herself, dumping books into a box. It's for me. Finding out somehow, getting some kind of answers; removing myself from what I've been the past couple of years. Starting over.

Gray had arrived back at the base at almost three in the morning after spending the evening and part of the night with Sam. It seemed he'd only been asleep for a few minutes when someone was shouting at him to get up, he was wanted in the crew room right away. He'd have turned over and gone back to sleep if that same voice, closer now, hadn't said, "Get on it, Marlowe! You're holding up the briefing. The rest of the men are already assembled."

He couldn't remember when he'd felt tireder, having participated in a daylight raid two days earlier, a nine-hour nighttime raid to Berlin the night before last. But he was ready to go out again. And he'd left his authorization note listing all the items of his personal kit that would go to Sam if he didn't make it back. All the men had done it.

Pulling on his battle dress, he paused to look out the window. Rain. Thick clouds. Perhaps, if the bad weather continued, they'd scrub the operation.

Immediately upon arriving at the crew room, he knew this was going to be a big one. Crews of twelve of the Stirling heavy night bombers were standing watching the squadron commander taking his pointer over the fourteen-foot wall map of Western Europe, telling them, "We're sending over three hundred aircraft ... a maximum effort. This squadron's been given the honor of being pioneers over Berlin with the new petrol-can type of incendiaries." He went on for some minutes, at last winding down, saying, "Make sure you get good photoflash pictures of target destruction."

The gist of it was that other squadrons would be closing in on Berlin from the south, east, and west in short relays. They were to bomb, get their photoflash pictures, then get the hell out of there.

He and his navigator, Robinson, went over the target site. Then Gray headed for the parachute section for number 56, his allotted chute. Carrying it, he went outside into the driving rain, to see the twelve four-engined Stirlings lined up at the rim of the aerodrome.

The seven other members of his crew were already on board, adjusting their gear. Ten thousand pounds of explosives ready to be dropped. As he sat down in the cockpit, he was overcome by a feeling of dread, almost of nausea. Something was going to go wrong on this one. He could feel it, taste it. He checked in with the eleven other pilots over the radio. Then instructions came through from control for quick-succession takeoff. Zigzagging the aircraft to the runway, he pushed the throttle forward, and they were up. The front gunner was joking with the wireless operator.

"Watch the skies," Gray told the crew as he always did. He was more on edge tonight than ever before, wondering suddenly what he thought he was doing. Not yet twenty-two years old, he was in charge of this aircraft, these men. Then the navigator, Robbie, came over the headset to give him the estimated arrival time at the bomb site. He automatically responded, "Okay, navigator," then addressed the three gunners, saying, "Keep your eyes peeled."

Entering over Holland, across Holland and into Germany, luck was with them, no incidents. Moving on through the tremendous vast emptiness of the sky, they flew deeper into Germany. His malaise faded. He felt comfortable, sure of his aircraft, his own abilities. Then a rapid series of explosions caused the bomber to shudder, rearing; flak rising all around, and the sickly fumes of cordite filling the interior of the cabin. Shell fragments pinged against the exterior of the plane. Gray came down hard on the stick and rudder bar and they cleared the flak after about five minutes. No injuries, no damage to the plane, nothing burning.

In a brief crew conference as they neared Berlin, they agreed that if no cloud clearance occurred after five minutes over the target, they'd dive below the cloud ceiling and risk a low-level sorting-out of position and subsequent attack.

Robbie, the navigator, was concentrating on locating the landmarks about Berlin, studying the small secret target map, noting the dispositions and guiding features. Their prime worry was the possibility of ground gunners boxing them in with flak and preventing them from making a dead-steady run over the target. Yet nothing came up at them. The crew gave their equipment a final check, then braced for action. Robbie told the wireless operator to swing open the bomb doors and slip a photoflash bomb into the tube, then gave Gray an alteration of course that would bring them over Berlin's northern sector. Robbie crawled up to the nose of the Stirling and stretched out on his belly, carefully polishing the bombing window, painstakingly checking, rechecking, and adjusting the half-dozen knobs and indicators before making identification of the sight.

Gray, looking ahead at the dull, reddish glow in the sky, said to him, "It looks as if some of our boys have already unloaded."

"It looks real enough," Robbie agreed. All of them were aware how clever the Germans were at camouflage, frequently setting false fires in order to encourage British bombers to drop their loads in harmless areas, even going so far as to erect mock built-up areas of considerable size to misguide target location.

Suddenly, flak shells exploded everywhere over the city, simultaneously.

"Never seen it so thick in thirty ops," the front gunner muttered, trying and failing to sound casual.

"No need to panic," Gray said over his headset, nevertheless feeling it like some exotic flower blossoming inside his chest; watching as one of their bombers was pounced on, held in a cone of light from half a dozen searchlights, the plane encircled by scores of bursting shells. Then came a tremendous crimson flash, superimposed upon the pale white of the searchlights, and the bomber exploded. In heart-thudding silence, Gray and the crew watched as flaming fragments of the bomber fell slowly down; continuing to watch as a second plane went up.

Shells bursting all around them, the interior of the cabin filled again with acrid smoke. He pushed down on the stick, taking them into a dive, then came up hard, turned a half-circle, and straightened out, saying, "Get pinpointing, navigator. Fast. Let's bomb the goddamned place and get the hell out of this!" His hands were sweating, the pulses in his temples throbbing, that feeling of dread in his mouth. His mind wanted to stop, just stop and think about Sam, about being in bed with Sam, making love to Sam, whispering in the dark. Sam.

Robbie pinpointed the site. Gray held them on course, waiting. Then a stream of shells came up at them, bursting wide, Robbie whispered, "Now!" and let go. The plane sprang upward as the bombs were released. Robbie talking to the wireless operator, advised him to signal base, say the target had been successfully bombed. Relieved, Gray was setting course for home when the upper gunner yelled, "Look!"

"Look what?" Gray asked, the panic blossoming anew.

"To port, sir!"

A great green-blue sweep of flame below.

"Looks like they've fired oil!" the front gunner yelled.

His hands wet, Gray held the course toward home until suddenly German flak gunners had them surrounded by shells.

"That's funny," Gray said, thinking aloud, "taking potshots at us now!"

He'd just got the words out when light burst on them and the plane was right in the center of a number of searchlights.

"Hell!" he swore. "Hold tight for evasive action!"

He twisted and dived, tried every trick he knew, to no effect. The plane seemed somehow attached to the end of the searchlights.

"I can't do a damned thing!" he shouted. "I'm diving! Open up with all guns straight down the beams! Let's see if we can knock them out!"

A shell exploded right in front of them, shattering the outer starboard motor, causing a staggering crash. The engine burst into flame as the petrol from the severed pipelines caught fire. A second shell burst in the near starboard section, causing the plane to lurch. Two more shells went off close to the tail and punched large holes in the metal skin of the aircraft around the photoflash rockets suspended on the fuselage wall. Gray took them down into a sickening, giddy dive. Then, with a monstrous groaning of the plane, and a wrench, he pulled up out of the dive, the port wing riding low. They were limping along at a dangerously low altitude, but at least they'd managed to escape the searchlights. The engineer was turning off the fuel flow to the destroyed engine, checking his readings.

"We've lost close to three hundred gallons," he told Gray. "We haven't got enough to make it back."

"Work out the shortest route to the coast!" Gray told Robbie. "We might be able to set down in the sea."

The plane was in bad shape. Very bad, Gray thought, keeping a death grip on both himself and the plane. Everything was shuddering, trembling inside as a result of the loss of the one engine, and the damage to the inner starboard one. They tracked a course that was the nearest line to the Dutch coast, but with every few miles the bomber was losing height.

Make it! Gray insisted, his hands slippery on the controls. *Make it!*

"Chins up, boys!" he said with forced good cheer. "If we can bring this old lady down in the Zuider Zee, at least we won't give the goddamned Germans the satisfaction of picking up the pieces. And somehow we'll make it in to shore. Check on your chutes and Mae Wests. We're losing altitude, so you'd better let all the loose gear, including guns and ammo belts, go overboard."

The inner port engine started coughing, spluttering.

We're not going to make it, he thought. We're going to have to come down in occupied territory. Come on, lady! Get us there! Just a little bit farther!

"Swing back the escape hatch, somebody!" he called out. "And bail the hell out while you've got a chance."

Robbie released the hatch in the floor, and there was an inrushing of cool, fresh air as the two functioning port engines suddenly choked and died and the plane started to plunge downward.

"Bail out!" he shouted. *"Bail out!"* Then the intercom went dead on him. Jesus! he thought. Sam. Sam. He held the controls another few seconds, then leaped out of his seat, dived back, braced himself against a metal stanchion with his body wound into a tight ball. He was the last of the crew on board, except for Robbie, whose chute had been damaged in one of the shell bursts.

A blinding flash, monstrous impact. They hit.

Sam! he thought. Oh, Jesus, Sam!

Leo telephoned the base, asking to talk to Gray, and after an unbelievably long wait was told he wasn't available. Mystified, she then called Directory Assistance for the number of the Tewkesbury house, got it, dialed, and asked to speak either to Lady Browning or to Mrs. Marlowe. A husky, quite beautiful voice asked, "Who is this, please?"

"Leonie Marlowe. Gray's sister."

There was an audible intaking of breath. And then the beautiful voice began talking very quickly, very quietly. An hour later, Leo was on the train.

Clarissa met her at the station. Extending her hand, she apologized, saying, "I'm sorry Sam couldn't be here, too. She's terribly upset."

"When did it happen?" Leo asked, going along with her to the waiting car. "How long have you known?" She wondered how her mother and father were going to take this, already trying to fit the appropriate words together.

"We knew fairly soon after, actually," Clarissa said, effortlessly handling the large Daimler. "I am so sorry to have to greet you with such distressing news. Evidently there was a large-scale raid. Quite a number of the crews failed to return. From what we've been able to gather, one of the lads from another bomber in the squadron saw them get hit. But he was quite adamant in insisting the plane didn't go down. I can't help feeling"—she turned to look over at Leo—"he'll turn up."

Dry-mouthed, Leo nodded; abstractedly absorbing the details of this woman, noticing her delicate, long-fingered hands on the steering wheel, the rather pointed look of her profile, redeemed from being too sharp by a pleasing roundness of chin and forehead. Beautiful, she thought distantly, trying to imagine Gray somewhere over there. A beautiful woman. She wondered what Sam would be like. She was unable to imagine Gray as a man with a wife. Her thoughts of him were as a little boy in knickers, perched in the fork of the tree cradling a heavy book in his lap.

"I'm afraid the only thing that's kept Sam even relatively calm about it all is the thought of the baby."

"She's having a baby?" Leo smiled instinctively.

Clarissa smiled back. "Just confirmed this past week. A pity he couldn't have known about it."

"You think he's dead," Leo said, her smile gone.

"No," she said consideringly. "I don't. Neither does Sam. She's in rather wretched shape just now. The upset over Gray. And being horribly ill with morning sickness. Perhaps seeing you will cheer her up a bit. Your letter to Gray"—she glanced over again—"arrived in this afternoon's post. We took the liberty of opening it. I hope you don't mind. All his things have been sent over from the base. Officially, they've declared him 'missing.' "

"I don't know how I'm going to tell them," Leo said

darkly, looking out the window, seeing an image of her parents' faces, anticipating their reactions to all of this. Grandparents. The father "missing." Herself an aunt. And this woman. She turned to take another look at the youthful profile. A grandmother. She looked not in the least the kind of woman one thought of as a grandmother. There was something about her. A casual elegance, an aura of wealth, a certain almost palpable sensuality. Like Rose's. But much, much stronger. Those hands and the definition of her mouth, the lift of her chin, the line of her throat, her skin. Leo found herself fascinated by Clarissa's beautiful throaty voice, her precise accent, the slight furrowing of her brow as she concentrated on driving. A small, exquisitely turned-out woman.

It was a considerable surprise, meeting Sam. Leo had been expecting her to ressemble her mother. But their only ressemblance lay in a similar shape to the eyes and that roundness of chin and forehead. Otherwise, there was none. Unnaturally pale, with a faintly greenish caste to the skin around her mouth and at the edges of her nostrils, her eyes large, bereft, Sam embraced Leo warmly, then held her away, saying, "You don't look like him. I'd expected you would. I'm glad, actually. I don't think I could have borne it if you looked like him." She embraced Leo again, then let her go, saying, "I'm so happy you're here."

"I understand," Leo said, at once drawn to her, thinking she could see the qualities in her that would have attracted Gray. An aura of intelligence, goodness, and the same somehow overwhelming sensuality as the mother's. "Have you been given anything for the nausea?" Leo asked as they continued studying each other.

Sam shook her head. A small child's gesture. "I feel vile," she said. "Positively vile."

"I'll fix something for you to take care of it."

"I forgot." Sam blinked several times. "You're a doctor, aren't you? I'd quite forgotten that."

"We'll have tea," Clarissa announced, having followed this exchange with interest, sensing the immediate rapport between Sam and Leo. "Do, please, sit down, won't you?"

Later that evening, after Sam had gone to bed, Leo sat with Clarissa in the small morning room at the rear of the house, drinking brandy, having a cigarette; silent for long minutes.

Finally Leo said, "I'll have a word with the pharmacist, arrange a prescription for Sam."

"The chemist, you mean?"

"That's right. I'll do it tomorrow before I go back."

"Very kind of you," Clarissa said. "You have your father's eyes."

"I understand you were friends. It's quite a coincidence, isn't it?"

"Yes, quite."

Another silence. Leo watched the way Clarissa smoked, the way she drank, the way she crossed her legs; knowing at once, intuitively, this woman had been her father's lover. She found herself intensely curious, studying Clarissa relentlessly—the loosely knotted hair at the nape of her neck, pearl earrings, the indication of small breasts under the cashmere sweater.

"You take after your mother, I gather." Clarissa spoke again.

"We look quite a lot alike, yes."

"We've become suddenly awkward with one another," Clarissa said with enviable candor, looking into her glass, revolving it between her hands. "I dislike when that happens," she said. "It's usually indicative of a good deal that's not being said. In this case"—she looked up—"there's everything to consider. All the possibilities."

"Who are you, really?" Leo asked.

"Oh, no one!" Clarissa answered seriously. "Really no one."

"No," Leo disagreed. "Tell me."

"*You* tell me something," she said, turning more toward Leo. "Tell me about your mother and father. There's a bit of a mystery about it that's always puzzled me."

"I'm not sure I know what you mean."

"Something happened. He changed so abruptly, became quite different. And stopped writing, of course. I've always suspected it had to do with a woman. Your mother, I think."

"How did you know him?" Leo asked, knowing.

"In a 'professional' capacity, one might say," she said wryly.

"When?"

"Before, during, and after his first marriage."

"Oh! My mother was his first wife's cousin. Did you know that?"

"I didn't. No."

Very quickly Leo told what she knew. Then again she said, "Now, tell me."

Clarissa drank down the last of her brandy and got up to pour another. "Will you have one?" she asked.

"No, thank you."

She poured more brandy into her glass, then replaced the stopper on the decanter and stood, her hand still on the bottle, looking down at the floor, at last raising her eyes to look at Leo.

"I've never made any great secret of my life," she said quietly. "Not that I went about flaunting it, either. Now, it no longer merits discussion. Certainly Joshua knew precisely what I was when we married. That was actually a part of the arrangement. I'd known him, too, you see, in a 'professional' capacity." She gave Leo an odd, touching smile, picked up her glass, and returned to the sofa. "Sam made all the difference, really," she went on. "I doubt I'd have cared especially. But Sam. Well, she altered my considerations. I'd always thought I'd one day retire to a small house somewhere in the country, perhaps near the seashore; live out the balance of my life reading all the books I'd never had time to read, listening to music. Living a very ordinary, quiet sort of life. I'd never thought of marrying. A great number of my friends spent their lives wanting nothing else. But to me it always seemed an aspiration beyond reasonable limits. After all, it takes a certain very real courage to marry a whore, to live with the knowledge of what she was, what she's been to so many men."

"Were you really?" Leo asked after a moment. "Or is that simply how you perceived yourself?"

"No, I was. Really."

"Didn't you hate yourself?"

Clarissa looked surprised. "Hate myself? No, not at all. Should I have?"

"I don't honestly know."

"I was reconciled to what I was. Just, I expect, as you're reconciled to being a doctor."

"You equate them on the same level?"

"They're both professions. You're very likely very good at yours. I was very good at mine. Not overly proud of it, you understand. There is that dark underside to it. But not unduly ashamed of it, either. Enough wasn't ever enough," she said very softly. "It was rather, at times, like a frightening disease; trying to fill something that refused to be filled. But I've never been ashamed of it. Never. I was daunted somewhat by my own capacities, saddened by the loss of my former 'respectability,' but reconciled, as I said."

"I envy you," Leo said. "I do envy you." I said this to Rose, she thought. Felt it, too.

"Why?" Clarissa sked.

"Because I think you have a lot of courage."

"Oh, nonsense!" Clarissa laughed. "I have nothing of the sort. There's a world of difference between being truthful and having courage. I'm the least courageous person I think I've ever known. I certainly wouldn't have the sort of courage you have; to volunteer myself into the service of another country, to face all that damage."

"I don't think of that kind of thing as courage," Leo said. "Not at all. It's just the job I've been trained to do. I simply want to do it where it'll be of some value."

"Precisely!" Clarissa smiled dazzlingly. "Just as I did."

"You're an incredible woman," Leo said all in a rush. "Absolutely incredible! I like you tremendously. Do you like Gray? Do you think he'll come back?"

"I adore Gray," she said. "I'm certain he'll come back." Impulsively, she took hold of Leo's hand. "You don't judge," she said. "And I greatly admire *you* for that. The only people I've told about myself in years have been you and your brother. Because I loved your father."

"Yes," Leo said. "I knew that."

"Did you?"

"When I saw you on the platform at the station, I knew. You met me prepared to love me because I was Gray's sister, my father's daughter."

"Yes," Clarissa said. "You're right."

"He'll come back." she continued to hold Clarissa's slight hand. "Gray always comes back."

28

The plane, going at about a hundred and fifty miles per hour, collided with the earth, bounced back into the air as if made of rubber, then hit again, shuddering and grinding as it came to rest in a small field.

Gray seemed to return to himself after an indefinite period of time, aware that he and Robbie were not the only ones who'd remained on board. In the darkness, he was able to distinguish the face of the engineer, who lay dead very close by him. Robbie, with a growing lump on his forehead and a severe cut on his arm, was sitting dazed and shaken, staring straight ahead.

"Come on, Robbie," Gray said, collecting himself. "We've got to destroy everything we can, burn it all." He unearthed the first-aid box and hastily wrapped a makeshift bandage around Robbie's arm after cursorily dabbing the deep-looking gash with iodine. Coming out of his stupor, Robbie climbed with him to the top of the fuselage, where, while Gray gathered together all the maps and charts and the air log and set fire to them, Robbie went at the instrument panel with the fire ax, taking special care to destroy the bomb sight. Before leaving the plane, they unlocked the camera magazine and set fire to the film that was evidence of their successful bombing operation. Finally, everything flammable was heaped on the fire in the cockpit, including their two unused parachutes.

Coughing and sweating, they dropped to the ground just as three red rockets flared in the sky and rifle shots cracked in the fields just behind them.

"We'd better get out of here!" Gray said, suddenly aware

of the danger they were in of being captured. "Can you make it?" he asked, taking Robbie by the arm.

"I'm okay."

"They've spotted our fire," Gray whispered. "Let's get out of here fast!"

They started off in the direction away from the rifle fire, eventually arriving at a narrow dirt road, and trotted along until they came to a ditch where they stopped to have a drink of water, a quick cigarette, while discussing their options.

"It's getting light," Robbie observed. "We'd better find someplace to hide."

"No, let's keep moving," Gray disagreed, thinking they were bound to come across people who'd be able to help them get back home; becoming aware of bruises on his legs, his arms. His back hurt. When he touched his fingers to his scalp, he felt a small lump just above his left ear, where his head must have bumped against the stanchion on impact.

They continued on, moving in the ditch, one or the other of them coming up level to survey the landscape every fifteen or twenty minutes; until Robbie spotted a small cottage about a hundred yards away. They huddled together at the bottom of the ditch, debating what to do.

"It looks abandoned," Robbie said. "Why don't I go over, take a look? If it is abandoned right enough, we could stop there, rest."

Just then they heard a dog barking quite close by and automatically began moving again, along the ditch. All thought of stopping gone for the moment. After an hour or so, Robbie muttered, "We'll get pneumonia if we don't get out of this wet, find someplace to rest, dry off."

Again they crawled to the top of the ditch to look around, and seeing and hearing nothing, scrambled up and across into a meadow, heading for a slight rise from which they correctly determined they'd be able to have a look in all directions. What they saw from the top of the hill was a patrol of Germans heading toward them.

"Let's run for it!" Gray whispered. "To those trees!"

Half-crouching, they made a break and ran as fast as they could toward a small stand of trees. The wood was fairly overgrown, with a number of large bushes that might provide cover.

"Hurry and help me gather some branches to fill in these gaps," Gray directed. The two of them worked quickly to thicken the natural growth of a large, very full bush near the edge of the wood that offered a clear area underneath where they might hide. Near the base, the earth was soft with leaves, and they crawled in one at a time, each taking a turn to observe if the other could be seen from outside.

"It's perfect!" Robbie said, crawling back in.

Within moments of surrendering their bodies to the soft cushion of dirt and leaves, they were asleep. Gray awakened to the pressure of Robbie's hand on his mouth.

"Germans," Robbie mouthed, shaking his head as he removed his hand from Gray's mouth.

His heart knocking crazily, Gray cautiously peered out through a peephole in the bush to see two German soldiers standing almost on top of them. One had a submachine gun, the other leaned on his rifle, looking around. Talking in undertones, they glanced about before making a brief search of the woods, then returned to stand in their original places. For close to an hour Gray and Robbie remained motionless beneath the concealing bush, scarcely daring to breathe, determined not to be captured. And finally the two soldiers moved on.

Waiting another hour to be sure the patrol was well and truly gone, Gray at last nudged Robbie, whispering, "Let's move out!"

"Where to?"

"Don't know."

"Bloody hungry," Robbie murmured, touching his bandaged arm.

"How is it?"

"All right, mate. No bother."

They crept out and began again following the ditch, stopping as the air began to get colder and the thin wafer of sun started to slip down. Coming to another small cabin, they again debated approaching it, when a man emerged from an outhouse off to one side, and fastening his trousers, made his way to the cabin.

"Maybe he's a loyal Dutchman," Robbie whispered hopefully.

"If he isn't, we're going to have to grab what we can, take him by surprise, then run for it."

"If he isn't, mate, I'll have him."

Gray looked at Robbie and nodded. Neither of them had so much as a pocketknife, all the guns and ammunition having been thrown out to lighten the plane. But he didn't doubt for an instant that Robbie would kill the man if he had to. He would himself, for that matter.

Waiting several minutes to make absolutely certain there was no one else around, they were making their way to the cabin door just as it opened and the man emerged to stand staring at them in perplexed silence for several seconds before beginning to talk rapidly in words neither of them could understand.

With the small amount of school French he could remember, Gray tried to explain who they were and why they were there.

The Dutchman brightened and proceeded in equally halting French to respond, explaining that everyone in the district knew about the missing British airmen. "Come," he said to them. "I give you food, get you dry."

Suspicious and uncertain, Robbie and Gray looked at each other as the Dutchman held open the door, beckoning them to come inside. It seemed to Gray the man was as nervous and suspicious of them as they were of him, and decided, indicating so to Robbie, that they should go ahead inside.

Astonishingly, once they were inside the warm cabin, the Dutchman beamed at them, in broken French saying, "We all help Winston Churchill's air flying men."

Smiling, the three shook hands, then Gray and Robbie collapsed on the floor in front of the fire while the Dutchman hastily produced a meal of cold sausages, half a loaf of coarse black bread, and strong black coffee. With difficulty he explained that a German patrol had already been through the area searching for them and all the patriotic Dutch had been rounded up and temporarily jailed until the Germans had thoroughly searched the countryside and satisfied themselves that the two men were no longer in the immediate vicinity.

While they ate and their clothes were drying, the Dutchman told them of a route they could follow that would bring them safely to a rendezvous where, upon exchange of a given code word, they would receive help. They ate, smoked two cigarettes apiece, thanked the Dutchman, again shook hands, and stepped out into the night.

Several times they waded across dikes, and the third time, Gray slipped and fell into the water, saturating his newly dried clothes as well as the few remaining cigarettes he'd been saving. They continued on a course parallel to the road, every so often hearing trucks passing very close to them.

Robbie checked the north star and decided they should

walk half a mile due east before striking a course in a northerly direction. They walked on for what seemed like many more hours; wet, stiff, in the darkness, straining to hear and see, when Robbie stopped suddenly, whispering, "Something ahead there, about thirty yards or so."

A dog began to bark. The something ahead they'd thought might be a bush cleared its throat. Gray's stomach jumping with fear, he tried out the password the Dutchman had given him. At once receiving the code word back. Then two more men materialized out of the shadows, clapping arms around their shoulders like old friends. Extraordinary, Gray thought, the way things were happening. From moment to moment, because of his extreme fatigue and the soreness of his body, he had trouble believing all of this wasn't some bizzarre dream. But it was real.

There was a farmhouse nearby, to which they were led. Buckets of hot water were brought out, along with bandages and disinfectant, food prepared.

The farmer and his wife, a couple in their mid-fifties, set to work stripping the two exhausted men of their filthy, dripping clothes, while one of the men they'd encountered on the road went off to find the local doctor to see to Robbie's arm, which was on its way to becoming badly infected. A second of the men went outside to keep watch.

Robbie's arm was cleaned and dressed by the doctor, and he dozed, half-asleep, while Gray talked to a local journalist who spoke excellent English and asked about the Berlin raid. In turn, Gray was told that the Germans had posted notices in the district offering a reward for information about the two British fliers still concealed in the district. "We will work," the journalist told him, "very proudly to get you out."

They stayed ten days at the farm, sleeping nights in an enormous haystack in the near field. Until the journalist came to tell them a special agent would be arriving soon to see them. Three days after that, the special agent came.

"A successful escape back to England," the agent told them, "will entail a lot of trouble, risk to many people. If we decide to help you, you must swear never to divulge anything you may see, hear, or learn about the Dutch underground. If you get hurt, or are captured, you must insist you know nothing at all."

Two days after that, they exchanged emotional good-byes with the Dutch farmer and his wife and followed the journalist at a safe distance until they reached a dirt road leading into the village, where he left them to continue on to their destination—a barn some kilometers away.

Inside, they found a parcel of food, and civilian clothing, which they quickly put on. They were locked into the barn by the journalist, who'd come by another route, after being told they would be collected in the morning.

Feeling doubtful again, they waited anxiously for several hours, wondering if it was possible they'd been tricked into making themselves so vulnerable. Locked inside a barn. It didn't feel quite right. Yet what else were they to do? Unable to rest, they sat out the time in silence until they heard the rattle of a key in the lock. Jumping up, they got well back into the shadows, hearing an English voice, asking, "Are you both ready to leave?"

They answered "Yes," and were again warned to keep all information they had and might gather strictly to themselves. "If you should get caught, you are to tell the Germans you stole these clothes and convince them you've both been elsewhere, not here. I'm leaving now. Leave in two minutes' time and follow me."

Closely keeping to the instructions, they left after two minutes, found their way to two bicycles, mounted, and nonchalantly rode away, keeping a good distance behind their guide. Cycling in silence, they at one point had to swerve wide to avoid a stationary German transport whose driver was leaning against the fender, surveying them coldly as they pedaled past.

"Froze my bloody heart, seeing that kraut," Robbie admitted some miles later.

"Scared me shitless!" Gray grinned.

They rode on, toward midnight arriving at the village of their destination. But they were stopped from proceeding as a convoy of German trucks came around a corner. Each truck was crowded with German soldiers in their greenish uniforms, stiffly erect, rifles between their knees, square steel helmets on their heads. Three escorting motorcyclists braked just in front of Robbie and Gray and casually stood watching the heavy transports go by. The two riders looking other-worldly, evil in their padded leather suits, black knee boots.

The convoy safely past, the two moved forward again, searching for their guide, becoming frightened as it seemed they'd lost him. Gray was unable to imagine quite what they'd do at this point to establish new contacts. "There he is," Robbie whispered. "Over there." The man was leaning on his bike, lighting a cigarette. Nearly sick with relief, they remounted their bicycles and followed the man up and down streets until it was indicated they should park their bikes and leave them. Their guide silently turned them over to another man, who casually fell into step with them, saying, "We'll be taking the train now, to just outside Amsterdam. If any of the passengers happens to be German and seems ready to start a conversation, or addresses you, pick your nose. They can't bear it." Again they were told, "If you are arrested, you are to say you have stolen these clothes, as well as the money for your rail tickets, and that you have been wandering around Holland without set destination."

Holding the tickets they'd been given, they waited on the platform for about fifteen minutes for the train to come in. A few minutes before it was due, the platform was suddenly filled by dozens of young Luftwaffe Germans. Gray and Robbie dived into the first compartment that stopped opposite them. Their new guide took a place some half-dozen seats away. In tacit understanding, Gray and Robbie at once pretended to go to sleep in order to avoid any possible confrontation with the young Germans who took the two vacant seats opposite them.

The German airmen made a tremendous amount of noise, drinking beer, eating bread and sausages from their knapsacks. Gray opened his eyes, to see the young flier opposite staring at him. Sensing the German was about to say something, Gray remembered what he'd been told and oafishly began picking his nose. The German's hand shot out and caught Gray across the side of the head, shouting an insult Gray thought vaguely deciphered into something like "pig." Everything in him wanted to strike back, but he forced himself to remain completely still, staring stupidly at the young officer until, in disgust, he turned away.

They arrived in Amsterdam late in the afternoon, and after following their guide along a circuitous, cautious route—to ensure that neither the guide nor Gray and Robbie were being followed—arrived at the apartment of the man they were told would oversee the next leg of their escape.

"It may take some time to arrange your return," their new host told them, another English-speaking Dutchman in his late forties or so. "And while you are waiting, we will undertake to teach you some of the ways of the underground, prepare you for certain actions you may be called upon to perform."

It slowly became clear to them that they were to be instructed in self-defense, as well as in cleanly, quickly being able to kill.

"It seems distasteful to you now," their host said understandingly. "But there may come a time when you are grateful for the instruction you will have been given."

In the middle of his seeming lecture, the telephone rang, startling all of them with its shrill noise. After a monosyllabic, very brief conversation, their host advised them "We are moving you at once. Please follow a short distance behind me."

"I'm becoming a nervous bloody wreck," Robbie confided as they left the apartment and trailed the man down into the street.

"I wonder what happened?" Gray mused aloud.

"Maybe better not to know."

They were conducted to a large house on the outskirts of town, introduced to their new hosts—a couple in their midthirties—and left there. For the next two weeks they remained within the house. They learned that the Gestapo were in Amsterdam in large numbers trying to ferret out the Dutch underground organization, take the main operatives.

Their training in self-defense and killing never did take place, for which both men were silently grateful, neither of them caring overly for the idea that they might have to resort to murder in order to survive. New, forged papers were prepared for them, establishing them as Dutch workmen. They spent their time in this house listening to BBC war reports via a receiver in the basement, and discussing with their host the various developments in the war. Unexpectedly, one evening, they were turned over to yet another man and told, "If all goes as planned, you'll leave for England tonight. A submarine is to rendezvous off the coast nearby to collect you."

Elated, Robbie and Gray exchanged good-byes with their host and hostess and climbed into the car with their new contact. The driver informed them they'd be stopping to collect new sets of identity cards and the various zonal papers they'd need to get them safely to the rendezvous point on the coast.

Feeling decidedly claustrophobic and anxious in the back of the car, the two rode along in silence. Gray thought if it all worked according to plan, he'd be seeing Sam in just a few days' time.

They stopped at a small suburban house, where they were

introduced to the man who would prepare their forged papers. A small, fragile-looking graphic artist who, with printer friends, provided forged documents for the underground when required.

The next day, back in the car, in possession of their new papers, they drove on; seizing up at the sight of a squad of German soldiers with brightly polished jackboots, carrying tommy guns.

At the barricade outside the Schiphol aerodrome, the driver presented his and their papers, responding to the questions barked out by the German officer with remarkable calm, saying, "We are workers at the Philips Radio Factory, Section Four, en route for Leyden." He spoke comfortably, fluidly in German, to which the officer responded with surprising amiability. They were all asked to leave the car while it was searched, and Gray was positive they'd never make it past this point. But the driver continued to chat with the officer while the car, and then each of them, was searched. The officer turned every so often to look doubtfully at Robbie and Gray, who made an effort to be looking elsewhere, playing up their yawning disinterest in the conversation. Finally they were back in the car, through the barricade, and once more on their way.

"Are you German?" Gray asked, impressed and somewhat confused by the man's fluency.

He laughed loudly, shaking his head. "Never! I attended school in Dusseldorf. *Swine!*" he said with passion, then fell silent.

Arriving in Leyden, they were turned over to still another young man, who, with his wife, was to shelter them until they were to leave for the rendezvous. They settled in to wait, anxious at the thought that in just a few hours they'd be home. It was so close they didn't dare speak.

But early in the evening, someone came to the door, and their young host held a hurried conversation, the gist of which was that the submarine was going to be unable to keep the rendezvous. "If the weather permits, it will return tomorrow night. It has happened before," he told them encouragingly. "One time we waited six nights. You will remain here. It is safe."

They waited out the evening, trying not to let their disappointment and anxiety show. But all Gray was able to think of was getting out of this small, overheated apartment and into that submarine. Six nights of this pressure, the intolerable waiting, were unimaginable.

At last he and Robbie went to the tiny bedroom they were to share. Neither of them undressed, both too keyed-up. Resisting sleep, they lay smoking side by side on the bed, speculating on just how long they might have to remain cooped up in this place; trying to be grateful for the great kindness they'd so far been shown, but riddled with nervousness and tension.

Near dawn, noise in the street below awakened them. Shouting German voices. Battering on the outside door. His heart going out of control, Gray looked out the window, whispering, "Christ! They've found us!"

"Let's make it up to the roof, get out of here!" Robbie urged, going to the bedroom door, throwing it open just as the street door splintered and feet came pounding along the passage, up the stairs.

"We're trapped!" Gray whispered, nearly sick with fear of what might happen to them now.

After a lengthy interrogation in the sitting room of the tiny apartment, during which Gray and Robbie were adamant in their insistence that they'd forced the young couple to provide them sanctuary, they were taken to Gestapo headquarters in the Hague for further questioning. And separated. Gray was taken into a small room and ordered to stand against the wall. After what seemed hours, he was invited to sit down by the Gestapo investigator, a tall thin man with piercing eyes, gray hair, and a Hitler mustache.

At this point, Gray was overtaken by a strange kind of outrage; a combination of frustration, exhaustion, disappointment, anger, and fear. They could do whatever they liked to him, but he'd tell them absolutely nothing. He was offered a cigarette, which he refused. And water, which he also refused; suspicious of the man's every offer, every gesture.

"I assure you the water is not poisoned," the officer told him with a sardonic smile, his expression saying: You're a fool to be so frightened.

Horribly thirsty, Gray put out his hand to lift the glass as the officer's fist crashed down on the desk and he screamed, *"Put it down!"* With a start, Gray obeyed, promising himself he wouldn't again fall into such an obvious trap. For the next two hours he gave his name, rank, and serial number over and over, lied about his movements and activities since the crash, giving the same story he and Robbie had given the arresting officers; the story the two of them had worked over until it was almost more real to them than the truth. He just hoped Robbie wasn't letting them get to him, forcing him to alter the story.

A second interrogator took over, asking questions about the Stirling, astonishingly technical questions about the aircraft and its navigational aids, its multiple engines. Gray had to struggle to resist the temptation to talk to this intelligent, even charming officer who displayed such impressive knowledge; finding himself thinking that at some other time this was a man with whom technical discussion of the merits of the bomber might be a most rewarding enterprise. He had to force himself to remember the number of lives that might be endangered as a direct result of information he might unwittingly give this man. So he repeated his name, rank, and serial number until the officer switched to questions having to do with British political and economic policy, to which Gray found it almost easy not to respond.

For several more hours, exercising a steel control over himself, he continued responding to the questions asked with his name, rank, and serial number, until the officer said, "We have established your identity, and that you are one of the British fliers downed in the Stirling. And we are satisfied that you are not an agent."

Believing now that it was ended, he went along with the guard who led him out to a van in which he was taken to a nearby prison. He was literally thrown—with a kick in the spine for good measure—into a small cell, and lay on the floor, falling at once into a deep, aching sleep. He was awakened some hours later by a guard throwing a bucket of water over him.

Given time only to relieve himself in a tin bucket, he was taken back to headquarters, where the questioning began again. He was hungry, thirsty; his head and body ached. But steadfastly determined, he repeated his and Robbie's story over and over, alert to trick questions, deviations; going back and forth over their actions following the crash, their fictional thefts of clothing and money, their meanderings. Until the third and last of the interrogators pounded his fist on the desk, spat at Gray in disgust, and summoned the guard to return Gray to his cell at the prison.

At dawn the following day, he was given a tin cup of thin black coffee, two pieces of coarse dark bread, allowed time to relieve himself, then was taken out to a waiting car. He was sitting in the back beside an accompanying guard when they brought Robbie out. Elated to see him, although shocked by how haggard and ill Robbie looked, Gray murmured, "They told me you were dead."

"Told me the same bloody tale," Robbie whispered, giving Gray's arm a fleeting squeeze.

The guard shouted, *"Silence!"* Deafening inside the car.

From the car they were transferred to a train, then changed trains at Cologne for Frankfurt. There they were taken to the Dulag Luft for further questioning. And, amazingly, were each given—they later discussed this, comparing notes—a fine meal consisting of stewed meat with potatoes; good light bread, heavily seeded, with butter; coffee with cream and sugar; and a fresh apple. They were also given two cigarettes apiece. Then, just when they'd relaxed, the questioning began again. The treatment returned to brutality, they were offered stale black bread and weak coffee, questioned again and again, until at last being advised they were to be sent in a few days' time to Stalag VIIIb in Ober Silesia on the East German border.

A purported Red Cross official came to visit the cell, attempting to persuade Gray to complete the forms he presented. "The Red Cross will establish your status as a prisoner of war," the supposed official told him, "and notify your family." Gray refused to put down more than his name, rank, and serial number. "Do you not wish your family to know you are alive?" the official argued. Gray shook his head and would not complete the forms.

Some instinct told him that it would be not only unwise but also dangerous to give the information requested on the forms. Details about the type of planes he'd flown, his missions; personal information. He didn't for a moment believe that any of it would ever get back to the Red Cross headquarters in Geneva.

The questionable official, obligated to carry on what Gray was positive was a masquerade, shrugged, picked up the incomplete forms, and left.

Two weeks later, after further cursory sessions of questioning, he and Robbie were marched to the station along with ten other POW's and herded onto a train. Each was given a loaf of bread and a bit of sausage—rations for what would be three nights and four days of train travel.

Robbie looked progressively sicker, devoured his rations in

one go, and sat huddled inside his clothing, his teeth chattering uncontrollably throughout the journey. Gray shared his food with him and finally held the man in his arms to share also his body heat. He was terribly afraid Robbie would die. And Robbie seemed his only, his last link somehow to Sam.

After countless delays, they left the train at Annaberg, near Breslau; a sick, reeking, exhausted group of men. With guards on all sides, the POW's broken down into groups of four, they were marched the five miles to the prison camp through a freezing rain. Robbie staggered along in a daze, and Gray longed to help him, but the one time he reached out to offer Robbie support, he received for his gesture a gun butt in the ribs and the screaming command in German to leave Robbie to walk alone. Not far from the camp they passed a field full of small dirty-looking crosses, and Gray ventured to ask the friendlier of the guards what kind of cemetery it was.

"Dead from the last war," he answered tonelessly. "British, Russian, French, American, Canadian. All who died in Stalag VIIIb."

At the main gate they were halted, counted. Then they passed through a second wall of fifteen-foot-high wire and were checked again. In front of the guardroom they were patted and searched a further time. Then they were left for close to two hours to stand at ease in the rain before finally being marched to the barracks.

Gray supported Robbie, murmuring encouragement as he helped him along. Thinking: I won't die here! I damned well won't die here! And neither will you!

29

When Leo was working, she was able to keep her mind active on a level that dealt effectively with the injuries and the best possible way to repair them. But in her free time, she found all her thoughts and actions pervaded by a kind of stealthy horror, so that in the midst of a hurried meal or riding the train to Tewkesbury—which she did as often as possible, choosing to spend what little off-duty time she had there—across the screen of her inner vision would drift a series of images that managed to almost completely destroy her appetite, upset her sleep, and generally distract her. Gangrenous limbs, partially severed limbs, shattered-beyond-repair limbs. Lost ears, lost eyes, lost noses. Burnt flesh whose odor stayed in her nostrils until, like some Victorian faint-heart, she took to carrying a handkerchief liberally dosed with perfume. Collapsed chest cavities, open suppurating belly wounds, lesions that reeked of rot. The smell of sickness, profound and unrelenting, struck the senses like an assault force every time she entered the wards.

Big injuries, small ones. The small ones no less painful than the large, obvious ones. A nineteen-year-old boy with shell fragments lodged in the middle of his palm, myriad bits of fragment caught in the ligaments, tendons, and bones, so that the slightest movement caused excruciating pain. A boy with an exquisite, almost angelic face. Rich brown hair, round blue eyes, pale skin with rubbings of color across the cheekbones and lips. Anthony Blake-Owens. She visited him two or three times a week, trying to schedule him for surgery. But he was being made to wait, because the more critical cases had precedence. So she visited him because he bore his pain with a touching stoicism and smiled so magnificently each time she parted the curtains he liked kept drawn around his bed so that he might, he said, "study undisturbed the fascinating cracks in the ceiling."

He sat an hour or two a day in the chair beside his bed, but felt the pain less when stretched out in bed, his bandaged hand propped on a pillow. He'd been a student at Oxford, he told her, and had quit the moment he turned eighteen, in order to volunteer into the army.

"My brother did much the same thing," she told him, gingerly reexamining the hand while he stared fixedly at her face and tried not to show how much it hurt.

One afternoon, while she was telling him she'd finally managed to get him scheduled for the first of at least two operations she'd probably have to perform on the hand, he put his good hand on her breast, then looked at her fearfully, waiting for some kind of rebuke. She wasn't quite sure what to do, looked at his one healthy hand where it curved over her breast, looked at his eyes, then removed his hand but kept hold of it as she bent over him and kissed him lightly on the mouth. His lips, she thought, were like a child's. Firm, yet soft, innocent. She straightened, released his hand, said, "I've left a medication order for additional painkiller if you need it," and, "I'll see you in surgery Monday morning," and slipped away through the curtains; to steal a few moments to herself in the deserted doctors' lounge, trying to understand both what had happened and why she'd done what she had.

Her actions seemed to have to do with a number of tangential factors: with the baby Samara was going to have very shortly; with Clarissa's impressive truthfulness; with her fear that Gray really might be lost for good; with her mother's surprisingly emotional letters that arrived with awesome regularity, invariably postscripted by her father and enclosing clippings he thought might interest her. It had to do with the damaged faces and bodies of the men she treated day after day; men being repaired as quickly as possible in order to be returned to some sort of duty—whether limited or active. Men, too, whose thighs had been shattered irreparably and whose legs she'd had to amputate. Two men with critical groin injuries. One who subsequently died. One upon whom intensive surgery had had to be performed. Penis and testicles removed. A young man who moved like a cripple up and down the hospital corridors with tears perpetually streaming down his face. And, finally, it had to do with an alarming emptiness inside her that seemed to grow a little more every day, with every additional surgical procedure in which she was involved or consulted, with each newly arrived partially destroyed young man whose eyes reflected a fear and horror—a crazed light—she longed to understand.

So did it matter if a young man sought to touch her in order to relieve his personal wealth of terror? Did it matter if she allowed herself to be touched in intimate fashion if it made both of them feel fractionally better for a few moments? Reliving that brief time within the curtained cubicle, she experienced a thrill of something like pleasure at the remembered pressure of that hand on her breast. Did it matter? She no longer seemed to possess the well-defined views she'd once had. Because nothing was as clear or as easily explained as it had once been.

She had thought her work here would satisfy whatever it was inside her that had nagged at her so unendingly, only to find that her efforts simply served to intensify the nagging need, the gaping emptiness, the weight of her unanswered questions. And Anthony's child-bold caress had made her aware, with frightening clarity, of how truly empty she was. She was merely making gestures, exercising her skills, performing small kindnesses; but unreconciled to the echoing emptiness of her hours alone wherein her questions rang with resounding definition.

She tried, finally, to explain it to Clarissa, who listened closely, thoughtfully, as Leo searched for words that might more accurately define the strange state in which she seemed to be living.

"It seems," Clarissa said when Leo had struggled to the end, "you're looking for some sort of permission, my darling."

"Permission?"

My darling. Every time Clarissa offered one of these endearments, it was like a flare being set off inside Leo's head. She knew the caring was sincere, but she couldn't comprehend why, or what she'd done to merit it.

"Someone," Clarissa said, "to approve of what, as yet—at least it seems so to me—is nothing more than a temptation perhaps."

"You're being too subtle," she said, frustrated. "I'm not sure what you're saying."

"It's war, you know." Clarissa paused to draw on her cigarette. "In the last one, I found myself studying the faces of the boys, men. Trying to imagine what it was they'd seen, experienced. I couldn't do it. I could listen to the tales they had to tell and empathize, but I simply could not make the sort of mental transposition needed to fully comprehend those experiences. So," she said, "I comforted them instead, with great caring; taking any number of young men into my bed, my body, with a tenderness I hadn't known I possessed. It seemed the best as well as the least I could offer."

"My God!" Leo said, feeling frightened. "Is that what women are? Cushions, comforters? I loathe the idea of that. As if we're too poorly equipped to appreciate the meanings of war."

"It's rather difficult, Leo, to appreciate what one hasn't experienced firsthand. One never has quite the grasp of the full meanings those who've lived it do."

"That doesn't mean I'm incapable of understanding. All I have to do is see them, see their eyes, and it's all very real, very understandable."

"That being the case," Clarissa said incisively, "I fail to see why you're doing such a lot of soul-searching because a young man put his hand on your breast and, instead of shrieking at him, you kissed him."

Leo stared at her hands, confused.

"I've embarrassed you. Don't feel that way. It'll resolve itself."

"It's just," Leo said hesitantly, "that it seems some sort of commitment . . ." She looked again into Clarissa's eyes, deep brown with gold flecks. One might drown in such sympathetic pools of light.

"What do you want, Leo? What do you *really* want?"

"I don't know. To have some genuine understanding of the things that are happening. To be able to make sense of . . . everything. Not to feel empty, I suppose."

"And is it that you need a man for that?"

"I've been married, you know. I hated having all those demands made upon me."

"We're not talking about marriage."

"No. We're talking about sex, and whether or not it's what I want or need or have to have. Jesus! I'm too old for this! It's idiotic!"

"If I don't consider myself too old for it, why should you think you are?" Clarissa looked a little angry.

Aware of how stupid her observation had sounded, Leo sat back, feeling precisely like a rebuked child.

"Women," she said confusedly, "like Rose . . . and you . . ."

"What sort of women is that?" Clarissa asked carefully.

"You know who you are, how to be what you want. I'm saying it all wrong."

"You're saying it right," Clarissa disagreed. "I suspect whoever Rose is, she's paid for whatever self-knowledge she possesses. We most of us have, Leo."

"My God!" she said softly. "That's true. It *is* true." Remembering how Rose had tried to kill herself, and the way she'd talked about her abortions.

"Of course it is," Clarissa said sagely. "And as far as the rest of it, I don't think one's ever too old. Unless one simply wasn't so inclined in the first place. If you're inclined, my darling, go ahead and do it. If you're not, don't. You are too old to be seeking permission, I'll grant you that. All this weighty soul-searching. We're in a *war*, Leo. Different rules apply because different emotions come into play. We've lived with such a lot of it," she said. "I expect we British rather shine when it comes to wars. We're so bloody good at *coping*. Food queues, rationing, petrol stamps, sleeping in tube stations, coming home to find home's been bombed. We're all past masters of the art of 'getting on with it.' I suppose that tends to make us rather callous to those like you who find it so difficult to deal with. It isn't my intention to be callous. But you are a grown woman, and a doctor. And beautiful, darling. Very beautiful. They're bound to respond to you. Especially in your capacity as ministering angel, as it were." She smiled. "And *you're* bound to deal with it, in whatever fashion you choose. Some things, Leo," she said slowly, importantly, "have meanings that come to us only when we finally stop driving ourselves halfway mad searching for them."

All the way home on the train, Leo thought about Anthony; his childlike mouth and unchildlike need; about his damaged hand and disrupted sensibilities. She'd come, she decided, perilously close to involving herself in a dangerous game of God-playing on a minor scale. She hadn't really anything to give to him, and seeking self-gratification by beneficently accepting his hand upon her breast, offering chaste little kisses, was both beneath her dignity, something of an insult to both their needs, and unkind, as she had no intention of further indulging in minor self-serving performances.

324 CHARLOTTE VALE ALLEN

The surgical procedure was a lengthy one. She was sweating heavily under her surgical garb, the cap, the mask; requesting more often than usual to have her forehead mopped as she picked among the damaged tendons and muscles with a long probe, each bit of fragment dropping with a ping into the enamel basin. One after another she removed the tiny particles of shell. At one point, near the end, she had to work with a large magnifying glass to locate and remove the smallest of the fragments.

Later, she visited him in the postoperative-care unit to say, "Once we've got the second round out of the way, you'll have sixty to seventy percent renewed mobility. I'm confident we got more than ninety percent of the fragments. But the muscles with a long probe, each bit of fragment dropping the second operation will enable us to repair the worst of it."

She very much disliked her empirical "we" and "us," but knew of no other way to communicate to him her decision. However, he seemed to understand and for the remainder of his stay at the hospital made no further advances toward her.

She was both disappointed and relieved.

What I do *not* need, she told herself firmly, is a semichild to further complicate my already complicated life. But that being the case, she wondered: What *do* I need?

Grayson quietly said, "I'd like you to take six months and stay home, spend the time with me."

"Six months? With you?"

"I've asked for the time. To try my hand at writing a book. I'd like you to do it, Leonie. The business will still be there for you to go back to."

It bothered her. There was something not quite right about it. But some stronger instinct told her to go along with what he wanted. "I'll talk to Rose," she said, studying him closely, as if for new, previously unnoticed signs; something to give her a better understanding of the situation. He'd never before made a request, even remotely similar, of her. Frightened, she acquiesced without further question, and arranged to have dinner in town with Rose to discuss the matter.

"Maybe he's right," Rose said guardedly. "Waiting until later is sometimes waiting until too late."

"Everything, including what you've just said, strikes me wrong just now. Why do you say that, Rose?"

"Simply because it makes sense. And why shouldn't you take some time to be together?"

"Fair enough. But what about you? Is it your intention ever to take time for yourself and Pat?"

"I've thought about it," she admitted. "I've been toying with the idea that if you take the next six months off, perhaps when you're ready to return, I'll take the six months after that. We could even work it out to spend six months apiece running Lion's." Rose smiled. "Why not?"

"Why not?" Leonie repeated, rubbing her hand up and down her forearm, her skin feeling peculiar. "I have this dreadful feeling, Rose, that reality isn't happening here. It's happening over there somewhere. With young Gray still missing, and Leo apparently working day and night at her hospital, and Sam about to have a baby at any moment. Now Gray wants to take six months, write a book."

"You're worried. That's perfectly understandable."

"It's not quite that simple, Rose. Leo's letters, for one thing, are very odd; filled with philosophical questions, riddled with anxiety. And the letters from Samara—it's very dear of her to write to us—such straightforward, affectionate letters. But the anxiety's there, too. Now, it's here. In full measure."

"I know it's not an easy time for the two of you," Rose said, caring. "So stay home and worry together."

"You manage," she smiled, "to tie it all up so neatly."

Initially the barracks seemed nightmarish, terrifying. The stink of burning wood, unclean male flesh, stagnant air; men squatting over fires made in open tins, cooking with homemade devices—herring tins with improvised handles. Empty tin cans for cups. Filth. And the stench of sickness underlying it all.

Two-thirds of the available space was taken up by three-tiered wooden bunks, the first tier resting directly on the cold concrete floor. Eighteen-inch alleyways divided the blocks of beds.

But they were warmly greeted by other RAF POW's, welcomed as if to some bizzarre reunion; asked for the latest war news, for details of how and where they'd gone down. The British barracks doctor was summoned to see what help he could offer Robbie. The men quickly indoctrinated the two of them into the camp routines. There was an extraordinary camaraderie among the men. The Canadians clubbed together, as did the British, the Australians, and the New Zealanders.

The English-speaking POW's segregated themselves from the non-English-speaking.

Quickly, alarmingly he fell into the routine of this sublife. The sometime—not to be counted on—distribution of Red Cross food parcels when they tried to make the contents last a week but too often devoured everything in one frantic meal because the daily ration of 350 grams of coarse black bread and a liter of cabbage soup—no cabbage, no taste of cabbage, no resemblance to cabbage—left all of them constantly hungry.

The mattresses fashioned of filthy straw, were breeding grounds for lice, vermin. Everyone had fleas, lice, and went about unconsciously scratching. Bitter cold, day and night, that penetrated their cloth shoes and ragged bits of clothing.

Every morning after roll call, four men came bringing a dustbin lid full of what the Germans called "mint tea," enough to provide each man with a small measure. No milk, no sugar. They hoarded the supplies of Red Cross tea that came in the food parcels and used the German "mint tea" to scald the lice out of their clothing, or as shaving water.

As the winter progressed and the temperature consistently remained below zero, the morale of the men in the barracks—and the camp in general—ebbed severely. Inadequately clothed, inadequately fed, they were freezing and starving to death. Weekends, they were each given a piece of fish cheese, a spoonful of turnip jam, and a very small piece of wurst made of raw meat. The British doctor warned the men to some way or other cook the meat before attempting to eat it, as the wurst was infested with tapeworm germs. The fish cheese, possessed of a thick slimy coating, smelled vile. Gray simply couldn't force himself to eat it. There was no shortage of men willing to relieve him of the cheese. He scraped it clean and fed it to Robbie, who claimed not to mind the taste or smell.

Months, and he couldn't quite believe he was becoming accustomed to this existence. But he'd fallen into the routines, went off on the work patrols, got through the days; and shared his meager portions of food with Robbie, afraid for him.

He dreamed of hot showers, fresh linen, as each morning after the "mint tea" the Germans turned on the water in the eight sprinklers in the wash house for exactly twenty minutes, during which time the men tried frantically to fill their tin cups, wash some portion of themselves before being taken outside for sixty minutes' marching practice in the snow. Before leaving the barracks, the men tried to work on the lice in their clothing, running lighted paper over the seams of their shirts in an attempt to burn out the vermin. Because the outdoor exercise heated the blood, thereby causing the lice to become wildly active. The practice marching was soon abandoned as more and more of the men collapsed in the snow.

Between midday and four in the afternoon, the men lay about in the barracks, idly talking, some halfheartedly planning escapes. Gray sat listening distractedly, noticing the flesh was beginning to leave his body, his legs becoming spindly, the knobs of his knees acquiring shocking prominence. He thought constantly of escaping, of Sam, of his mother and father and Leo; wondering if, as they'd promised he would be, he'd been reported back home as a POW. He decided to pay closer attention to the whispered escape plans.

Sam went into labor when Leo happened to have an entire weekend free and was spending it in Tewkesbury, keeping Sam company while Clarissa was in London for a few days. She never discussed what she did during her visits to the city, but returned home afterward looking tired and worn.

When Leo suggested they telephone her mother, Sam excitedly said, "*No!* Unless it's an emergency, we're not to!"

"But don't you think this is something of an emergency?"

"No." Sam sighed. "Not the sort to ring her about."

"What the hell is she *doing*?" Leo asked after listening to the baby's solid heartbeat with her stethoscope.

"Helping Joshua," Sam gasped, her face contorting as she went into another contraction.

"Helping him how?"

"Just *helping* him. Is it going to be soon, do you think?"

"A little while yet. You're not dilated."

"Oh!" She sagged back against the pillows and looked at the ceiling. "I wish he knew about the baby. I do wish he knew."

"He'll know soon enough once he gets home."

"We only got to be together fourteen times," Sam said. "I counted it up from my diary. Still, I suppose that's a lot better than most of the others, who only had two or three times, perhaps. Fourteen is quite a lot if you think about it. Do you feel strange being here?"

"Strange?"

"My being your brother's wife. Having the baby. Your not having seen him for—how long?—three years?"

"Closer to five."

"I hadn't realized it was that long. Doesn't it feel strange to you, really?"

"Does it to you?" Leo asked, holding her hand through the next contraction.

"Yes and no," she answered consideringly. "It seems now as if I actually know you better than I do Gray. I've seen more of you. And that is strange."

"I suppose it must be."

"What a funny woman you are!" Sam observed. "Always so distant, holding yourself away somehow."

"Is that how I seem to you?" she asked, intrigued by Sam's view of her.

"It's as if you do care. Terribly. About any number of things. But something seems to drop down in front of you when you begin caring too much, or too obviously. And you're so frightfully angry." Sam smiled as Leo bathed her face with a damp cloth. "Why is that, Leo?"

"Not a very pretty picture you're painting of me," she said lightly, returning her hand to Leo's, thinking the description sounded very true of her father. Have I become like him? she wondered.

"That's part of what's so strange, you see," Sam attempted to explain. "The way you look. You're so lovely. Really! Mother and I have talked about it quite often. The way you look. And the things you do. But what you say is so different. Not at all in keeping with the way you look and the things you do. Oh, bloody hell!" Her face suffused with color, she stared unblinkingly at the ceiling, taking short shallow breaths until the contraction ended.

"I can give you a shot if it's too bad," Leo offered.

Sam looked at her in surprise. "It isn't bad," she said earnestly. "Have you delivered babies before?"

"A few. During my internship. It isn't my first time, if that's what you're worried about."

"I'm not in the least worried about anything. That's one of the things about you," she said breathlessly. "You're so bloody competent. It shines off you."

"You're wrong, Sam," she said quietly.

"I'm not, you know. I'm really not."

Sam bore the pain in silence. She swore several times but otherwise contained everything, as if refusing to allow any involuntary sign of weakness to show.

"If it helps," Leo said gently, "make a little noise."

"Do you suppose they torture the prisoners?" Sam asked suddenly.

"I don't know," she responded, immediately and deeply bothered by the question. "I wouldn't think so."

"They do the Jews, you know. Frightfully. Joshua . . ." She didn't finish what she was going to say, caught in another spasm of pain. "They seem to be coming quite close together now."

"Will you let me telephone your mother after the baby comes?"

"*No*! She'll be home in the morning. It can wait until then."

"You're dilated," Leo said, signaling her to lower her legs. "It won't be long now."

Something was happening to her, a feeling sweeping over her that, unlike Sam's pain, couldn't be contained. A recognition and a painful infusion of caring for this swollen naked girl spread upon her bed, heaving her way into motherhood; whispering at some moments, talking loudly at others; communicating her way into delivery and somehow obligating Leo to care, and care very deeply. She was doing it by clinging to Leo's hand, by smiling that dazzling smile from moment to moment, by talking so hopefully about someone she loved deeply who might very well be dead.

Leaning on her elbows, pushing forward against the stonelike mound of her belly, straining, crimson-faced, she hissed, "Come on, come on, *come on*!" before collapsing back for a moment, trying to catch her breath. Incredibly, she started to sing as she lay looking at the ceiling. In a pure, high soprano. Some childhood song unfamiliar to Leo. Then she stopped, raising herself, beginning to push again. Catching Leo's startled expression, she smiled at her, saying, "We love you, you know, Leo. Even though you hate feelings, having to feel. I'm happy you're here with me now."

For a while there wasn't room for further conversation. Sam was too busy trying to push the baby out. She gave a massive heave that finally moved the baby out of her and into Leo's waiting hands.

"What is it?" she asked tearfully, wiping her eyes and nose with the back of her hand. "Is it a boy?"

"It's a boy," Leo answered, choked; awed by the reality of the bloodstained infant she held. *The son of my brother. My mother's grandchild. A part of me.*

She heard Sam's voice whispering and looked over.

"Is it so dreadful, caring?" Sam asked.

"No." She shook her head. "No. I don't know why it hurts. It shouldn't." She put the baby in Sam's arms, pulling herself together to finish the job at hand. *Why does it hurt?* she asked herself, massaging Sam's stomach to encourage the final contractions. *Am I crippled in some fashion, that caring should be so painful? But, God, it could've been my baby—mine I killed.*

Clarissa returned from London wearing dark glasses, which she kept on during her visit upstairs to see Sam and the baby. Leo sat drinking a cup of tea on the sofa in the lounge, watching her come in, light a cigarette, then sink into the armchair in front of the coal fire, saying, "Thank you for being here with Sam, for all of it. We're very grateful."

"Don't thank me! For God's sake, please don't *thank* me!"

Clarissa's hand lifted to the dark glasses, and she slowly removed them, her eyes meeting Leo's. Dark, almost purple circles ringed her eyes. Her entire demeanor was one of utter exhaustion. "Stop fighting," she said, her voice huskier than ever. "It's what you have to have: being needed. None of us is above it, Leo." She sat back and held the cigarette to her mouth, her hand trembling visibly.

"I'm going to give you a sedative, put you to bed."

"No!" Clarissa said strongly.

"But you're—"

"No, Leo! Finish your tea! I want to sit here and have my cigarette."

"What have you been doing?" Leo asked boldly, fed up with guesswork.

"What the bloody hell do you *imagine* I've been doing?" she snapped. "Fucking soldiers in Trafalgar Square?"

Shocked, Leo went silent.

"You exhaust me at times," Clarissa said more quietly. "You're an exhausting woman to be with. I'm sorry I barked at you."

"It's all right. I understand."

"No." Clarissa gave her head a slight shake. "You *don't* understand. I was helping my husband smuggle in two political refugees. We spent the night getting them to a safe house. And then we returned to the flat and made love. I got on the early train and came home. I'm *tired*, Leo. My husband is almost ten years younger. He simply has more energy than I do. I'm fifty-three years old and I'm tired and you're an exhausting woman. It's difficult. It's *all* difficult. They were three hours late. I was terrified they'd been caught. Terrified. I *love* him. It's very *tiring*, living constantly on the fine edge of fear."

"What can I do for you?" Leo asked helplessly, feeling deeply ashamed, inadequate.

"You should have made love to that boy, Leo," she said sadly. "It does mean something. It's all such a frightful waste. I'm going up to bathe. I think Sam would enjoy your company just now."

Leo put out her cigarette and got up. But instead of going to the door, she came across the room and stopped in front of Leo, placing a tender hand on her face. "You've given so much of yourself to us, darling. Won't you relax and accept us, let us know you? Is it really so impossible for you?" Without awaiting an answer, she withdrew her hand, saying, "Do go up and have a visit with Sam. She'd like it very much."

She managed to contain herself sufficiently to sit chatting with Sam for half an hour before getting up, saying, "I'll just look in on your mother, then go out for a walk." She drifted out, drawn against her will, down the hall to tap quietly at the bedroom door before opening it, stepping into what felt like Clarissa's world. Softness, dreaming colors, a fragile-looking woman sitting against the pillows drinking neat whiskey from a crystal tumbler, smoking a cigarette. Her hair unfastened, it fell about her shoulders. Waiting. Leo went to sit down on the side of the bed, asking, "How do you feel?" feeling it rising from her chest, into her throat, strangling her. Clarissa tossed down the last of the Scotch, set aside the glass, leaned over to stub out her cigarette before opening her arms, beckoning Leo into them, stroking her hair as Leo cried and cried, unable to stop; like a small child, sobbing, soaking the front of Clarissa's nightgown with her tears. While Clarissa held and stroked her, murmuring, "I know, I know. It's all right now, all right." Caring breaking its way into her like a wedge being forced between her ribs, driving itself relentlessly through her like a fever. She felt as if she was emerging from more than a decade of life encased in concrete.

30

Leonie enjoyed her time at home far more than expected. She put the bulbs into the garden, supervised the exterior repainting of the house, worked with Amy in the kitchen and went with her to town to do the marketing. There were long unhurried dinners, and evenings spent listening to the radio for the latest news, games of chess she and Gray played before going upstairs early to make love for hours. It was as if he'd suddenly rediscovered, totally, his passion for her and couldn't bear to allow even one evening to go by without actively, heatedly demonstrating it.

In the mornings, he closed himself into what had been Gray's bedroom and was now a study, and banged away at the new portable typewriter he'd bought upon deciding to write the book. Emerging midday, he sat down to lunch in the kitchen with Leonie and Amy, then went up for an afternoon nap. By three-thirty, Leonie was downstairs on the telephone with Rose, getting the daily report of the business. And he was back at the typewriter.

Amy went about pulling at her lower lip, shaking her head, muttering to herself; initially causing Leonie to laugh, asking, "What's the matter, Amy?"

"Nothin'. Not a thing."

Amy couldn't put into words the feeling she had nowadays. It was like waiting, but not knowing for what. Just waiting for whatever was due to happen. There wasn't any doubt in her mind that something was sure enough going to happen. And it felt wrong, didn't feel any way good.

Gray seemed calmer, more content than Leonie had ever known him to be. And sometimes while he worked, she read and reread the children's letters, studied the photographs of the baby, and unknowingly, also found herself waiting.

In bed one evening near the end of her third month at home, they were talking quietly, discussing the chance that young Gray might still be alive, and about the improved tone of Leo's letters, smiling together over the photographs of the baby. And for the first time, she ventured to ask, "How is the writing coming along?" He frowned, then said, "I'm about ready to throw it into the trash."

"It isn't good?"

"The truth is," he said slowly, "I threw it all out several days ago."

"But why?"

"Because I *used* to be a writer, Leonie. I'm not anymore."

"I'm sorry," she said, not sure quite how to deal with this.

"Don't be. I know you want to get back to work. Why don't you?"

"I want what you want, darling. If you'd like the two of us to continue on this way, I'm quite happy—"

"You need it," he said, drawing her over close to him. "Selfish of me to deprive you of something you need."

"I need *you* more."

"Years ago"—he sighed—"I'd have derived the greatest satisfaction in hearing you say that. But a bit of wisdom's bound to come with age, I suppose. And the truth is, you need both. So go ahead, get on the blower with Rose tomorrow and tell her you'll be coming back."

It didn't feel right. None of it.

"If it's all the same to you"—she smiled—"I'll just keep my part of the bargain, see the six months through."

He sat silent for several minutes, stroking her hair, his arm secure around her. "God," he said after a time, "we've had some times, haven't we?" He laughed softly.

"I'd say so, yes."

"And the children," he went on, as if continuing some monologue she'd missed parts of. "Splendid children. Fierce, independent, unique children."

She lay still against him, waiting.

"You," he said, going on. "It's been very high and very low, but never boring. The very first time I saw you. Do you remember? That afternoon you arrived on the boat train. Old Gus wouldn't even consider going to the station to meet you, wanted to send the butler. What was his name?"

"Benson."

"That's right. Benson. I said, 'Like hell!' and went myself to meet you, stood on the platform and saw you step down from the train. It was as if the sun had come out suddenly. The brightest, most beautiful sight I'd ever seen. Seventeen years old, looking terrified; yet so bold in the face of it. Offering me your hand, looking me straight in the eye, saying, 'I am Leonie. Dr. Benedict's daughter. From Africa.' And I wanted to say, 'Yes, you are. Yes.' Africa. My African." His hand continued to stroke her hair, and she lay without moving, not wanting to disturb him his reminiscing. He laughed again, saying, "Drove poor Gus round the bend those first six months. Poor Gus, poor stupid Gus. She deserved better than that. Being blown to bits by a stray shell. Poor old Gus, putting all those years between you and me. *God, I love you!*" he said with sudden ferocity. "He'll be all right," he said after a moment, switching tracks. "That boy's a born survivor, no fear. He'll turn up. Odd about children. Gray's far more your son than mine. And Leo's cursed, I'm afraid, with my nature. Bad enough for a man, but hellish for a woman." He sighed again and stopped stroking her hair, placing his other arm around her. "I love you, Leonie."

"And I you," she whispered, afraid to say more and shatter the spell.

They went to sleep without making love. And she awakened in the morning feeling unusually cold. She put her hand out to touch Gray, startled by the coldness of his skin. Sitting up, she leaned over him, then straightened slowly; remaining sitting, staring into space for a long time. Her brain was somehow caught, unable to tick forward; like a stopped clock. She wet her lips and lowered her head to her knees, closing her eyes. Unable to react except with agonizing slowness, as if frozen in body as well as mind; aware of the texture of the bedclothes, of the dampness of the sheet beneath her, of the substance of his body weighing down his side of the bed.

It seemed to take hours. She simply couldn't react, and remained with her head on her knees, holding herself together until Amy came tapping at the door, carrying the morning tray with the coffee and the one cup they liked to share. Carefully she set the tray down on the dressing table as with narrowed eyes she looked at Leonie curled in on herself and then at the lifeless bulk in the bed beside her.

She touched Leonie's shoulder, startled by the coldness of her skin; just as Leonie had been startled by Gray's.

"You better get up," Amy said softly. "Get outta the bed, come sit in the chair."

She shook her head, grinding her forehead against her knees, her teeth clenched. Brain locked unticking, fingers gripping her upper arms, holding herself together. Until Amy's warmth came around her like a blanket, Amy in a deep whisper murmuring, "Come here to me, come on, now, you come here to me, honey. Just you come on here to me, now."

They'd planned it for fifteen months. And at the last minute asked Gray if he wanted to go along. He said yes. And they went, making it out of the camp under cover of sheets stolen from the hospital, white against the thick-falling snow, cutting their way through the wire fences with improvised wire-cutters; bellying their way out to freedom. Gray and the two others. All RAF men.

The only part of the plan that went as it should have was their passage out of the camp. After that, everything fell apart. After hiding by day, traveling by night for three days and nights, they were captured. And taken to Gestapo headquarters, separated there. In a small interrogation room, while the interviewing officer watched, casually smoking a cigarette, the guard twisted Gray's right arm slowly higher up his back. A question. Another twist. No answer. Another twist. They said it was an accident. "If you had been more cooperative," the officer said, "this would not have happened." But he'd told them nothing. And the last slow twist pulled his shoulder right out of its socket. He fainted.

He was returned to the stalag, and spent three months in the camp hospital, his arm and shoulder slowly mending. But, according to the British doctor, "Not right at all. Bastards! If we ever get you back to England, lad, we'll set this properly. Much pain?"

"Not too bad."

"I'll see to it you have some morphine." He gave Gray a cigarette, lit it for him, then went off, looking down at his feet.

Back to the barracks.

At Christmas they decorated the barrack room with bits of colored paper, stolen branches of fir trees smuggled back by the work patrols, pictures drawn on the wall with homemade charcoal. The lines of washing were down for once. The men sat at the long, bare tables talking quietly, having had their first decent meal in months. Outside, the snow fell thickly, and from one of the other barracks, could be heard faint sounds of voices singing "Silent Night." The dogs barked out in the compound, there were the muffled sounds of guards making their rounds, searchlights turned the falling snow yellow as they swung back and forth.

He lay on his bunk touching the ceiling with his fingers, trailing them back and forth over the cold, damp wood; thinking about Sam, about home. All the Christmases. Almost two years of days marked off in rows, with a nail, on the ceiling. Rows and rows of lines marked off.

Robbie was dead, had died after Gray's abortive escape attempt. First dysentery, then a twelve-foot-long tapeworm. He'd been close to death before the escape. And he died. An 84 pound skeleton, shot full of morphine, when it was far too late, by the German doctor who supervised the hospital.

Russian POW's had been brought into the next camp, bringing with them a new breed of vicious lice, and typhus. The Russians, jammed into their quarters and sick, died like flies. The British and Allied prisoners, too, were dying. Even some of the Germans. Just a day or two was all it took. One started out feeling seedy, feverish, as if with a common cold; then aching all over, trembling, shivering; finally unconsciousness as the typhus took over. The entire stalag was under quarantine, each compound strictly segregated, locked, and closely guarded to prevent the men from mixing, spreading the germs.

None of them was worse off, though, than the Russians, who, with no Red Cross aid, received only their bits of bread and meager portions of soup. No medicines, no treatments. The Germans did attempt to save British and Allied lives by treatment, and there were special serums flown out from the Red Cross in Switzerland, along with other medical aids.

Gray and half a dozen of the others hit upon the idea of collecting the virulent Russian lice in matchboxes, saving them. And when the guards came in, three of the men would lie in the shadow of one of the top bunks while some of the others stopped the guard on some pretext so that the men in the bunk could carefully tip out their matchboxes of lice onto the guard; hoping the lice would drive the Germans crazy as they carried them back to their quarters.

Thinking about that, he laughed aloud. A sound that had no volume, didn't travel, contained little humor; but all the anger in the world was in it as he ran his hand over his shaven head. Everyone in the camp had been issued razors and told to shave off all their body hair, in an effort to get rid of the lice.

After the new year, he again requested permission to write to his wife. The others regularly wrote and received heavily censored letters. But part of his punishment for refusing to divulge the details of his and Robbie's time in Holland, as well as for his attempted escape, was the withholding of his privilege as a POW to communicate with his family. They still refused to allow him to write. But they did say he had finally been reported as a POW. And perhaps soon he might write.

Soon.
If I'm a good boy.
Sam?

Barely able to speak, Leo requested a week's leave. When asked why, she placed the telegram on the chief surgeon's desk and stood watching him read it; wanting desperately to get out of there, away from all the sickness and putrefaction, to deal with the numbing grief and total helplessness she felt.

"Of course, of course. My sympathies. By all means. I'll arrange ten days at once."

She was able to say, "Thank you," retrieve the telegram, and get out of the hospital. Throwing her coat on over her blood-spattered surgical suit, not caring, she walked out into the fresh, breathable air, moving mechanically; wishing she were able to go home to her mother. It had been the first thing she'd tried to do. Impossible, she'd been told.

She went into the first pub she saw to drink a triple brandy straight down. Then, back out in the street, she continued walking without direction; moving backward and forward up and down the years, the brandy partially soothing the ache in her midsection. She felt dangerously close to some sort of explosion. She'd been unable to say good-bye to either one of them—Gray or her father.

Her days and nights were spent trying to patch up, put together, pieces of men of all shapes and sizes; dealing with the blood and broken bones, torn flesh. She thought of Clarissa, what she'd said. She was right, I should have. He was beautiful, young, and we'd both have felt better for the contact. Something, someone. Not to feel this way.

She'd go up to Clarissa and Sam. But not yet. Not until she was able to establish some more substantial grip on her ravaged emotions. She felt raw, like one of the wounds she too often cleaned before suturing; open, her vulnerable parts dangerously exposed to the unclean air. She didn't know what to do, went into another pub, ordered a single brandy, and sat down in a corner, smoking one cigarette after another, nursing the brandy; afraid of getting drunk and possibly going completely out of control.

Someone came to sit down beside her. She could feel eyes darting against the surface of her skin and, irritated, jerked her head up to look, see who was attempting to intrude upon her too-rare moment of privacy. She looked into a pair of hazel eyes that seemed improbably sympathetic.

"You look awfully down," a deep, cultured voice said. The voice came from below a blond, carefully trimmed mustache. She looked at where the voice had come from. Pink lips, the lower one possessing an interesting fullness; the upper one masked by the mustache. "Will you have another?" he asked.

"How the hell old are you anyway?" she asked sharply, drawing her brows together.

"Rather too old," was the answer. It came with a sad little smile.

"What are you?" she asked. "A what? Captain?"

"Major, actually. *You're* a captain, I see."

"Bingo! We'll send you your prize."

"Medical corps," he went on, unperturbed. "Nurse, are you?"

"I'm a surgeon."

"Sorry. Should've known better. Nurses don't make captain."

"They probably should."

He agreed. "Probably."

"A major," she repeated, looking again at his mouth. "How old *are* you?"

"Thirty-six. Do I qualify?"

"Damned right! No more children," she said, crushing out her cigarette, at once lighting another, waving away his hand with a lighter. "You're on leave," she said, sloshing the brandy around inside the balloon glass. "With a wife and three darling children in Sussex."

He took his time lighting a cigarette. "Half-right," he said. "On leave."

"What? No wife and darling little kiddies?"

"Did have," he said, something altering in his eyes. "Went down the entire street, back and forth. Not a bloody house left standing."

"Oh, Jesus!" she whispered, starting to choke again. *"Jesus!"*

"Let me buy you another drink," he said. "I'd like to, very much."

Mute, she gave him her glass.

"Brandy, is it?" He sniffed her glass.

She nodded.

He went away and came back, sat down, returned her her glass, said, "Cheers!" and took a swallow of his drink.

"What were you," she asked, "before you were a major?"

"A banker. International finance."

"A banker. I've never thought of bankers as people with the potential to kill."

"We all have it," he said soberly. "Or they give it us, rather like an endowment."

She looked at him again. He was profound, she thought. Very profound.

"How long have you got?" she asked, blinking at her second contact with the hazel eyes. It seemed to hurt in the distanter regions of her body.

"Five days," he answered.

"Have you got somewhere to go?" she asked.

"I haven't, actually. I find myself forgetting, thinking I'll run along home. But home isn't."

He finished his drink. As an afterthought, as they were leaving, she picked up her glass and tossed down the contents. Then she took him back to her tiny flat and defiantly yanked the blackout curtains closed before turning on all the lights.

"What's your name?" he asked, looking for somewhere to put his greatcoat.

"Just call me doctor," she said coldly.

"May I tell you my name?"

"For God's sake, no! Please, don't! Just as long as you're not a child." If he was clumsy, heavy-handed, insensitive, she'd probably want to die after. She could feel a deathly desire creeping through her bloodstream.

Her defiance evaporated in the bedroom.

He said, "You're very beautiful," and touched her lovingly, shocking her. Both the quality of his initial caress and her own response were unanticipated. She hadn't expected to feel anything. But she did. She felt everything. Her need had a short fuse, and his hands on her breasts, his mouth on her throat, were fire to the fuse. She twisted out from under his caress, beginning to cry convulsively. He held her, attempting to comfort her. Another shock. At last he defeated her utterly by quietly crying with her, as if her tears had a contagious quality. Or perhaps it was simply that she'd failed to credit him any capacities whatsoever—most especially the one for grief.

After quite some time, having cried themselves out, he said, "My name is Colin Davison," and sat up. "I'll make us some tea."

She turned her face into the pillow and fell asleep. He woke her with a steaming cup of too-milky tea and a plate of bread and butter and cheese.

"Took the liberty of raiding your larder," he said. "Hope you don't mind."

"No."

"It's a beautiful name." He clinked teacups with her.

"What is?"

"Leonie." He gave it its proper French pronunciation. Lay-o-*nee*. "Beautiful," he said.

"How . . . ?"

"It's on your postbox, doctor. I saw it when we came in."

"My father died," she said in a voice quivering with emotion. "My brother was shot down over Berlin more than two years ago. He's probably dead, but I don't want to believe it. He has a son he doesn't even know exists. I spend all my time trying to save bodies, but can't do anything about minds or souls. None of it makes any sense."

"No," he agreed. "What part of America are you from?"

"Connecticut."

"I'm a Londoner."

They finished the meal without further conversation. He collected the cups and plates, returned them to the makeshift kitchen that took up a corner of the lounge, then came back and sat on the edge of the bed. The two of them shared a cigarette.

"I haven't been . . . I haven't . . . made love in four years," she admitted.

"And if you hadn't had several drinks," he finished for her, "I wouldn't be here."

"Probably not."

"Would you prefer me to leave?"

"Do you want to leave?"

"I'd like to stay, actually."

"Then stay." It didn't matter, did it?

"I haven't ever made love to anyone but my wife," he said, passing her the cigarette. "I suppose that puts us on about the same square."

"When did you find out?"

"Last leave. Three months ago. Found one of the neighbors digging about in the rubble. He told me."

"I'm sorry." She lay back and covered her face with her hands, trying not to start crying again. It didn't matter a damn if he saw her body, but for the moment she couldn't bear to have him see her face, look into her eyes. His eyes contained that crazy bewildered light the men in the hospital all had. That same sadly astonished too-quickly-aged quality. The sirens went off, and she said, "Turn out the lights, will you, please?" from behind her hands.

"Hadn't we better strike out for the shelter?"

"Does it matter?" she asked, daring to put the question to someone at long last. "Does it really matter?"

"Not terribly." He turned out the light, then put his hand on her breast, gently squeezing her nipple. She uncovered her eyes—safe in the almost complete darkness—and tried to see him as his other hand traveled over her. She opened her legs, and his hand moved up the length of her thighs.

"You've wonderful skin," he said, his hand stroking back and forth along her inner thigh.

Painfully, hating to admit it but needing to say it, she whispered, "I like the way you touch me."

"I like touching you. I'm not altogether sure I believe any of this is happening." He sounded bewildered, too. So it isn't, she thought, something solely contained in the eyes. "It's been nearly seven months since the last time." His voice had leveled down now. "And it wasn't good. We talked mostly. About starting a family once the war was ended. I'd always been selfish, you see, not wanting to share her. But then, we both of us thought . . . Being apart. And all this going on and on, years and bloody years. Changing everything. I thought how wrong, how selfish. Wanting to have the children . . . Well . . ." He sighed. "I find myself forgetting from moment to moment. Then I come back to myself, realize who you are. Not her."

She could sense from his hands how much he'd loved his wife, how much of a capacity for caring he had. Because she was someone he didn't know at all, yet he was offering the very best of his caring for these moments. And surely, she thought, remembering too clearly Clarissa's same words, the least I can offer is the best of myself.

"Are you bothered by this?" he asked, moving down between her thighs, lowering his head.

"No, no. Not . . . bothered."

His tongue lightly striking made her clench her fists and moan softly, so that he slid his hands beneath her and lifted her closer, striking harder. She unclenched one hand, then the other, stroked his hair; her hands saying: Thank you, yes; her hands indicating he should stop. Floating, raising herself to accommodate the pillow he placed at the base of her spine so that she was tilted toward him dizzily and wanted to say: It isn't any good for me this way, it never is, I don't come this way, but never mind. Teasing his way into her body, long lazy thrusts that made her reach greedily, kissing his mouth; the mustache grazing her breasts, shoulders. He whispered, "Tell me when you're going to come," and she thought she couldn't possibly say aloud what he was asking, it never happened this way; but it did, she could, cried, "My God! I'm going to," and fell into amazed spasms as he paced himself to end with her. Gasping, they held each other with unbelievable tenderness. Loving strangers. He remained inside her, and after resting, made love to her again before withdrawing slowly, causing both of them to sigh. She held him close until they both slept.

On the last day of his leave he said, "If I make it back, I'll come for you."

"You don't have to say that," she said.

"I'm well aware of what I *have* to say and what I *want* to say."

"It's only because . . . your wife . . ."

"No. It's because of you. I've learned you, know you. Sounds ridiculous to say that after just a matter of days. But it's the truth."

"I can't make promises."

"I know you," he said without smugness.

"Yes," she agreed. "I honestly think you do." How did this

happen? she wondered. Four days and nights and it happened. Making love, talking, making more love, talking more, talking, talking. Up and down the years of their two lives, exchanging the pain and pleasure, creating something out of the rubble. Was that possible?

"I'll make it back," he said. "And I will come for you."

And then he was gone.

She was able to pack her bag, go to the station, and get on the train. To discover Sam had had a letter from the Air Ministry.

"He's *alive!*" Sam laughed. "I knew he was! I *knew!*"

Staggered, Leo sat down heavily on the sofa, caught between tears and laughter. Losses, gains. Clarissa came to sit down beside her. "I don't even know what to feel," Leo told her. "My God!"

"We had a telegram about your father." Clarissa's rich voice was close to her ear. "I'm sorry, darling. But it was very quick. He simply went to sleep. I'd choose that, if it was a matter of choices."

Dry-eyed, she breathed in Clarissa's perfume, instinctively reaching out to hold on to her; trying to sort through all the meanings. At last saying, "It really *does* matter. I shouldn't have said I wouldn't promise. I should have given him something more to go on with. There was no price to it. Only the price I put on it. It was so wrong of me not to."

"Whatever it is," Clarissa said, "it's an impossible time to try making promises. We all know that, Leo."

"No." She sat away, shaking her head. "The whole point is, I *didn't* know that. This is a hell of a way and a hell of a time to be finding things out. I'm not a child. I'm thirty years old. What's *wrong* with me? I loved Colin more in four days than I *ever* loved Adam. I actually loved him. That doesn't make any sense. Not a bit."

"What makes you think there's any 'sense' to love? It hasn't anything to do with that. You give a bit of yourself away, Leo, then drive yourself mad wondering if you're wrong to do it. Yet you could no more prevent yourself giving those bits away than you could see someone bleeding to death on the pavement and walk past him. Now you feel vulnerable because you allowed someone to see you, showed yourself. Let it be, darling. None of us is going to capitalize on your vulnerability. It's the most attractive part of you."

Outside, Sam was laughing with the baby. Thoughtfully, Leo and Clarissa listened. Leo was thinking of her mother, of what she'd say in the letter she'd write home in an hour or two; to follow up the telegram she'd sent immediately upon receiving word of her father's death: DEVASTATED STOP I LOVE YOU STOP WITH YOU IN MY HEART AND THOUGHTS STOP CANNOT GET HOME STOP LETTER FOLLOWS STOP LEO.

31

The only way to escape, he decided, was by not escaping. By becoming so seriously ill the Germans would repatriate him. So he studied the illnesses of the men who were already classified for repatriation and decided to enlist the help of a very amicable chap in the next bunk who was suffering from acute nephritis and had already been scheduled, classified, for repatriation.

The external symptoms of the disease manifested themselves in a dreadful yellow color in the face, and badly swollen ankles.

After making a slow, careful study of his friend's case and eliciting his promise to help, Gray went after the aid of several others of the fliers he knew could be trusted to help while maintaining secrecy.

Since the orderly in the doctor's office was under the barrack commander's thumb, it was fairly easy to have him engineer it so that Gray's specimen would tie in with the evidence of other tests the German doctors were bound to carry out. Then with the help of a particularly artful and clever rear gunner named Brody, between them they fashioned an imitation penis from a smooth length of appropriately sized rubber hose purloined from the camp kitchen. One of the ends was a piece of wood carved carefully by Brody and plugged at the tip by the insertion of a shaved matchstick. The other end was stoppered with a cork, thereby safely allowing fluid to be carried inside. The whole thing was meticulously painted flesh color and then given a trial run. Filling the mock organ with nephritis-laden urine, Gray strapped it on and pretended to give a urine sample. It worked without a hitch.

With the further help of the imaginative Brody, who flicked Gray's ankles with wet towels for hours, they managed to cause him to swell up most effectively. He then swallowed several pieces of soap, which gave his complexion a pale green tinge. This was enhanced by a die concocted by Brody, who scalded a few bits of crepe paper, thereby producing a usable yellow dye.

Prepared to brazen it out, Gray went along to the camp hospital, where the German doctor examined his ankles, then spoke to his orderly, and Gray was taken into the doctor's office, where he was told to undress down to his shorts. The orderly then handed him a beaker and snapped, "Pass water!"

Taking his time, he managed to get enough into the beaker for test purposes. And the following day he went again before the doctor to be told the result of the examination. He was suffering from an advanced disease of the kidneys and was to visit the sick bay every other day for further tests. From then on, he became more adept at camouflaging the mock penis, as well as gaining generally in confidence.

In order to be further convincing, for three days he smoked dried sunflower seeds, which produced a tremendous wheezing when he breathed. In truth, he was getting thinner and thinner, and this fact, along with the quietly told tale that he was also suffering night sweats and other symptoms of tuberculosis, sounded very convincing.

X rays were taken. The medical orderly, properly primed, saw to it that the markings on Gray's plates coincided with his additional symptoms.

Then it was a matter of returning to the barracks to wait for the arrival of the medical commission that would be coming from the Red Cross in Geneva in a few weeks' time. Eating no more than one slice of bread a day, he succeeded in making himself look positively haggard and genuinely ill when it came time to face the medical board.

The group of doctors examined his X rays, scrutinized him closely, conversed among themselves in solemn undertones. They carefully examined the records that showed the many tests he'd been through, and again conferred. A uniformed Swedish doctor asked Gray to remove his shirt, and listened at Gray's chest and back while the sunflower seeds produced their audible wheezing. Another of the Swiss doctors walked around the table and pulled up his trouser legs to look at

Gray's ankles which were puffy from another two hours of Brody's work with the wet towel.

Yet another conference. And then the spokesman said, "Thank you. You will go home."

The entire examination had lasted less than ten minutes.

Ten minutes to decide that after two years, eight months, and some days, he'd go home.

Thirty of them passed the repatriation board, then waited another month before they were removed—at very short notice—from the camp and taken to Leipzig, where they remained for two more months with other repatriated British and Allied prisoners from camps throughout Germany. As the weeks passed, his initial spurt of happiness dimmed.

Then, with as little notice as they'd been given at the stalag, they were hurriedly put on a train for Sassnitz, the German Baltic naval base. There they boarded the German ship *Deutschland* and, eight hours later, arrived at Trelleborg in Sweden, where they remained for a week. They were fed and treated magnificently by their Swedish hosts.

Finally they sailed from Sweden and arrived six days later at Liverpool. A great number of the men broke down and cried at the sight of the cheering crowds waiting to welcome them. Gray found himself glad that Sam didn't know he'd returned. He was suddenly deeply frightened at the prospect of seeing her or any of his family. All his perceptions had undergone drastic changes. They wouldn't have recognized him. He scarcely recognized himself. A shaven, gaunt man with a misshapen shoulder. He was grateful to be sent directly from the ship to the hospital. He needed time, essentially to come to terms with the man he had become. He was no longer sure of his identity, and he'd have to find that out before he could even begin to think about facing the people he loved.

Sam had been notified, via a formal letter from Red Cross headquarters in Geneva, along with one from the Air Ministry, that Gray was in the process of being repatriated for medical reasons and that she would be further notified as to when she might expect his return. Ecstatic, yet worried about those "medical reasons," she rang Leo at the hospital to tell her. Leo then sent a telegram home to advise her mother. And with no more time to stop to examine her reactions to this extraordinary news, she hurried back into surgery.

At the flat, much later that evening, she collapsed onto her bed with a glass of brandy and a cigarette, weak with fatigue;

trying to think. Her thoughts wanted to fly in all directions. None of them was distinct. Relieved and happy at the prospect of seeing Gray, yet she was concerned, as was Sam, about the medical reasons. Her experiences with repatriated soldiers from the camps led her to expect Gray would either be suffering from some terminal illness or so critically injured as to be almost completely incapacitated. Either way, the men returned by the Germans were all but useless. A slap in the British face, as it were; sending men home nearly ready for burial.

Her thoughts of Gray seemed to get mixed in with those of Colin, and she found it was sometimes Gray and sometimes Colin she was anticipating seeing. And that surprised her. She had, in fact, given more thought to Colin in the past few months than she'd imagined she might. She didn't want to think about him, or any man. What she wanted, she told herself, was the war to end so that she might return home, establish a private practice, and try to live some sort of calm, sense-making life. But when she projected herself into that life, the images evoked were unsettling, deeply disturbing; as if she were blatantly lying to herself, being monstrously dishonest.

The war was winding down, and everyone knew it. She wanted to see her brother, her mother, go home. It would all happen now. Why did she still feel so beset by these unanswered questions? Living was the point of living. Why couldn't she just get on with it and stop confronting her continuing doubts and questions?

Gray was coming back. That was wonderful. Wasn't it? And she was happy at the prospect. Wasn't she? Yes, of course, of course. Happy. Yes.

She'd been in England close to three years. Gray had been gone all that time. Now he was returning. He had always come back. That was Gray. And she was glad. She was. If she could only be glad about herself, her life. . . .

Sam was jubilant.

"He's to be released from hospital in a fortnight!" she told Leo, her energy transmitting itself through her jiggling knee that had Gray Three—as they all called him—giggling and clutching at his mother's protectively encircling arm. "He'll be so surprised! About Gray Three, I mean. And Mummy's coerced the butcher into a decent-sized roast. We'll have a proper celebration, the lot." Her smile losing some of its brilliance, she said, "Is something, the matter, Leo?"

"No!" she said too brightly, aware peripherally of Clarissa's head turning in her direction. "I'm just so tired."

"You do look awfully . . . faded, actually," Sam said, thinking she'd never seen Leo look so hollowed-out. "I expect a lie-down and a good meal will put you right."

"I expect," Leo agreed, her eyes meeting Clarissa's.

"Time for your nap!" Sam set Gray down and stood up. "Say ta-ta, Gray!"

He chortled, piped, "Ta-ta," and ran out on fat little legs, his crystalline laughter echoing down the stairwell as Sam chased him up the stairs.

Clarissa studied the lit end of her cigarette, then took a hard drag on it and put it out, asking, "What is it?"

"They're putting together special medical teams to go in with the first liberation armies."

"And they've asked you to go," Clarissa guessed.

Leo nodded. "The thing is, all this time . . . I don't know. I've wanted to know, really *know*. Now I've got a chance, and I'm terrified. It's so stupid. I tell myself I've seen all there is to see. But this isn't going to be the same. I know it."

"Why must you always put yourslf through so much?" Clarissa asked. "Forever testing, probing, looking for something you might've missed the last go-round. You're quite right, of course," she said. "You'll most likely find it all out now. And then what will you do? Will this satisfy you, Leo?"

"There always has to be the thing you do after you've done the something you've got to do next."

"Rather like a child's set of building blocks."

"I suppose."

"Have you heard again from your major?" Clarissa asked.

"No. But I don't expect to," she lied.

"Yes, you do," Clarissa said softly.

"The only thing I know right now is that the moment all this is over, I'm going home. I need to see my mother." She said "my mother" and felt anguished, wanting more than anything else to be close again to the one person on earth about whom there were no undisclosed secrets, no unanswerable questions.

"I should like one day to meet your mother. She sounds an exceptional woman."

"My mother . . ." she said, breaking into choking tears.

"My mother"—she began to cry noisily, horribly—"is beautiful. *Beautiful*."

He thought he'd gone far beyond simple, basic emotions, that whatever natural instincts he might once have possessed had been burned out of him just the way, day after day, he'd burned the lice out of his clothing. But the sight of Sam and the little boy hiding behind her, peeking out at him, undid him more effectively than any inflicted torture could have. He looked at his son, then at his wife. She came into his arms, and he cried like a baby. Everything flooded forward, surfacing. He cried with Clarissa, with Leo. Their embraces, their reality were what had sustained him all that time, and all he could do was weep.

A five-day pass from the hospital wasn't long enough. Five years, he thought, might do it. It would probably take that long just to acclimate himself to the fact of the nightmare's end. His brain seemed to have tremendous trouble accepting the sight and feel of Sam and Clarissa and Leo, the existence of Gray Three.

Every so often he'd find himself staring into space, traveling out of the present tense; believing himself to be still on the top tier of the bunk, touching with his fingertips the rows of marks indicating the passage of months and years of his life.

He needed, among many other things, to get past his awe of Sam's healthy body, his fascination with her "otherness," to accept that this reality was also his. Sam had grown into a woman, a mother; and done it all without him, while continuing to believe he'd come back. Not like the dozens of other women whose letters had been read aloud in the barracks with grim gallows humor. How so-and-so had happened to fall in love with someone else and was ever so sorry but . . . And how such-and-such had just happened to be coming out of the cinema in Golders Green one evening and a dark stranger had shoved an infant into her arms, whispering, "Take care of the baby," before disappearing back into the darkness. But not Sam. Sam had waited. And he couldn't perform.

"It doesn't matter!" she insisted. "Do you think that's all I care about? I don't care a damn! Not a damn! *It doesn't matter!*"

He cried a lot. Taking Gray Three out for a walk, looking down at the boy, he'd think, "my son," and find himself crying. He lay down with Sam and had to get up after a few minutes, go close himself into the loo because he had to cry.

The hospital psychiatrist said, "Give yourself time, lad. You've been through an experience that's not going to quietly go away with a few good nights' sleep and some decent meals. And," he added very sincerely, "there are far worse things than tears."

It helped.

On his next pass, he was able to make love to Sam, and to say, "I love you."

Seeing that light in her own brother's eyes made something break inside Leo's head. Something that had, for years and years, remained impenetrable in the face of everything, simply cracked and disintegrated upon recognizing that whoever *they* were and however *they* went about it, *they'd* managed to reach all the way into the heart of her family and, beyond, into her. She left for Germany with what felt like a permanent flutter in her chest; constantly quaking, but determined, even dependent, upon this final step. She traveled by train, by boat, by truck, unaware of anything but the continuing motion inside her chest.

She went by jeep, in army fatigues, with a Red Cross badge, up to the gates of the camp. The Germans had fled only hours before, but not before hastily setting fire to their files in an attempt to destroy the evidence of their activities. The fire had failed to take, so that the soldiers were able to rescue the bulk of the documents.

With a small group of soldiers—one of a number of similar other groups—she moved tentatively toward the barracks. The air was foul with sickness and death as they stood in the doorway accustoming their eyes to the gloom, their senses to the filth within.

Her heart seemed to be trying to lift itself out of her body as she turned to see, at last, what she'd always known. She was rooted to the spot, as were the half-dozen accompanying soldiers, as first one, then another of the prisoners moved out of the shadows and into the light.

A whisper seemed to travel through the place, and more and more of them appeared. And her heart gushed up into her throat, came out of her eyes. There were no more questions, none. She was face to face with all the world's reality in its starkest, most horrific form. And it came to her with such caring, such a depth of sorrow that it no longer mattered who saw what part of her. Eyes, face, body. *She* didn't matter. She sobbed aloud, the sound startling her. She looked to see tears on the faces of the soldiers. They all wept as hands reached out questioningly to them and the soldiers moved forward, she moved. Her own hands, her arms reached out, seeking to say with her previously taken-for-granted hands and arms what the barriers of language prevented her from saying with words.

She looked into eyes that searched hers for the question of her humanity. She touched the cadaverous faces and bodies of these people who had somehow survived, meeting the ultimate crazed light of knowledge in their eyes; understanding that the light would always be there. Understanding, too, that it was going to be in her own eyes now. Because she was seeing, finally. She opened her mouth to say, "It's going to be all right now." Smiling, sobbing, she went among them, touching, loving. "We're going to take care of you." Thinking: God—there isn't any; how could there be? No so-called God, all-embracing, would allow this to happen.

Every additional death after their arrival was a loss she took personally. She worked, drawing upon some previously unsuspected inner strength, eighteen, twenty hours a day to help medicate these people, feed them, heal them; hearing their stories—in translation, or from those who spoke English; hearing it all. And she thought: My life has been a fairy tale of limitless pleasures. Any imagined inequities precisely that: imagined, in comparison to the true and crippling torture these few survivors had known. Few, because those undestroyed records listed tens of thousands. And so those who did survive really were merely a few.

She wanted more than ever now to go home. First to England to see Gray again, and Sam, Clarissa, Gray Three. And then to her mother. To tell all the important people how very deeply she loved them. Before it was too late. And Colin. She wanted terribly to see him. This man who'd one night shared his tears with her. I should have given my promise, she thought again and again. Because I loved you, too.

She returned to London when replacement medical staff came in, and dreamed nightly of that moment when the first of the prisoners had detached himself from the shadows to stand in the light. All the hollows and prominences of his face glaringly defined by the unrelenting light. The anguish caused her, in her sleep, to curl into a tight knot in the empty bed.

Miraculously, a lot of red tape got cut, and transport was being arranged for her, Gray, Sam, and Gray Three to travel home together.

But not Clarissa. Leo wanted to say: You'll come, won't you? You'll visit us?

"Joshua," Clarissa told them, "is working now to get people to Palestine." She smiled. "I'll help him."

Leo nodded, knowing Clarissa would never come to visit. She'd go with Joshua, wherever he went, helping him do whatever he chose. Because she loved and believed in him. It was easy to understand, really. So why had it taken Leo the better part of her life as well as a war to see it?

After sending a telegram to say they'd be coming, she began packing her few things. And resigned herself to the fact that Colin probably hadn't made it back or she'd have heard from him. She added him to the store of people she knew she'd remember the rest of her life; caring more about him after the fact than she'd been able to at the time.

Leonie asked Rose to come up and wait with her, because she needed to share the occasion. And only Rose really knew just how much of what had seemed like manic energy had actually been grief and desperation she'd struggled to put into the business. Now they were coming home, and there had to be someone's hand to hold, someone she loved to welcome the children home with her.

Rose, Leonie thought, was traveling out the far side of middle age. Fifty-five. It didn't seem possible. But then, so little, these days, seemed possible. And I, too, she thought, must seem to Rose very much changed. Aging women, running a business. But time had done well for Rose. She'd evolved into someone soft, and very much in tune with her own feelings and those of the people around her; someone who'd acquired the ability to articulate and display her thoughts and feelings. It was this, along with Rose's determination, that had forcibly lifted Leonie out of the confused spiral of loss and set her back to work. Now the children were coming home.

"Do you imagine"—she smiled—"we'll one day be two old crones, sitting out here on the front porch, rocking away, wondering how so much time managed to get past us?"

Rose laughed. "What do you call *this*? All that's missing is your knitting and my crocheting."

"No." Leonie shook her head. "Actually, you look far too sophisticated for the picture."

"It used to be me," Rose said, "who was fixated on age. Now I think you're the one. I keep getting the impression you think you've gone past it, that you're trying to settle into some sort of graceful old age."

"Maybe. I have the feeling I've earned a bit of that."

Impatiently Rose said, "You *know* you're never going to allow it to happen. And no one in his right mind could possibly look at you and start getting a room ready at the old folks' home. My God, Leonie! You haven't changed a bit in twenty years. I sometimes think if I didn't love you as much as I do, I'd hate you for the way you look."

"The way I look," she said dismissingly, "hasn't anything to do with anything. It never has. It's how one feels."

"Spare me! Don't tell me how old you feel!"

"Only occasionally. Most of the time I simply can't understand why I'm unable to do the things I did at twenty. But my resources simply aren't there. At least, not the way they once were."

"When are they supposed to get here?" Rose asked.

Leonie stood up and walked to the front window. "Soon now," she said, looking out at the snow. "Are you cold, Rose?" She turned. "Shall I turn up the heat?"

"It is a little cold in here."

She raised the thermostat, then went back to the sofa, on impulse taking hold of Rose's hand, with a smile saying, "I'm horribly nervous. Isn't it absurd?"

"No," Rose said softly. "It isn't. Not one bit."

"I *feel* absurd." She turned to look again at the window. "Like an anxious schoolgirl waiting for a good report card. I miss him so terribly, wish he was here for this." Her hand tightened around Rose's as her head turned slowly back. "It's the way it was. At the beginning, when I first came to this country. The feeling I had, waiting. But not really the same, I suppose. Because now I know I'll never see him again. And all during those years, I believed always that he'd come to me, find me somehow, some way. I do admire you, Rose. You always said you'd never allow some man to pin you down, put a child inside you, then go off, leaving you alone to grow into a replica of your mother. You've managed to keep complete control of your life."

"Are you trying to say you haven't?"

"Not at all. We're very different, we two. I *wanted* the children. I did think briefly of aborting Leo. At the very start. But I couldn't. And I was right, you see. Because I still have his children."

"My God! Let's have some coffee or something. This is all too dramatic and profound. I know you're nervous about them coming, but . . . I'll go put on the coffee."

"Amy will do it. Why do you hate it so when I say that sort of thing?"

"It's real to you, I know. But it's so damned . . . I don't know. I just can't deal with that."

"I loved him, Rose. I know you've never really understood why. You tolerated Gray, just as you tolerated Jimmy; believing, I think, that because I seemed to have a need for these men, you'd go along with whatever it was I needed, but always somehow disapproving. Why?"

"I've never 'disapproved.' I just know you could've done everything on your own, without them."

"You're so wrong," she said quietly. "Oh, I *thought* I could. But I could no more have succeeded initially without Jimmy than I could have had the children without Gray. I've always needed both. The challenge and the loving."

"So you'll find yourself someone else."

"I think not."

"Oh, you will!" Rose said confidently.

"No," Leonie said in a way that made Rose suddenly believe her. "I couldn't possibly allow someone who hadn't traveled through all these years with me to see and know the damage."

"But that's just physical," Rose argued.

"It isn't, Rose. It isn't just the scars or a breast that's not as it should be. Perhaps 'damage' isn't quite the right word. I simply haven't any desire left. None at all. Lust sometimes. Frighteningly. When I feel I'll scream if someone isn't here to hold me, see to my needs. But the other's gone. Just gone."

Rose said nothing.

Leonie's first reaction was: They're not children. I can never again think of them as children.

Leo was tall and lean and no longer young, possessed of haunted eyes and a new way of smiling, an altogether different way of speaking and touching. But still Leo. And her father's anger still sparked from her greenish-gray eyes.

Gray had aged twenty years. Shockingly. Sunken-eyed, harried-looking, and no longer private, he went into her arms with tears on his face. She held him, awed at the realization that this was the little boy who so adamantly had refused to cry; this tall, alarmingly thin stranger.

Sam, though, was the catalyst, bringing warmth and laughter and her little boy into the house; bringing her healthy roundness, her ebullience, her goodness in all around them; making the reunion less shocking, less chokingly emotional altogether.

Gray Three ran through the downstairs rooms finding things, bringing them back to show his mother; discovering Amy in the kitchen, standing gazing up at her, in his piping little English voice asking, "Why are you so brown?" so that Amy's laughter, too, returned to the house. "How come you-all so white?" she asked, scooping him up into her arms while he tested her springy hair, peered up her wide nostrils, ventured to poke his finger into her ear.

Leonie wanted to open her arms and in one encompassing embrace hold them all. Leo and Gray, Sam and Gray Three, Rose, Amy. Hold them, keep them. Knowing that, at best, it could be for only a moment. Because always it was a matter of opening again, letting them go.

Leo studied her mother, realizing it was only the third time she'd seen her mother cry. She remembered vividly that her mother hadn't cried when Uncle Jimmy died. No, she thought. That was me. I was the one who cried. But when Daddy came to us, she cried then. And when she was ill, nearly dying, she cried; angrily. She wondered about the times when her mother must have cried privately; those times neither she nor Gray—nor possibly anyone else—would ever know about.

Looking at her mother, she was reassured by her sameness, her consistency a soothing buffer to her own changed self. We are changed, she thought, but she has remained the same. The fires of time have merely tempered her surfaces, made them even stronger. Or perhaps—could this be the truth?—we were simply too involved with our own personal fires to be aware of her subtly altering through the years.

"I nearly forgot," Leonie said, keeping her arm around Leo as she wiped her eyes. "There's a letter for you. It came special delivery yesterday. I'll just fetch it for you."

"Probably more paperwork from the medical corps," she said, reluctant to allow her mother out of her sight, following her into the dining room, where Leonie picked up an airmail letter off the sideboard.

"I don't think so," she said, handing Leo the letter. "It's handwritten."

"Handwritten." Leo turned over the letter to look at the return address, experiencing a start of pleasure at the unfamiliar handwriting, the so-familiar name. "My God!" She laughed. "It's from Colin. I don't *believe* it! How did he . . .?" She tore open the flap to quickly scan the contents, saying, "He went to corps headquarters to get my address. Says he's coming over. I'll read it later," she said, returning the letter to the envelope.

"You've found someone," Leonie said, touching Leo's hair.

"The truth . . ." Leo caught hold of her mother's hand, holding it with both her own. "The truth is"—feeling she might just lift off the ground—"I think he's found me."

Gray Three finally climbed up and went to sleep on Rose's lap.

Leonie, looking over, thought: Children always know where the love and comfort is, and go to it with an instinct as pure and unrestrained as water seeking its own level.

"Do you *know* what he called me?" Rose said later, a high flush of color in her cheeks, after Gray Three had demanded she be the one to put him to bed. "Granny Rose. I nearly hit him."

Leonie laughed, putting an arm around Rose's shoulders as they went out to the kitchen to help Amy prepare dinner. "Don't fight it, Rose," she said, hugging her. "You know you adore it."

"*Granny Rose,* for God's sake?"

"Better," Leonie said lightly, "than Granny Lion."

It was Rose's turn to laugh. Loudly. "*Granny Lion?*"

"When I find out which of them taught him that . . ." she threatened.

"Granny Lion," Rose said again, savoring it. "That's marvelous!"

ABOUT THE AUTHOR

CHARLOTTE VALE ALLEN is the author of many novels, among them *Running Away, Gifts of Love,* and *Acts of Kindness,* all available in Signet editions.

After thirteen years in the United States, she has recently returned, with her young daughter, to her birthplace, Toronto, Canada.

More Bestsellers from SIGNET

- [ ] JO STERN by David Slavitt. (#E8753—$1.95)*
- [ ] BALLET! by Tom Murphy. (#E8112—$2.25)*
- [ ] LILY CIGAR by Tom Murphy. (#E8810—$2.75)*
- [ ] ASPEN INCIDENT by Tom Murphy. (#J8889—$1.95)
- [ ] WINGS by Robert J. Serling. (#E8811—$2.75)*
- [ ] CITY OF WHISPERING STONE by George Chesbro. (#J8812—$1.95)*
- [ ] SHADOW OF A BROKEN MAN by George Chesbro. (#J8114—$1.95)*
- [ ] BEDFORD ROW by Claire Rayner. (#E8819—$2.50)†
- [ ] JUST LIKE HUMPHREY BOGART by Adam Kennedy. (#J8820—$1.95)*
- [ ] THE DOMINO PRINCIPLE by Adam Kennedy. (#J7389—$1.95)
- [ ] FEAR OF FLYING by Erica Jong. (#E8677—$2.50)
- [ ] HOW TO SAVE YOUR OWN LIFE by Erica Jong. (#E7959—$2.50)*
- [ ] FLICKERS by Phillip Rock. (#E8839—$2.25)*
- [ ] LUCETTA by Elinor Jones. (#E8698—$2.25)*

* Price slightly higher in Canada
† Not available in Canada

Buy them at your local bookstore or use this convenient coupon for ordering.

THE NEW AMERICAN LIBRARY, INC.,
P.O. Box 999, Bergenfield, New Jersey 07621

Please send me the SIGNET BOOKS I have checked above. I am enclosing
$_____ (please add 50¢ to this order to cover postage and handling).
Send check or money order—no cash or C.O.D.'s. Prices and numbers are
subject to change without notice.

Name _____

Address _____

City _____ State _____ Zip Code _____

Allow 4-6 weeks for delivery.
This offer is subject to withdrawal without notice.

SIGNET Books You'll Want to Read

- [ ] **NATURAL ACTS** by James Fritzhand. (#E8603—$2.50)*
- [ ] **CARRIE** by Stephen King. (#J7280—$1.95)
- [ ] **NIGHT SHIFT** by Stephen King. (#E8510—$2.50)*
- [ ] **'SALEM'S LOT** by Stephen King. (#E9000—$2.50)
- [ ] **THE SHINING** by Stephen King. (#E7872—$2.50)
- [ ] **TWINS** by Bari Wood and Jack Geasland. (#E9094—$2.75)
- [ ] **THE KILLING GIFT** by Bari Wood. (#J7350—$1.95)
- [ ] **KINFLICKS** by Lisa Alther. (#E8984—$2.75)
- [ ] **THE FRENCH LIEUTENANT'S WOMAN** by John Fowles. (#E9003—$2.95)
- [ ] **MANHOOD CEREMONY** by Ross Berliner. (#E8509—$2.25)*
- [ ] **RIDE THE BLUE RIBAND** by Rosalind Laker. (#J8252—$1.95)*
- [ ] **WARWYCK'S WOMAN** by Rosalind Laker. (#E8813—$2.25)*
- [ ] **A GARDEN OF SAND** by Earl Thompson. (#E8039—$2.50)
- [ ] **TATTOO** by Earl Thompson. (#E8989—$2.95)
- [ ] **CALDO LARGO** by Earl Thompson. (#E7737—$2.25)

*Price slightly higher in Canada

Buy them at your local bookstore or use coupon on next page for ordering.

NAL / ABRAMS' BOOKS ON ART, CRAFTS AND SPORTS

in beautiful, large format, special concise editions—lavishly illustrated with many full-color plates.

- [ ] **NORMAN ROCKWELL: A Sixty Year Retrospective** by Thoma_ C. Buechner. (#G9969—$7.9_
- [ ] **THE PRO FOOTBALL EXPERIENCE** edited by David B_ with an Introduction by Roger Kahn. (#G9984—$6._
- [ ] **DALI . . . DALI . . . DALI . . .** edited and arranged by _ Gérard, with an Introduction by Dr. Pierre Roumeguère. (#G9983—$6.95)
- [ ] **THE TIN CAN BOOK** by Hyla M. Clark. (#G9965—$6.95)
- [ ] **FANTASY: The Golden Age of Fantastic Illustration** by Brigid Peppin. (#G9971—$6.95)
- [ ] **THE FAMILY OF MAN: The Greatest Photographic Exhibition of All Time—503 Pictures from 68 Countries** created by Edward Steichen for The Museum of Modern Art with a Prologue by Carl Sandburg. (#G9999—$4.95)
- [ ] **THE GREAT AMERICAN T-SHIRT** by Ken Kneitel, Bill Maloney and Andrea Quinn. (#G9972—$5.95)
- [ ] **THE WORLD OF M. C. ESCHER** by J. L. Locher, G. W. Locher, H. S. M. Coxeter, C. H. A. Broos, and M. C. Escher. (#G9970—$7.95)
- [ ] **MAGRITTE: Ideas and Images** by Harry Torczyner. (#G9963—$7.95)

Buy them at your local bookstore or use this convenient coupon for ordering.

THE NEW AMERICAN LIBRARY, INC.,
P.O. Box 999, Bergenfield, New Jersey 07621

Please send me the SIGNET and ABRAMS BOOKS I have checked above. I am enclosing $_____ (please add 50¢ to this order to cover postage and handling). Send check or money order—no cash or C.O.D.'s. Prices and numbers are subject to change without notice.

Name _____

Address _____

City_____ State_____ Zip Code_____

Allow 4-6 weeks for delivery.
This offer is subject to withdrawal without notice.